The Faith Healer's Daughters

KEEPER OF
THE LIGHT

BY
SHEILA ENGLISH

PROLOGUE

PAIN RIPPED THROUGH ABIGAIL, ending in a long and exhausted scream. They'd told her it would be difficult, dangerous even. She was only eighteen and very petite. Her size worked against her, but her age, her health, these were on her side.

A faint dizziness replaced the pain for the moment. It was nearly midnight, and she'd been at this for twelve hours. She'd gone through two midwives, both of them sister-wives loyal to her husband, their husband, Zachariah Williams. Loyalty carved from fear of the most powerful man in the secluded community, a man no one crossed and the strongest faith healer anyone had ever seen.

The sister-wives had been called away to give an update to Zachariah, and only Abigail's cousin, sweet, caring Patricia, herself only sixteen, remained to tend her. Patricia would risk the wrath of Zachariah tonight. They both would. They had to if they were to save Abigail's unborn children from a fate no one should have to endure. Life in the community. Life with Zachariah.

Thunder roared outside, so loud and close it rattled the bedside table. The water in Abigail's glass swayed, almost pitching over the lip. Almost, but not quite was the story of her life. She'd almost escaped so many times that they finally married her to Zachariah to keep her in her place. That was two years and six attempted escapes ago. Married at sixteen to a man who looked to be seventy, who could blame her for trying to escape? But they did blame her. No one left the faith healer community, Zachariah and his crazy brothers made sure of that.

The pain began to build again and Abigail reached out for Patricia's hand. She was afraid she might break Patricia's slight fingers, but she couldn't help it. She needed Patricia and always had. Her younger cousin was her only real friend, the only one who not only understood why she'd wanted out of this place, but wanted out herself. And though Abigail had failed so many times, Patricia had devised a plan. One that would likely work, if they could just get out of this house. She gripped Patricia's hand tighter, but the younger girl never complained. She knew what she was in for the moment she'd offered her hand.

The pain built, rolled over her, pulled out another scream and then began to subside, this time, taking a small bit of her will with it. The lights flickered, but finally determined to stay on. It was as though the heavens cried out for them, or perhaps the heavens also feared Zachariah and were doing all that could be done to stop their escape tonight. Abigail knew Patricia feared the thunder, but she feared Zachariah more. *Smart girl*, Abigail thought of the young blonde with huge, round blue eyes staring at her as though she were caught in a trap and knew it. Patricia could be gone already, but she refused to leave Abigail and her unborn children behind.

"Patricia, you need to go. This is taking too long. We'll be found out," Abigail kept her voice a whisper, whether from fear or from screaming herself hoarse, it was hard to say.

"Not gonna happen," Patricia squeezed her hand and let it go. She reached over to the bedside table and took the cold, damp cloth left there by the midwives and used it to wipe the sweat from Abigail's brow and upper lip. "Those babies are coming soon and as soon as you are able to move, we'll be out of here."

"The problem is," Abigail broke off to take in a deep gulp of air. The contraction took its course. "The sister-wives already said my babies are high risk. Triplets, Patty. I may not live through this. They may not."

"Stop it! You're going to live and we're going to get these babies out of this place." Patricia started to say something more, but another contraction stopped her. She held on to Abigail's hand with all her strength until Abigail released her death grip. "As soon as they come back for you I can leave long enough to do what needs done. All you have to do is have that litter of munchkins, and I'll take care of the rest."

Abigail managed a smile. Patricia had teased her about having *a litter* ever since they discovered she was having triplets. She helped Abigail see the beauty and wonder of her pregnancy, regardless of who the father was. Patricia was like that, full of hope. Even when she was told she had been promised to Zachariah as a new wife, she continued to be hopeful. Hopeful that they would escape. Hopeful that it wasn't too late to have the life they had always wanted.

Creaking brought their attention around to the only door in the room. Ethel, one of the two midwives attending Abigail walked in and quietly closed the door behind her. She spared a glance to Patricia and for just one moment her face made Abigail's blood run cold, but another contraction brought her focus back to the task at hand.

"Where are you going?" Ethel's attention was torn between the screaming Abigail and Patricia who was about to walk out the door.

"I need a break," Patricia said, her heart beating wildly now.

"Brother Zachariah says to stay put."

"I'll be right back. Need to use the bathroom." Patricia took a moment to look out into the hallway. No one was there. Why would there be? Abigail was the only one known to run away and she certainly was going nowhere in her condition. But, on the heels of that thought she heard footsteps down the hall, coming up the stairs, several footsteps.

"Stay put! You can use that one," Ethel pointed to the closed bathroom door inside the birthing room and was clearly confused as to what to do, but when Abigail screamed out Ethel chose to leave Patricia to her own fate.

In an instant Patricia was gone. The door didn't quite close all the way and Abigail could see out into the hallway. Lights flickered again, but held fast. Lightning, which couldn't be seen in the boarded up room, cast light and shadow through the window down the hall. With the sound of thunder crashing around her, Abigail gave birth to her first daughter, Ivy.

Another crash, but this time it wasn't thunder. The door was thrown open just as the lights gave up the battle and threw them all into darkness. Lightning lit the hallway causing the tall figure to stand out in silhouette. His arms were inordinately long, almost long enough to be considered a malformation, and his profile was unmistakable with the bulbous nose and pointy chin. Abigail's husband, Zachariah. She would have feared the dark, angry expression on his face if she hadn't been delivering their second daughter, Amber. He knew. Somehow, he knew they were planning to escape.

Zachariah's footsteps fell hard on the floor, as he strode in to the room powered by anger and purpose. He glanced around the room briefly, then his hard gaze fell to Ethel who wisely took a step back from him.

"Where is Patricia?" he demanded.

"She wouldn't listen to me. I had to tend to Abigail and the babies. She walked out right before you got here." Ethel blanched.

The tall, older man pierced Ethel with is steely gaze.

Abigail almost felt sorry for Ethel in that moment. Zachariah's punishments were as creative as they were cruel, and no doubt Ethel already knew that. Abigail didn't have time to worry about Ethel as another contraction wracked her body with pain.

Ethel turned her attention so fully on Abigail and final baby you would have thought Ethel herself was the baby's grandmother. Perhaps she was. Abigail would never know, since it was forbidden to know who your biological mother was in the community. Fathers were known, but never mothers. All the sister-wives acted as community mothers and some of them didn't care for that at all. Some children looked similar enough to one of the sister-wives that it wasn't a stretch to guess who the parent was, but you guessed in silence.

Abigail gave birth to Elizabeth nearly half an hour after Patricia left. Patricia didn't return and Abigail hoped she'd made her escape. But as Ethel put the tiny babies into a large carrier someone knocked on the door that Zachariah had shut as he awaited the final child's birth. And Patricia's return. Zachariah opened the door slightly, but it was enough that Abigail could see and hear what was going on.

"We've spotted an old truck across the ridge on the west property. It's gotta be her." The man was in his late twenties, armed with a gun and enough sense to keep his eyes on Zachariah and not gaze at the leader's nearly naked young wife.

"Go get her," Zachariah's voice was calm, almost serene. That was never a good sign. The man nodded and walked away. Zachariah turned to Ethel. "Leave us." And with that Ethel sighed her relief and moved faster than Abigail had ever seen her move before.

Zachariah walked closer and towered over Abigail beside her bed. He glanced once at the basket filled with his three daughters, but showed no joy. Why would he? He had fathered so many children she doubted he would even miss these three, if she ever got away. Yet, she sensed there was something more going on here and she willed herself to look up into his face.

"Abigail," his voice was nearly soothing, but she knew not to believe anything he said. "For two years we've tried to have a child together. Two years, two miscarriages." His eyes raked over her body which was now covered, but not clean. "I healed you. I made you fertile. My power kept these babies in your womb. And you plotted to repay this gift by taking them from me?"

Abigail remained silent. She didn't care that he used his faith healing powers to keep the babies alive in her womb. She was happy to have her daughters, but nothing about their father made her proud or grateful.

"Did you know, Abigail," he began as he sat on the side of her bed, trapping her between him and the carrier on the other side of her, "my power, given to me by the Divine One, that which I use to heal the sick and injured, it is only one side to a very powerful coin." He sighed, a sound that she thought, in her exhausted state, could be one of sadness. "The other side of that coin, my girl, the other side of life, well, it's death."

Abigail found she still had some adrenaline left in her body and it flooded her, increasing her heart rate, making her already dry mouth feel as though she'd been trapped in the desert for weeks. Energy surged through her body as she considered the soft cries of her babies in the carrier next to her. Within arm's reach of Zachariah.

"It's forbidden to harm your own children!" Abigail started to push herself upright, but Zachariah put his large hand on her shoulder and she couldn't move past it.

PATRICIA STUFFED HER FIST in her mouth to keep from crying out and giving away her position. Abigail made her promise to save the children even if Abigail could not be saved. Patricia couldn't stop Zachariah. She could only look on and pray Abigail might be spared.

"I have no intention of harming our children," he said as his hand moved slowly from her shoulder to her chest, resting over her heart. "You wanted to leave me, and so you will. But, before you go I want you to know that these innocent girls, our children, these final reminders of you, will be the most miserable creatures this community has ever known. They will be less than slaves here. Never loved. I will forbid loving them." He paused for a moment, studying her face, assuring himself of her utter misery. He wiped at one of the tears with his free hand, unaffected. And with the other he pulled the energy, the very life, from Abigail Williams. If he were sure there would be no consequences he would have killed the babies, too, but of course even Zachariah Williams had something to fear.

An explosion sounded outside, dwarfing the clash of the thunder. Zachariah stood without a glance to the crying babies or a final parting look at his young wife and hastily strode out the door, closing the door behind him. He had no idea another door had opened as he made his dark promise to Abigail. Patricia was careful when she had circled back, climbed the trellis and come in through the small bathroom window. Her heart shattered at the lifeless Abigail. She couldn't stop staring at her. Her cousin, best friend, confidant. She thought living in the community was the worst tragedy of her life, but she had been wrong.

She focused on the large carrier filled with three tiny babies. Even a sixteen-year-old girl such as her could see the babies were far too small. The smallest had to be Elizabeth. They'd chosen the names together, and Elizabeth was to be the last one born. The tiny thing was almost surreal and it wasn't breathing as well as the other two. Patricia lifted the carrier, finding it much lighter than she had anticipated. Abigail had chosen the carrier herself, and Patricia already knew it would fit out the bathroom window.

Patricia quickly ran to the door and turned the lock. She needed a little time. Most of the men would be running after the old truck she set fire to, but the women inside the house could be plenty dangerous in their own way.

She ran back to the bed and placed her hand on the side of Abigail's face. It was still warm. She silently mouthed the words, "I love you." Then she grabbed the carrier, threw a blanket over the babies and ran.

Chaos both man-made and nature-made served to keep Patricia hidden from the eyes of any who might call attention to her. She knew some saw her slinking around with what appeared to be a large, covered basket, but not everyone in the community was as loyal as Zachariah liked to think. She headed southeast to a long stretch of tall fence that had been cut the previous day. It wasn't until she began to peel back the chain link fencing that the car on the other side could be seen. No lights came on when the door opened and someone came running toward her. A woman dressed entirely in black took the carrier, trusting Patricia would follow.

The woman placed the carrier gently into the backseat and then got into the driver's seat. Patricia got in the back with the babies and tapped the driver on the shoulder, which put the car into motion. Next to the woman driver sat a man who also wore dark clothes. His shoulders were wide, his hair black and tied back. His features much like those of the men at the Sioux reservation nearby. Patricia knew at once this had to be John, Helena's husband, the man who helped her escape the community nearly ten years ago. He turned around, offered her a kind smile and glanced toward the carrier.

"Where's the mother?" His voice was deep, gentle but concerned.

"Zachariah killed her." Patricia's voice caught on a sob and she stifled it. It wouldn't help anyone to have her lose it right now. She turned around and watched the lights of the community begin to fade in the distance.

"I'm so sorry, honey," Helena's eyes reflected in the rear-view mirror. Patricia nodded, knowing not to trust her voice. "How are the babies?"

"I don't know. They're so small. The tiny one is Elizabeth and she's not breathing right." Patricia wasn't sure she could take another death. She loved these little ones before they were ever born. She would die before she would let something happen to them.

"Patricia, we need to drop Elizabeth at a hospital. It may be the only way we have to save her life." John thought of every contingency. They knew it was possible there would be complications.

Patricia nodded, picked up the tiniest of the girls and held her close. They drove through back roads for over two hours, eventually coming back to the main highway. They'd get as far away from the community as they could, but Patricia knew leaving Elizabeth was a gamble. As Patricia cuddled the small bundle in her arms she finally let the tears fall. There were hospitals that took in newborn babies, no questions asked. As Elizabeth struggled to breathe Patricia knew they would have to leave her behind.

Patricia kissed Elizabeth's tiny head. The baby's skin was ashen, her breathing labored. Helena was the one to drop her off. Elizabeth might actually be the lucky one in the long run. Zachariah was known for hunting and capturing those who escaped the community. With Helena, Patricia and the girls together, he would likely double his efforts to find them. Elizabeth would have no tie to the community. It was the only consolation Patricia had.

Helena and John would raise the girls as their own, but in her heart those were her girls. She reached out and softly caressed first Ivy and then Amber lightly on the cheek. It was the first time she noticed that Ivy had a small heart-shaped birthmark high on her cheekbone, near her right eye. Patricia's thumb moved over the tiny heart with a feather light brush across the softest skin she'd ever felt. The girls would be hunted their entire lives. Their childhood would be different from normal children, but at least they wouldn't belong to Zachariah Williams. They would need to be strong, like their mother. They would need each other to survive.

CHAPTER 1

GABRIEL HENNESSEY FLIPPED IVY Jones over on her back, but not for long. Ivy was up, sweeping his leg with a roundhouse kick, putting him on the floor she'd just got up from. She'd always pulled her punches with him, but the memory of last week took control over emotions she had been trained for years to hold in check. As he jumped back up with a smile on his face, certain of his years of training—top trophy wins for martial arts competitions, an eighty-pound difference in their weight, and a height advantage of nearly a foot—he took his stance like he had for the nearly ten years they had both trained at this dojo. But, this time, history would not be repeating itself. The warnings she got about not standing out, not showing off, were overridden by the recent events of the summer and his dismissal of her just as school started up again. She moved into a defensive stance and instead of throttling back so he could take her down as usual she threw a punch, unchecked and unencumbered by warnings, training, or any sense of self preservation.

The loud crack caused a few of the others to stop and stare. Gabriel was the top student at this dojo, and no one even came close to being able to beat him, so when he hit the mat, nose bleeding profusely, it didn't take long to gain the attention of everyone there, including a very concerned and unhappy sensei. The sensei grabbed a rag on his way over for.

Gabe to put on his nose and helped him up, sparing a very disparaging look in Ivy's direction.

"Miss Jones, please clean this up and join me in my office when you're finished," the small Japanese man instructed in soft tones, which did nothing to quell Ivy's fear of him. Not that she feared he would hurt her, but she didn't like disapproval of any kind from someone she respected. Accidents happened of course, but when they did you always got a talking to so he knew you understood where things went wrong and how to avoid such accidents in the future. Ivy hoped he'd think it was an accident and a lucky hit, because she had no other story prepared for him, at least nothing she wanted to share.

Ivy turned toward her sister, a mirror image of herself except for the slight red hue to Amber's blonde hair, and the birthmark on Ivy's face. Amber gave a quick frown of disapproval, a slight shake of the head and then she turned back to her sparring partner. Ivy got herself into this, so she would own up to the consequences. But the feeling of satisfaction from even a tiny bit of revenge was a balm to her damaged pride and broken heart. So she cleaned the blood off the mat with little concern. But, as she made the trek to the sensei's office, the first tingle of regret nudged her. Was it really worth it? Ivy thought about the long, wonderful summer filled with picnics, movies, and long walks with Gabe, laughing and holding hands and her first kiss. Sparks, fireworks, butterflies and all the romance her sixteen year old mind could hope for in a single summer. Then school started, and Gabe informed her the starting quarterback dated cheerleaders, not the geek girl from AV club. Okay, maybe he didn't put it that way exactly, but she knew what he meant when he broke things off with her.

His words echoed in her mind as she came to the door and put her hand on the doorknob. "There's nothing that really holds us together, Ivy. You have no interest in my friends and I won't give them up." Now that his popular friends came back to town from their expensive vacations and wildly exciting stories, being with her was boring. Ivy pushed the door open and saw Gabe sitting, head back, rag still in place and she realized that, yes, it was worth it. Cause now he'd been humiliated too.

The lecture was what she expected, the punishment not too severe. There seemed to be some question as to just how "accidental" the punch was, and she wondered if Gabe had said something to the sensei about their recent falling out. Ivy would call it breaking up, but Gabe assured her they were never going out officially, so it was just a "falling out" or "moving on."

Jackass. She seemed to think that a lot these days. Every single time she looked at Gabe Hennessey she thought it. Every time she thought of his brown hair with the blond streaks, his blue eyes and perfect smile. Every time.

She'd gotten dressed, met up with her sister, and made her way out of the dojo and into the sunshine, but not without passing by Gabe and getting some weird look from him that she couldn't even fathom. He didn't appear angry like she thought he would, but that expression was not one of respect for an opponent either. Accusation? Whatever it was she didn't care. He could have his cool friends, pretty cheerleaders and limelight. She was done. Over. Finished. Tonight she'd go all night long without thinking about him one time. Without crying herself to sleep. Without wishing her life could be different so she could be what he needed her to be at school.

Wishing wouldn't change anything. She knew that more than most. She'd been wishing for a different life ever since she realized that not all kids spent their weekends learning to shoot guns or build smoke bombs.

Amber walked in sync with her, silent at least for the moment. A vintage Camaro pulled up and the driver signaled for them to stop. Ivy couldn't think of a single reason why she should be rude to Gabe's cousin Ryan, but she wished she could think of a way to avoid what she was sure he wanted to talk about.

"Hey Ivy!" He said.

The passenger window was down and Ivy dropped her duffle next to her sister and walked over to lean in a little so they could talk. He was an older guy, eighteen, and had graduated already then came to Coalville, Kentucky to spend the summer with Gabe. Gabe was mad that he couldn't go to Europe with his friends over the summer because of some family issues, so he talked his cousin into hanging out for a while. Ryan was what Patricia, her god mother, called a beatnik. John, her adoptive father, called him a hippy, but that might be because Ryan's dark hair was just a bit past his shoulders and often in a ponytail. Or because he had a pretty decent goatee going on. Or because he was artistic and unemployed. Either way, Ryan was all about fun and he'd spent a good part of the summer trying to convince Amber he was the most fun she'd ever have. Amber was never one to be easily impressed by a hot guy and never gave him much attention, which only seemed to make Ryan like her more. He'd tried to get her to pose for some pictures and followed her around for a few days with his new camera until she threatened to do something Ivy felt pretty sure was anatomically impossible. A few days later and Ryan went back home, but like magic he showed back up right as school started, surprising everyone by getting an apartment in town and setting up a tattoo shop there. And that was where she'd gotten herself into trouble.

They'd all been at a bonfire when she and Gabe first started seeing each other, or hanging out, or whatever, and Ryan showed Amber a tattoo on his left forearm of a grim reaper and told her he'd done the tattoo himself. It was really good and Ivy didn't believe he'd actually done it himself. She thought he was trying to impress her sister. After some discussion, Ryan told Ivy he'd do a tattoo for her if she wanted. If she wasn't afraid. The power of the pinky swear was invoked in front of witnesses, and Ivy bravely announced to all that she loved tattoos and she would certainly let Ryan do one for her when he had a shop of his own. How could she have ever guessed she'd be held to that promise so soon? Ryan needed people to tattoo so he could build his reputation in town and he planned to start with her. It was ironic really. Gabe didn't want to be with her anymore because she was a nobody, and Ryan wouldn't leave her alone about being his first client because it would somehow impress a bunch of people. Such was her life. A conundrum wrapped in an anomaly.

"Hey Ryan!" She threw on her best fake smile and told herself to man up. She'd made a promise, and a Jones always kept her promise.

"We still on this week?" He spoke to her, but his eyes wandered past her to where Amber stood, ignoring him in a most obvious manner.

"Yeah." She answered, then rallied when he glanced back at her. "Of course!" She smiled and hoped it looked better than it felt.

"What about you sunshine?" He asked Amber, who continued to ignore him, though Ivy was certain she'd heard him.

"I think it's just me," Ivy said when Amber didn't answer.

"Not just you." The voice was masculine and familiar and annoyed her in direct proportion to how much it made her heart feel like it'd dropped down into her toes.

"Gabe," Ivy said by way of acknowledging him. She moved away from the door so he could get in. This time when she leaned back down to talk to Ryan she was sure not to touch the car in any way, as though it were now contaminated. "You're getting a tattoo?"

"No," he answered, buckling his seat belt, checking his hair in the mirror and flashing her one of his infamous half-smiles that used to make her knees weak but now served only to remind her to throw her shields up where he was concerned. "I don't want a tattoo. But, I know how you love them." His smile widened as he not-so-subtly referred to her proclamation at the bonfire. "I planned on being at Ryan's to check out his work. And I get to see you squirm. That just might make us even for today, right?"

"I won't squirm," she assured him, "And today *did* make us even. You remember that the next time you want to spar with me. Or humiliate me." She'd hoped to show him that she wasn't so easy to hurt, but sometimes words have power not fully realized until they leave your lips. The end of her tirade was more sad than tough and she hated that.

His smile faded and a slight frown held what she took as pity. She didn't want his damn pity and she straightened, took a step back so she didn't have to lean in. She lifted her chin and squared her shoulders.

"Do what you want," she told him, her voice stronger and under her control again. "I could care less if you're there." What was one more lie at this point? She lied when she told him she understood why they couldn't see each other and she lied when she told herself she was over him. This one seemed pretty small compared to some she'd told this week.

Amber stepped up beside her and she leaned down, pushing herself forward so that she leaned in through the window, forcing Gabe to move out of her way. Her shoulder hit his sore nose and he yelped, grabbing it and giving

Amber a look that would wither most people. Amber didn't acknowledge him or apologize. She acted like she didn't realize she'd done it even though that noise Gabe made was close to her ear.

"I guess I'll come too." Amber smiled, winning a grin from Ryan, albeit a cautious one, as he glanced at Gabe holding his nose.

Amber nodded and moved away from the car, giving Gabe a smile that had nothing to do with humor. At least nothing *he* would find humorous. Gabe frowned at her again, but then Ryan put the car in gear and they slowly rolled away from the curb.

"You did that on purpose." Ivy didn't bother posing it as a question as she picked her duffle up.

"You betcha." Amber didn't bother denying it.

"We've got archery class at home." Ivy began walking home. "Let's get going."

They walked side by side, quiet at first, but Ivy knew her sister couldn't let it drop. If Amber had her way, they would have blown up Gabe's locker the first day of school. To say her sister was a bit protective would be like saying she was just a little vindictive. "Just a little" was not how Amber did things.

"Ivy, I'm sorry he hurt you. I'm sorry he's an ass." Amber drew in a deep breath as though she were just getting started. "But you need to pull yourself out of this funk and you need to not go through with this whole tattoo idea. John and Helena will kill you and kill me for knowing about it and not telling them."

"If you do, it will all turn into a life-lesson philosophy speech and more training on how to stay invisible. I just don't need that right now. You're protective enough it's like I don't even need parents!"

"That's not really fair, Ivy. After all they've been through to take us in, adopt us, keep us safe. If not for John and Helena taking us and Patricia in, things could be really bad," Amber scolded.

Ivy hated this speech and knew it by heart. "I know, I know, and I do appreciate all they've done for us. I love our home. We couldn't have asked for better parents. But, between Helena and Patricia mothering us and John's constant train-till-you-drop it's hard to fit in a regular life. It's hard to fit in at all." Ivy wondered for the millionth time if things would have been different between her and Gabe if her life allowed her to have a lot of friends like he did. She'd underestimated how many people would be curious about them as a couple. She couldn't afford that kind of attention and Gabe refused to choose her over his friends. Something had to go. That something ended up being her.

"You know there's never going to be a regular life for us. At least not until we're adults and can keep anyone from forcing us to go back to our biological father. Rules keep us safe. Keeping a low profile keeps us safe," Amber continued. "Standing out in any way is a beacon for trouble." She quoted Helena.

The day was warm and bright, completely opposite of Ivy's mood. They walked leisurely, in no hurry to spend the rest of the day in the heat training.

Ivy sighed loudly. "Helena doesn't want us to do anything that brings attention to us, but doing *nothing* does bring attention to us! We'll always be outcasts at this point. We'll never fit in."

Amber's eyes reflected the pity Ivy hated to see there. "You want to be popular because you think that's how you'll get into Gabe's life," Amber said. "Well, Ivy, not only can that not happen, but if you have to be popular to have him stay with you, he isn't worth having. I almost wish Helena wasn't friends with his mom. He's the only boy you've really ever known well. The only one ever allowed to hang out with us. You put too much stock in the history you have with him and how cute he is and how popular."

Ivy slid a glance to Amber, thinking about those days. Amber had never fallen under Gabe's spell. It had always been Ivy who wanted to be with him every possible chance she got. At first, Gabe said she was too young to hang out with, and years later she wasn't popular enough to hang out with.

Maybe Gabe was right and there really wasn't anything to tie them together, not time, age, friends, or social status. How this past summer happened was purely fate, or bad luck, depending on how you look at it.

Amber's pace quickened, her steps slapping the pavement hard enough to echo in the street.

"When John and Helena find out about the tattoo, you better cover for me! That's all I'm sayin'." Amber continued voicing her train of thought. "And don't even ask me to lie to Patricia for you, cause I won't."

Ivy picked up her pace. "Patricia is the only one likely to not care. She would understand that I just want to do something for myself."

"Uh, huh. You keep telling yourself that. But if she gives me the guilt-ray stare you know I'll fold."

Ivy had to smile. They always teased in secret that Patricia's super power was her shield-of-honesty, kind of like Wonder Woman's golden lasso, and her most diabolical weapon was her guilt-ray. No one wielded guilt like Patricia did when she really wanted to get her way. It was a gift.

"No worries, sis," Ivy assured her as they turned down Appleseed Lane. "I'd never draw you into a web of lies." She glanced at Amber, whose expression told her she was not buying into anything she was saying. "We'll stick with tradition and we'll sneak out. No one will ever even know what happened and I'll have the tattoo put somewhere they'll never see it."

Amber frowned at that. They'd snuck out of the house a couple of times during the summer for bonfires and midnight movies. They'd never been caught, so Ivy felt sure that Amber would go even if she didn't like it. Even if it meant having to listen to her sister complain the whole three mile walk to Ryan's place.

"One day, Ivy, you're going to get caught," Amber warned.

"Are you really going to give me the 'Ivy you take too many chances' lecture? I mean, do you do it for your own plausible deniability if we get caught, or because you think if you say it enough times I'll actually listen?" Ivy sighed, hoping this would nip that particular lecture in the bud.

"You're reckless," Amber said, dashing Ivy's hopes that the conversation was ending. "One day it may be more than just you that pays the price."

Ivy waited for more. She knew the lecture well enough to give it herself. Amber was all about survival and doing what was right. She didn't seem to understand that life without fun, without adventure, without something to live for, was no life at all. They'd just have to be at odds about this one thing. She just wished it wasn't such a big thing to have between them. She wished Amber didn't need to be coaxed or guilted into every idea, every adventure.

Honeysuckle, lavender, roses and other scents she couldn't name but loved just the same, hung in the air, and she breathed them in like they could feed her soul. They had been trained to take a different route each day and there were several they took, but this was by far the best one. The weather was perfect and the colors of autumn had begun to paint with passion everywhere. The leaves weren't ready to give up just yet, but soon they would carpet lawns in red and gold and dance as the September winds came and orchestrated the music of Fall. In that moment, Ivy didn't mind that her life was void of adventure, excitement, or attention. The sun kissed her skin and the cool breeze of late afternoon soothed it before she felt the burn from a Fall sun that had already turned her skin a lovely bronze, nearly as dark as her whiskey-colored eyes.

The birds chirped and Ivy could hear the sound of lawn mowers announce the commitment of husbands and gardeners. The day was so serene and perfect she immediately felt the need to cheer herself by needling her sister.

"So, you're going to be at Ryan's lair," Ivy said, doing her best to sound neutral. "Right where he's wanted you all along."

Ivy smiled and wriggled her eyebrows, but the laughter died on her lips as she watched Amber's shoulders tense, her eyes narrow and her lips set in a serious line. Ivy immediately went on alert, but she continued on as though her heart wasn't pounding hard in her chest. Ivy knew immediately what was up when she looked ahead, and now adrenaline poured into her body. She'd noticed the white van parked outside the dojo when they arrived. She hadn't seen it when they came out, but it hadn't gone far.

"Montana plates," Amber whispered.

"Tinted windows," Ivy added. "Parked away from the houses. Can't see if anyone is inside."

"Take Richardson Avenue and cut through the Wheeler's old place." Ivy smiled as she instructed her sister of their plan. Outwardly they looked like a couple of girls chatting and enjoying the day. No one would suspect they had gone on alert. Richardson Avenue was an alternate route that had an emergency duck-and-run route built in.

Once they turned onto Richardson Avenue they picked up their pace just a bit. The sound of an engine starting up had Ivy glancing at her sister to confirm she had heard it too. Ivy's breathing was shallow, heart racing, adrenaline pouring in, and she moved her feet even faster, bringing the Wheeler house closer. The house was empty and had been for sale for the past few years. The only fence was in the back and separated the yard from the forest beyond.

"Now!" Ivy started running for the fence, sparing a quick glance back to ensure herself that Amber was keeping up. Ivy dropped her duffle right before she hit the fence, launching herself as high on the fence as possible and then throwing herself over to land gracefully on the other side. She had momentum on her side and took off at full speed. She heard Amber hit the fence but was pulled up short when her sister's gasp stopped her in her tracks. She turned to see Amber was already up, but limping as fast as she could toward her. Ivy ran back even though Amber was shaking her head.

"Just go," Amber told her. "I'll catch up."

"Put your weight on me!" Ivy put her arm around Amber's waist and her sister put her arm around Ivy's shoulders. Ivy was grateful that Amber was smaller than her and though Amber was only about fifteen pounds lighter and maybe an inch shorter it helped Ivy to move her sister faster through the next two miles of forest.

Ivy saw the house in the distance and found some reserve energy to help her pick up the pace again. Her side hurt, and Amber was leaning harder. She needed to get her sister help more than she needed relief from the pain.

Ivy heard the deep baritone voice of John as he called out to Helena. John was big and he was fast. He'd grown up on a reservation where they hunted for food and spent a great deal of time running in the woods. In no time he was there, picking Amber up, carrying her swiftly through the trees. Helena joined them, but her attention went from Amber to the forest behind them in a split second. Ivy kept up with John, but she had no doubt Helena was assessing the threat, searching for anyone who may have followed them. Ivy chastised herself for not knowing if they had been followed. She scanned the area from time to time, but her energy and attention had been on Amber and getting her home.

They'd reached the porch at the rear of the house, and Patricia had the door standing open for them to come in.

"What's happened?" Patricia asked, her eyes wide. The petite blonde woman pointed to a chair just inside.

John put her gently onto the chaise lounge in the family room. Ivy's eyes struggled to adjust to the darker interior of the house. She stood at the foot of the chaise lounge peering down at Amber's swollen ankle as Patricia ran to get an ice pack and some pain medication.

"There was a white van," Ivy started as soon as she heard the door slam shut announcing that Helena had joined them.

"Where?" John asked. His dark eyes grew intense, though his large hand gently rested on Amber's shoulder.

"Not even a quarter mile west of the dojo off Richardson," Ivy answered for Amber.

"No one was following you," Helena assured them and walked over to stand next to John. Immediately the two joined hands. They were each other's touchstone. "Did you get a good look at them? A license plate number?"

"White van, Colorado plates, tinted windows," Ivy cataloged. "I think I remember the plate number, too. But, I didn't see anyone."

Ivy heard Amber's quick intake of breath as Patricia placed the ice pack lower on Amber's ankle where swelling had started to highlight an oncoming bruise..

"It did have one of those license plate frames," Amber interjected, then stopped talking again when Patricia handed her some pills to take.

"Right!" Ivy recalled the license plate frame now. "It had dollar signs all around it in black and silver." How could she have forgotten that? But immediately she knew—she had been distracted by boys and tattoos. Her desire to have a normal life could result in putting everyone she loved most in danger, just as Amber had warned, and she didn't want that.

"John and I will go into town and find the van," Helena said. "Patricia and Ivy, be on alert."

Patricia snorted and gave an exaggerated scowl at Helena. But Ivy knew Helena hadn't said it for Patricia's benefit. Patricia was always on alert. Ivy knew it had been said for her benefit, for not paying closer attention, and the shame of it burned all the way down to her toes. Helena made her point and then signaled to John and walked out of the room.

A warm, strong finger touched the bottom of her chin, pulling up until she was forced to look into John's eyes. His black hair had recently made room for strands of gray. His Native American heritage gave him high cheek bones, darker skin and aura of patience and wisdom Ivy found comforting. Or perhaps, she thought, it was his gentle nature housed inside a large and powerful frame that caused her to feel comforted. John had a way of seeing you in a way that made you feel right about yourself and Ivy needed that more often than she cared to admit.

"You got your sister here safely," John peered into her eyes and she was sure he saw her soul, "I'm proud of you." He smiled, tapped his finger gently on her chin and was gone.

Ivy heard them in the next room, gearing up, though you'd never know they were packing deadly weapons if you just passed them on the street. The door banged shut and soon the rev of a car engine sparked to life and Ivy pushed away the threat of tears at having let everyone down.

"No one wants to be the one to tell you that you should have been paying better attention," Patricia spoke gently, "Especially not when it's so obvious that you already know that. But, it's Helena's duty to make sure you hold yourself accountable for the things you know you're responsible for." Patricia always spoke to her as though she were an adult and it made Ivy want to be that for her, but sometimes it was hard to live up to that.

"I know." Ivy glanced from Patricia to Amber when Amber tried to move and let out a little yelp of pain.

"Let's get that ankle elevated a little more and get a bigger ice pack on it." Patricia had removed Amber's shoe and sock and had pulled her pants leg up. "I'm afraid a trip to the hospital may be in order." Patricia left the room to find something else to prop up Amber's ankle.

"Ivy, I'm pretty sure it's broken." Amber was pale and her breathing was labored with pain. She'd done a great job hiding that from Patricia, and Ivy knew why. "Can you do anything?"

Ivy considered the swollen ankle and was pretty sure Amber was right. Her mind jumped back to that day six months ago in the barn. One of the barn cats had been attacked by something and was crying out in pitiful screams. They'd been headed there to work the punching bag and the wooden training dummy when they heard the sounds and rushed in to find the sad creature. Ivy loved cats, she loved going out to the barn and hanging out with them after a workout. She'd even named the injured cat. This was Tink, one of her favorites. Immediately she went to it but was afraid to touch the little thing for fear of making things worse. She was already crying when she reached out to gently pet the cat's back leg, the only spot she saw that didn't have an injury. She wanted Tink to live. She didn't want her to suffer. It was all she could think of as she felt Amber's arm go around her shoulders and her sister pull her close.

But something happened in that moment that would change her life forever. A warm current of energy, smooth as water, fast as lightning, flowed from the center of her being, down her arm, and out her fingertips into the cat. She could actually feel the power moving into the cat's body as if they were one being tied together through that warm power. Ivy sat there marveling at the sensation when she realized the power had also moved to Amber, who was also petting the cat. Amber's quick intake of breath told her that she felt it too. But this time the power grew warmer as it grew in intensity, flowing back from Amber, through her and down into the cat. Ivy wasn't sure what it was doing to Amber so dislodged herself and moved away from them both.

Ivy breathed hard and fast. It felt as though she'd gone on a long run without eating anything. Her heart raced, but her energy waned. It wasn't a painful sensation, but it was foreign, uncomfortable, and frightening. Immediately she turned to Amber, who was staring at her as though she'd grown a second head.

"You alright?" Ivy hoped she hadn't shared that feeling with her sister. "Did you feel that?"

"I felt it alright," Amber answered, still staring at Ivy. "What was it?"

"I don't know."

The cat moved and both girls turned their attention to it. Her fur was still matted with blood, but she was standing and licking at the blood as though her only care was to get clean.

"Tink?" Ivy moved a little closer to examine the small cat that had moments earlier been in the throes of a very painful death.

Tink stopped and eyed Ivy, then Amber, dismissed them, and went back to cleaning herself.

Ivy picked Tink up, eliciting a sound of displeasure, but not one of pain. Ivy ran her hands over the cat but found no wounds, no breaks, nothing. She put Tink down, who took off in a heartbeat down the length of the barn and around a corner, disappearing from sight and reach of the annoying humans. Ivy and Amber had not spoken of that day again. Not until now.

"I don't know if it'll work." Ivy looked from Amber's hazel eyes to her swollen ankle and back. "But, it can't hurt to try, right?" Oh, she hoped that was true. The cat was still alive and full of mischief, and neither she nor Amber experienced any negative repercussions from the healing except that it had made them tired for a short while.

Amber just nodded. Ivy crouched down at the foot of the lounge chair, took a deep breath and gently laid her hands on Amber's hot, swollen ankle. She shut her eyes, searching within herself for that place where that power lived. She envisioned Amber and her ankle as she felt the center of her being begin to warm. The energy moved out in a fluid motion. Her heart began to speed up even though she felt very relaxed and calm. She felt it leave her fingertips and enter Amber. Amber's ankle warmed to the touch and Ivy felt connected to what she could only think of as Amber's energy. The fluid energy covered the ankle, grew warm, and Ivy knew instinctively that it was healed.

The sound of a deep intake of breath caused Ivy to open her eyes. As Amber cast a worried glance at the kitchen door Ivy realized what she thought was a sign of relief, was far from it. It was the sound of shock. She slowly turned her head to see Patricia standing there with a pillow under her arm, an ice pack in her hand and her fist closed around what Ivy assumed were more pain pills. Patricia's mouth hung open.

"What have you done?"

CHAPTER 2

PATRICIA MOVED HER SLENDER fingers over Amber's ankle so tentatively Ivy wondered if she were concerned she'd catch something, or that there'd be some kind of electric shock involved in touching the place where she'd healed her sister. Ivy glanced at the clock for the third time since Patricia sat next to Amber. Time was moving so slowly Ivy fidgeted, wishing she could hurry it along and get it all over with. There was a really good reason why she and Amber had said nothing about her gift.

"How long have you been able to do this?" Patricia set Amber's ankle back down gently, as though she'd forgotten it was healed. She wrung her hands as she started pacing in front of the lounge chair, her eyes going everywhere but to Ivy.

"How did you plan on explaining away the injury?" She stopped pacing.

Ivy stared down at her shoes, seeing only the scene at the barn playing out over and over until she was dizzy from it. She half sat, half fell onto the end of the lounge chair, her hand falling naturally to Amber's now-healed ankle. She gripped the ankle so tightly that Amber moved, bringing Ivy out of her self-reflection.

She sat in the safest place she knew of—home. The furniture was modest but comfortable with little items collected over the years displayed on shelves, side tables, and walls. The faint smell of cedar mingled with the wonderful peach cobbler aroma coming from the kitchen. They had nothing fancy, by choice. Nothing to make them stand out in any way. Nothing they couldn't leave behind. What some might consider quaint or old fashioned was a clever disguise for the fortress that was really here. Ivy could see three places from her peripheral vision where weapons were hidden. She knew every escape route in the room, in the house, within a mile radius of the place. Fight or run. That was all there was to life for her and her sister.

And she knew why: Zachariah. Her father. A man who wielded such power that he could give or take life, just as he had given life to her and Amber and taken it from their mother. A power no one understood, but everyone feared. Now she had a power she didn't understand. She was her father's daughter and it set her apart from everyone else in this house, in this family.

"Ivy!" Patricia raised her voice enough to snap Ivy out of her inner reflections.

"Not long, maybe a month," Ivy spoke quietly, not daring to make eye contact. Prolonging the inevitable judgment she was certain was coming, "I didn't think about how I'd explain it."

A slight pressure, warm and gentle, on her shoulder brought her head up to meet Patricia's eyes. Patricia seemed to be searching for something, her eyes moving back and forth over Ivy's face, looking for something with such an expression of raw emotion that Ivy felt the burn of tears behind her eyes. Then Patricia pulled her close, held her tight and stroked her hair.

"Baby," Patricia always called her that and secretly Ivy liked it. "I love you. Everything is going to be okay."

Ivy melted into her and the tears broke free. Patricia continued to gently stroke her hair, waiting, as patient as John, for her to speak.

"I thought you'd worry that I was going to be like my father," Ivy admitted, bringing more tears and a hot ball of dread into her stomach. "I don't want to be like him."

"Listen to me," Patricia let go and stepped back just enough to peer into Ivy's eyes. "You are nothing like him. Not where it matters. This power you have will be a gift, because of how you use it. You have a heart for people, for animals, for lost causes." Patricia's smile was gentle and sincere.

"That's the thing with power, any kind of power. It, in itself, is neither good nor bad. How you use it determines whether or not it is good or bad, blessing or curse. You know what I mean?"

Ivy nodded, the ball of fire in the pit of her stomach began to cool. She wiped the tears from her eyes as she stepped back, arms falling away, but somehow, in some real and important way, she was closer to Patricia than any embrace could ever bring them.

"She saved one of the barn cats." Amber's voice was quiet, but steady. "But, healing makes her tired. Drains her."

Ivy nodded. "When I was saving the cat I got tired, then I touched Amber and it was as though she were a living battery that I could pull energy from." Ivy told Patricia exactly what had happened the day in the barn.

"You need to understand, Ivy," Patricia gazed at her pointedly, "that kind of power always comes with a price. One way or another. I never saw Zachariah look tired after a healing, but his brother, who I believe is my grandfather, Eze- kiel nearly died from trying to heal a child whose cancer had progressed really far before it was discovered. They say he was in a coma for weeks afterward. I wasn't born then, but I remember the sister wives talking about it. So be careful."

"Amber?" Ivy hadn't considered that using Amber as a living battery might have dire consequences. "Did it hurt when I touched you? When I took your energy?"

"Not hurt, not exactly," Amber replied. "I could feel something like an electric current, but it didn't hurt. It kind of hummed through me, if that makes sense. And it made me really tired. Exhausted."

Consequences had always been Ivy's enemy. Going to school, she wanted to be on the swim team, or maybe be a cheerleader so Gabe would notice her, but when Helena laid out the possible consequences of being found, it seemed unfair to everyone else for her to want those things.

Ivy's heart picked up its pace. "Do we have to tell John and Helena?"

"Why wouldn't you?" Amber's quizzical expression left no doubt as to where she stood on the matter.

"You don't understand," she glanced back to Amber. "You're always the good one. You always do what you are supposed to. You're careful. I'm the one everyone has to worry about. Now, there's more to worry about. What if they pull me out of school until we know more about this power?" No more Gabe. A prisoner in the home she loved. That was *not* going to happen.

Ivy shook her head before Patricia could speak.

"Just give me a little time to figure out what this…" she focused on her hands, then back to Patricia, "…power is. You can help me. Then, when we tell them we can let them know all the facts. They won't have to worry. They won't have to put me under a microscope. Please, Patty?"

Patricia scowled and did that thing with her eyes like she was reading as she looked into Ivy's face.

"I don't like keeping secrets from John and Helena." Patricia relaxed her stance and the scowl disappeared. "One week. That's it. And no keeping secrets from me. We work on trying to figure out as much as we can about your power, then we go to them and tell them everything. Deal?"

Ivy already had her arms around Patricia, hugging her with a quick squeeze, trying on a tentative smile.

"If we're going to hold this information back we need to do two things now." Patricia considered both girls. "First, no experimenting without me there, got it?" Both girls nodded, so she went on. "We had better wrap that ankle or they're going to know something is up."

Patricia wrapped Amber's ankle and cleaned up all the supplies lying around the lounge chair. Patricia hated to talk about the community. Helena and John talked about it more than Patricia did and they had been away longer by nearly five years. No one ever pressed her to talk about it. Ivy knew Patricia had seen their father kill their mother. Patricia saved her and Amber that night. But, she never wanted to talk about it in detail. And she never spoke about family and friends she'd left behind. Hearing her talk about her grandfather was like getting a peek inside a forbidden treasure box. She wasn't about to push her on it though, not when she'd just been given a huge favor.

Ivy followed Patricia and Amber into the kitchen. The peach cobbler was sitting out, perfuming the air with goodness.

CHAPTER 3

THIS IS WHERE GABE'S cousin moved to?" Helena's tone rode the line between incredulous and angry. "This is not the best part of town. I think we need to change our plan and do this once we know the area more."

Ivy's heart sank as she listened to Helena. Since they'd been followed from the dojo security around the house tightened making it impossible to get in, or out, without John and Helena knowing. So, she'd told them they were meeting Gabe at Ryan's to help Ryan get his new place set up. Helena refused, Patricia argued that cancelling plans at the last minute were unfair to Gabe and Ryan and John suggested a compromise. They could go, but not alone.

The houses were a mix of in-need-of-repair and in-need-of-demolition. Fallen gates, windows held together with silver duct tape, paint peeling away to expose ailing wood, overgrowth in some yards, roof partially fallen in. The neighborhood gave Ivy a mix of dread and sadness as they saw house after house in states that appeared uninhabitable, yet curtains pulled back to watch them as they drove slowly toward the next block.

"Poverty doesn't make a neighborhood bad. But desperation can cause anyone to do things they wouldn't normally do. Just be careful." John continued to drive slowly, watching the people who walked the streets or sat out on porches.

"Gabe's cousin is up a block and a half and down an alleyway." Ivy would be amazed if they let them go to Ryan's house at this point.

"As long as it looks safe." Helena said

They saw the name of the alleyway that Gabe had given to Ivy and John slowed the car, pulled over and stopped, letting the engine idle as though the final decision had not yet been decided and they could easily just drive away.

Patricia leaned forward slightly, reached around behind her and produced a small handgun. She leaned back as she handed the gun to Ivy.

The thing was heavier than one might think, and Ivy balanced it on her palm for a moment before gripping the handle, index finger outside and away from the trigger. Ivy double checked the safety, found it to be on and leaned forward just as Patricia had done when removing it. She tucked it beneath her blouse at the small of her back.

All the training they'd had over the years—the martial arts, archery, target practice and weapons training—was for moments like this. She doubted they might actually need that training, but wondered if Amber's heart was racing as fast as hers. The moment of uncertainty passed as Helena got out and opened their door. Amber got out, then Ivy and they stood waiting for Helena's final instructions.

For all of Helena's intrusive training, harping and ability to really frustrate Ivy, Ivy never faulted her. She relied on Helena, not just to keep them safe, but to know that they were ready to keep themselves safe. If Helena let them go it was because it was as safe as it could be, or because she trusted them that much. Ivy realized that she depended on Helena and her commitment to them and their safety. She needed Helena. So when Helena looked at her as though she were trying to read something deep within her, then nodded her approval to go, Ivy's heart swelled with pride just as her nerves steeled themselves.

"Gabe is there, right?" Helena confirmed.

"Just texted him," Ivy answered. "He's there."

"You're right. This area isn't as bad. But remember that we have no idea who was following you. Remember your training," Helena added.

Ivy turned toward the alley trusting that Amber would follow and that Helena, John, and Patricia would be nearby somewhere. A slight niggling of guilt tapped at her heart knowing they'd not have allowed her to get a tattoo, but they'd trusted her to go, thinking she was helping a friend.

Once they stepped into the alleyway, Ivy's senses went on high alert and she searched for exits, potential dangers, and listened to everything going on around her.

Unlike the rest of the dreary neighborhood, the alley had a cheerful, bohemian feel to it with plants hanging outside of windows, cute little signs decorated with symbols or dried flowers inviting people to come in for palm readings, tarot cards, jewelry, homemade arts and crafts or music lessons. They finally came to a door with a sign that simply read "Tattoo You." Ivy thought that might be an old Rolling Stones song, or album. She wasn't a hundred percent sure and would have to ask Patricia later.

"You know you don't have to get the tattoo," Amber, like Jiminy Cricket, took a shot at being her conscience. "We can say our parents changed their minds."

"And look like a child?" But, maybe Amber's idea was the way to go. If Helena wasn't so strict, Ivy thought she wouldn't have to hide things from her. Helena was as much to blame for this as Gabe.

"This is it." Ivy felt more excitement than anxiety now. They'd made it to Ryan's unscathed and could hear music blaring from within, where Gabe would be waiting for her. Okay, maybe he wasn't actually waiting for her, but he was expecting her. Wasn't that close enough?

Ivy knocked on the door and it swung open. Gabe stood there smiling a disarming smile, and Ivy's heart stuttered just a little.

"You made it! Come on in!" Gabe stepped aside and as Ivy walked by him she wondered what cologne he was wearing. It was something masculine and wonderful, just like him, and she hoped she would be near him most of the night, smelling that cologne and feeling the heat coming off of his tall, athletic body.

"Great neighborhood," Amber said with no enthusiasm at all.

"I told you I'd pick you up." Ryan walked out from the kitchen that doubled as the tattooing room. "Cute little girl like you coming to the shady side of town. Living life on the edge."

Ryan was as tall as Gabe and some people thought they were brothers, but Ryan's hair was slightly curly and darker than Gabe's. He had more of a devil-may-care look to him where Gabe was definitely athletic. The smile he gave to Amber might have melted the heart of your typical teen girl, but Amber was tougher on a lot of levels, and Ivy figured Ryan was going to have to try a bit harder if he wanted to impress her sister.

Gabe leaned back against the wall next to where Ryan stood, and the double whammy of hotness was definitely enough to get Ivy's heart racing. Gabe was wearing a short sleeved shirt and his biceps were about the size of her calves. He flexed just a little, bringing her attention abruptly to his face. She felt a bit flushed and hoped she wasn't red-faced, though she had a feeling by the way his dimple deepened when he grinned that that was exactly what was going on.

"So, you want a tattoo, huh?" Ryan asked Ivy. "What do you want? A flower? Heart? Some kind of Celtic love knot maybe?" He elbowed Gabe when he said that last part and then wiggled his eyebrows, earning him a frown from Ivy.

"No. Nothing like that. I want small angel wings on the back of my right wrist. But, I want you to thread in raven wings like this." Ivy pulled out a piece of paper and handed it to Ryan.

Ryan glanced at the drawing, then again, this time giving careful consideration to the picture.

"This is pretty amazing and by the colored pencil work it appears to be an original. Did you draw this?" Ryan glanced from the drawing to Ivy.

"No, I'm not the artsy type, I'm more girl of action type." Ivy laughed. "I told Amber I wanted something beautiful with wings. She drew that. I love it."

"You did this?" Ryan asked Amber.

"Don't act so surprised." Amber shrugged as though it had been easy to come up with the idea of raven wings peeking through black raven feathers.

"This is amazing." Ryan's tone was more respectful and he stopped posing in the doorway of the kitchen and motioned for them to come in.

Ryan pointed to a chair that sat next to a small chrome table with the items Ivy figured he'd need to do the tattoo.

"Did you get the paper signed by your guardian?" Ryan sat down in front of the small table and took Ivy's hand, extending it toward him so he could easily access her wrist.

"Of course," Ivy assured him. She took her arm back, dug in the front pocket of her jeans and produced the necessary, and forged, document. Helena might trust them in a questionable part of town while under her keen supervision, but a tattoo? No. And it was best to ask forgiveness than permission when it came to Helena. Ryan studied the document, set down on a counter behind him and reached for her hand again, pulling it back into place.

He flipped her hand so her wrist was bared to him and ran his thumb across her skin.

"Nice skin. Soft. Great canvass."

Ivy wasn't sure if he was complementing her or even speaking to her directly, but before she could respond Gabe sat down next to her.

"Yeah, well, look with your eyes, not with your hands, bro." Gabe leaned back tipping the chair onto two legs as he balanced himself next to Ivy. He wriggled his eyebrows at Ivy, smiled and slid a glance back to Ryan. "I'd hate to have to hurt you to protect her honor and all."

"Well, first of all...bro, I'm not scared," Ryan laughed, "Second of all, I actually do need to use my hands if she wants a tattoo. Besides," Ryan added, "It's not my fault if your girl here has exceptionally soft skin."

Gabe frowned at his cousin, took Ivy's free hand, and ran his thumb over the back of her forearm.

"This is ridiculous!" Amber interrupted, getting a scowl from Ivy. "We don't have all night and that tattoo is pretty intricate. What I want to know is, how safe is all this? I mean, we're in your kitchen."

"Temper, temper, now," Ryan smiled at Amber, "I thought we planned on having some fun?"

Gabe let Ivy's hand go, winning Amber another scathing glower from her sister.

"I use disposable needles. I'm very, very careful. It's safe," Ryan told them, then added, "I promise. You can trust me."

As Ryan put everything together Ivy heard the sound of scraping across the kitchen floor. Gabe moved just behind her where he'd have a great view of the tattooing. The heat of his body penetrated through her shirt, warming her back and shoulders. It was so distracting.

"So are you doing any martial arts competitions this summer?" Ivy asked without turning to look at him.

"This summer I'm training for my first professional MMA fight. I've gone as far as I wanted to go with the competitions. I'm ready for something more challenging." Gabe leaned in closer, putting one hand on the back of her chair. She could feel him breathing into her hair, heard his intake of breath as though he were smelling her hair. All she could do was fidget in her seat.

"Your mom is okay with that? It looks pretty brutal." Ivy finally found her voice.

"I'm eighteen now, so she'll need to be okay with it. But she understands it's my choice. She may not like it, but she doesn't give me grief over it." Gabe was so close his warm breath in her hair and down the back of her neck gave her goosebumps. "My mom is easy to figure out. I totally get why she feels that way. Not all women are so easy to understand."

It wasn't the first time Gabe brought up his inability to understand women. Well, one woman. Young woman. Her. Ivy hadn't been able to explain to him why she couldn't just be part of the popular crowd. His crowd. Without the ability to explain to him that she had to remain unseen as much as possible, he simply accused her of making him have to choose between his friends and her. And that had not ended well for her.

"Your mom lets you do whatever you want?" Ivy decided Gabe was kryptonite to her brain and better judgment.

"Right now she's not even at home. She totally trusts me to do the right thing." Gabe leaned in closer. "Do you?" That last part was softly spoken into her ear and sent a shiver up her spine.

Amber cleared her throat.

"Uh, yeah, let's trust the guy with dreams of a career in violence and no supervision at home. You're lucky my sister has a filter for crazy when it comes from you. As in, she can't seem to hear the crazy in half the crap you say!" Amber sat down at the table and rested her chin in her hand.

"So where's your mom then?" Ivy asked, keeping the conversation away from Amber's silly commentary.

"My little cousin, Mia, Ryan's baby sister, she's really sick, so my mom flew out to Colorado to help take care of her." Gabe leaned back, taking his warmth with him. His tone changed slightly and Ivy saw Ryan peer over to him and then go back to his preparation which looked about ready. Neither of them said anything for a time, causing Ivy to wonder just how bad things were with Gabe's cousin.

"I'm sorry your sister is sick." Amber said sincerely.

"Thanks." Ryan's mouth was a thin line, no smile and something in his eyes made Ivy want to change the subject.

"Is this gonna hurt?" Ivy asked. She knew it wasn't going to feel good, but honestly wasn't worried about the pain. She'd always had a high pain threshold. She was more worried about Helena's reaction to the tattoo.

"A little at first, but then your endorphins kick in and it's not bad. Afterward it will feel kind of like a sunburn for a little while. The skin will flake and I'll give you something to keep your skin moist. I've got some instructions written up for you for aftercare." Ryan's mood seemed to lift as he concentrated on something other than his sick sister.

"Ivy heals pretty fast, right Ivy?" Amber referred to Ivy's plan to attempt to heal her own wound as soon as they left.

"Something like that, yeah," Ivy responded.

"I've seen you take some pretty hard hits at the dojo and wondered how you could bounce back so quickly when I would see you at school." Gabe leaned in again.

"That's not because I heal quickly," Ivy said. "That's because I rarely let anyone get a good punch in." She turned her head to smile at him, but he was closer than she thought, their faces so close he could have leaned in another inch and kissed her. She quickly turned back around, flustered, forgetting what she had been talking about.

Amber sounded like she was close to laughing when she said, "Ivy really is pretty good at all that physical stuff." Ivy wanted to kick her under the table, but Amber had been smart enough to sit too far away.

"Here we go," Ryan interrupted.

Everyone seemed mesmerized as Ryan worked for an hour on the tattoo. He'd offered to give Ivy a break at the half hour mark, but she declined. She wanted to get it done. They only had a couple of hours to be there, and she hoped the tattoo would be finished by the time they left.

Ryan had the outline done at the half hour mark and the next half hour started adding the the black of the raven feathers. An hour and a half later, Ivy had a beautiful tattoo on her wrist and she stared at it in awe.

"You did a wonderful job. Thank you! I love it!" Ivy couldn't stop admiring it. It was just as beautiful as Amber's drawing.

Gabe gently took her arm and brought her around to face him as he examined the tattoo. Her hand lay relaxed inside his much larger hand as he examined it.

"Beautiful," was all he said before releasing her arm and smiling until she worried if she'd be able to stand up without fainting at his feet.

Ryan went over the aftercare directions and told her to come back in a couple of days so he could take a look at it.

They walked out into the sitting area right outside of the kitchen. Ivy sat next to Amber on the couch as each boy took an armchair at opposite ends of the couch. Gabe sat closest to Ivy and she wondered if he wanted to be near her or if it was just fate that he took that chair. She'd promised herself she wouldn't read too much into it, but he did seem interested in her.

"What brings you back here to Coalville?" Amber asked Ryan.

"Needed a change of scenery."

"While your sister is sick?" Ivy couldn't help herself. It just came out. She would never leave Amber's side if Amber was so ill that another family member had to fly out and help take care of her.

"My mother has been preoccupied with Mia's care, and I'm no good with stuff like that, so it was better for me to just stay out of the way." Ryan shifted in his seat.

Ivy and Amber exchanged a glance.

"How long have you been here?" Amber changed the subject.

"About a week and a half. Right, Gabe?"

Gabe nodded. "About that. Mom's been at your place two weeks, so that seems right."

"May I ask what's wrong with your sister?" Ivy asked. She found she liked

Ryan a little less knowing he'd left his family at such a crucial time.

"Some kind of rare cancer. I'm not really sure." Ryan's gaze slid to the floor and Ivy thought there was more to it than he was saying.

"What are they doing for it?" She pressed him even though he was uncomfortable, or maybe because of it.

"Everything. Anything." Ryan's eyes shined intense for a moment. "I'd do anything for my sister." It was the first glimmer of real caring about his sister's condition, and the look in his eyes was startling.

"But, you're not there." Ivy reminded him, holding his gaze.

"That doesn't mean I wouldn't do anything within my power to help her." He broke their gaze, shook his head at some internal dialog that Ivy couldn't even imagine then added, "I mean, if there was something I could do, I'd be doing it. There's not, so I'm here and out of the way. It's what was asked of me and it's what I can do."

Ivy was even more intrigued by this bit of information and was about to ask why he'd been asked to leave his sick sister's side, but Gabe interjected.

"It's personal family stuff. Boring. Let's talk about you instead."

"I didn't realize you two are orphans. What's that like?" Ryan's question made them all stare at him.

It wasn't like people didn't know they were adopted by Helena and John. Some people knew it. The doctor knew it. The school. But, it wasn't easy knowledge to come by, so having someone know anything at all was disconcerting.

"No. We're adopted." Ivy kept her cool. "Orphans have no parents at all. But, Amber and I, we have a family who cares for us. Who would never leave us. Even if someone told them to."

The barb hit the mark and Ryan frowned, but backed down.

"Where did you hear we were orphans?" Amber interjected.

"Gabe's mom." Ryan offered, quickly averting his eyes. "She mentioned something along those lines."

"That's not true." Gabe's tone lost its easy going charm and his glance at Ryan was not friendly. "My mother would never divulge any personal information like that."

"She didn't mean to spill the beans," Ryan tried to smile and change the mood, but it didn't seem to be working on anyone. "I overheard something and put two and two together. And obviously, I was wrong. Sorry if I hit a sore spot. I didn't mean to."

"Let's just drop this." Gabe said. "I'm sorry Ivy. Amber."

"Well, it's time for us to go anyway." Ivy smiled, checking her watch, knowing that if they didn't follow Helena's rules they'd never be allowed to come back. Time was up.

"Already?" Gabe stood as well and walked the girls to the door while Ryan remained seated but waved his goodbye. "I'd hoped to get a chance to talk to you, alone."

"If you want it bad enough, you'll make it happen." Ivy said as she opened the door.

"Okay then, how about we go out to dinner after Ryan checks on your tattoo in a couple of days and talk then?" Gabe reached out to tuck an errant strand of Ivy's hair behind her ear.

"I think we can make that happen." Ivy said and then quickly corrected herself. "If you're not worried what people think?" Before the door shut, she thought she saw something in Gabe's face, the tightening of his lips, a tilt to his head, but he said nothing more.

CHAPTER 4

HELENA STOOD ACROSS THE street at the mouth of the alley. She turned south and started walking, so Ivy and Amber turned in that direction as well, but on the opposite side of the street.

Helena walked at a faster pace, but was always within sight. John and Patricia had to be close by, but Ivy didn't see them yet. She had the feeling Helena was about to go knocking on Ryan's door if they'd been even a minute late.

Ivy had only walked half a block when she felt it. The hairs on the back of her neck stood up and the feeling she was being watched was so powerful she had to fight her natural inclination to look around to see who was there. Amber continued to walk as though nothing were wrong and it wasn't until her sister reached up to twirl her hair that she realized Amber knew something was up as well. She and Amber had secret signals and code words they used that no one else knew about, not even Helena, John or Patricia. Amber twirling her hair always meant danger. Ivy signaled in kind, a quick flip of her hair in response. They picked up the pace just a little and started talking so no one would know they had caught on.

"See anything of interest?" Amber wasn't quite whispering, but her tone was low and her voice soft.

"Not yet. But, I feel it. Someone is watching us, I just can't tell from where."

Ivy moved like she was a little tipsy and bumped into Amber, knocking her slightly off balance.

"Ivy, knock it off, you almost made me fall!" Amber pushed back a little, her eyes roaming the area as though she wanted to make sure no one had seen her near-fall. Ivy laughed a little and looked as well.

There were two men, one about a block back and one coming in from a side street, both shadows of large men. Helena had turned the corner before Ivy saw them and she wondered if Helena was going to get John or if she'd just not seen the threat.

In less than a minute, she and Amber would pass the man on the side road. She thought to cross the street, but the man behind them was catching up and he was on that side of the road. It wasn't exactly a trap, but it potential danger. She and Amber still had some options, but as soon as they began to run they became prey and she didn't want things to go down that way. They would just stay the course, hope for the best, be prepared for the worst.

Ivy could almost see Amber tightening up, ready to run, ready to fight. She was ready too. Her heart raced. She tried taking in as much as possible without letting on that she was worried. They passed the man on the side street. He was smoking one of those thin and fruity cigars. He wore a ball cap pulled down in front of his face.

It was only a few steps more, and Ivy heard it. Footsteps running toward them. She turned just as the man with the ball cap pushed Amber down hard and made a grab for her. It was then that she saw there were two men, one with long hair close by the guy with the ball cap who was rushing over to Amber, and then the man that was further back. Where was Helena?

No time to think. Ivy maneuvered so that the man with long hair trying to grab her got nothing but air, followed by a swift kick to the groin.

"Son of a bitch!" He yelled. He staggered, but was back upright in seconds.

The man attacking Amber had his hands full, but he got a good punch in and Ivy forgot everything as she ran to help her sister.

Ivy tried her best to stay focused. She'd made her decision as to her next move, but then two things happened all at once. John appeared from seemingly nowhere and went after Amber's attacker. He was on top of the long hair guy hitting Amber, and though Ivy's first impression was that the guy hitting Amber was big, he was small compared to John. Then the ball-cap guy who tried to take her grabbed her hair, yanked hard, but then let go as someone else took him down. It was the guy following them up the street. And, he seemed just as deadly as John as he started beating the man with the ball cap until that man wasn't moving anymore.

She didn't recognize him at first because he was wearing a jacket she'd never seen before, probably Ryan's. Gabe had donned a beanie and Ryan's jacket, but she recognized him once he was closer. Well, recognized who he was, but she wasn't at all sure she recognized the Gabe that beat that guy perhaps to death.

"Stop!" She ran to him. She didn't use his name just in case people were watching this play out. She was pretty sure there were. No one that would help, but someone might talk later.

Gabe was already slowing down when she yelled. He stopped, reached in to take the guy's pulse, then kicked him one more time for good measure.

"He's alive." Gabe glanced over at John who was checking on Amber. Her assailant was a heap of blood and mess on the street. Gabe knew John from when he'd pick the girls up at martial arts class and he nodded at the large man, but turned his full attention on Ivy.

"Are you alright?" Gabe started to reach for her but noticed his hands were bloody and pulled them back. He stood there staring down at her with such intensity Ivy wasn't sure she knew this Gabe at all.

"Yes," she finally found her voice.

"I was pissed at Ryan for being such a douche and wanted to give him hell for it. Then I realized that I'd not asked if you had a ride home or wanted me to walk you. So, then I felt like a douche and well…" he spread his hands out at the scene around them as though to say "and this is how it all ended."

"You're not a douche." Ivy wanted to say he was a hero but she was certain that would come out as lame as 'You're not a douche' had, so she just added, "Thank you."

John and Amber walked over and Ivy could see Amber's lip was bleeding. She ran to her sister and hugged her, eliciting a cry of pain.

"I'll take care of this as soon as we're home, okay?" Ivy whispered. No way would she let Amber suffer when she had the power to fix her.

John shook Gabe's hand and looked over at the man in the ball cap who was still unconscious on the ground.

"I knew you did martial arts competition, but that was more than any martial arts there, son." John nodded toward the man on the ground.

"I'm training for MMA fighting." Gabe glanced over at the man as well, then back to John with a smile. "I think I just won my first match."

"I'd say so." John smiled as a car drove toward them.

Ivy recognized the SUV immediately and put her arm around Amber's shoulder to help walk her toward it. Helena was driving and stopped where the girls stood. Patricia jumped out of the car and ran to the girls. John and Gabe walked up behind them as Helena also got out to meet them on the other side of the vehicle.

"What happened?" Patricia asked. "Helena said someone was following you and John got out to see if he could catch someone. Then all hell broke loose."

"They attacked us! I thought Helena would come back, but she didn't!" Ivy looked accusingly at Helena, who only frowned back at her.

"I wasn't the one with a gun. You were." Helena's voice was not apologetic at all. She was angry. "I went for back up thinking you could hold your own because you have a gun."

Ivy froze for a moment and felt around to her back where the gun was still in place.

"I totally forgot I had the gun!"

"A weapon you don't think to use is no weapon at all, Ivy. Look at your sister!" Helena nodded in Amber's direction.

"You're saying this is my fault?" Ivy's voice rose an octave as she felt both angry and guilty.

"Let's just simmer down for a minute." John moved in between Ivy and Helena. "If Ivy was unsure of using the gun it was best not to pull it out. One of those guys could have gotten it and…" John's attention went out toward the street as he talked about the badly beaten men and then stopped. "They're gone."

They all turned back to the street to find it empty.

"Either they were faking being unconscious, or there were a lot more people here that carried them off." Patricia said.

"Hell!" Helena breathed out, obviously mad at herself now as well. "We need to know who they are and why they're after the girls."

"Really?" Patricia asked. "You need to ask that question?"

"I'd like to know." Gabe said. "If this isn't random violence, then what is it?"

"It's just a mugging gone wrong." Helena moved and helped Amber get into the car. She buckled her in even though Amber was perfectly capable. She turned to John, who nodded, and he and Patricia got back into the vehicle. They waited there for Ivy.

"I'm so sorry this happened," she said to Gabe.

"You're sorry? For what? You didn't ask to get mugged." Gabe leaned in to whisper, "If that's really what happened here." She knew it was a thinly veiled question, but he didn't press her on it.

"Are you okay?" she asked him, taking in for the first time his own injuries. His hands were bloody and she wasn't sure how much of that was his blood. It looked like he'd been hit at least once in the face as a goose egg was starting to form near his left eye high on his cheekbone. "I think you need to get some ice on that right away."

Gabe reached up and touched the spot, nodding. "Will the police be by for my statement?" he asked.

Ivy knew no one would be calling the police, but she wasn't sure how to tell him that. She did the only thing she knew to do, she lied. "If they need your statement, they'll be by."

"If?" Gabe's questioning expression held an entire conversation in it that they just couldn't have right then.

Ivy raised up on the tip of her toes and placed a soft kiss on the side of Gabe's face that didn't appear painful. Perhaps it was the adrenaline still pumping through her veins that gave her the courage, but there it was.

"Thank you," Ivy whispered as she backed away, finding it difficult to break away from him when he was looking at her like that. So serious. So concerned.

"Do you want a ride home, Gabe?" John had rolled down his window to ask.

"No. Thank you, sir." Gabe responded, only then taking his eyes off Ivy. "I'm going back to my cousin's place. It's close. I'm sure I'll be fine."

John nodded, rolled up his window, and they began to drive away. Ivy turned to watch Gabe out the back window until they turned the corner.

They walked into the house and everyone headed for the kitchen. It wasn't that anyone was hungry, though John opened the refrigerator out of habit, coming back empty handed. The kitchen was always the meeting room when you wanted to feel comforted. Ivy never questioned why that was, she just knew it to be true. Perhaps it was the never ending aroma of pie or cake or cobbler. Whatever it was, she found herself calming, reflecting and worrying more about getting Amber healed than anything else.

"How did they find us?" Helena sat down slowly as though she were sore, or maybe just tired beyond her ability to deal.

"Are you sure it's someone from the community?" John asked.

"Who else could it be? They're following Ivy and Amber. They've tried to abduct them. They're violent. They're stealthy. Need I say more?" Helena didn't need to. John and Patricia looked so serious, so concerned, Ivy knew it must be true.

"It could be your run of the mill kidnappers, white slavers, and I know no one wants to hear this, but rapists. The girls are beautiful. They're young, and someone who doesn't know them might think they're easy targets." Patricia was nodding as though she were trying to convince herself. Run of the mill criminals were not something to scoff at, but they were easier to get rid of. Easy to deal with. They weren't an organized community already proven to be comfortable with killing.

"It's possible," Helena said. "We've been so careful to stay under the radar. There's no reason I can think of that we'd be found now."

"Let's keep the girls home from school while we try to figure this out." Patricia's expression turned to one of apology. "We have to be certain of what's going on."

"I keep running it over and over in my mind. What might have happened to bring attention to us? What might we have done?" Helena's voice was almost far away, as if she were somewhere other than there in the kitchen. Her face seemed sad and Ivy felt compelled to walk over and hug her. Helena grabbed onto Ivy with such fierceness Ivy was taken aback.

"I won't let them have you," Helena promised. "They will have to kill me first."

Her words shoved adrenaline into Ivy's veins, and brought Amber to tears.

"It's not going to come to that." Ivy patted Helena's back wanting to offer the reassurance that had always been offered to her.

"It's possible that there was a catalyst to bringing them here," Patricia said and sat down across from where Helena usually sat.

It took a moment for Ivy to consider what Patricia might be trying to say. Then it hit her. It hadn't been that long ago that Ivy had discovered and used her powers. Then she used them again tonight. Could there be some connection between her power and the community being able to find them? Was her power like a beacon to her father? Was she the reason they would all suffer?

"No," Ivy whispered. If she could have begged Patricia not to let it be so she would have, but it wasn't really up to Patricia. Patricia didn't control that. And Patricia couldn't be faulted for thinking it.

"What is it?" Helena asked as she moved to sit across from Patricia.

Patricia's guilt showed and Helena looked at Ivy. "What is it, Ivy?"

Fear stole her words, her breath, even a heartbeat for a moment. This was her fault. Somehow she knew it. So did Patricia.

Amber got up and walked to her, took her hand and gazed into her eyes.

"This isn't your fault. No matter what, this isn't your fault."

Ivy examined Amber's swollen face, the dried blood Amber had missed wiping off at the corner of her mouth. There were bruises all over her face, her knuckles and God knew where else. Ivy couldn't stop herself. She reached out and gently touched her sister's face. And, it began to heal.

A sharp intake of breath came from behind Ivy, and she knew it was Helena. By the time Amber was fully healed Ivy was tired and totally unprepared for whatever she'd have to say or do next now that they all knew.

"How long have you been able to heal?" Helena was still sitting, and Ivy wondered if that was by choice. Helena's face was white as a ghost.

"A month or so. Not long," Ivy answered and she followed Amber back to the table where they both sat.

"When were you going to tell us?" Helena asked and then immediately glanced at Patricia. "You knew?"

"I knew. I found out today," Patricia admitted.

"Why didn't you say anything?" Helena she asked.

"It was Ivy's secret to tell. And she wasn't ready yet." Patricia held Helena's gaze.

Ivy wasn't sure she wanted to know what Helena was thinking as she sat there with that look on her face.

"Helena, I was going to tell you, but I just needed time to figure out how." Ivy hoped this wasn't going to blow up in her face.

Helena sat there as quiet as John had been the entire time. John reached out and took Helena's hand.

"Can you feel him?" Helena asked.

It took a moment before Ivy understood. If the community, or more likely, her father, could track them using her power, then perhaps she could somehow feel him through his.

"I don't think so. I mean, I don't know what I would be feeling for."

Helena nodded as though she understood, and perhaps she did.

"We need to figure out if he can track you through your power whether you use your power or not. Or find out how they did find us and make sure that doesn't happen again." Helena's color came back slowly. "If he can track us through Ivy then we have to gear up for a battle. If he tracks only when Ivy uses her power then we just need to not use it." Helena watched Ivy nod in agreement. She would not be using her power if that is what kept them safe.

"And if it was something else?" John asked.

"Then we need to figure out what that is and fast," Helena answered and then added, "There's no use running until we know how we're being tracked. At least here we have home field advantage."

John and Patricia were nodding, somber but resolute.

"No school, no powers, no going out on your own." Helena said. "We need to set up traps around the house, alarms, make sure all of our weapons are ready. Patricia, I may need you to go to the safe house and make sure there are provisions and weapons ready there. It's been a while since we've been there."

Patricia nodded. "I can do that tomorrow."

Ivy knew the safe house was by the lake, but it had been years since she'd been there.

"John, you take first watch. I'll relieve you around 0400 and once it's light out, we need to do some recon." Helena was more herself now that she had a plan. She turned to Ivy and Amber. "I know it's hard, but I need you to try and get some rest. The next few days are going to be tough."

Ivy didn't need a second invitation to leave. They both went up to their bedroom.

"What are we going to do?" Amber asked.

"Try to keep our home if we can," Ivy answered. "But if they're able to track us through me, Amber, I'll have to run. Without you."

"No! That's not how this is going to go down. We stay together!" Amber was adamant. "If you leave, I leave."

Ivy nodded. There was no sense in upsetting Amber further. She knew what she had to do to keep her sister, her family, safe. Like it or not, she would do it.

CHAPTER 5

THE SUN CAME IN BRIGHT and warm through the parted curtains in her bedroom. Ivy lay staring at the stripe of white on her ceiling the sun had put there. She watched as that stripe grew and got brighter and now she was sure this would be the last time she'd look up at that ceiling and greet the sun there. This room, the room of her childhood, was like a treasure box of memories and she took them out one at a time in her mind, marveled at them, visited with them and put them back, all but one.

She recalled the day that Patricia told her and Amber about the death of their mother. She told about how much their mother wanted to protect them. How she begged Patricia to take her and Amber away from that place. She told them of what she saw their father do, his promise to make their lives miserable. She cried that day at the loss of a mother she never knew and would never know. How brave she must have been to go against such a powerful and dangerous man. And to be willing to give her life to save her daughters. Now Ivy knew it was her turn to be brave. It wouldn't even be as hard as what her mother had to endure because she wasn't being held by a mad man. Not yet at least. She wasn't pregnant. She wasn't surrounded by people willing to betray her.

Ivy quietly sat up, careful to be silent and not wake Amber or anyone else in the house. She already had a bag packed for emergency escapes. It was kept in the closet just in case they ever had to leave at a moment's notice. Amber had one there too. But, Amber wasn't going with her. She couldn't because it was too dangerous. Amber had to be protected. If they took her away, away from this place, away from her, she could still have a relatively normal life. Amber didn't have some kind of freakish power that their father could track. Only Ivy had that. So only Ivy would leave. Like her mother, she would give anything to keep the people she loved safe from Zachariah.

Softly, she moved bare footed across the floor to the closet, opened it without making a sound and picked up a backpack that sat on the floor under her hanging clothes. She brought it out, set it on her bed and looked around the room for items she wanted to add to her pack. There were pictures of her and Amber through the years, but the one she wanted to keep was one when they were around ten years old and Patricia had wanted to dress them up alike. The only thing they could agree to wear that was alike was their softball uniform. Then, just as Patricia snapped the picture they made faces at her not realizing they were making the same exact silly face. It looked like they planned it because it was so exact, but they hadn't. It had just happened that way. She loved that picture and that memory, so she put the framed picture into the backpack.

There was a necklace from John that she got when she turned thirteen and an amazing set of throwing stars Helena got her when she showed a proficiency in using the ones they trained with. They were titanium, but they were colored pink with Hello Kitty on them, something Helena had customized for her. Ivy picked them up and shook her head. Who gives deadly weapons with Hello Kitty on them? Helena. She picked up a scarf Patricia had made her. It was so ugly, but she wore it every winter since she was nine. It was the first one Patricia had ever made and since she wasn't sure it would turn out she had used some unwanted yarn that she'd gotten on sale. It was a pea green with burnt orange entwined in it and it was everything but symmetrical. But, Patricia was so proud of completing it that Ivy asked for it, making Patricia all gooey sentimental because she knew Ivy would wear the ugly thing with pride.

She didn't really need to bring anything to remember Amber by. Not only because they looked so much alike, but because she wore something on her skin that was from Amber. Ivy inspected the healed tattoo. The colors peeking through the black feathers were vivid and beautiful. She loved that Amber drew it for her and that she would have that forever now.

Ivy changed into some sweats, put on a ball cap and a pair of sunglasses, and threw the pack over her shoulder. She spared one last glance at her sleeping sister, so peaceful and beautiful, then slipped out and down the stairs.

Her stomach protested as she walked past the kitchen door and she thought it might be wise to pack some snacks and maybe grab some banana nut bread that she knew Patricia had stayed up late baking. Who knew when she'd get banana nut bread again and she was sure no one would begrudge her taking half the loaf. She walked into the kitchen toward the loaf that sat there on the cutting board beneath a glass cover. She removed the glass cover and quietly sat it down on the counter. The sun reflected off the glass as it streamed in through the kitchen window above the sink. There was movement in that reflection and Ivy quickly turned and gasped as she came face to face with Patricia.

"I figured that, if you thought about it, you might think we'd all be better off without you. And if you thought that, you might try to leave. Then I thought, the only way I can really catch her is to lay out bait I know she can't live without. Thus, the banana nut bread." It was all said very matter-of-fact, then Patricia sat down and just waited.

Ivy sighed, thought about her best course of action and either way she played it out in her mind, she'd be taking banana nut bread with her, so she took a knife from the drawer and cut a hunk off. She put bread on a napkin instead of getting out a plate and sat down at the table, dropping the pack to the floor.

"You know it's the best solution." Ivy took a bite and the bread was still warm.

Patricia got up, got a glass out of the cupboard and got milk that she put in front of Ivy. Ivy smiled and took a drink, closing her eyes as the cold, sweet milk mixed with the banana flavor. Surely heaven had banana nut bread and milk and none of it had calories.

"The best solution is to stick together. We don't even know if your power has anything to do with what's going on." Patricia was back in her seat calm and well-rested, which Ivy suspected was a lie.

"If there's even the chance that I might put us in danger, put Amber in danger, then I need to leave." Ivy met Patricia's calmness with her own, which was also a lie.

"What if it's not you and you aren't here to save your sister when they come for her?"

Ivy's hand stopped with the milk glass nearly to her mouth. "That's not fair."

"Nothing about this is fair, Ivy. You may be able to heal people, but you can't see into the future. You don't know whether staying or leaving is what is truly best. And if you aren't sure, then you should just stay put and gather more data, right?" Patricia nodded toward the glass of milk just as the milk was about to run over the rim of the glass and onto Ivy's clothes.

Ivy set the glass down before she spilled the milk. Staring at Patricia didn't elicit any response. She would never be able to change her mind on this. And maybe she was right. What if she wasn't what brought those men here? What if she left and they got Amber because she wasn't here to save her? She thought about Amber's bruised and bloody face last night. What if something happened to Amber and she wasn't here to use her power to save her?

Ivy took another bite of the bread then looked up as the kitchen door swung open and Amber walked in still in her pajamas. She seemed sleepy. She took in the scene, regarded the pack on the floor, walked over, picked it up and slung it over her shoulder.

"Dork."

Amber only had the one word for her sister, but it was enough. She left the kitchen and Ivy realized that she needed to stay at least long enough to know if she would be more of a help than a danger to her family.

"Listen, why don't you come with me to check on the safe house?" Patricia changed the subject and like that everything changed.

Ivy loved that Patricia could just let things go. She didn't feel the need to harp on her about her decision or lecture her about not saying anything to anyone about that decision. Patricia got her. And Amber. Somehow she just knew what they needed, or didn't need. Ivy's heart swelled with love for this woman who had saved her life when she was a baby. The woman who knew banana nut bread was far too much of a temptation and used it as bait to keep her from leaving home.

"Yeah, I'd like that. Maybe we can get Amber motivated to get dressed and go with us?" Ivy popped the last piece of bread into her mouth and stood.

"Go motivate." Patricia gestured for her to hurry.

Ivy heard Helena, John, and Patricia talking in the kitchen as she approached. Amber was in tow, though she wasn't exactly happy about going to the safe house because it was on the lake and Amber didn't swim. She was actually afraid of the water because she'd almost drown at that lake house when they were seven years old. But, she did want to get out of the house, and it only took a little groveling to get her to agree.

"I'll keep the girls with me today while you two do recon and set out traps around the house." Patricia's voice carried, and Ivy looked to Amber, who just shrugged.

It didn't really matter what they did today. It was going to be very little and nothing fun. May as well go on a road trip to the lake.

Ivy pushed through the door and she and Amber took their seats at the kitchen table. Breakfast was set out for them, and regardless of the banana bread Ivy felt certain she could put away the eggs, bacon and toast without any trouble.

Patricia was packing a lunch, and John was loading their vehicle with bags and boxes. Ivy walked out to help, but stopped in the driveway as she watched a white Mustang drive toward them. John walked over and stood in front of Ivy, and she had to peer around him.

"It's Gabe and Ryan!" Ivy stepped out, but John turned, frowned and pushed her back behind him.

"Hey! Gabe helped us last night!" Ivy protested.

"He did. But he was also the person who knew where you'd be. And I don't know the other boy at all." John was calm, of course, but she realized he was taking no chances.

"Ryan is Gabe's cousin. I've known Gabe all my life! Don't you think if Gabe was working with my father we'd have had trouble long ago?" Ivy reasoned and stepped out again. This time John let her remain at his side.

The car stopped near the SUV, several feet away. Ryan got out of the driver's side door as Gabe got out.

"Hey!" Gabe called out.

"Hey!" Ivy answered and waited for him to get closer so they wouldn't have to yell to each other.

"I thought I'd come see for myself that you're okay. And maybe offer you and your sister a ride to school?" Gabe shook John's hand and nodded his salutation, then looked back to Ivy.

"Well, you should've called. We're not going to school today. We have some family business to attend to." Ivy glanced at John, hoping she could handle the situation herself. She wondered what John would want to know, what questions he'd want asked of two boys who just decided to show up after an attack like the one from last night.

"Where are you going?" Ryan walked up and offered John his hand. "Hi! I'm Ryan, Gabe's cousin."

John took it and introduced himself and then Helena as she stepped into the circle they'd formed.

"Ryan thought you might say 'no' if I called since I was pretty sure Amber would be all messed up today." Gabe's smile faded into genuine concern. "Is she okay?"

"She's fine. She's getting ready for our little road trip." Ivy knew Amber wouldn't come out. She couldn't explain how her injuries had gone away without raising suspicion.

"Where you headed?" Ryan asked, his gaze searching for Amber, then looked back to Ivy.

"Why do you need to know?" Helena asked.

Ryan considered her for a moment, then Ivy and John and back to Helena.

"I don't go to school any more. I thought maybe I could tag along?" Ryan smiled but his charm was entirely lost on Helena.

"You want to go on family business with us?" Helena questioned, then added. "You don't go to school?"

"GED." Ryan replied. "I don't mind tagging along on family business. I don't have any plans today."

"Well, this is private."

"No problem. We can always do something later." Ryan said.

"Well, I just wanted to know you're all okay. I need to get to school." Gabe smiled at Ivy then turned to get back in the car.

Ryan looked around the place as though admiring it. He nodded his goodbye to everyone and joined Gabe. They turned around and drove away.

"Don't you think it's strange that all this time Gabe has never come here, but he stops by today to see what we're doing?" Helena asked.

"Not what we're doing," Ivy corrected, feeling a bit defensive of Gabe, "How we're doing. There's a difference. And you have to admit that having a near kidnapping might be the most excitement this town has known in ages, so of course they're going to be curious. Nothing ever happens here! Now something has happened, and you act like being curious about it is some kind of admission of guilt."

"Ivy, you need to be more on guard right now." Helena warned. "If anyone is watching us, they've now seen Gabe twice and his cousin too. They may think Gabe is helping us. Keep him away." With that she turned and went back inside.

"I hadn't thought of that." Ivy could feel the burn in the pit of her stomach that she recognized as guilt. She peered out across the forest and wondered if anyone was looking back at them. Would they think Gabe was somehow part of their group? Might they use him to get at her? She shook her head as though she could clear it that way. Didn't work. Now she just had more people to protect. And more people she was putting in danger.

"The sooner we figure this out, the better you'll feel and the sooner you'll get back to your regularly scheduled life." John put his arm around her and gave her a half-smile. "We're packed up and ready. Why don't you go get Patricia and Amber?"

T**HEY SET OUT AND** an hour later had made good time. Patricia put them in charge of making sure they weren't being followed. They weren't.

"How can anyone follow us at the rate of speed you're willing to drive, you speed demon!" Ivy teased.

Patricia just smiled. "I've got mad driving skills, girls. No one is going to out drive me."

Ivy rolled her eyes and laughed. She heard Amber in the back snicker and glanced in the rearview mirror to see her sister smiling.

"Music?" she asked Amber. Amber nodded.

Ivy reached out to turn the radio on, and her long sleeve moved back, revealing her new tattoo.

"What is that?" Patricia's quick intake of breath and high pitch startled Ivy and she withdrew her arm, sitting back against the seat.

Silence.

More silence.

"I'm not talking to myself." Patricia's tone was less surprised and more angry.

"I got a tattoo." Ivy figured the less said, the better. Keep it simple. Maybe it will go away if it's downplayed?

"Ivy, of all the things you've been taught. Of all the disrespectful things you could do…" Patricia broke off. Her face was red and the red on her neck was becoming more and more splotchy.

"It's my body. My decision." Ivy spoke softly, hoping not to set off a bomb in the car. A bomb named Patricia.

"When you turn eighteen you can do what you like. Until then you do as you're damn well told." Patricia's grip on the steering wheel tightened.

"I'm not your typical teenager. I give up a lot. Why can't I have something in return for what I give up?" Ivy had this argument in her mind even before she got the tattoo. It just wasn't as convincing saying it out loud.

"You don't know what it's like to give up a lot." Patricia snapped.

"It's just a tattoo." Ivy knew it was lame as soon as it came out of her mouth.

"It's a sign that you don't care about the people affected by what you do. It's a sign of disrespect because you didn't discuss it with me, or Helena or John. And I'm pretty confident that you did not get either of them to go for this, right?"

Ivy nodded.

"You've had your mind on boys so much that you forget the family that sacrifices for you, takes care of you, loves you. You need to get your priorities figured out, Ivy. And fast." Patricia shook her head, but said no more.

"I do everything I'm asked to do, even when I loathe doing it," Ivy answered. She caught sight of movement in the rearview mirror and glanced up to see

Amber shaking her head, trying to dissuade her from what she knew was coming. "I'm sixteen years old and I have never been on a date. I've never even been kissed! I'm going to be a virgin forever!"

Ivy heard Amber's quick intake of breath. but much feeling flowed through her and she wasn't able to stop herself.

"I'll be seventeen before the end of this year and I'm the only girl in my class who has never made out. I'm a pariah at every school social function we're allowed to attend. No one will date me. Everyone thinks I'm a geek or a dork or a loser!"

"Ivy…" Patricia started.

"No, Patricia," Ivy interrupted, "I finally have done something cool and Gabe noticed me. I'm not sorry I did it."

"You think Gabe thinks you're cool because you got a tattoo?" Patricia asked.

"Because I had the guts to get the tattoo, yes." Ivy had wondered why Gabe had taken an interest in her all of a sudden, and the only thing she could figure was that it had something to do with the tattoo and being a bad girl, living on the edge. It was exciting and it made him notice her. Why else would he take notice of her just now when she'd been trying to get his attention since she was in the seventh grade and finally got into an A-cup?

"Ivy, if you need to prove yourself to someone in order to get them to like you, they're not the person for you. You should just be who you are, and some-one will find that person wonderful, and they will like you for just being you." Patricia sounded less angry.

Ivy sank down in her seat. Being trapped in the car, unable to escape what-ever lecture Patricia chose to give, was just one of the many reasons to never take a road trip with parents after doing something they disapprove of.

"Sometimes it's better to ask for forgiveness than permission," Ivy muttered. But, of course Patricia had some kind of super hearing and heard every word.

"Maybe it would be best for us to give this a rest right now?" Patricia sug-gested. She leaned over and turned on the radio.

The rest of the trip was done without conversation. Patricia listened to '80's music, which Ivy was sure was a form of punishment. They arrived an hour later. The driveway was hard to see until you were on it, then it wound around deep into the forest for another half hour before opening up to a clearing where a two story cabin sat facing the lake.

"Wait here till I get back," Patricia told them. Ivy and Amber stayed put as Patricia did the initial walk-through of the house before signaling to them.

They carried in everything John had packed in the car and started putting those items away. Food, water, ammunition, extra blankets and a myriad of other survival type items. Within the hour everything was ready. Patricia wanted to dust and sweep and make sure the place was livable before everyone was forced to stay there. Ivy finished with her assignments and went to find Amber, who was in their room washing the windows on the French doors that lead out to the balcony over the lake.

"Could you sweep the balcony?" Amber asked glancing out the French doors to the lake beyond.

"You really need to learn to swim, Amber. Then you wouldn't miss out on the wonderful view off the balcony." Ivy didn't press her beyond that.

She and Amber had reacted differently to an accident on the lake many years ago when they were little. Their canoe had capsized and neither were strong swimmers. Amber had been caught beneath the canoe when it turned and had panicked. Patricia was there with them and got them back to shore safely. When they got back, Amber was so terrified that she refused to even go out on the balcony any more.

Ivy vowed that she would become a great swimmer and would never fear the water again. And she did. Ivy knew she could win swimming competitions if she were allowed to compete. Her physical education teacher had practically begged her to be on the team because she was so good.

Ivy walked out into the gentle, warm breeze and inhaled deeply. She loved that smell of clean air, water, and forest. She stood there soaking up the sun for a moment and set the broom down so she could lean over the rail and catch more of the aroma of honeysuckle that was nearby. But as she leaned her weight onto the rail it gave and she lost her balance nearly falling over the broken railing.

"Crap!" Ivy looked down at the wood dust and flaking paint that adhered to her shirt from leaning onto the railing. The wood was old and broken near where the main railing met the side railing. It gapped just a bit at the corner and Ivy noted the crack at the bottom was fairly significant as well.

"You okay?" Amber called out.

"Yeah, we're going to need to bring something to fix the railing is all. Let's not tell Patricia right now though, or she'll keep us here all night building a new one. John will fix it when we move in."

Ivy finished sweeping off the balcony the best she could, and that finished their assignments. They went downstairs where Patricia had sandwiches and chips waiting, ate a good but late lunch, and packed it all in.

As they made their way to the SUV, Ivy's phone vibrated and she pulled it out. A text from Gabe!

Meet up 2nite?

Ivy had to be careful not to come across as too happy or Patricia might realize something was up. She texted back.

Where?

Ivy glanced to Amber, who was getting in. Patricia was locking everything up.

Ryan's?

Ivy could hardly suppress her excitement. Amber gave her a quizzical expression. Ivy shook her head, a signal that she couldn't talk about it right now.

Sounds good. When?

Ivy had reached the vehicle and opened the door to get in. The phone vibrated, drawing her attention from Patricia, who now walked toward the SUV.

8?

Butterflies took flight in her stomach, and she wasn't able to keep the smile entirely away.

C U then!

Ivy sat down and closed the door. She buckled up as Patricia got in. A quick glance and smile to her sister promised more when they got home.

Ivy looked out at the cabin and the lake. It was beautiful here. She hated to be so far from Gabe, but it wasn't so far she couldn't see him on weekends. Besides, if all went well it would be temporary.

CHAPTER 6

A NEW TEXT CAME IN from Gabe on the ride home, but Ivy didn't dare check it. If Patricia insisted on seeing the text, they could be restricted to their room all night. So as soon as they arrived home Ivy signaled to Amber to follow her upstairs to their room.

Ivy sat down and pulled out her phone.

Need ride?

Ivy showed the texts to Amber as she sat down on the bed next to her.

Not sure yet. Will let U know soon.

"How do you plan on going to see Gabe when we're on lock down?" Amber asked. "Patricia is already unhappy with you."

"I don't plan on asking Patricia." Ivy smiled at her sister. "I'm enlisting Helena."

She smiled at the perplexed expression on Amber's face, but she had a plan she was sure would work.

An hour later and Ivy sat in the kitchen next to Helena as they shared their plan with the family.

"It's a surprise attack," Ivy began. "This time when they come for us, we'll actually be ambushing them. We show them we're prepared and not afraid to fight back. So far they've been trying to be stealthy. Obviously, Zachariah doesn't want a big scene."

"A show of force isn't going to stop Zachariah." Patricia stated.

"Maybe not, but he'll see we're not afraid of him. And we send a message telling him we're willing to go to the press and say anything we have to say in order to stop him."

"Helena tried the press route and no one would listen." John interjected.

"But, I wasn't a young girl. I was grown. It was my word against Zachariah's and no one was willing to go against him. Ivy has a point." Helena took John's hand. "They're young girls who have someone who is actual family on their side, someone who lived in the community, willing to testify for them."

"I don't know how much my testimony will help if Zachariah accuses me of kidnapping." Patricia said.

"The fact is," Ivy continued, "it would make the media. It would. If Zachariah is more concerned with staying under the radar so he can keep his little kingdom intact, he may just let us go."

"What if this time they just use a sniper and shoot someone?" Patricia asked.

"They had the chance to do that the other night. They obviously don't want to call too much attention to themselves." Helena sounded confident. "You and I both know the girls are important to Zachariah, but more important than keeping out of prison? He may decide it's not worth it."

"Knowing Zachariah, that's not a comfort," Patricia answered. "He's unpredictable and willing to kill."

Ivy hadn't considered that everyone else could be a moving target that her father would be willing to eliminate if they got in the way.

"What do you think?" Ivy asked John.

"It's a gamble." He said. "It's possible that enough time has gone by that Zachariah would let the girls go if the price seemed too high. We show we're willing to make a stand, send the message and the girls could be taken off of Zachariah's most wanted list."

Silence filled the room for what felt to Ivy to be an eternity. Finally Patricia spoke up.

"I don't like it." She said. "But the alternative is to keep running. Keep hoping they don't find the girls while we're not around to fight for them. We make a stand now and maybe you're right, John, maybe the price will be too high and Zachariah will leave us alone."

Ivy asked, "Now what?" She held her breath as she awaited the final decision.

"Gabe and Ryan are expecting the girls. We drop them off like we did before, but we'll hide out on foot in different areas. We all have cell phones and will communicate that way. You girls will stay with Gabe and Ryan the same amount of time as before and leave just as you did last time. They'll likely sense it's a trap, but they won't miss the opportunity. We'll all have to be on high alert." Helena checked her watch. "If we're going to do this, now is the time."

They all got up and as Ivy was leaving someone tugged on the back of her shirt. She turned to see Patricia scowling, a look she'd grown accustomed to today.

"No more tattoos." It was not a request.

Ivy figured that if that was the only problem she was going to have, then she'd promise. "No more tattoos."

They were silent on the ride over until they got about a block away and Helena brought out a revolver.

"Amber, this is for you."

Amber took the gun, tucked it at the small of her back and continued staring out the window which was all she'd done the entire time they were in the car.

Ivy waited, growing frustrated and a little embarrassed that Helena wouldn't entrust a gun to her.

John shook his head, but said nothing. He pulled out a pistol, checked the safety and handed it back to Ivy. His gun was heavier than Ivy was used to, but she could handle it. It would be pretty bulky tucking it behind her, but she did the best she could and realized she'd have to leave her sweater on the entire time they were at Ryan's.

They stopped, and she and Amber got out at the alley, walked to Ryan's, and knocked on the door. Amber kept looking around for signs of danger. Gabe opened the door and smiled. The only danger Ivy was in at the moment was making a fool of herself while trying to impress the hottest guy in high school.

Ryan was sitting in the same chair near the couch that he'd been in last time.

"Welcome!" Ryan stood until the girls sat and then took his seat. "So, how was your family trip? Get a lot done?"

"We did everything we needed to," Ivy said then looked to Gabe. "How was your day?"

Ivy cringed internally a little as she wondered if she sounded like a wife. Who asks that? A nosey wife, that's who. Gabe didn't seem to care.

"Same old stuff. School work, football. Oh! Well, I did do my first sparring session for MMA training today!" Gabe lit up as he talked about the session. "I laid him out flat!"

"Right on!" Ivy punched him in the arm playfully.

"So Ryan, other than tattooing, what do you do all day?" Amber asked and Ivy knew she was trying to get more information on Ryan than what they were able to get online. They found out he'd had a few run ins with the law over the last couple of months, mostly online stuff, and he'd been kicked out of school. He did get his GED, but that was about all they knew.

"Ryan here is a genius with mad hacker skills," Gabe shared.

"Is that right?" Amber asked. "What kinds of things do you hack?"

"I'm pretty good with computers, game systems, GPS systems, anything electronic." Ryan smiled, ignoring the question. "Unlike my cousin here, I'm a lover, not a fighter." With that he threw a small stress ball at Gabe who caught it. "I leave all the fighting for my man Gabe."

"You're just jealous cause I'm a lover *and* a fighter. And I'm freakin' smart, which makes me a triple threat." Gabe threw the stress ball back and Ryan caught it.

"And a braggart and a smart ass." Ryan laughed.

Ivy watched the two cousins and had no doubt there was genuine affection there. They were both eighteen, but Ryan was three months older than Gabe and claimed the right of "oldest" which somehow meant he got his way most of the time. Ivy wasn't sure how that worked, because it certainly never worked for her.

"Why would you need to hack something?" Amber wouldn't let it rest. "Doesn't that get you into trouble with the law?"

Ryan shrugged it off.

"So what would you lovely ladies like to do tonight?" Gabe asked.

"Whatever," Ivy answered, unsure and more than a little nervous.

"How about a little truth or dare?" Ryan laughed when Ivy scowled at the suggestion. "Don't tell me you're a little goody two-shoes? Never played? What?"

"Shut up," Ivy said. She started to remove her sweater since she was growing warmer by the minute, then stopped herself as she remembered the gun that would certainly be visible if she stood without that sweater on.

"You cold?" Gabe asked.

"No. Not really." Ivy wasn't sure what else to say and she glanced to Amber for help.

"Are you worried we'll get the wrong idea if you start to take your clothes off?" Ryan laughed, winning him a dirty look from his cousin. "I'm kidding!"

Truth or Dare and juvenile teasing, all of a sudden, Ivy didn't want to be here anymore. This wasn't what she thought it would be.

"Hey! What about a drink? I have some beer, or wine for you ladies who are more sophisticated." Ryan stood to get some drinks.

"Look," Amber started and her voice stopped Ryan. "We don't want to take our clothes off. We don't want to play immature little games. We don't want to get high or get drunk. If you called us over for that, you called the wrong girls." Amber said. "Let's get out of here."

Ivy felt the knot between her shoulder blades relax. They both stood up and headed for the door.

"Wait." Gabe jumped up and glared at Ryan. "Wait, I'm sorry Ryan is being a jerk. We do want you to stay, and I thought it might be fun to play the new martial arts game on Ryan's new game system."

He sounded sincere, and Ivy hated to leave things like this when they might not see each other for a while. Amber shrugged her shoulders, and they both sat down.

"Hey! I was just trying to be funny. I'm sorry. Come on back before Gabe starts crying." Ryan tried to appear repentant and the girls needed to spend a little more time there to ensure the mission timeline was correct, so they came back.

"I get to beat the crap out of Ryan though," Amber said as Gabe handed out the controllers.

"I'm really good at this game. I've been playing for days," Ryan said as he settled back into his chair and got comfortable with the controller he was handed.

"I wasn't talking about the game," Amber said, but Gabe turned the game on and they were naming their characters, getting ready to rumble.

"What are you doing tomorrow?" Gabe asked as his character threw Ivy's to the ground.

"Looks like ICU for me." Ivy laughed. She brought her character back up, swung around and swept his legs out from under him. "Maybe I'll see you there?"

Gabe frowned, stood up and wedged himself between Amber and Ivy on the couch.

"It's on, girlie. I'm taking you down." Gabe nudged her shoulder playfully.

"Don't cry when I kick your butt." Ivy laughed and nudged him back.

"Want to make a little bet on this then?" Gabe smiled.

"Winner gets what? To punch Ryan in the head?" Ivy felt herself flush a little and hoped the red kept to a bright pink that she could blame the excitement of the game on.

"Hey! I'm right here you know! I can hear you." Ryan was busy fighting off Amber who wasn't even breaking a sweat as she beat his character into submission.

"They call that a bonus." Amber laughed.

"The winner can name their prize after they win, how's that?" Gabe grinned which should have put Ivy on alert, but only served to deepen the red in Ivy's cheeks.

"You got it." With that Ivy elbowed the controller out of Gabe's hands, laughed when he complained and fumbled around for it, and got to kicking butt.

An hour later and laughter filled the room as they finished the game.

"Bro, we just got our butts handed to us by a couple of cute girls." Gabe laughed. "If we're going to lose, this is the way to go."

Ryan stood up and stretched. "Anyone want some juice, water or soda pop?"

"I'd love some water, please." Ivy said.

"Get me a diet something, will ya?" Gabe asked.

"I'll help you." Amber stood up, quickly glanced at Ivy, and followed Ryan into the kitchen.

"I think she likes him." Gabe leaned back on the couch and stretched his arm along the back.

Ivy looked at the arm and for a moment was unsure as to what to do. If she leaned back, it'd be like he had his arm around her, and she wasn't sure if he'd like that or not. He was probably just getting comfortable. But, what if it was an invitation and she missed out? Her heart pounded in her chest as she decided to lean back and do her best to act like she didn't even notice his arm there.

"I wouldn't bet on that." Ivy smiled up at him.

"She just followed him into the kitchen." He smiled back, leaving his arm in place.

He was intoxicating. She felt a little dizzy as her heart raced at his nearness. She felt daring and leaned back a little more until his arm touched the back of her shoulders. He didn't move, and she struggled to stay calm and cool.

"That's because she doesn't trust him." Ivy smiled. "She's making sure he doesn't put anything into our drinks."

Gabe's smile faltered just a little and Ivy realized her mistake. She needed to talk less about her and ask more about him. That's what Patricia had said to do, but all that wise advice had left the second Ivy felt Gabe's arm against her shoulders.

"That's pretty harsh." Gabe said. "You really don't trust us?"

"It's not that." Ivy tried to force her brain to function properly. "It's just something our parents have instilled into us. If you're somewhere that you're not familiar and someone offers you a drink in a glass, don't drink it, or be sure you watch what goes into the glass yourself. Our parents are a bit paranoid."

She hoped he knew enough about John and Helena's over protectiveness to give her a pass on this. His smile grew again, and she felt herself relax.

"They do seem pretty concerned about you two," Gabe said. His hand moved to her shoulder and he gave it a friendly squeeze, but left it there. "So, what's the prize?"

"What?" Ivy was confused again.

"You won the game. Winner picks the prize." Gabe smiled, his dimple deepening.

Ivy would have bet anything that he knew what kind of effect he had on her, and he was enjoying her discomfort. She admitted to herself that she could be reading into it, but with all the girls she'd seen him date, she figured he knew what he was doing. Right now, he was making her forget her name. He probably knew that, too.

"I can have anything?" She hadn't meant to whisper it. It just came out that way.

Gabe nodded and his thumb began to caress her arm in slow, methodical circles. "Just tell me what you want, and it's yours."

Ivy realized she was holding her breath and did what she could to release it slowly. Her heart pounded so hard she was afraid he would hear it. He leaned in close enough that she felt the warmth of his body along the front of hers. The hand on her shoulder pulled her toward him, gently. His other hand came up, his thumb caressing the line of her jaw. He leaned in closer, pulled her closer.

"Say it." His voice was low and soft and pulled her in with its hypnotic spell.

"Kiss…" Ivy didn't get a chance to say the rest as his lips, warm and soft touched down lightly on hers.

It was everything she wanted and nothing she expected. She thought it would be wet and wild and crushing, but it was soft and tender and sweet. His hand guided her, adding pressure with his thumb against her jaw, tilting her face up, opening her mouth ever so slightly. He moved his lips and captured her top lip between his, then her bottom lip and as his hand moved around to the back of her neck, supporting her head even as he drew her closer, she felt the wet warmth of his tongue gently caress her bottom lip, slip in between and taste the inside of her mouth.

He pulled back and looked down into her eyes. His hand came back to caress her jaw. He studied her face until she was uncomfortable, not knowing what to say. Struggling for words she said exactly what was in her mind.

"I win."

That made him smile and he winked at her. She thought he was about to say something, but noises from the kitchen announced incoming company and Ivy moved back as Amber returned to the room with a couple of glasses in hand.

Amber stopped in mid stride and looked at them with a quizzical expression. Her eyes darted from Gabe to Ivy a couple of times, and then she frowned as though she couldn't figure out the puzzle. She began walking toward them, slower, tentative. She handed one glass to Ivy, the other she kept as she sat down.

Ryan walked out with two glasses in hand, but he didn't seem to notice anything amiss. He handed a drink to Gabe and then sat down with his own.

"What's next?" Ryan asked.

"I don't know, I thought maybe we could watch a movie. I'm pretty sure you've pirated anything worth watching." Gabe smiled at Ryan and Ivy. "Ryan can get us anything we want to see."

"You realize that's illegal," Amber said, then sipped from her glass. "How would you like it if someone stole your artwork to mass produce commercial fake tattoos? Or what if someone saw one of your originals and copied it onto someone else? Would you like that?"

"You're a real Debbie Downer, Amber." Ryan sat his glass on the low coffee table in front of the couch.

"Just keeping it real." Amber was entirely unapologetic. "You think you're not hurting anyone with what you're doing, but it does. Just because you don't have to see how it hurts them, doesn't make it less awful to do."

Ivy wondered what had gone on in the kitchen that had caused Amber to be anti-Ryan. Or perhaps Amber was just baiting him, trying to get him to say if he knew anything about what happened to them last night.

Ivy watched Ryan. His jaw muscle twitched and he didn't even seem aware of it. His lips were a straight line, not smiling, not quite frowning.

"I guess I'll have to walk the straight and narrow around you, doll." He turned his sharp eyes and charming smile to Amber.

"That might be best for everyone," was all Amber said.

"Okay, what about something not illegal. Who's up for Firefly?" Gabe stood, walked over to the small entertainment center that held Ryan's surprisingly large television. Gabe opened the cabinet, fished for some discs and pulled out what he was looking for. He plugged it in, and made his way back to the spot on the couch next to Ivy. This time there was no pretense. He put his arm around her and pulled her close. She snuggled into him, sparing a fleeting glance to Amber, who was tapping the watch on her wrist. Ivy frowned at her, but she knew they had a limited time. They would have to leave in an hour, but Ivy had every intention of enjoying it.

TIME. WHEN YOU WANT it to last, flies fast to spite you. At least Ivy felt that way as Amber stood, signaling it was time to go. They'd gotten little information from either Ryan or Gabe, but that hadn't really been Ivy's main reason to be there. Now it was time to get her head into a more serious game. Disappointment over leaving Gabe when things were going so well between them was replaced by the very real need to do this mission and claim her life back.

"Sorry, but we have to go." She didn't sound sorry, but Ivy couldn't blame her. Amber and Ryan seemed to have zero chemistry, and Amber wasn't the biggest fan of sci-fi, so she figured Amber was just as excited to have the time pass as Ivy was afraid it would be over too quickly.

"I'll walk you out." Gabe stood up and held a hand out to Ivy. She took it and stood. He turned and helped Amber up too and then began to walk the girls to the door.

"Dude!" Ryan stood up. "I thought you and I were going to watch the MMA match tonight. It's about to start."

Gabe frowned at Ryan. "Record it. I'll watch it with you when I get back. We can fast forward through the commercials that way."

Ryan appeared frustrated, but Ivy couldn't figure out why. Did he really dislike her and Amber so much as to not want them walked safely to their ride?

"It's fine." Amber said to Gabe. "We have someone waiting out on the street for us. We're good."

Ivy looked to Amber, knowing that wasn't true but realizing that they needed to walk out alone if they were to stand a chance of luring out the men who were after them and doing it while also keeping Gabe out of danger. Gabe was a good fighter. Great even. But, he didn't have a weapon. And he didn't know what was going on. He'd be a liability, and that was dangerous to everyone.

"She's right. We're good. John is waiting for us." Ivy smiled at him, but he was frowning.

"You're sure?" he asked. "With everything that happened last night, I just need to know you're safe."

"I will be. But, I will text you in just a minute and let you know we're with John." Ivy promised. She hated to lie to him, but it was necessary to keep him out of harm's way.

From out of nowhere the small stress ball came zinging through the air to hit Gabe in the temple. Ivy gave a little yelp, then laughed, and Gabe slowly turned to give Ryan a withering look. Gabe launched himself toward his cousin leaving Ivy and Amber to make their way out onto the street, their laughter dying once the door closed behind them

"We need to be on alert," Amber said.

"I know." Ivy answered, searching every shadow.

They reached the mouth of the alley and started to turn in the same direction as last night. Just a few feet away on the opposite side of the street sat a white van.

Things were about to get interesting. But, this time, Ivy remembered that she had a gun.

CHAPTER 7

IVY PULLED THE GUN from behind her and tucked it in the front of her pants so it would be easy to grab. She didn't see anyone, but that didn't mean they weren't out there. Helena's instructions had been crystal clear. If you have a choice in the matter, run.

Her training told her that any direction was a gamble. If they wanted them that badly, they'd have covered all their bases. What they may not have counted on was two armed teens and John out in the park undercover, where he'd been since they'd dropped them off. Since this was exactly what they were hoping for, Ivy was sure Patricia and Helena were out there somewhere, waiting.

At the first sign of trouble, Ivy and Amber were to take off toward the park. If someone came from the park they were to go south, but since the van was sitting south of them they would have to improvise. Regardless, they knew where to meet up if they got separated. Not that Ivy had any intention of letting that happen.

A noise coming from the park alerted them to movement. A splash behind them like someone stepping into a puddle caught Ivy's ear. The only place she'd seen standing water was in the alley. It was starting to feel more like they were boxed in, and Ivy rested her hand on the top of John's gun.

They kept walking. They gave the white van a wide berth nearing the park in less than a block. Amber looked from the corner of her eye and Ivy could see fear there. That was good. Fear always made Amber more alert. Ivy chanced a glance behind them and saw him. He was a hulk of a man, well over six feet tall and she guessed him to be over 300 pounds. If she had turned back around a millisecond earlier, she'd have missed the tall skinny guy behind him. They were about the same height, but the hulky guy was so large it was easy to miss the guy behind him.

Ivy nodded. They began to run.

As they passed the park, John ran out of the shadows. He was limping, but still moved faster than most men his size. Up ahead was Helena. Ivy didn't see her because she was dressed entirely in black from top to bottom. Once she stepped into the light, Ivy recognized her immediately. They didn't slow down. They ran past John, past Helena, and kept going. Ivy finally turned around and could see John and Helena fighting the two tall men. She stopped to think, but Amber kept going a few feet, and then she stopped.

"Stick with the plan!" Amber hissed at her. Then the shot rang out and the night went silent.

Ivy watched John fall to his knees as someone new ran from behind and jumped the hulky guy while Helena continued to struggle with the tall skinny one. The newcomer immediately started pounding and kicking at the large man and Ivy knew who it was. She started running back, gun in hand, a certainty that she would use it to save John, Helena, and Gabe.

She trusted that Amber was behind her, but she never turned back. The large man picked Gabe up and threw him several feet where he connected with the cement and went completely still. The large man bent down, picked up a gun and pointed it at John's head. Helena screamed, but was knocked back.

A shot rang out so loud it hurt Ivy's ears. She had her gun up, but she hadn't fired it. Staring at the tall man holding out his gun, at the still form of John on the street, Ivy thought her heart would burst from the adrenaline pumping hard through it. She'd stopped when the shot rang out. Her eyes felt as though they would bulge out of their sockets as she tried to take in what had just happened.

Then he fell. The large hulking guy fell, first to his knees, then face down into the street.

Reality washed over her. There would be no message given to Zachariah. No deals. They'd underestimated either Zachariah's absolute need for power or their importance to him.

The shock of gun fire distracted the skinny guy, and Helena kicked him so hard in the groin that he fell. She kicked him in the head and he went perfectly still. Helena looked over to them, first at Ivy, then past her.

Ivy turned, and there stood Amber, gun still in her hand, arm still extended, obviously in shock. She was like a statue, but as Ivy walked toward her she could see that her hand was starting to shake, a tear spilled over and down her cheek. Ivy took the gun gently from her hand, put the safety on and held her sister close.

"We need to get out of here." Amber's voice trembled, more like she was cold than she was frightened or crying.

Ivy knew she was right. The cops would be there in a matter of minutes. And as though the thought could call them to her, lights from a car shown bright as it turned the corner and approached them. Ivy realized it was only car lights, no siren, no red or blue. She recognized the car as their SUV and knew it was Patricia.

Patricia stopped, and the whir of the electric powered window sounded as the passenger side window came down.

"Get her in the car. Hurry!" Patricia told them.

Ivy put Amber in the car and then ran to John and Helena as the car slowly moved forward in that direction.

"Was he shot?" Ivy felt the sting of tears as she asked the question.

"No, stabbed. Must have been someone in the park. I didn't see what happened. We need to get him home, get him stabilized."

Patricia jumped out and together she and Helena sat John up. Ivy was relieved when John said something even though she wasn't sure what he'd mumbled.

"They're fine. They're both fine," Helena whispered to him.

Ivy realized that Gabe had not moved yet. She ran to him, the trauma finally catching up to her, tears running down her cheeks. He'd been there for her again and it had cost him dearly this time.

Ivy fell to her knees next to him and started to pat him down, look for blood. His head was bleeding badly from where he'd hit the corner of the sidewalk. Ivy put her hand on the wound and felt the energy within her stir. She closed her eyes, the warm electric current flowed through her, into him and spread. She could feel it moving, working, healing. She opened her eyes to find him staring at her, confused.

"What's going on?" Ryan ran from the alley and fell to his knees next to Ivy. "I told him to stay put. I told him not to go."

"I'm okay, man." Gabe stirred, then tried to sit up.

"I heard shots. Were you shot?" Ryan grabbed Gabe's shoulder to bring his face around so Ryan could see him. Gabe didn't want to look at Ryan. He kept trying to look at Ivy.

"He isn't shot. He hit his head. He needs to go to the hospital. Can you take him?" Ivy knew Gabe would be okay. She also knew she'd have a really hard time standing up, let alone moving on her own two feet.

"Ivy, we have to go." It was Amber and she pulled her up with surprising strength.

Ivy thought it had to be the adrenaline. She let her sister pull her up and turn her toward the SUV that was only a few feet away with the back passenger side door standing open. Ivy peered out at the street. The large man was gone, the van was gone. Like nothing had happened. But, she could hear sirens in the distance growing louder. She cast one last glance back at Gabe who was now standing, still looking at her.

"I'm sorry." She mouthed the words, turned, and got into the vehicle.

They backed away and tore off down the street in the opposite direction of the siren sounds.

"Is he okay?" John asked, his eyes sliding to the side mirror.

"He will be." Ivy nodded.

"We need to get home and grab our gear," Helena said, drawing Ivy's attention to the opposite side of the back seat.

"Was it the community?" Ivy asked.

"Yes."

"Are you sure?" Ivy didn't want it to be true.

"I saw the mark on him. They all have this tattoo on their wrists," Helena told her.

Ivy glanced to Patricia, but Patricia didn't seem to think much of the coincidence.

"What kind of tattoo is it?" She needed to know.

"Raven wings on either side of a caduceus."

"Raven wings?" Ivy asked and she looked to Amber, but Amber was staring off out the window, in her own world. She'd just killed a man. In comparison, Ivy figured her tattoo wasn't such a big deal.

"Where did the two guys go?" Ivy didn't want to say 'dead guy' since Amber was obviously struggling with what happened.

"The white van pulled up, two guys with guns got out and took the other two." Helena sounded calm like she was just reciting some casual fact. The sky is blue. The Earth revolves around the sun. Two guys with guns pulled a dead dude into a white van.

"So they know we know." Patricia spoke for the first time since Ivy had gotten into the SUV. She glanced at Helena. "There are things the girls should know. Just in case."

Ivy wondered what it was they didn't already know.

Helena frowned at Patricia and shook her head.

"Not yet."

Ivy filed it away for another time. Healing Gabe had taken everything she had. Regardless of everything that had just happened, the fight, the guns, everything, Ivy wanted to sleep. She rested her head on the cool glass of the window and closed her eyes.

The SUV stopped and Ivy heard doors open and close. She opened her eyes and struggled to focus. Her door opened slowly and Amber stood there with her hand out. Together, they walked into the house. Amber led her to the kitchen even though Ivy desperately wanted to go to bed. But, there was something in the back of her mind telling her she had to stay awake. There was something unfinished. Something was still wrong, but it was too far away for Ivy to recall it.

As they stepped into the well-lit kitchen Ivy found enough energy to stand on her own two feet. John was laid out on the kitchen table, Helena cutting away a red soaked spot on John's shirt.

The sound of a sharp intake of breath from Patricia who stood behind John told Ivy things were bad. She stepped closer and saw for herself, the knife wound bubbled blood each time John inhaled. He was pale and breathing shallow. Ivy sat down, wondering if she had enough energy in her to heal him. Helena's unguarded expression was enough to make her try.

Ivy reached out and put her hand on John's forearm. She searched inside herself and pulled at what energy she could find there. She pushed hard until it moved into John, traveled to the wound both inside and out. Ivy felt some kind of glitch, her vision faded, went black, came back over and over again. Nausea hit her, and she leaned her head onto the kitchen table, keeping her hand in place, trying to push more energy into John.

"She's killing herself!" Amber's voice was like a distant echo in Ivy's ears.

A hand touched her shoulder.

"I think it has to be bare skin." Amber's voice again.

The hand slipped under her shirt near her neck and rested on her bare shoulder. A spark, like a tiny electric jolt entered Ivy's body where the hand touched her skin. Ivy's body reacted to it, pulled on it, sucked energy from it as though her life depended on it. A second, smaller hand, Amber, she could tell it was her sister, not just from the hand, but from the energy that flowed immediately into her, like an old friend. It was like she could taste that it was Amber, but taste wasn't really the right word. She could sense it. She knew who it was because it felt familiar to the flow of her own energy. Ivy wondered if using Amber before, then healing her twice, made her energy signature more recognizable to her own. The thought was fleeting and then she let it go as the power of two fully charged people flowed into her, through her and into John.

Ivy heard John take a deep breath, felt his body respond to the energy she was pushing into him. Amber said it didn't hurt, but would it be the same if two people, two different energy signatures pulsed through someone?

Ivy felt John heal, slowed the flow of energy and then took some for herself. She just needed enough to function. She took it, and even though they were still touching her, she was able to turn it off. She'd found a switch inside herself and she knew now that she could control it.

Ivy felt so much better. She raised her head, saw that it was Amber, as she suspected, and Patricia. Helena still stood where she'd been when Ivy rested her head, only this time she wasn't looking horrified at John's wound, she was staring straight at Ivy with an expression Ivy couldn't identify. If she had to give it a name she would call it, weary.

"Thank you," Helena whispered, but Ivy thought it sounded almost like a question.

Ivy leaned back from the table, and John's hand snaked out to grab hold of her wrist.

"Thank you." John's voice was strong, his tone unmistakably grateful.

John sat up, threw his legs over the edge of the table and stood up. He still looked terrible, but only because he was still covered in blood. The wound was gone, not even a scar remained.

Amber and Patricia were clearly both exhausted. They still smiled, big and genuine. Ivy smiled back, now confident that she had mastered her new power. She wasn't sure that it would be of much use as a weapon, but it was useful just the same.

"I'm going to stay on watch, the rest of you get some sleep. We need to rest and leave at first light." Helena kissed John on the cheek, put a finger to his lips when he started to protest and shook her head.

Ivy walked out with John, Patricia, and Amber and headed upstairs, ready for a good night's sleep. She dressed slowly, but not more slowly than Amber. They got into bed around the same time though and turned their lamps off like they'd synchronized it.

"I'm sorry we have to leave." Amber offered, sounding as tired as Ivy thought she must be.

"Me too." Thoughts of Gabe, the kiss, the expression on his face when he woke up to see her doing, what? What did he think he saw? She'd healed him, but wasn't sure it was enough. Ryan had interrupted her but at least Gabe was able to stand and talk. He surely had to be okay. She wanted to see him before they left, but the chances of that were slim to none. She lay flat on her back, hands behind her head, staring at her ceiling in the darkness. Her last thought wasn't of blood and bullets or the community or kidnapping. She fell asleep without really giving sleep any thought, thinking of a soft kiss and a boy who made her feel alive.

Dreams flowed through her mind, vivid and unpredictable. She saw Gabe, his eyes staring into her as she healed him.

"Thank you," he whispered. But, it wasn't his voice. It was John's, and the dream changed to the kitchen where John was bleeding out and Helena screamed at her to save him. She put her hand on John, but nothing happened. She tried, but she had no power. Then someone stepped out of the darkness in the corner of the kitchen. It was a tall man, older with dead eyes that bore right into her. "It's my power and I'll take it or give it as I see fit," he said.

She'd never seen her father, but she knew instinctively that this was him. He took her power away and he was going to let John die, but somehow Helena would blame her for it. Then, from behind her father a young girl stepped out. She was about Ivy's age and Ivy wondered if this was her mother. The girl looked like her, but she had dark hair. That caused her mind to glitch a little in the dream because she had already been told by Patricia that her mother was blond with a touch of strawberry red. Who was this girl? The girl stared at her with such hatred that Ivy took a step back from her. Fear crept into Ivy's body, turning her blood cold and making her heart race.

"Who are you?" Ivy asked the dark haired girl.

"Elizabeth," the girl answered, but she sounded like Amber.

With a start, Ivy sat straight up in her bed. It startled Amber awake and she sat up too.

"What is it?" Amber asked, looking around the dark room frantically.

"It's okay," Ivy promised, but she felt out of breath as though she'd run a mile. "It was just a dream."

Amber remained upright for a few more seconds, then laid back down and was snoring softly before Ivy put her head back on her pillow. The sun wasn't up yet, but it wouldn't be much longer. Ivy continued to stare at the ceiling until the first hint of light streaked lines across the ceiling through the curtain.

Had that been her father she'd seen in her dreams? Had he found her somehow through her power? Was that some version of her mother that was at his side? Ivy kept seeing the face of the girl, thinking it was so much like Amber, so much like herself, but different somehow. The hair was dark, the eyes dark, but it was the look in those eyes that convinced Ivy she hadn't been dreaming about her mother. There was anger, hatred, and maybe even cruelty there in that girl's eyes, and Ivy was certain that her mother was none of those things. So, who was it? Was she real? Did it matter?

Ivy didn't remember falling back to sleep, but when Helena came in to wake them up, she was grateful to realize she'd had no more dreams.

CHAPTER 8

I VY HADN'T MEANT TO oversleep, but by the time she got up and down
to breakfast everyone was packing, checking weapons, and gearing up. A
stack of pancakes sat on the table, presumably for her. Nearby was a box
of ammo, and at the other end of the table was a black backpack. Nothing said
home like pancakes and bullets.

"We need to make a run into town for just a few items, and then we'll meet
up with Helena and John at the safe house." Patricia put the plate of pancakes
into Ivy's hands. Apparently, Ivy would need to eat quickly or not at all.

According to Patricia the plan was that John and Helena would take the
SUV and they would take Patricia's car, an old Plymouth Duster John had
restored for her. Ivy secretly had hoped it would be hers when she got her license.

A faint sound caught Ivy's attention and she made her way outside, thoughts
of pancakes and cars forgotten.

Ivy turned toward the gravel driveway when she heard a car approach.
Patricia had gone outside earlier to put things in the car and was already sitting

in the driver's seat, but Ivy saw her shake her head and open the door to get out when they both realized who the visitors were.

Ryan parked behind them and both he and Gabe got out. Ivy felt concern for Gabe at first, but seeing that he was perfectly fine as he walked toward her, she felt the rush of heat to her cheeks as she thought of their kiss.

"Good morning." Gabe acknowledged Patricia, then turned to Ivy. "I think we need to talk."

"Gabe, we don't have a lot of time," Patricia told him.

"Where you headed?" Ryan asked as Amber got out of the car.

"Nowhere worth mentioning." Patricia stared hard at Ryan, and Ivy realized she didn't trust him.

Ryan put his hands up in a defensive gesture and smiled. "Just trying to be friendly."

Looking at Patricia, Ivy decided the timing couldn't be worse. She was certain Helena and John were watching. Then it occurred to her that there could be others out in the forest watching as well. Seeing Gabe in the light of day could just put him in the crosshairs of the community.

"Gabe, it's not safe here. You need to go," Ivy said as she walked closer to him so she could talk to him without everyone else hearing.

"I'm not an idiot, Ivy," Gabe said. "I know you're in some kind of trouble. Attacked two nights in a row? Those guys meant business and it looked to me like you are that business."

"It's not something I can talk about. Not because I don't want to, but because it could put you in danger," Ivy told him. He looked like he was about to say something and she added, "Gabe, you're in danger just being here."

He stared down at her, pursing his lips, then biting at the corner of his lower lip. Whatever he wanted to say wasn't coming out easily. Or at all.

"We really need to go boys, so if you don't mind..." Patricia forced a smile that was so fake she may as well have just said, *"Get out of the way."* But before she could say anything else Ivy watched her head jerk to the left, eyes scanning the forest.

The hair on the back of Ivy's neck rose up. She knew better than to look, it was bad enough that Patricia had been so obvious. Ivy had no doubt Amber knew something was up. Something bad.

"Get in your car boys." Patricia's tone had changed from frustrated to so commanding in such a way that even Gabe took notice.

"What's going on?" Gabe asked.

Ivy took his hand, bringing his full attention back to her, and she squeezed hard. She didn't want to alert whoever was out in the forest watching them, but she needed to convey the urgency of the situation to Gabe in a way that would get him to move. Unfortunately, the look in his eyes was more obstinate than understanding, and Ivy knew she would need to do something quick or things could go badly for all of them.

"We need to get out of here. Now!" Ivy whispered, squeezing his hand again, then threading her fingers through his, moving as she pulled him toward Ryan's car. She glanced at Patricia as if to say, "This is the only way." Patricia was not pleased, but she didn't try to stop her either.

Ryan didn't move. He was either not happy to have Ivy join them or he was the worst person on Earth at reading body language. She mouthed the words, "Let's go!" at Ryan, but he just stood there, gazing out into the forest. Ivy hadn't heard anything, but her heart began to beat harder, faster, as she got into the car and slid over so Gabe could get in.

"Dude!" Gabe closed the car door and leaned over her to look at his cousin. "Let's go."

Ryan cast one final glance out at the forest, then nodded and got in. As they began to back out, followed closely by Patricia and Amber, Ivy chanced a glance into the forest. Adrenalin filled her veins as she saw, not one, not two but four figures in camouflage outfits moving toward the cabin.

"Did you see those guys?" Gabe had noticed them. She had hoped she wouldn't have to lie to him. She hoped he didn't have to be involved at all. Hoping was a fruitless exercise today it seems.

"Listen," Ivy began, her brain moving on fast forward as she searched for what to say. "You're right. Those guys from last night are after me, and Amber. But, the more you know, the more danger you're in." So far she hadn't lied. At least there was that.

"Well, they saw us. Saw Ryan's car. So, you may as well tell us what's going on," Gabe told her as he glanced at Ryan then back down at her. Ryan didn't seem to have anything to say.

"All I can tell you is that there are some people who would take Amber and me, and maybe even Patricia and Helena if they could. They're bad men, and we've been trying to keep a low profile for years so this wouldn't happen. Now it has, and we need to deal with it." Still, no lies. Ivy wasn't sure why it was so important, but she didn't want to lie to Gabe. It mattered that she be honest with him.

"Just call the cops, Ivy." Gabe's brows knitted together. He pulled out his cell phone, but Ivy put her hand out to stop him.

"We can't. It's more complicated than that." Ivy said to Ryan, who continued to drive even as Patricia passed them and stayed right in front of them, leading them, Ivy was sure, to the safe house. But, before they got too far she slowed down, and pulled over. Ryan pulled in behind her.

Patricia got out and hurried to the passenger side of Ryan's car. Gabe rolled the window down.

"Ivy, you need to get in the car with us." She opened the door, but Gabe didn't move. "Boys, you need to go home now. Go home and lay low for a while. I need to take the girls and leave town for a bit, but we'll be in touch soon."

It seemed easy for Patricia to lie to Gabe. The safe house would most likely be the first step to leaving their old lives behind and getting new identities and a new home. Ivy thought they might stay and fight, but the panic she saw in Patricia's eyes told her they were in more danger than they first thought.

Patricia opened the door wider, glanced down the road behind them, a worried look on her face as she squinted against the glaring sun.

"I need to go." Ivy moved, which forced Gabe to get out of the car. Turning back to Gabe Ivy looked up into his troubled eyes. "Don't call the police. It would only make things worse. Patricia is right. Lay low, stay away from our place. We won't be there."

"Where will you be?" Gabe asked. "When will I see you again?"

Ivy felt the heat sting behind her eyes. Her throat went dry as she looked at him. "Soon." She lied.

She followed Patricia back to the Duster and got in the back seat. The sting behind her eyes became heated tears that blurred her vision. It was so unfair. All of it.

She watched Ryan's car pull back onto the road and head toward town as their own car moved slowly toward town, then veered off onto an obscure back road.

PATRICIA APPEARED DEEP IN thought for the first hour they were on the road. She shook her head, drawing Ivy's attention.

"Crap. Girl, you need to dissemble your cell phones. Take out the battery. We don't want anyone to be able to track you." She said. Patricia massaged her temple and sighed. "John and Helena should be at the safe house by now."

"Do you think those guys are from the community?" Ivy finally found her voice.

"Yes, I do." Patricia kept her eyes on the road.

"Do you think Gabe and Ryan are safe?" It was the question that haunted her most. She couldn't live with herself if something happened to Gabe because he was with her.

"Let's hope so." Patricia's voice was quiet and reflective.

"Maybe we should check on them later," Amber suggested, bringing Ivy's gaze to the side view mirror where her sister was looking at her in the reflection from the backseat.

"You two will stay at the safe house," Patricia told them, then quickly added, "But, I'll ask John to check on the boys in a day or two, okay?"

It had to be okay. It was the only choice she'd been given. Ivy wondered how long it would be before she and Amber would be allowed to go anywhere at all. Ivy's fear had come to life. She was a prisoner. She wasn't in the community, but the community was still ruling her life.

Patricia took out her cell, and Ivy and Amber powered down and started the process of ridding themselves of what could potentially be a tracking device. She watched as Patricia called a couple of numbers until finally someone picked up.

"Hello, John?" Patricia asked, then went silent. "Yes, it is. Yes, they are." There was such a long pause then, Ivy had enough time to worry, then become afraid. "I'll be there in an about an hour and a half." She hung up, dropped the phone to the seat and slowed the car, pulling over and putting the car in park.

Her breathing had gone from fast to unnaturally slow and she rested her head against the steering wheel.

"Patricia?" Amber put her hand on her shoulder. "What is it?"

"That was a cop who answered John's phone." Patricia didn't look up.

Amber glanced back to Ivy her face blanched as though she were ill. They were smart enough to know their world was crumbling. Now they just needed to know how big a chunk was just lost.

Patricia sat up, glanced in the rear view mirror at Ivy, then over to Amber. "I need to drop you girls off at the safe house and head back home. Apparently, John and Helena changed plans and went back to the house for something." Patricia scowled. "I should have called them right away. I should have thought about it. I really thought they were at the safe house." None of the words were for them and Ivy knew it.

"Are they dead?" Ivy whispered into the car, unsure she wanted to be heard.

"I don't know," Patricia answered. "The police just asked me to return home."

"Are you sure it's not a trap?" Ivy asked.

"I know the officer who picked up the phone. But, we won't take any chances. I'll drop you off and go back to see."

"That's not going to happen." Ivy was tired of running already and tired of being treated like a child. "If they get you, what will happen to Amber and me? We stick together. We can call the police station and check with them, and we go back together. If the police are really there, those guys in the forest won't try anything."

Patricia sat there for what seemed like an eternity. She nodded, more to herself, Ivy thought. She put the car in drive and turned around.

Since they didn't need to go to the safe house, they'd get home in an hour, less if Patricia treated the car like the bad ass ride it was meant to be.

Amber called the police station and got confirmation that something had happened, but they wouldn't give her any more details on the phone. Time stretched out. Ivy could almost feel the minutes ticking by. None of them spoke, and Ivy imagined her sister and Patricia were locked within their own nightmares, just as she was as she wondered what had happened to John and Helena. The fact that no one would give them any information at all only fueled the nightmares playing across Ivy's mind.

By the time they pulled into the driveway, Ivy couldn't sit still. She leaned forward, removing her seat belt. There was a police car just as they turned in and Patricia stopped, gave her identification and got clearance to move farther down the long driveway. Three more police cars, one unmarked but unmistakably law enforcement, filled the parking area in front of the house. Several people in uniform wandered around the property, but Ivy only had eyes for the front door that was standing open. She strained to see inside, but only saw darkness and the outline of familiar things within.

Patricia pulled over and Ivy was out the door, running into the house before Patricia had turned the engine off. Someone tried to stop Ivy as she ran through the front door and followed the line of uniformed men and women who moved along a path like ants toward the kitchen.

Someone grabbed her shoulder, but Ivy spun around and got free, moving forward with what felt like unnatural slowness. She could hear her own heartbeat. Her mouth went totally dry as she shoved away hands and arms that tried to block her. The door was propped open and the kitchen table was in view. That view stopped Ivy in her tracks like no person could. She stood at the threshold of the kitchen that had just recently been full of the smell of pancakes and sounds of laughter. Her world went askew, her sight blurred. It felt as though the walls were shrinking and expanding, the floor felt as though it moved even though she was standing still.

One more step and she could see everything. But she couldn't force herself to do it. She was glued in place and everything around her began to spin.

Her mind registered what her eyes were seeing, and that seemed to signal something to her heart, then her eyes.

There was so much blood.

CHAPTER 9

"WHERE ARE THEY?" The screaming increased, but the words were the same over and over. Ivy turned to Amber who had been let in, accompanied by Patricia, a police officer and someone in plain clothes. Ivy heard herself screaming, but she felt disembodied from it all. The pain in her chest became white hot and made it difficult to breathe. Or maybe it was the screaming that hurt so much.

Amber broke away from the others and ran to her. Something about the warmth of Amber's embrace, the tight hold of her arms, made Ivy stop screaming, but her breaths were fast and shallow. She was drowning right here outside their kitchen. The room spun, and she leaned hard into her sister. She heard Amber take in a gulp of air, and they moved in unison in a heap to the floor.

The smell of Murphy's Oil Soap tinged with lemon registered in Ivy's mind as she continued to breathe in quick bites of air. The smell of cedar followed just beneath that and then the shampoo Amber used wafted through her nose. Green apple and clean water. She pulled Amber in so tightly, she heard her sister grunt.

She buried her face into Amber's hair because the underlying odor beneath all those homey smells was the bitter copper of blood, and Ivy felt hysteria knocking around inside her looking for a good place to spread itself. She couldn't take that smell. She leaned closer into Amber and forced herself to slow her breathing.

The floor was cool where the hard wood wasn't covered by the large area rug that covered most of the living room area outside the kitchen. Ivy put her hands down and touched the surface of the wood. Like a touchstone, this was home, this was safety. But, in an instant, it wasn't and Ivy felt only the cold wood, and that cold spread up her fingertips to her hand, up her arm and down her chest where it rested in her heart and stilled that racing muscle.

Her training, the training John and Helena had spent years instilling in her, had to mean something. She needed to search her mind, her memory, and call on that training just like they had taught her. Ivy closed her eyes, took in a long breath and let it out slowly. She tried willing herself to stop trembling, then realized it wasn't her, but Amber. Amber was falling apart. That thought brought Ivy back to the present. She opened her eyes and looked at her sister's face. The shock, horror and grief there caused Ivy to feel more determined to call on her training.

Think.

What next?

Ivy pulled Amber's face around to look straight into her own. Amber's eyes struggled to remain on the horror in the kitchen, but Ivy pulled her head far over, putting her own directly in the way of the kitchen door. Amber took a moment before she stared into Ivy's eyes.

They were not telepathic. People always asked them if they were, or if they could feel what the other was feeling. It was never like that. But it was close. They were close. They shared everything. Ivy didn't have to wonder what Amber was thinking or how she was feeling because she knew. She knew because Amber loved John and Helena, too. Amber saw the blood as well. For a split second and for the first time Ivy looked into Amber's face and saw her own reflection staring back at her.

"Think," Ivy whispered. It was a command, and she shook Amber just slightly as she said it.

Amber's breathing slowed, but her eyes remained glued to Ivy's. She blinked.

Blinked again. Tears filled up, giving way at the same time so that dual teardrops spilled over and ran down her cheeks. Amber lifted her hands up and gently wiped at the tears on Ivy's own face.

Then Patricia was there helping them both up. The man in plain clothes was asking Patricia something, but Ivy could only hear the sound of her own heartbeat in her ears. A distant sound of the ocean pulsing in time with that beat came next. She willed the room to stop spinning as she leaned slightly into Amber. She pulled back, standing entirely on her own. Deep breaths steadied her, but she couldn't look back toward the kitchen. Not yet.

"Are you okay? Why don't you sit down on the lounge chair?" Patricia said. At least she'd heard the words. The room stopped spinning. She glanced at Amber, who was standing upright as well, regarding the house as though she were taking inventory of it. It caused Ivy to look around.

People in white jackets, police uniforms, serious looking plain clothes, men and women walking around the house, taking pictures and notes. Some were talking to each other, some were staring at them.

"I'm okay." The words came out, and Ivy was grateful that they sounded even normal.

"I need to sit down." Amber stepped back and nearly stumbled on the area rug. The plain clothes gentleman that had come in with Patricia grabbed her arm and steadied her. He walked her the few steps to the lounge chair and sat her down. He crouched down and started talking to her, but Ivy couldn't make out what he was saying, so she turned back to Patricia.

"It may not be their blood. There are no bodies in there," Patricia said. "It may not be *just* their blood."

Ivy considered it. John and Helena spent every single day training for an ambush, for a fight. Hell, for Armageddon it seemed. Patricia was right. They could still be alive. If the community didn't want anyone to know they'd killed them, they would have cleaned up the mess. If they wanted to make a point and scare the hell out of them they would have left the bodies. Where were the bodies? Wouldn't they be more valuable alive? The thought gave Ivy strength and she looked over Patricia's shoulder and into the kitchen through the open door. There was a lot of blood, the room in total disarray.

Ivy started for the kitchen. She needed to see inside. Patricia put her hand on her shoulder to stop her.

"I looked already. There's no need for you to see that."

Ivy shook her head. She walked toward the door, but a police officer stopped her.

"This is as far as you can go right now." He said gently.

Ivy could still see the majority of the room. She didn't see bullet holes. But, she couldn't see everything. She looked for some kind of markings in the blood to indicate that bodies were dragged out, but couldn't find any. Whoever had lost all that blood had either walked out or they were carried out. Ivy turned back to Patricia, who had come up behind her.

"They could still be alive." Ivy felt the first pangs of hope.

Patricia nodded.

"Why would they come back here?" Now the training was kicking in.

Patricia shook her head, then scanned the room with her eyes and shook her head again. They couldn't talk here. Not now.

"They want us to look around the house to see if anything is missing or out of place," Patricia told her. "Then they want us to come down to the station to give a statement. They just need to hear that we were getting ready for vacation and that John and Helena were supposed to meet up with us later."

Ivy understood. They turned together and walked over to Amber. The next hour, going through the house, through the memories, seemed like the longest hour of Ivy's life. Nothing had been touched that they could tell. Nothing taken. The question that raked through Ivy's mind like fingernails on a chalkboard driving her mad was: *Why had they come back? Why?*

"Ivy, Amber, this is Detective Arnold." Patricia introduced them.

Detective Arnold was the investigator that had come in with Patricia and who walked with them around the house. He was tall, slightly older than Patricia, piercing light blue eyes and a calm voice that invited you to trust him. Ivy couldn't decide if she should or shouldn't, so by default she didn't. But, Patricia answered his questions with as much honesty as she could and wasn't giving off any vibe that told Ivy not to trust the detective.

They followed him to the station where another long and difficult hour slowly crept by. They had been put into different areas for questioning, which grated on Ivy's nerves a little. A woman who had to be fresh out of the academy was assigned to question her and the questions seemed pretty straight forward and simple. At least, they were questions Ivy expected would be asked. She hesitated for just a moment when the woman, Carla, asked who they had seen or spoke to that day, and Ivy realized she had to tell her about Ryan and Gabe. She wouldn't say anything about the visitors out in the forest since that would only complicate things, but she figured Amber and Patricia would stick as close to the truth as possible, and that meant giving them this information.

Carla took down Gabe and Ryan's names and addresses, excused herself and returned with a glass of water that she handed to Ivy. Ivy took a sip just to realize she was dying of thirst and downed the entire glass.

"What happens next?" Ivy asked.

"I'm taking you to Detective Arnold where you'll be with your aunt and your sister. He can let you know what's next."

Carla walked her to a small corner office, and she saw Patricia and Amber as she walked in. Patricia was standing even though there were enough chairs for everyone. Ivy nearly collapsed into a chair next to Amber.

As Detective Arnold told them they would need to find somewhere else to stay, but had to remain in town, Ivy peered around the room, then stole a glance out the window that made up half of one wall. Her heart nearly skipped a beat when Carla walked into view with Gabe and Ryan trailing behind her. Gabe seemed to sense her, or perhaps he was just looking around himself when he caught sight of her, but their eyes locked for just a few seconds and Ivy tried to fit all the "I'm sorry" into that look as she could.

Patricia was talking, but Ivy hadn't paid attention. Then a hand rested on her shoulder and she nearly jumped out of her skin. Patricia scowled at her, but it was more of a question than a reprimand. She stood up and followed Patricia and Amber out of the office.

"Let me get someone to walk you to your car," Detective Arnold offered.

"I appreciate that, but I think we'll walk over to the diner first and just try to regroup. I just really need some fresh air, and the walk is best I think." Patricia shook his hand.

Ivy nodded her farewell and followed Patricia and Amber out of the police station.

"Where are we going really?" Ivy asked when they got outside. The sun was still out and Ivy squinted while she waited for her eyes to adjust.

"We're going sit down and come up with a plan before we do anything else." Patricia had her cell out. "Plus, the diner gives us a good vantage point to watch the area around our car and make sure no one followed us here"

"What's next?" Amber stepped in sync with Ivy.

"We find John and Helena. That's what's next," Ivy said.

"No, first we get you girls somewhere safe." Patricia said.

"All these years of training, and now that we actually need to use it, we are going to hole up somewhere hiding?!" Ivy could not believe it. This went against everything she was ever taught. You stick together. You help each other. This is family.

"Do you think we need to go to the safe house and wait?" Ivy asked Amber.

"I think we have no idea where to start, Ivy. The best thing to do is make sure we are safe, regroup and come up with a plan." Amber sounded calm, but Ivy doubted that she felt that way.

"I know exactly where to start! We need to go back to the house and fortify there. They'll come back. When they do, we'll capture one of them and get them to tell us where John and Helena are."

"That's not going to happen, Ivy." Patricia had hung up and her tone was like steal. "The police are still going back and forth to the house. I have no doubt that place is being watched. They'd be on us before we could fortify ourselves inside. It's a bad idea."

"I'm not running!" Ivy hadn't meant for the words to come out so loud and she immediately regretted it as she saw a few passersby slow and gawk at them.

Patricia winced, scowled and gave Ivy a warning look that needed no interpretation.

"Let's head over to the diner, it will get us out of the street. Right now we're like fish in a barrel." Patricia didn't wait for a response, but turned toward the diner and walked as fast as she could without running.

Amber followed suit, not even caring to look back, so Ivy followed, then caught up with her sister and walked into the diner.

They sat at the last booth in the back, putting them near the back exit and facing the front doors of the diner. Patricia sat facing the doors and

Amber scooted in next to her, leaving Ivy to sit facing away from the door, which she loathed.

Stephie, the waitress who had served them for as long as Ivy could remember coming to this diner walked up with a big smile on her face. She looked at them and the smile melted just a little. She dialed it down to "pleasant, but guarded" and asked what they wanted.

Patricia managed a small smile and ordered herself a coffee. Ivy ordered apple juice, as did Amber. No one wanted anything to eat.

Stephie stepped away to retrieve their drink orders and the table grew silent.

Ivy contemplated several scenarios, some that included ditching Patricia and Amber to find John and Helena on her own, and some that were more a fantasy where she was able to talk Patricia into seeing things her way. Nothing that sounded sane was forthcoming, so Ivy shook her head as though to clear it and started to talk.

"I understand that we need to regroup. We need to be safe," Ivy started. "But, I need to know that the plan will eventually include finding John and Helena."

Ivy looked pointedly at Patricia and waited. Patricia had been peering out the window that made up the entire east wall of the diner. Ivy wondered if she was looking for danger, or seeing something in her mind that only she could see. Either way, she got no response and that only frustrated her more.

"If you're not going to do something, I will," Ivy said and got the response she was looking for: Patricia's total attention.

"You're going to do as you are told." Patricia lowered her voice, but there was still sting to it. "You're going to think of someone other than yourself and what you want. You will stay with Amber and me. You will go to the safe house. And, you'll do what you're told once we get there. Understand?"

It was rhetorical, and Ivy knew it. She burned, partly with embarrassment for being treated like such a child and partly with anger and for the same reason.

Ivy searched her mind for a reply that wouldn't confirm Patricia's assessment of her, but before she could gather her thoughts a sound caught her attention. Beyond the initial exit door in the back was an alcove. One side of the alcove took you to the restrooms, the other was storage and beyond that was a back door. It wasn't unusual to have someone drop something when they came out of the storage area. It was a bit dark and people going to the restroom didn't always pay attention the door opposite them. But, Ivy heard a sharp intake of breath. A woman gasped. Ivy waited for the sound of something dropping, or perhaps a laugh or apology from whoever had bumped into the woman, but immediately there was nothing but silence.

Patricia was staring out the window again and Amber looked up at her with a confused expression on her face.

Patricia sat up straight, her eyes focusing on something outside. Ivy swung her legs out so she could stand easily. Amber had her hands on the table pushing up when all hell broke loose.

The back exit door swung open hard, causing Amber to flinch and bringing Patricia's startled gaze to the immediate threat. Ivy was standing when a tall albino man in a white suit walked through the door. Ivy watched his movements, graceful like a predator as he walked fully into the diner, scanned quickly and immediately locked his eyes on them.

"Daniel." Patricia breathed out the name in a tone that made the hair on the back of Ivy's neck stand straight up.

Daniel was less than three feet away, but he had a silver Beretta 9 millimeter in his hand and he swung it toward them as he took a step forward. His eyes went straight to Patricia, and that was all the invitation Ivy needed.

Ivy launched herself forward, kicking the gun out of his hand. She heard it hit the floor and mentally noted the direction it has skidded. She stepped forward, spreading her feet apart to give herself the leverage she needed for hand to hand. Daniel was still stunned, and Ivy took that millisecond of surprise to hit him as hard as she could in the nose. He stumbled back and she stepped forward again, but this time when she swung, he caught her hand and used her momentum to pull her forward.

Ivy lost her balance, then recovered enough to step as hard as she could on his instep, causing him to cry out and lose his grip on her. She moved forward and away from him, gaining her stance again, locking eyes with his. Angry, pink eyes stared at her, still watering a little from the blow to the nose. He didn't even try to wipe away the blood, but let it pour down his face where it spilled over the sneer of his lips.

Amber moved away from the table, which freed Patricia up to join them, but they were facing the front of the diner, which let Ivy know that Daniel was not the only threat they faced.

Ivy took a deep, steadying breath as she assessed Daniel, listened to the mayhem behind her and realized she could see the gleaming silver butt of Daniel's custom pistol between two stools near the long counter that sat opposite the booths. She stepped back, feigning fear and Daniel took a step forward. One more step and she would be within reach of the gun, but she'd need to buy herself enough time to actually pick it up.

From her peripheral vision, Ivy could see where someone had recently vacated one of the stools at the counter. A plate of eggs and a pork chop. A knife. Ivy changed her stance to bring around her full weight when she kicked out at Daniel. She knew he wouldn't just stand there and take the kick and she was counting on it. Daniel grabbed at her foot, caught it, and pulled hard as he twisted. The pain in her ankle shot up through her leg, but it only served to wake up her senses. As she fell she reached out to the counter as though it could help her from hitting the ground, her hands slipped, and she fell hard to the ground, between the stools.

Daniel looked at her and one side of his mouth lifted in a half-smile. He started to bend down and scoop her up when Ivy turned, reached around one of the stools and plunged the knife into Daniel's shoe. He screamed and stumbled back, the knife standing there in the white shoe like a statue in the snow.

Ivy grabbed the gun, pushed herself away from the counter and was up on her feet by the time Daniel had pulled the knife out.

She pointed the gun at him and he stopped in his tracks.

"Back up." The safety wasn't on and he knew it, so he backed up. She motioned with the gun and he backed up more.

Ivy moved so she could keep the gun on Daniel but also look around the diner and see how bad things were. She'd heard Amber cry out at one point as she stabbed Daniel, but she didn't dare split her attention then. Looking toward the front of the diner, she saw Amber fighting a young Asian woman, and Patricia was just stumbling back from a tall, thin black man who had pulled a gun on her.

The training took over. That's why you train, so you have muscle memory and your body just knows what to do. Ivy turned the gun on the tall, thin man and fired. The sound was deafening in the small diner. Ivy heard noise behind the counter, she was pretty sure she heard Stephie scream back there. The sound of pots and pans clanging together added to the symphony of mayhem and terror. Ivy immediately checked Daniel, who hadn't moved, then slowly she started moving toward Patricia and Amber.

The Asian girl had her hands up in the air and was backing away very slowly from Amber. Patricia moved to her, checking on Amber as she crossed the space between them. Her hands felt hot as she laid them on Ivy's wrist and gently took the gun from her grip.

"The police are dealing with a couple more of them outside the diner. We should head out the back and hope to get away before they detain us." Patricia put her other hand on Ivy's shoulder and gave a gentle squeeze. "We can't let them detain us, Ivy. It could be dangerous for everyone."

Ivy felt her body disengage from the violence that had stolen it. She walked silently to the man she had shot, reached down touched him. He would live. It wasn't as bad as she'd feared. She studied at the Asian woman for just a moment, so she would never forget her face, then turned and grabbed Amber's hand, pulling her along as they exited the back of the diner.

The fresh air and sunshine hit Ivy as they stepped out, followed immediately by the sound of gunfire toward the front of the diner. There wasn't much space between the back of the diner and a six foot chain link fence and Ivy hoped she could make it over as she stepped gingerly on an ankle that she was certain was swollen.

The sound of a car to the left caused Ivy to turn in that direction. It was Ryan and Gabe in Ryan's car. The relief washed over her as she grabbed Amber's arm and pulled her toward the car.

"Let's go!" Ivy yelled out and was rewarded when Amber moved ahead and Patricia came around to offer a shoulder for her to lean on.

Amber threw the door open and waited for Patricia to get her to the car. Ivy practically dived into the back seat, then pulled herself up and made room for Amber and Patricia to get in.

The car was in motion before Patricia closed the door all the way.

Ryan's tires squealed as he pulled out, kicking gravel back before the tires hit asphalt. The car swerved as all tires hit the road, Ryan straightened it and hit the gas, taking them down the middle of town at about sixty miles an hour.

"Where are we going?" Gabe asked as he glanced back at Ivy.

"Take the old highway south for now," Patricia answered.

"How did you know we were at the diner?" Amber asked. She was looking into the rear view mirror, staring at Ryan.

"A couple of crazy druggies came in while they were questioning us. I've never seen them here before," Gabe explained. "They saw us and started a commotion. One of them got to Ryan and asked where you were. He just said that you'd already left."

"The detective you were with came out and told them you had refused a ride so no one knew where you had gone," Ryan added. "One of the guys tried to leave, which just caused total chaos in the station with both of those dudes fighting the cops, trying to get away."

"I knew you were on foot and figured you might go to the diner," Gabe added. "I've seen you in there a lot." He shrugged like it was nothing that he knew where she spent her time. Ivy wasn't sure if that was cool or creepy, but for the moment, given that he just saved them, she was going with cool.

"Makes sense," Patricia said, but when Ivy looked at her she was staring out the window, not really talking to anyone in particular.

"How so?" Ivy asked, seeing Patricia through the reflection in the window.

"There were only three that came to the diner," she said. "They must have split up to look for us."

"And that explains why the police didn't get there sooner," Amber added.

"What I want to know," Gabe interrupted, "is who are these people and what do they want with you? Why would they harm John and Helena? Are they alive? Do these people have them?"

Ivy glanced at Patricia, but Patricia was staring out the window again. Briefly, Ivy wondered if Patricia was in shock. It was a scary thought so she dismissed it.

"These people are part of a commune, a cult of sorts. My mother used to be married to the leader of the cult, and when she died Patricia, John, and Helena helped Amber and me escape that place." Ivy glanced again to Patricia, then back to Gabe.

Gabe looked at her as though he were waiting for more information.

"The leader of the cult is our father." Ivy peered into Gabe's eyes, waiting for it all to register, waiting for the judgment that would come. She had pulled him into some crazy cult fight that could endanger his life and for what? Because she had a crush on him. Because he was willing to be her friend.

"Seriously?!" Ryan's voice rang out as though the word was profanity. "So, if these people find you, there's nothing anyone can do to keep them from taking you?"

"What are you talking about?" Gabe frowned at Ryan. "These people are freakin' crazy! There's no way they're going with them!"

Gabe didn't get it, but Ryan did. Ivy felt the heavy burden of truth burn inside her. It was helplessness and fear. She hated that she felt vulnerable around everyone.

"Ryan's right." Ivy could hardly raise her voice above a whisper. The defeat in admitting the worst case scenario caused the back of her eyes to burn and her vision to blur. "With our mother dead, our father has every right to take us. All he has to do is tell them Patricia kidnapped us, which she did, and poisoned us against him."

"Well, no offense," Ryan said, "But, how do you know for sure she didn't do just that? What if you father has been searching for you all this time wanting you back because he loves you?"

"He doesn't love them." Patricia sat back and looked directly at Ryan. "He doesn't love anyone. I watched him murder their mother. I know what he has in store for the girls. John and Helena knew too. And they believed so completely that he would harm them that they were willing to give their lives to keep him away."

"I'm just saying that there are two sides to every story." Ryan added, causing the tension in the car to rise.

"I trust Patricia," Amber added, anger giving an edge to her voice.

"The question now is," Patricia sat forward a little more so she could see more of Ryan, "what are you going to do, Ryan?"

Ryan didn't try to look at her. He didn't say anything for a few seconds, and Ivy wondered if he was going to answer at all when Gabe looked over at him, causing Ryan to actually squirm.

"What do you mean?" Ryan asked.

"Are you saving us? Or turning us in?" Patricia asked.

Ivy caught Ryan's glance in the rear view mirror. He didn't look at Patricia, but at Amber. Another moment passed and Gabe turned around.

"We're with you," Gabe answered for them both. "Right?" He glanced at Ryan.

Ryan turned his attention solely on the road. "Right."

"Here's the thing." Patricia looked toward both boys. "If we're going to let you come with us to the safe house, you need to give me your cell phones."

"That's not going to happen," Ryan answered.

"Why?" Amber asked.

"Okay, let's have a reality check here." Ryan began. "There are people, dangerous people, doing what they can to kidnap you and when anyone gets in the way, there's bloodshed. Do I want to have no way to call for help? I think not."

Ivy could see his point, but she knew Patricia didn't totally trust them and there was no way she would bring them to the safe house without them giving up their phones.

Gabe sat forward for a moment, glanced meaningfully at Ryan and pulled out his cell phone to hand it back to Patricia.

"Dude," Gabe said as Patricia pocketed his phone, "We're out in the middle of nowhere. These people seem pretty organized to me, so there's a good chance we won't see them coming until they're right up on us anyway. Do you think calling 911 is really going to help before the damage is done?"

Gabe had a point. Even if they did call for help it would take so long for help to arrive, and these community soldiers, they were definitely trained soldiers, or assassins as far as Ivy could tell, would be in and out before anyone could save them. Besides, Ivy could appreciate Patricia's dilemma as well. Even if help arrived, they would find that she was a kidnapper and turn her and Amber over to their father, or at least put them into state custody until Zachariah would figure out how to get them back. Patricia didn't want anyone to call 911 even if they did need help.

Ryan reached down beside him and picked up his phone. He held it for a moment, then handed it back to Patricia.

"You realize that because of you guys, Gabe and I are in just as much danger as you are. These people have seen us. And they seem to be pretty resourceful since they were able to get into a police station and cause a brawl. I'm taking a big leap of faith here," Ryan said.

Gabe frowned at Ryan. "They're victims. We just got caught in the crossfire. It's not their fault."

Ryan seemed unconvinced. His expression was part sneer and part exasperation. Ivy could see him grip the steering wheel more tightly as he put his focus back to the road in a way that seemed to dismiss everyone in the car.

Patricia gave Ryan directions to the safe house and within the hour they had pulled up in front of the cabin, parking near the tall pile of fire wood on the side.

Ivy got out and watched as Gabe scanned the area. She wondered what he was thinking, not for the first time that day, not even for the fifth.

They followed Patricia inside without a word. Walking in the side door brought them directly into the kitchen.

"Why don't you boys get a fire going, and then we'll meet in twenty minutes here in the kitchen to discuss what to do next."

Gabe gave a short nod and stood up. Ryan followed him out to get some firewood. Ivy seized her opportunity.

"Patricia. Who is Daniel? I heard you say his name when he walked into the diner." Ivy realized that Patricia would know some of these people, but the way Patricia had said his name held some emotion to it that Ivy didn't understand.

"Daniel," Patricia said as she finally sat down at the table with her and Amber, "is my brother."

CHAPTER 10

IVY WAS STUNNED. She had always thought of Patricia as an only child. Why had she thought that? Ivy chastised herself for being so thoughtless. Other than how Patricia's life at the community affected her, other than Patricia's connection to her own story, she hadn't given much thought to Patricia having a family she cared for at the community. Patricia rarely talked about it, and when she did, it was always negative, so Ivy just assumed she had left behind all the horrors of that life and had been happy to do so. But, a brother?

Of course that brother had attacked them. Might have killed them! Ivy's mind raced as she relived that scene at the diner. Daniel had certainly been there to do something on behalf of the community. Ivy had no doubt about that. He hadn't come in with flowers. He had a 9 millimeter pistol. He had *not* been friendly.

"Daniel is very loyal to the community. Very loyal." Patricia seemed as though she were trying to read her. "If Zachariah gave the order to kill me, Daniel would not hesitate to do so."

Ivy felt both relieved and sad. She was relieved that she hadn't hurt someone Patricia cared about, and sad that Patricia's own family would hurt her and that Patricia knew that. Something like that, a family that would harm you, wasn't entirely foreign to Ivy. She knew her father had killed her mother and would likely harm her and Amber as well, but she hadn't seen it close up and personal. She had been told. She believed it. But, she hadn't had to face it in the flesh. Everything she knew about family was learned from Patricia, John, Helena, and Amber. She only knew love, trust, caring, and respect. She couldn't imagine what Patricia felt when she saw her brother walk in.

"I'm sorry," Ivy said. What else could she say? She wanted to ask her how she felt, but the boys would be walking in any minute, and there was no way Patricia would discuss such things once they came back.

"We can talk about it later." It was as if Patricia could read her mind.

Hadn't it always been like that though? Ivy thought about her family, what she considered her real family, and realized that Patricia knew her better than anyone other than Amber. The slow building heat of shame filled her as she realized that she'd never really taken an interest in Patricia's own life story, her own loss, her own tragedies, nothing beyond the story of how Patricia watched Zachariah kill Ivy's mother.

Ivy's thoughts were interrupted when, Gabe and Ryan, walked in carrying wood. Patricia led them into the main room of the cabin where the wood stove stood. Ivy and Amber followed and sat down. Ivy watched Gabe build the fire with surprising ease and efficiency. She wondered if he camped a lot and realized that for someone who had a crush on this guy she knew little about him beyond what she saw at school and in the dojo.

Had she really been that self-centered all her life? Ivy wondered how she could go through life knowing only how people affected her, but not really knowing people. Even Amber, whom she loved more than anyone in the world, who knew her so completely, well, what did Ivy really know about Amber's hopes and dreams? Yeah, they talked about finding boyfriends, getting good grades, school gossip and one day getting married and having a family, but it was all kid's stuff really. She had no idea how Amber was feeling at this very moment. She hadn't even asked Amber how she felt about the power they'd discovered she possessed. Ivy just assumed Amber thought it was cool and appreciated that she could heal her. But, she didn't really know how she felt deep down inside.

It was well past time to stop being so self-focused and be more aware of the people around her. It was past time to realize not just where they were or what they said, but who they really were and to care about what matters to *them*.

"You day dreaming?" Gabe asked as he sat down next to her on the small couch. He leaned over with a half-smile and whispered, "About me?" Then winked and the smile spread.

Ivy smiled faintly, but genuinely.

"Come on," he elbowed her lightly, "I'm just trying to lighten your mood." He peered into her eyes, his smile fading. His eyes raked over her face, but he said nothing else.

"Listen, we have most of what we need here," Patricia said, bringing everyone's attention to her. "But I'm sure the boys need to let someone know where they are, give some story and get about a week's worth of clothes. You can stay with us while we sort everything out, then we need to arrange to keep you safe after we leave. At least until Zachariah's people realize you have nothing for them. So information, no value."

"Aren't you afraid we'll make a phone call or give away your position if you let us out of your sight?" Ryan chimed in and earned scowls all around.

"That's why I'm coming with you," Patricia announced. "Gabe your mother is still out of town, right?"

"Right," Gabe replied.

"I'll call her and let her know I've asked for your help while we figure out what's happened to John and Helena. A small town like ours, everyone must know by now that something's happened." Patricia then turned to Ryan. "I know you have your own apartment since we've already checked you out. I assume there's no one we really need to contact regarding what you're doing for the next week?"

"No one will even miss me." Ryan assured.

Patricia nodded. "We should go ahead and leave tonight, as soon as it's dark. I have a few loose ends to tie up in town, you boys need to get your things together and we need to be quick about it."

"It's about to be dark." Gabe said glancing out the window.

"Then I guess we better get to it?" Patricia motioned for them to move, then stood in Ryan's way for a moment. "I'm trusting that you two need help and that you want to help us. Don't do anything that will make me regret that trust."

Gabe nodded, but Patricia waited for Ryan to acknowledge her words before she moved out of his way so they could leave.

Ivy gazed outside the window to see a light stripe of purple cutting across a light gray sky. The wind was just enough to move the leaves in the trees, but not strong enough to move the heavier limbs. She thought of the light caress of cool air that had greeted her when she got out of the car and could imagine the temperature dropping in rhythm with the falling sun. The thought of the cold night ahead made her shiver. Gabe gave that half-smile and put his arm around her shoulder, rubbing his hands up and down her arm to warm it. She shivered again. Ivy smiled, wanting to melt into him, but moving away instead.

"Girls, why don't you go up to John and Helena's room and make it up for the boys to share?" Patricia instructed.

Ivy was glad to have Gabe here. But, her focus needed to be on what was needed of her.

Just like at home, John and Helena's room was at the very end of the hallway. They went inside and Amber quietly closed the door behind them.

The room was rustic. Helena loved autumn colors regardless of the season. Their bed was large and made of a sturdy, heavy oak. The dresser, chest of drawers and a night stand on either side of the bed all matched. The burnt orange, brown and green of the comforter blended with the coffee-colored walls and falling leaf décor. The room was masculine, Ivy realized. She'd never thought about it before. But, it definitely had touches of Helena everywhere from the extra pillows on the bed to the lacy curtains and tall mirror standing in the corner that held several scarfs draped over it. Helena loved beautiful scarfs, and they were everywhere at home, so Ivy found some solace in them being here too. They would prepare the room for the boys, but those scarves would remain. Besides, Ivy knew that preparing the room really meant they needed to sweep the room for anything they knew John and Helena wouldn't want others to see. And of course, for weapons.

"You can't keep this up, Ivy," Amber said as she went to the closet and started going through, picking out weapons and personal items and setting them on the bed. There were pictures, a box that they both knew held Helena's personal items, little reminders of John and Helena together.

"What do you mean?" Ivy asked.

"You know what I mean." Amber stopped long enough to give Ivy her best 'you know better' glare. "Even if the guys do decide to stay and help us, once we find John and Helena we'll be on the run again. And they won't be able to go with us. Not when we won't be coming back. Not when we're most likely going to have to change our names, our state, maybe even the country we live in."

"Amber, I realize that. But, what if we can figure out a way that lets us stay? What if we don't have to run?" Ivy needed to believe that there was hope, even when she knew the odds were not with them.

"Don't you think that if there were a way to keep the community away that someone would have done that by now?" Amber asked.

"But, we've never spoken to Zachariah. We've never tried to get them to leave us alone," Ivy said as she went through the dresser and then the chest of drawers. She pulled out a .38 Special and walked it to the bed where the pile of weapons was becoming quite impressive. "What if there's something we can offer him in exchange for our freedom? What if there's something we can say or do to make him leave us alone?"

"Like what?" Amber had moved on to the night stands.

"I don't know yet, but we shouldn't stop trying. We should never stop trying." Ivy cast her eyes toward the bed. The weapons there reminded her of the training John and Helena had insisted on putting Ivy and Amber through. It was a reminder that John and Helena meant to keep them safe at any cost. Now they were paying that cost and nothing was going to stop Ivy from trying to rescue them. She would never stop trying to find them.

Amber was staring at the bed as well and Ivy imagined her sister's thoughts were running along the same path as her own.

"No, we shouldn't stop trying," Amber finally agreed, then went back to do a final sweep of the room. "But it's wrong to lead him on when you know the odds."

"Me *lead him* on?" Ivy might've laughed if the circumstances were different.

"I've crushed on him for as long as I can remember. He finally sees me. Actually sees me! And, for his trouble he's drawn into our drama, his life is in danger and he ends up having to help save us? I think I'm doing fine at pushing him as far from me as possible, and I'm not even really trying!"

"Well, you have the worst timing of any relationship I've ever heard of," Amber said as she pulled a box out of the closet and started putting the weapons and other items into it. "Gabe has always been flirty with you, but you are so thick…"

"He has not!" Ivy interrupted, considered how much her voice carries and immediately lowered it. "He is just friendly is all! He's friendly to everyone. Other than at the dojo, he barely notices, well, noticed me."

"Puh-lease!" Amber closed the box up and lifted it with a little grunt.

Ivy figured with all those guns that box had to be a little weighty. She thought about offering to help her sister with it, then figured carrying it on her own may cause her to reconsider having a lengthy conversation, so she kept silent. Amber walked at a brink pace from John and Helena's room—well, technically is now Gabe and Ryan's room—and into Patricia's.

By contrast, Patricia's room was totally girlie. The small room had flowers, pastels, and antiques. A tall standing mirror just like John and Helena's was tucked in the corner, a queen sized bed with a light blue comforter and a wardrobe close to the only window in the room, which was at the foot of the bed and on the east wall. An area rug that was large and blue with green and yellow flowers covered most of the small room's floor. A small bathroom directly opposite the end of the bed was a luxury add-on, one of the few they'd made to the upstairs rooms.

Amber put the box in the wardrobe then turned and put one hand on her hip.

"Gabe has liked you for a long time, but I'm not going to argue with you over that. He likes you and now you know." Amber was just getting started. "It's just a crush, something you can walk away from, so…walk away from it."

"Easy for you to say!" Ivy plopped down on the end of the bed. "The only crush you've ever had was on our freshman PE teacher, Mr. Davis! And he was married! To a man!"

That got Amber to smile, which made Ivy smile, and they both broke out into laughter.

"Talk about bad relationship timing!" Amber laughed "I have bad relationship everything! I can't even tell a guy is gay."

"Listen, I know what you're saying is the smart thing. I really do." Ivy sobered. "But I can't stand the idea of the community, of Zachariah, taking everything that makes us happy! That's what he wants. That's what he told our mother he was going to do. He wants us to be miserable. We have to find a way to win."

"Right now we just need to find a way to stay alive and keep him from getting his hands on us."

"Girls, we're leaving," Patricia called from downstairs.

Ivy sighed and walked to Amber, taking her hand and pulling her along. They walked downstairs where Patricia, Gabe, and Ryan stood ready to leave. She glanced out the window and was surprised at how quickly the day faded into the early evening. By the time they got to their first destination, it would be full dark.

"I have my phone," Patricia told them. "You know the drill."

Of course they did. Fortify the house, turn on the trip lights, power up a burner phone, turn on the outdoor and the indoor security system and keep a gun close by. Ivy had known this drill by heart by the time she was seven years old. She nodded at Patricia and noticed Gabe was staring at her. She offered her own rendition of a half-smile and he gave one back, turned, and walked out behind Patricia and Ryan.

She heard the door close and turned to Amber, but then someone walked back in.

"If anything happens to me, there's a lock box at the First National bank in San Francisco. It's on Mission street and it has your name on the account, Ivy," Patricia told her. "I'm going to get the key for you and I want you to put it somewhere safe. Understand?"

"What's in the safety deposit box," Ivy asked. Her curiosity peaked at finding out something new that had never even been discussed during any drills in the past.

"New identities, access to money, a key and directions to another safe house back east. Letters from me, John, and Helena to both of you girls."

Ivy's heart raced and her blood felt hot in her veins.

"You're going to be fine. We're going to find John and Helena. And we'll figure this all out." Ivy promised, but to Patricia or herself she'd best not say.

Patricia smiled at them. Amber walked up and hugged her tight, then let her go. She turned back to Ivy and brought her hand up to caress the side of her cheek.

"You both look so much like your mother. So beautiful." She smiled, but there was sadness there. "Be careful while I'm away. Use your training. Be careful."

"You already said that." Amber tried to laugh, but it just came out as a whisper.

"Well, I mean it," Patricia said. "I love you girls."

"We love you, too." Ivy said.

It all felt so final. As Patricia walked out the door, Ivy was overcome with the need to chase her down and hold her tight. She felt like a little girl needing the reassurance of her mother. But, by the time she moved toward the door she heard the car door slam and the engine roar to life.

She wanted to say so much to Patricia. She had questions. But, they would have to wait for another time and for someone else to answer them.

CHAPTER 11

"NOW WHAT?" AMBER ASKED while they watched the tail lights grow smaller as Ryan, Gabe, and Patricia drove away from the house.

"Let's get everything locked up, security cameras double checked, throw another log on the fire and then triple-check the doors and windows. That way, when Patricia calls, and you know she will, we'll have something to tell her that will make her happy."

Amber nodded and headed over to the monitors. There were two; one that pointed toward the house from the forest at different intervals, and one that pointed from the house out to the forest, the road and the lake. Each monitor was sectioned into six blocks representing each camera. Amber was the more technically savvy, so she took the tech stuff and Ivy started checking the doors, throwing the log on and putting on some hot chocolate.

As she warmed some milk, she turned on the stereo that was under the cabinet where they kept their dishes. One of John's old '80's CDs was plugged in, and Ivy made a mental note to get her iPod from her room to plug into the stereo. In the meantime, she listened to Cyndi Lauper sing about girls wanting to have fun and smiled at the irony.

"All clear," Amber said as she walked into the kitchen. "Including my stomach. Can you make some grilled cheese sandwiches for us?"

"Girls just want to have fu-un, oh girls…" Ivy picked up the spoon that was lying next to her cup of hot chocolate and started singing into it, serenading Amber, who could only roll her eyes, shake her head, and finally join in the chorus.

The song ended and Amber walked over to turn the volume down before anyone could start singing again. She was still smiling when she sat down and started drinking her hot chocolate.

"Do you think Ryan acts a little suspicious?" she asked.

"I think we live a life where we critique the behavior of everyone we come into contact with," Ivy answered as she sat to drink as well. "If you suspect everyone, then how to you differentiate between normal behavior and suspicious behavior?"

"You just know," Amber answered, but seemed thoughtful as she took another sip. "I mean, things start to get weird just after he moves to town. He seems to be around when bad things happen. I know you don't want to think badly of him because of Gabe, but you can't deny that something doesn't quite add up with him."

"I know." Ivy sipped her drink. "But, they've been seen with us. They've helped us. Do we just leave them to a bunch of crazy people and hope nothing happens to them?"

"No," Amber agreed. "But bringing them to the safe house?"

"Where else were we going to bring them? At least here they are safe and we can keep an eye on them," Ivy said. "We're damned if we do, damned if we don't. If they're innocent we need to help keep them safe since they're in this mess because of us. If Ryan is up to something, we'll find out soon enough."

"If Ryan is up to something?" Amber raised one eyebrow in question. "You don't think Gabe would help his favorite cousin with whatever it is they may be up to?"

"No, I don't." Ivy suddenly felt angry, even though she knew this was a logical line of questioning and for their safety, a necessary one.

"How long until they get back?" Amber asked, then took the drink.

"I'm thinking it will be no more than six hours for Patricia. I'm assuming the guys will come back when she does."

"You don't think Patricia will want to keep them under her watchful eye the entire time?" Amber bugged her eyes out and smiled.

"Yeah, I guess so. But, I don't know if Gabe will need to go to school himself to get checked out for a few days or not," Ivy said. She hoped he could just leave a message, but something told her that may not be so easy.

"Do you think Patricia already has a plan to find John and Helena?" Amber stood up and went to the sink where she rinsed out her cup.

"I hope so."

There seemed little more to say after that. Amber became quite and Ivy guessed she was as worried about all this as Ivy was herself. Ivy rinsed her cup and started pulling out some bread, cheese and butter. She started cooking as Amber slipped out. She could hear her walk up the stairs, her footsteps light as she went from room to room checking doors and windows. By the time Amber came back down Ivy had fixed them her rendition of dinner: grilled cheese sandwiches and tomato soup.

They ate in companionable silence. Ivy wondered what Gabe was doing then, and what might be happening to John and Helena at that very moment. That only brought her spirits down and though she tried, she couldn't stop thinking about it. They ate, cleaned up and turned off the stereo even though Aerosmith was finally on and that was music Ivy could definitely tolerate from the '80's.

Ivy walked out to the main room and Amber joined her. The fire was roaring, but Ivy felt tired all of a sudden and thought she'd throw one more log on to last them until morning.

Glancing over at her sister, she watched the gold and red from the fire dance across Amber's face. She's always thought her sister was so beautiful, but when you're a twin it's a little awkward to keep saying it. Amber had more red in her hair, just enough that the firelight picked out those colors and brought them to life in a way the sun never could. Beautiful, geeky, smart, talented Amber. Ivy wished she had her patience, her organizational skills and her ability to think of others before herself. Ivy's heart swelled with love. She would do anything to keep Amber safe. Anything. Even if that meant having to leave Gabe behind.

"You don't think that'll get too hot do you?" Amber asked, and like that the spell was broken and Ivy fell back to annoyance, which was as comfortable to siblings as love.

"I've set up a lot of fires in my time and we're fine." Ivy frowned as she fake smiled so big there was no mistaking the sarcasm.

"I've set up a lot of fires in my time..." Amber mocked. "I'm just so old. In my time we had to rub two stones together."

Ivy smiled then laughed and threw one of the pillows from the couch at Amber who ducked, picked it up, and threw it back. Ivy put it back on the couch and turned to shake her head at Amber.

"You're a goober." Ivy laughed.

"You're an old fart," Amber shot back.

"Well, this old fart is tired." Ivy turned to walk up the stairs.

"Should I get your cane?" Amber followed behind her. "Maybe you should lean on me so you don't fall down the stairs?"

"Ha. Ha." Ivy continued to smile as she continued to climb.

"Oh no! I've fallen and I can't -" Amber was laughing.

"Don't even go there!" Ivy interrupted. But she laughed too and they reached the top of the stairs and turned to go into their separate rooms. "Good night Amber. Brat."

"Good night, Ivy. Sassy pants."

Ivy walked inside her room and closed the door. Slowly she put on her pajamas, while she waited for her computer to boot up. She checked the security cameras remotely from her computer and imagined Amber doing the same.

She started to put on her pajama bottoms then changed her mind and threw on some shorts instead. Heat climbed upward making it warmer upstairs than she thought it would be. She'd swallow her own tongue before admitting Amber was right about that last log. She walked over to her window and opened it a crack. The wind blew in brisk, but not overly cold. It brought the light scent of pine and the heavier scent of the lake, which wasn't unpleasant. Ivy breathed in the cool air, closed her eyes and did her best to empty her mind for just a few seconds. It wasn't exactly meditating, but it did help keep nightmares at bay.

Growing tired, she breathed in deeply once more and opened her eyes. Her light was on, so it made it difficult to see anything outside. But the security system was on, and if there were any intruders she'd know about them in time to gear up and give them a fight to remember.

She glanced at the monitor on her computer again. Everything was fine. She left it on but turned off her overhead light. She threw the comforter to the foot of the bed and covered with only the sheet. And then, she was asleep.

SO MUCH FOR KEEPING dreams at bay. Ivy realized immediately she was inside a dream. She was burning up with a fever maybe. No, it was the fireplace. Had the cabin caught fire? She couldn't smell any smoke, but if this was a dream, could she expect to smell anything?

Ivy watched herself get up and walk to the window. Only, it wasn't her single paned window that she'd cracked before she fell asleep, it was French doors. And she wasn't' watching herself, it was Amber. Her sister threw open the doors. Ivy could see the sweat on her body as she passed in front of her computer monitor, then she disappeared outside. Then Ivy could see the stars. The night was clear, but pale. It occurred to her that dawn must be approaching. She felt panic slip inside her skin as Amber walked further out on the deck. Something was really wrong, but she couldn't recall what it was. She just knew that Amber needed to go back inside.

She tried to tell her to stay away from the railing, but no words would come out. Amber usually stayed back because of her fear of the water, but the lake was so cool and the wind off the lake felt so glorious. Amber braved another step and leaned against the rail. The wind picked up, and Amber closed her eyes, leaned into that wind and took one deep breath before the railing gave way, and Ivy heard the sound of breaking wood, her sister's surprised and horrified scream, and the splash below as Amber's body hit the water.

She can't swim!

Ivy knew she couldn't swim. But it was just a dream. A terrible, horrible, awful dream. She tried to force herself awake. She closed her eyes tightly in the dream and willed it. But, it was like the adrenaline coursing through her veins nailed her inside the dream instead of waking her up. She rushed to the broken railing, looked over and saw nothing. So she jumped.

Ivy heard the sound of her own gasp as she sat straight up in bed. She was drenched in sweat, from the heat in the house or the fear from the nightmare she wasn't sure. She threw the wet sheet back and jumped up. Something caught her attention out of the corner of her eye. On her monitor there was movement in the lake.

"Amber!"

Ivy ran from her room to Amber's room where the French doors stood open. Just like in her dream, she rushed to the railing. How long had it taken to wake up? How long had Amber been in the water? It was light enough that she could see Amber's body floating, no thrashing around, no motion at all. Lifeless. Ivy wanted to be sure she cleared Amber's body and didn't jump on top of her. She took a few steps back and then ran and jumped out as far as she could.

The lake was like ice compared to the temperature of her skin. The shock nearly stole her breath away and stunned her for just a moment. She came up from under the water gasping for a breath that was more of an inhaled scream. She pushed her hair away from her face and swam toward Amber.

She had always prided herself on her swimming skills. She grabbed Amber and turned her over so that she wasn't face down. She already looked dead to Ivy, but that didn't slow her down. She grabbed Amber around the shoulders, slipping her arms through Amber's from behind. She pulled her closer and started swimming. She swam backwards, with Amber's back near her chest, but not on top of her. Ivy didn't have time to think, only move. The beach wasn't far, and it took only a minute to get there, but it seemed like a lifetime. She got out of the water, pulling Amber up and out as well.

Ivy would be picking gravel and rocks out of her kneecaps for days, but as she bent over Amber's still body going through the motions of getting the water out of her lungs, breathing for her, over and over, she felt no pain. She didn't feel the cold as the wind whipped across her wet body. She didn't even realize she was crying out Amber's name at first. But, when a warm hand fell on her shoulder Ivy turned wide eyes to a familiar face. Patricia had come home. She must have come home last night because she was in her baby doll pajamas. She hadn't even put on a robe.

The expression on Patricia's face when she stared down at Amber said it all. Amber was dead. Patricia fell to her knees beside Ivy, her hand slipping from her shoulder down her arm to her hand. She looked up into Ivy's eyes, tears already rolling down her cheeks and whispered so softly Ivy might have missed it if a puff of gray air hadn't come through Patricia's lips, the cold giving her words substance.

"Heal her."

Ivy looked at her, then to Amber. She forced a calm she knew she'd fabricated in order to keep her mind focused. She pulled inside herself calling that energy that was her power, her ability to heal. She grew warm from the inside, then a spark of what felt like electricity moved through her, warm and coursing like blood. She put her free hand on Amber's heart and she pushed into her. But, it was like filling a deep well with a thimble of water. Amber was so far gone there was no way Ivy could heal her with just her own energy. She turned to Patricia and she tightened her hold on Ivy's hand. That was all the invitation Ivy needed. She reached out her energy to Patricia and pulled. Patricia was strong, still young, and full of such life it rocked Ivy as it passed through her and into Amber. Ivy looked back to Amber as though she could see the line of energy moving into her, but she couldn't. She could only feel it.

As it began to fade and Ivy felt the waning of her power something hot moved, but this time from Amber to Ivy. It was hot as fire, not like an electric jolt. It burned, and for a split second Ivy thought the heat would consume her, but just like that it was gone. Ivy wondered what had happened. Had her power malfunctioned in some way?

Then, Amber coughed and water ran out of her mouth. She gasped and her head rolled to the side. She breathed in again, coughed again and opened her eyes. Ivy dropped Patricia's hand and the faint line of energy that was still flowing stopped. Ivy grabbed her sister and pulled her into a sitting position. She put Amber's head between her hands and studied her face. It wasn't much color, but there was a little, and Amber was breathing on her own.

"Amber? Can you hear me?" Ivy shook her slightly, trying to get her to focus on her.

Amber blinked her eyes hard twice before she focused on Ivy. Her eyes grew wide as she looked around her, saw that she was wet, and remembered what had happened.

"It's okay." Ivy hugged her. "It's alright. Everything is alright."

"Patricia," Amber managed to say.

Ivy leaned back enough to see Amber's eyes looking beyond her. She turned and let Amber go. Amber remained upright, but Ivy no longer paid attention. Patricia lay there, her hand still out toward them, her eyes fixed in their direction, open and dead.

CHAPTER 12

"PATRICIA!" IVY SCREAMED, BUT her voice cracked. It was as though she had laryngitis, but she wasn't sick. She was exhausted, or at least her power was. She realized she had completely depleted her own power and then pulled from Patricia's energy.

"No! No! No!" Ivy tried to scream again, but it came out like a low octave whisper from a winded singer. She fell more than leaned toward Patricia. Her body seemed to betray her as punishment for what she'd put it through. She crawled with her hands, elbows and knees until she was over Patricia's prone form. She laid hands on her and tried to call her power, but nothing came. Basic self-preservation could not be overcome, and just like she was unable to stop her heart from beating by willing it to stop, she could not will her power to come. Her body was giving up.

A cold, wet hand on her bare leg brought Ivy around to Amber. She looked better physically, but the emotion on her face was terrifying to look at. There was such tragedy in that look, such grief. Amber shook her leg.

"Use me," she whispered as though her throat hurt then coughed uncontrollably for a moment.

And in that moment Ivy had a decision to make. Try to save Patricia and risk losing Amber, or let Patricia sacrifice her life and live with that forever. For all she knew, if she tried to take Amber's energy she could lose them both. Amber was dead, or at least she was nearly dead, and the energy that was Patricia's life force jump started Amber, but it didn't put her back to a hundred percent healthy. Nowhere near it.

"You can't let her die! Not if you can save her!" Amber pleaded and shook her leg, gripping it with such force that Ivy knew there would be a bruise there later.

They locked eyes and that one moment, held in a suspension of grief and fear, was all Ivy needed to make up her mind. She grabbed Amber's hand and put the other hand over Patricia's heart. Then she prayed Amber's energy would spark her own.

She felt something stir, some power deep and cold and dark and she pulled on it. She'd expected the warmth to come, to flow through her, but this was cold and it began to burn. The heat ran through her veins like a lightning strike and she cried out in agony. She moved away from Amber and Patricia as though her life depended on it. She didn't even realize she'd moved. She was there, and then she was several feet away. Her leg burned and she looked down to see a handprint on her leg near her ankle. Blisters had already formed. It throbbed, but the heat was already fading.

Ivy looked to Patricia who lay there motionless, eyes still open. It hadn't worked. Patricia could not be saved.

Ivy slowly stood and walked the few feet to Patricia's body and then collapsed on the other side of her. She sat directly across from Amber, Patricia between then.

Ivy didn't even have the energy to cry. She stared down, finally reaching out to gently close Patricia's eyes.

"She's dead because of me," Amber whispered, uncovering her face, but still looking down at Patricia's body. "I should be the one who is dead. I was the one who was careless. I should be dead, not her."

"She wanted to help you. She wanted to help us both." Ivy wasn't sure who she was trying to convince. "She gave me her hand. She wanted me to use her to save you. She wanted me to."

Ivy reached out to her sister, but as her fingers grazed her arm Amber recoiled as though the touch might kill her.

"You had no right!" Amber glared at Ivy, tears pouring down her cheeks, falling on her wet clothes. "You had no right to exchange her life for mine! I didn't want that!"

Ivy froze as she listened to Amber's voice struggle to scream. Her hand remained suspended over Patricia's body and she slowly pulled it back to her side.

"I never meant for that to happen," Ivy promised. "I had no idea it could kill someone!"

"Not *someone*, Ivy! Patricia! It killed Patricia!" Amber's voice broke and the last of what she said came out on a squeal. She rose to her feet and took a step back.

"I would never have intentionally hurt Patricia! I love her!" Ivy stood quickly. The speed of her movement and the low energy made her sway, and she stumbled back but righted herself before she could fall.

Amber looked down at Patricia's body again then back up at Ivy.

"No, you accidentally killer her, didn't you? Since it's just an accident, it doesn't count, does it?" Amber's voice cracked again, but there was no mistaking the hysteria there. "But there she is!" She pointed to the body like a witness would point to the accused. "There she is. Dead just the same."

Ivy had no words. Nothing she could say could ever change this. Nothing she could do would ever change this. All she had thought about was how to save her sister. She didn't consider what her actions might do to Patricia. Hadn't she just promised herself she would be more aware of others? But she wasn't. And Patricia paid the price for that.

For a few minutes, they stood there saying nothing. Amber turned and went back into the cabin, leaving Ivy and the rising sun to stand sentinel over Patricia.

Ivy felt the hysteria rising from the darkness within her. She could see herself inside her mind, standing in the middle of a long tunnel. In the center, everything was dark except for the light at either end of that tunnel. The darkness wanted to consume her. It became hard to breathe, and she sucked in the air as though it was heavy and wet. The harder she tried to breathe, the thicker the air seemed to get. The light at the end began to close, and it got darker. She swayed as she breathed faster and harder. She took one step and the darkness swallowed her up.

A LIGHT FLICKERED. IVY'S eyelids felt so heavy she had to will herself to lift them at all. Ivy opened them just slightly and could see that she was inside the cabin. For one fleeting moment she thought everything had all been a dream, and her eyes flew open wide and she sat up. She was on the small couch, a light blanket thrown over her. She was still wearing wet clothes that smelled of lake water. She pushed back her hair and the movement caused her already throbbing head to scream an echo of pain throughout her entire body.

The door to the kitchen swung open and Ivy turned to face Amber, but it wasn't her sister. Gabe walked in with a cup in each hand and looked surprised when he saw her sitting up.

"I made hot chocolate," he said quietly, which she appreciated as her head promised to split open at any moment.

"Aspirin?" It was all she could manage to say. "Where's Amber?"

He set the cups down on the coffee table in front of her and disappeared into the lower level bathroom under the stairway. He came back and placed two pills in her hand and handed her a small paper cup filled with water. She took it gratefully, and felt the pills scratch all the way down her throat despite the water chaser.

"Ivy, Amber told us that Patricia hit her head when she came to help pull you both out of the water." Gabe sat beside her on the couch and waited for her to talk. "I had an issue with the school and wasn't sure how long it would take before they agreed to let me have some time off. Patricia said she couldn't leave you and Amber alone any longer and trusted me to stay safe and be careful. I should have been here to help. I'm sorry."

What was she supposed to say? 'Actually, I saved my sister's life by sacrificing Patricia's. She would have wanted it that way, so it's really okay.' No, she didn't think that was what she was going to go with. Instead, she did the one thing she hadn't wanted to do.

"I'm sorry, too."

Gabe waited for a few moments. Ivy felt sure he was waiting for her to elaborate, but that wasn't going to happen.

"We need to call the police," he told her.

"No police!" Ivy felt herself snap awake as she set down her cup and grabbed Gabe's arm. "If we call the police they will put us in foster care! Or worse, the community. Our father, could find us and our lives would be ruined. Miserable! John, Helena and Patricia would have sacrificed everything for nothing!"

Her voice no longer cracked. It wasn't normal yet, but close enough that she doubted Gabe would think it anything more than grief.

"We can't just leave her like that. We have to do something." He sounded so calm, but she could see his pulse, his heart beating hard, throbbing in his neck. He kept gritting his teeth, flexing his jaw muscles.

"It was an accident." When she said it, she immediately heard Amber's voice. *"She's dead just the same."* Tears filled her eyes and she put her hand up to let Gabe know that she needed a moment.

She struggled between tears, fear and guilt. They couldn't just leave her. Gabe was right. She deserved better. She deserved not to be dead. Ivy was determined she would at least get a good burial, even if the authorities couldn't be involved.

"We'll bury her on the property. Amber and I will take care of it so you and Ryan don't have to be involved, okay?" It made sense, and it felt surreal.

"Ivy, I'm pretty sure that it's illegal to bury someone after an accident and without contacting authorities. I understand your dilemma, I do, but you need to understand that if Ryan and I help you, or even if we just know that you did it, we are accessories after the fact." Gabe leaned in and took both of her hands. "Listen to me, Ivy. Really. Listen. I would do anything for you. And I'll do this, too if that's how we're going to keep you and Amber safe, but we need to get help. We need to figure out what to do next. Ryan is the only one of legal age and the one who stands to get into the most trouble here. We need to cover our asses and not let this spiral out of control any more than it already has." He searched her face, leaned in and kissed her forehead gently, pulled back and let out a big breath. "You need to trust Ryan and me. And you need to share the decision making with me, understand?" He lifted his eyebrows in question and Ivy nodded.

"Why?" Ivy finally managed to blurt out the question that was plaguing her since the second time Gabe came to her rescue.

"We've known each other forever. We may not have hung out in school a lot, but we had the same sensei, we hung out in some of the same places. You're familiar to me, like home. My mom has always had a lot of respect for John and Helena and she always thinks Patricia is one of the most interesting people in town, with all of her hippie ways and overly-positive attitude." He stopped for a moment and she wondered if he caught that he'd referred to Patricia as though she were still alive. He cast his eyes down for a moment, his face going slack as though he was deep inside his own thoughts.

"Helena liked your mom most of anyone in the town outside of our own family." Ivy filled the silence because she needed to. "Once they realized they were both book worms, they really did form a solid friendship."

Gabe nodded, but still said nothing. It should have occurred to her that he might feel something about Patricia's loss. Their families may not have been super close, but they knew each other, had been at each other's homes, exchanged Christmas cards and laughter and books.

"I know mom asked John to keep an eye on me while she was away. I mean, she trusts me, but she's a mom, ya know?" Gabe half-smiled and shrugged, as though that said it all.

"Well, I did wonder why John was so interested in MMA fighting all of a sudden," Ivy said. "I mean, he was a weapons guy mostly. I'd never seen him watch any of those fights, but when he started talking to you about it I figured it could be that your mom asked him."

Gabe nodded and grew quiet again. They sat there like that for a while, then Gabe stood.

"You tell Ryan and I where you want the grave and we'll go dig it for you. Maybe you can make some kind of marker. I don't know how to do all of this, not under these circumstances at least, but you tell me what I can do and I'll do it."

"Thank you." Ivy felt the burn of tears behind her eyes, but held them in check.

Gabe walked out of the room, presumably to find Ryan and let him know what was going on.

Ivy sighed and stood up. She was a little unsteady, but the vertigo was less and she ventured a few steps forward, then stopped. She glanced at the stairs and her eyes trailed up where she imagined Amber was holed up in her room. She slowly made her way upstairs and knocked on the door. There was no answer, but she walked in anyway.

Amber sat cross-legged on her bed. She'd changed her clothes, but her hair was still wet and stringy. Ivy sat on the corner of the bed, afraid to get closer, but needing her sister.

"Where should we bury her?" Ivy finally asked. "I was thinking back by the shed, near all those yellow wild flowers."

Amber nodded but said nothing.

"Amber we have to talk. We have to be able to work together. We're sisters. We're all we have left."

Amber's eyes flicked over at her then darted away and toward the French doors. The doors were closed, the curtains pulled shut. "I know."

Ivy realized that was all she would say. This was all going to fall on her shoulders and she figured that was only right.

"I'm going to clean her up and put her in one of her summer dresses," Ivy offered.

"The one with the tiny daisies." Amber suggested, still looking toward the French doors.

"That's a good choice. We'll put her in my cedar hope chest. That will have to do."

Amber only nodded, so Ivy continued.

"I'll go down and tell the guys. It will take some time to get everything ready." Ivy waited for any more input, but when nearly five minutes went by and Amber was still staring at the stupid French doors she realized she'd been dismissed from the room. And she was fine with that, she couldn't escape the added guilt her sister threw at her with her silence.

It took longer than she thought it would to get everything done. The guys brought in Patricia's body and lay it on her bed, then left to dig the grave. Ivy brought out the dress, jewelry, a hairbrush. She busied herself with the preparation in order to ignore the actual event.

Finally, she sat on the bed, her task complete. Patricia looked so pretty in her summer dress with matching crystal daisy earrings that Amber had given her and a locket John and Helena gave her last Christmas that had pictures of her and Amber in it. She even put on a little make-up and tried to set her hair the way Patricia liked it, straight back away from her face. Ivy marveled at how young Patricia looked, and it only made her more melancholy.

"I'm so sorry," she whispered into the room and glanced over at Patricia lying on the bed.

There was no talking to the dead, but Ivy imagined Patricia forgiving her because she needed to be forgiven, and it didn't seem that Amber would forgive her for a long time. She slipped out and went to her own room where she gathered how own clothes, something nice and respectable. She went into the upstairs bathroom and got into the shower.

The warm water felt wonderful on her skin, her muscles, but when it hit the burn above her ankle she winced. Her power had somehow backfired and it caused a burn to happen where Amber's energy had entered her body. She wondered if that had been the moment that Patricia died. Had stealing the life force from someone somehow changed her power? Would her power always burn like that now? Would she even be able to use it ever again after this? She wished for a moment that her mother were alive to help her figure it out, but immediately on the heels of that thought was that her mother wouldn't really be able to help her. She wasn't a faith healer. Or, at least Patricia never said she was. Her father was the faith healer, and he would have been the one to help her. Now she had no one. She certainly would never betray Patricia's memory, her sacrifices, and seek out her father for help. It was best to never use the power again. It was unpredictable, unstable, and dangerous. She wished she never had the power, but then it would be Amber who was dead and not Patricia. So she changed the wish to wishing nothing had happened to anyone. A childish wish, but she just couldn't help it.

The burn would leave a scar and Ivy wanted it that way. Patricia was dead, so the least Ivy could do was face the scars surrounding that death. She finished showering and got out. Her routine felt unnatural even though it was exactly as she had always done it. She'd dry her hair, use her toiletries, put on a little make up, curl her hair and then put her clothes on. She felt like a robot as she spoke to herself quietly, inside her own head, leading herself to do these mundane things as though she were leading a sleep walker to safety.

She was ready. She went back into her room and glanced at her computer where she could see the guys were finished digging. They had the chest next to the hole, the lid was open, ready to swallow up one of the most important and amazing people Ivy had ever known.

Another twenty minutes ticked by and Ivy remained sitting on the corner of her bed. Moving meant the finality of Patricia's death was upon them, so she did her best not to move at all until a light tapping on her door brought her to her feet. Still, she couldn't step forward and she couldn't open her mouth to invite the person in. After a minute, Gabe opened the door quietly and peeked inside.

"Ready?" he asked.

Ivy nodded and took that first step. The vertigo had left before she got into the shower, but that step forward brought her room out of focus, and it began to spin. She reached out to steady herself and found a strong shoulder, Gabe, and then his arm went around her waist and he steadied her. He just stood there allowing her to get her bearings, and when she stepped out again he was there to support her. Within just a couple of minutes they were downstairs. Five minutes later and they were standing at the graveside next to the chest. There were chairs there and Ivy wondered if Gabe set them there or Ryan. No matter. She needed to sit and was grateful for the chair.

Gabe excused himself when Amber sat in the chair next to her. Neither of them spoke. Five more minutes and Gabe and Ryan gently laid Patricia's body into the chest. They struggled a little to get her in there, but it wasn't horrible, or at least Ivy didn't think so. Of course, her idea of horrible had changed of late, so perhaps she wasn't the best judge.

The guys had straps on the chest that allowed them to pick it up relatively easily. Ivy thought for just an instant about how John had those things at home too. They were handy.

They lowered her into the ground with some difficulty, but again, it was not horrible. When they were done, they retrieved the straps and set them aside. They stood, Gabe at the head of the grave like he was a reverend about to read her eulogy.

His eyes found Ivy's. Ivy stood, not sure where her courage was coming from, but determined she would say a few words.

"Some people are driven by passion," Ivy began and then cleared her throat and waited for a second before she could begin again. "Some people are driven by money, power, self-preservation. Patricia was driven by love. She was willing to sacrifice her life to get our mother out of a terrible place. And when our mother couldn't make it," again her voice cracked and she had to hesitate, "she risked the same fate in order to save my sister and me. She could have taken off and started a whole new life and had a family of her own, but her love kept her with us, caring for us, keeping us safe. She was everything good that you can imagine. She became our instructor, our advisor, our friend and family. She was generous and loving and kind. She will be missed, but not forgotten."

Ivy sat down and waited for Amber, but after a few minutes she finally turned to her sister to see her sitting there quietly absorbed in her own thoughts, tears streaking down her face. She took a chance and reached out, but Amber stood abruptly and ran back into the cabin, leaving Ivy's hand outstretched.

Gabe walked over and took her hand to pull her up and into his arms. They stood there quietly, his brow touching lightly to hers, eyes closed.

Ivy took in his warmth, his comfort. She heard Ryan moving around, concentrated on shutting him out when she realized he was filling in the grave. She made herself as small as she could inside her own mind, withdrawing until there were no sounds at all except for Gabe's breathing and the sound of her own heartbeat. Time lost any value as her heart began to break in ways she'd never experienced. Patricia was like a mother to her. She'd let her down. She'd let her die. Her own sister had passed judgment, and as usual they agreed.

How long they stood there she couldn't say. It had to be nearly an hour because when Ivy came back to herself and opened her eyes Ryan was gone.

The grave was covered. Gabe's eyes were still closed, his forehead still touching lightly to hers. The wind was cool coming off the lake. She shivered and he tightened his hold, brought her closer, warming her with his body.

"I don't know what's going on with you and Amber," Gabe spoke softly, but didn't open his eyes. "I can tell there's more going on than what you've told me. There may be a lot I don't know, but what I do know is that Patricia loved you and she wouldn't want you to suffer."

Ivy felt the heat of a single tear spill over, followed by another. Her nose began to run and she pulled back from Gabe, watching his eyes open and look deep into hers. His hand lifted slowly as though he were afraid she'd spook at the movement. He wiped the tears with his thumb, his eyes never leaving hers. The gesture only seemed to fuel the tears and they kept falling until he finally gave up trying to wipe them all away. Instead, he moved his hand around to the back of her neck, his fingers caressing her skin. He paused just before his lips touched hers and looked into her eyes for just that heartbeat of time before gently kissing her.

The kiss was warm and salty and gentle and reassuring. She closed her eyes and melted into that soft comfort. He didn't know enough to reject her, and she knew it was wrong to let him offer her such peace, but God she needed it so desperately. A few gentle seconds and she pulled away. He moved his hand again and gently caressed her face.

"I'm going to take care of you, Ivy," he promised. "I won't let anything bad happen to you."

The illusion of peace, the promise of it, shattered her resolve. She didn't deserve his compassion. She didn't deserve him. She was a killer and a monster, and the last thing she deserved was his comfort.

"You don't understand." Ivy took a step back, and the space between them filled with cold air. "Amber is angry because I'm the reason Patricia died."

Gabe frowned down at her. "You'd never harm Patricia. I know that much."

"No, not on purpose. I didn't know that I would kill her. But, I needed to save Amber. I was so focused on Amber, I didn't realize Patricia was dying."

"You're right. I don't understand." Gabe said.

"All you need to understand is that I did kill Patricia. And the fact that I didn't mean to doesn't mean I'm not guilty. It means I'm dangerous. It means that I could kill anyone." Ivy took another step back and all the peace she'd felt moments ago was emptied out and fear, self-condemnation, and grief filled that void. "I could kill you."

CHAPTER 13

THE FOREST WAS COLD, and the further Ivy ran into the dense trees and shrubs, the darker it became. A branch caught at her face, scratching a long bloody line down her cheek. She barely noticed. Her lungs ached, her side ached and her heart ached. The more pain, the faster she ran. She tripped as she came into a small clearing. She felt her wrist break when she tried to reach out to keep her body from hitting the ground too hard, a natural instinct she couldn't avoid. The sharp burning caused her to cry out. She felt nauseous and remained there on the damp ground trying to absorb it, actively feel it, hold on to it, embrace it as the punishment she wanted it to be.

She rolled to her side, pulling herself into a fetal position. If only she could wish it all away. If only she could turn back time. Instead, she lay there wishing it had been her and not Patricia who had died.

Gabe had reached out to her, offering to comfort her, but when she told him what she was capable of, he stopped. She couldn't blame him of course, but knowing that one last sliver of peace was gone from her was just too much.

What she wanted to do was flee from herself. Since that was impossible she just fled. She needed to put as much distance between herself and that cabin and those people and that memory as she could before she exploded from all the feelings inside her.

The aching in her wrist intensified. She could see the broken bone pushing against her skin. She didn't care. The pain was a blanket that she wrapped herself in and it was the only comfort she would accept. In the comfort of pain, you can cloak all transgressions. You can hide there from even yourself. The pain took over everything and pushed out all thought.

"Ivy!"

Her eyes snapped up, and found Gabe hovering above her. He reached down and scooped her up into his arms as though she weighed nothing. He looked around the small clearing and carried her over to a fallen tree. He kneeled down in front of her and pushed the hair from her face. He then scanned down her body and stopped when he got to her wrist, grimacing as he saw the damage.

She pulled her arm from him, which caused a fresh burst of pain that stole her breath.

"Stop it, Ivy!" Gabe didn't touch her arm again, but his eyes bored into her with such fierceness they pinned her in place. "You need to get a grip on yourself. Stop torturing yourself! Stop running from me. And stop blaming yourself."

"You don't understand," Ivy whispered.

"You said that already," Gabe lowered his voice. "Now make me understand."

Ivy looked at him for a moment, wondering what the best course of action would be. She didn't have the energy to fabricate a lie. Perhaps the best way to make everyone stay away from her, the best way to ensure everyone was safe from her, was just to tell the truth.

"Look at me," she said calmly.

Gabe looked at her. She had his undivided attention. She pulled lightly on her energy, focused that power and watched Gabe's eyes widen as the bloody scratch healed. The look of confusion, the frown, the way his eyes moved over her face. She knew she needed to make a clearer point. She raised her arm and he backed away just enough so he could clearly see. Her wrist was contorted from being so severely broken. She pulled on the energy a little harder this time and focused on her wrist. The energy hummed in a way that kept her from feeling any pain as she watched the bones twitch and move back into place.

Gabe sat flat on his butt, still staring at her now-healed wrist

"How?" It was his turn to whisper.

"My father is a faith healer. And so am I. I can use energy to heal people. But, when it's really bad I need more energy than just my own, so I take other people's energy. I use them like a battery. Amber was dead, or nearly dead. She'd fallen from her balcony. She doesn't know how to swim. I was trying to save her, but she was so far gone and I was so tired. Then Patricia showed up. She told me to use her energy. I was watching Amber the whole time. I should have been watching Patricia too."

There it was. Her crime, her sins, her curse. She waited for him to digest it all, judge her, leave her. She watched him and wondered how he was processing it all. She closed her eyes against the coming pain. Pain that had nothing to do with bleeding scratches and broken bones. As the silence stretched out, she opened them again. He still sat there, but now he looked at her with such intensity, she frowned and clenched her fists.

"You can heal people by touching them?" he asked.

She couldn't trust her own voice, so she simply nodded.

"You can heal yourself. You can heal other people." He stopped abruptly, his eyes cast down as though searching for something in his mind. "Did you heal me?"

Again she nodded.

"I knew something had happened the night of that fight. I just wasn't sure..." he trailed off, again casting his eyes downward. He finally looked back at her.

"Amber was dead?" he asked.

"Nearly," She answered.

"Patricia told you to use her, to heal Amber?"

"She did, but she had no idea...I had no idea." Ivy's breath caught as she bore down on the oncoming pain.

"It was an accident." It wasn't a question. It wasn't a judgment. Gabe's voice was soft, calm. "A tragic one, but still an accident."

Ivy nodded, the burn behind her lids giving way to hot tears.

Gabe stood and walked to her. He kneeled down in front of her as he had before, but this time he leaned into her, his forehead touching hers once again.

"Ivy, if you'd told Patricia that using her like that might cost her her life, what would she have said?"

Her shoulders hunched over, the weight of her guilt bending her toward Gabe. He wrapped his arms around her as she began to tremble, the tears pouring down. She knew he didn't require an answer, because they both knew. Patricia would have given anything to save Amber, even her own life. Ivy wished she could have given Patricia the choice, but she knew with absolute conviction what the answer would have been.

She couldn't remember ever sobbing so hard or for so long. She felt drained by the time she was able to breathe normally. She pulled back from Gabe so she could look at him. He dried the last tear with his thumb, reading her face like a book, looking perhaps for her to be okay, which she wasn't, but she was more in control.

"We should go back to the cabin." Ivy made to stand up and Gabe was there pulling her up, holding her again, briefly. They turned back toward the cabin and Gabe took her hand, entwining their fingers, keeping her steady.

"Is that why these people want you?" Gabe asked as they walked deeper into the woods to the path, that led back to the cabin. "They want to use your gift?"

"Curse you mean?"

"I suppose it's all how you look at it," Gabe said. "Or how you use it."

"I guess." Ivy figured him a few answers, but she really didn't have the energy for an interrogation. She hoped it wouldn't turn into that. "But, no, that's not why they want us. They don't even know about my ability."

Ivy hoped that was true. She didn't know how long they'd been watching her, what they'd seen. And of course if they had John and Helena, …well, she didn't want to think about what would had to happen to pry that kind of information from them.

"So they want you because…" Gabe glanced at her questioningly.

"Because my father hated my mother and promised her he would make us miserable right before he killed her." How tragic her life sounded to her own ears. She'd never thought of it that way before. You couldn't live long without death or heartache touching your life in some way. But, for the most part she loved her life. Perhaps she'd not given much thought to how shielded she'd been or how thoughtless. Either way, the looming sense of danger that had been used to keep her working hard on her training and kept her alert and aware at all times, was easily replaced with a sense of melancholy if she wanted to take it there. Which she didn't. Sadness could become an addiction if you let it, and where would that get her?

Pushing aside the sadness, the grief, and the desire to simply feel sorry for herself was not going to be easy, but she had lived with some of the strongest people she'd ever known. She was more like them than she would ever be like her father. In her heart she was sure of that. If she never used her ability again she would be even more like them, and less like him. She had more to offer than just her healing power. She would find John and Helena the old fashioned way—through hard work, perseverance and training. If she could save John and Helena, she could be redeemed. In an instant her resolve fell into place. She had purpose and she knew what to do next.

"I need you not to tell anyone about me," Ivy said as she looked at Gabe. He nodded, glanced at her, nodded again.

"I won't."

"Not even to Ryan." She needed him to understand that no one could know. Not ever.

"Especially not Ryan." Gabe agreed.

The way he said it caused her to slow her pace and she looked at him, finally stopping altogether.

"Why especially not Ryan?"

"Because, Ivy, he would use you." Gabe's jaw clenched before he spoke again. "Ryan's sister is dying. If he knew you held this kind of power, I'd be afraid of what he would do to force you to use it on her."

"I'm so sorry," Ivy didn't need to imagine how it would feel to know your sister was dying. She knew exactly how desperate that could make someone. How you would do anything to save her, not considering the cost. Desperate people were dangerous people. Still, she felt compassion for Ryan and for Gabe. She knew from listening to them talk that Ryan's sister was much younger. She recalled the conversation at Ryan's place when Amber had gotten upset with him for not being with his family.

"If she's dying, then why isn't Ryan with her?"

"It's complicated." Gabe started walking again. They were no longer holding hands and his pace was faster than hers, so she had to speed up in order to keep from speaking to the back of his head.

"Whether or not you want to be with your dying sister does not seem complicated to me," Ivy told him when she'd caught up. "Especially when you make it sound like he'd do anything to get me to heal her."

"Ryan got into some trouble at home," Gabe said as they walked side by side. They were nearly to the cabin now. "His mother told him he couldn't come back until he could get his head on straight. She just couldn't divide her time and energy between her dying daughter and a son who was getting put in juvenile hall, then jail almost every weekend. I don't know what the final straw was, but there was some kind of blow up between him and his mom. All I know is that she called my mom and asked her to come there to help, and Ryan decided he'd come here and hang out with me."

"Your mom has been there a while now, hasn't she?" Ivy couldn't help wishing she could help him. But, who would pay the price for that little girl's life? Would her mother ask her to take her life in order to save Ryan's sister's? Would Ryan give his life? Ivy couldn't take that chance. It was not up to her to take one life in order to save another. She wouldn't put herself in that position ever again. She would never take another person's life. She'd been given a gift, but that gift, but sometimes the price was too high.

"Yeah, my mom will probably stay till the end." Gabe's voice was quieter, not a whisper, not exactly, but very quiet.

"There's nothing that can be done?"

"They were trying some new kind of therapy, but it didn't work. The last call I got from Mom she said it was only a matter of days."

"How long ago was that?"

"Three or four days ago."

They stepped out of the forest's edge and stood at the side of the cabin. They stopped for a moment and Ivy's eyes trailed their way to the grave nearby, then moved out to look at the horizon over the lake. The day was warm, but the breeze was cool. The birds chirped and life went on despite Patricia dying and despite what was happening to a little girl hundreds of miles away.

She could help, if it wasn't too late. But, at what cost? She thought of one of Patricia's favorite sayings, "Damned if you do, damned if you don't." There was just no way to win, even if you didn't play.

She waited for Gabe to ask her to save his cousin, but he didn't. She figured he didn't want her refusal to be there between them. She didn't want that either. They walked into the cabin to find Ryan and Amber sitting at the kitchen table, a pile of papers spread across the table. Ryan had a map in front of him, and Amber was looking through what appeared to be phone records and other bills.

"What are you doing?" Ivy joined them at the table. Gabe followed suit and sat next to her.

"Patricia said there was a safety deposit box with new IDs and information," Amber said, not looking up from whatever task she was at. "I'm going through all the papers I found in her room and around the house in various drawers."

"Right. In San Francisco." Ivy said.

"Don't you wonder what else they hid from us? Why would they have all that and not say anything to us? Don't you find it odd?" Amber did stop then, frowning at the paper in her hand.

"Find anything helpful?" Ivy asked.

"Nothing." Amber threw the paper down, sat back in her chair and took in a big breath, letting it out slowly.

"It's just another fail safe. There needed to be more than just one safe house. There needed to be more of a plan than just holing up here. I mean, normal people prepare for the worst, but don't really think it will happen. We're not normal people. Why are you so uptight?"

Amber just looked at her for a long moment, as though she wanted to say something but wasn't sure if she should.

"What do you know, Amber? What are you hiding?" Ivy leaned in a little closer to her sister as though she could will her to tell her what she wanted to know just by being closer to her.

Amber reached inside her pants pocket and brought out an envelope. The paper had yellowed just a bit, and Ivy could make out handwriting on the front as Amber unfolded it. Patricia's handwriting.

"The key was in this envelope that I found in Patricia's room." Amber tried to rub the creases out of it, but it was a lost cause. "And the paper with information about the box and the bank."

"Okay?" Ivy was starting to feel frustrated. She wanted to force Amber to just tell her what was going on, but she knew that would just put more strain on their fragile relationship.

"The paper also had a note scribbled on the side. Looks like Patricia added it later and in a hurry.

"What did it say?" Ivy felt her nerves stretched tight, grow tighter, and she had to force herself to breathe evenly, be patient.

"It said, 'Find Elizabeth'." Amber looked up at her now.

"Who is Elizabeth?" Ivy asked, waiting for more details.

"I don't know. That's all it says." Amber finally relinquished the envelope.

Ivy looked at the bank information and could see where the key left an indentation in the paper. Amber had to have it on her, but that didn't bother her. The scrawl was definitely in Patricia's handwriting, but why she added such a mysterious message to one side of paper was what really made Ivy wonder.

"It must be a contact. Maybe someone who will help us out if we get into trouble and are on our own." Ivy handed everything back to Amber.

"Why would they ask us to trust someone they never even told us about?" Amber asked.

"I don't know, Amber. I suggest we pack up tonight and get ready for the trip to San Francisco. Maybe then we'll find out who Elizabeth is."

SHE WOKE DRENCHED IN sweat and groped for the lamp beside her bed. The click of the switch brought light that flooded her small room. She immediately checked the room for any immediate threat, but there was none. Regardless, her heart still beat so fast it was painful, and her throat was dry from fast breathing. She usually only felt like this after a long run. Of course, after a long run she also felt exhilarated. Sitting alone in her room in the middle of the night recovering from a nightmare she couldn't quite recall left her drained and tired, though she was no longer sleepy.

For one brief moment, something flashed across her mind. Girls crying for their mother. Or perhaps they were crying because they felt so alone? She wasn't sure. She squeezed her eyes shut as tightly as she could then opened them wide as though she could wipe away the haze that kept her from remembering her dream.

It worked. Or, at least she got another flash. The girl's faces came into focus and she gasped. She reached for the phone next to her bed and punched two digits. The phone on the other end rang once, twice and on the third ring someone picked up.

Her heart beat faster, but for different reasons now. This was dangerous. Calling this late at night was a quick way to find herself in solitary. But, not reporting this right away could result in far worse. She was damned either way, so she decided to go with the lesser of two evils.

"What?" The voice sounded irritated. But, then again, it always sounded irritated. Zachariah was moody and unpredictable. She hated to be on the receiving end of that moodiness even though she should be used to it after all these years.

"I had a dream," she told him.

The pause was long enough to make her squirm. He had to understand the significance of her calling this late over a dream.

"What did you see?" he asked, but his tone had changed and was less severe.

She felt her stomach unclench and realized she really needed to pee. She'd made the right decision. She could tell by his tone.

"The girls are going to San Francisco." The dream was coming back to her in bits and pieces, but she knew this was true. And this was just the kind of information he was looking for. Relief gave way to pride.

"Where at in San Francisco? When?" he demanded.

Her heart sank. She didn't know, at least not yet. She should have waited to call him.

"I don't know yet, but this dream was clearer than the last one. I'll do what I can to figure out the details."

"You do that, Elizabeth. And when you have *all* the information, then call me."

"Yes, father."

CHAPTER 14

 T'S A TWO-DAY DRIVE if we take turns," Gabe explained to Ryan. "They need our help."

"This is the end of the road for me, Gabe," Ryan told him as he plopped down on the small couch. "I buried a woman yesterday. I think the best thing for both of us to do is get as far away from those girls as possible."

"Shhh!" Gabe frowned at Ryan as he sat in one of the chairs facing his cousin. "They'll hear you."

"That's the very least of their worries, don't you think?"

Gabe frowned hard at Ryan and nodded toward the stairs. Ryan had every right to want out of this, but Gabe needed him. Ryan was one of the best computer guys Gabe had ever seen. Not that he knew a lot of computer guys, but he did know that Ryan was good at more than just tattooing. Gabe just wasn't sure why Ryan didn't do something with that skill set when it could make him so much more money than tattooing. He'd created a fantastic state of the art website when Gabe decided to move from martial arts tournaments to MMA fighting and wanted to establish himself online so he could promote his own fights. The guy was a genius.

"Look, once we know what's in that box we can get them somewhere safe and try to figure out exactly who their dad is, where he is and see if there's any way we can find John and Helena. I need your help tracking this guy down."

"There's no way I am tracking this guy down. He makes people disappear!" Ryan pushed a hand through his hair.

Gabe sighed in exasperation. He knew Ryan had a right to feel that way, but he thought his cousin would want to help these girls out. He never thought of Ryan as someone who would turn away like this. Ryan looked away from him and out the window. Gabe knew the ploy, but he wasn't going to let Ryan off the hook that easy.

"I'm going to help them," Gabe said with conviction.

Gabe wondered how he and Ryan could be so much alike growing up and be so different now. Sure, they still had a lot of the same traits, but there was something fundamentally wrong with Ryan that Gabe attributed to Mia's illness.

"No!" Ryan stood up and walked the two steps it took to stand in front of Gabe. "You need to get far from them too. You don't need to be their knight in shining armor, Gabe. You need to stay alive."

"I'm not afraid and I'm not going to get myself killed." Gabe clenched his jaw and willed himself to unclench his fists.

"Don't be an idiot!" Ryan's voice rose and octave and several decibels, "Their entire family is dead or missing! I'm leaving here today, and you need to go with me".

Gabe knew their chances of finding John and Helena could be affected if Ryan bailed. Sure, there might be information in San Francisco that would take them right to where they needed to go, but if not, they'd need Ryan to help put the pieces of the puzzle together that would lead them to Ivy's family. He felt the beginning of a headache form between his eyes, and he rubbed there with the palm of his hand.

"Listen, I realize you don't want to go." Gabe stopped rubbing his head, but the pain persisted. "I know you have a lot of stress right now with your sister, the fight with your mom, now this. But it's the right thing to do. We can help them. And then we can get you home to say goodbye to your sister."

"You don't know what you're talking about." Ryan's voice rose. "The best thing for me to do is get back to my own life! I don't need you dragging me into someone else's drama and I don't need you psychoanalyzing my issues with my family."

"Ryan you make no sense!" Gabe's voice got louder in response and he stood up, forcing Ryan to take a step back. "Something's been eating at you since you came back here to live. I thought it was Mia's illness or maybe the fight you had with your mom, but now I don't know. It's like I don't know you at all."

"All you need to know is that I'm doing what's best for Mia, my mom and even you! If we don't get away from those girls, I can't promise any of us will be safe." Ryan took a half-step forward and was nearly nose to nose with Gabe. "We leave in an hour."

"No, *you* leave in an hour. I'm staying."

"Dammit, Gabe! You're going with me. You have to. If you don't, things are going to get bad."

"Things are already bad." Gabe jabbed a finger in the center of Ryan's chest. "But they're not anywhere near as bad for us as they are for Ivy and Amber. You can take your car and leave. We'll take Patricia's car and head to San Fran. And right now, you leaving soon sounds like a really good idea."

"Listen to me." Ryan's tone changed, and Gabe could hear the desperation there. "We need to protect our own, right?" When Gabe just stared at him, he continued. "We're family. We protect each other. We help each other. If you were dying, I would do anything to help you. Wouldn't you do the same?" Ryan swatted Gabe's finger away and stepped back.

"What are you talking about? You'd do *anything*?" Gabe felt something click into place, and it burned in the pit of his stomach like acid. He stood there looking at Ryan, the way his eyes darted everywhere but directly looking at him. He was fidgeting, which Ryan rarely ever did. Gabe had spent years learning to read body language on the tournament circuit. When he changed over to MMA fighting his training focused on that the whole first few months. How had he missed the signals? Easy, he hadn't known there was a fight. He hadn't been looking for signals.

"What have you done?" Gabe's voice was low and steady. "Ryan?"

Ryan stopped fidgeting, though his heart pounded hard in his chest. No one could understand what he'd been through. It was always judgments and accusations.

"I did what I had to do to save Mia. No one was supposed to get hurt." Ryan's voice had calmed, lost its volume to the point Gabe had to pay close attention.

The sound of a chair moving brought both of them around to see Ivy and Amber standing near the chair closest to the fireplace. Gabe chastised himself for not hearing them come down and wondered how much they'd heard. Either way, he was certain that whatever Ryan was about to share, Ivy and Amber needed to hear too.

"Ryan was about to tell us what he's been up to lately. Right, Ryan?" Gabe turned his attention back to his cousin, who stood there like a deer in headlights as he looked at Amber's accusing face. "Ryan!"

Ryan turned from Amber to Gabe, stepped to one side and sat down on the couch.

"You have to understand. I didn't think anyone would get hurt," Ryan began. "He told me you two had been kidnapped by your mother's family and that they had poisoned you against him." Ryan paused, looked around the room, anywhere but at the people in the room. "He said he just wanted his family back and if I helped him, he would help me."

"He who? Who would help you?" Gabe asked.

"Zachariah." Ivy released the name into the air like it was a curse to be exorcised.

Ryan nodded. "He came to town with a big tent like an old revival or some kind of dark carnival promising that he and his people could heal anything." Ryan looked at Gabe. "Anything."

"A faith healer?" Gabe asked.

"Not just any faith healer," Amber added, "but our father. Right, Ryan?"

Ryan nodded again. "They would be there the entire weekend. I went the first night and saw things..."

Ivy felt her heart sink as understanding dawned on her.

"Miracles?" Ivy prompted, already knowing what Ryan saw because she'd been told about how her father traveled and what he did in the places he stopped. They had to be on the lookout for anything that looked like gypsies or a revival or as Ryan had aptly put it, a dark carnival.

"I knew this girl from school. She'd been burned when she was little. Her face was so scarred that she had a hard time speaking. He put his hands on her and…"

"The scars went away." Ivy finished for him.

"Yes. Over and over again he healed people. So when it was over I asked him what it would take to come to my house and see my sister. There was no way she could make it to him. He asked me what I had to bargain with, how much money did I have? I knew how to get into my mother's savings. I knew how much she had there. If he could really heal Mia, she wouldn't care if the money was gone."

Ryan paused again, one hand moving to brush away the stray hair that had dropped down into his face.

"Then what happened?" Amber asked, finally taking a seat.

"We agreed on the amount for a house call. He came over the next day while my mother wasn't home. Mia slept most of the time because of her meds. He came in and we went into Mia's room. He just stood there next to her bed for a while, I don't know, assessing her maybe? Anyway, I had my laptop sitting there on a table next to her bed and when he looked around the room he zeroed in on the laptop and that's when he refused to help her."

"Why would he refuse? Not enough money?" Gabe asked.

"Sort of. He already had the money. I had to hand it over before he'd even look at her. I'd already transferred all the money to my personal account and got cash earlier in the day before mom left," Ryan told them.

"Then what was it? Why did he refuse after he got the money?" Gabe asked as he leaned forward toward Ryan.

"I was working on your website. It was the page of pictures I was putting into a widget so they would show one at a time in an infinite loop. Some of them were from the dojo in town. One had a picture of you sparring with Ivy. I don't know how he knew it was her, but he did."

"So," Ivy said, and they turned to her, "he wanted the money and he wanted me and Amber. He wouldn't heal your sister until you helped him find us."

"He healed her, but just enough to keep her going while I helped him." Ryan continued. "It was the best she'd looked in over a year." He paused, tears filling his eyes, but refusing to fall. "He could really do it. He could save her life. And all I had to do was reunite him with his kidnapped daughters."

"You didn't tell anyone?" Gabe asked and Ryan shook his head. "Because no one would believe you. And the fight you had with your mom?"

"The money I stole. Mia wasn't completely healed, and I really had nothing to show for the money I took. She knew it was me. The money had been transferred to my account. She thought I was doing drugs, but it was never that. The money was for Mia's medical care. It was for experimental treatments that her insurance wouldn't cover. As far as my mother was concerned, I'd taken away the only chance Mia had at getting better."

"You made a deal with the devil and threw us under the bus because you're no good at deals." Amber's voice quivered. Her cheeks were flush and tears pooled in her eyes, defying gravity for as long as they could before giving in to fate.

"It wasn't like that," Ryan's face flushed with anger. "He said you'd been kidnapped. I was helping you."

"Really?" Ivy asked. "If you told him where we were and everything he said was true, why didn't he just come and get us? Why didn't he just call the FBI or the cops and report Patricia or John and Helena and come get us?"

"He said you'd never believe him. Not after being brainwashed all of your lives," Ryan answered. "He said they needed to deprogram you first."

"That's crap, Ryan and you know it," Amber said as she stood abruptly and stepped toward him, arms at her side, fists clenched tightly. "The second it got dangerous, the second one of the jerks from the community hurt your own cousin, you had to know something wasn't right!"

"Why didn't you tell me?" Gabe asked.

He sat there calmly, but Ivy knew better. The clenched jaw, the rigid posture. Gabe was anything but calm.

"By the time I figured out things weren't exactly right it was too late. I was in too deep. I had to see it through or he was going to let Mia die." Ryan's voice finally broke. It was the first sign of any inner turmoil, and the red from his cheeks made a path down his neck disappearing beneath the collar of his shirt. "He told me that if I didn't keep track of you he wouldn't help Mia. And he said it was up to me to keep Gabe safe. I was to keep him from getting involved, but we all know how successful I was at that."

"So, why are you leaving Ivy and Amber on their own now? Did you tell them where we are?" Gabe's tone changed with the realization that Ryan had betrayed them, had betrayed him.

"They're supposed to be here in less than..." Ryan paused to look at his watch, "two hours. They told me to get you out of here and they'd handle the rest."

"Oh my God!" Ivy stood so fast her chair fell backward and crashed to the ground.

Amber stood and ran as fast as Ivy had ever seen her run. She darted upstairs where Ivy could hear her footfalls move from her own room to Patricia's then to Ivy's room.

"We need to get out of here now," Ivy told Gabe. She couldn't look at Ryan. She understood his desperation, but it didn't help her to forgive him.

"I'll pack and meet you out at Patricia's car," Gabe told her and started toward the stairs.

"I have your stuff in my car already," Ryan said.

Gabe and Ivy looked at him, but there was nothing to say at this point.

"Just go," Ivy told Gabe.

"I'm not going with him. I'm going with you." Gabe placed his hand on her shoulder and gave her a light squeeze.

There was instantly a lump in her throat and she couldn't say anything. She nodded and turned to run upstairs and help Amber get them packed.

Ivy found Amber back in her own room cinching up some backpacks. Every movement seemed exaggerated, quick, hard movements. She said nothing, so Ivy came in and picked up the backpack that had her name on it.

"Your power. Your boyfriend's cousin. You're got to think about consequences." Amber's voice was harsh at first, then she softened. "We have to depend on each other, be responsible to each other. Being a family is about considering what your actions to do those you love."

Ivy flinched as though truth itself slapped her.

"Amber?" but she wasn't sure what to say after that, so she let the name hang there in the air.

"It's hard not to be mad." Amber slung her backpack over her shoulder and moved toward the door. "I love you, Ivy, but I need some space."

Ivy watched her sister, her closest friend, walk out the door without another word. She stood there in the room they'd laughed in, played in, cried in, and conspired in. The walls were a pastel green, Amber's favorite color, and she had wall appliques on them full of inspirational words like *dream, hope, dance.* Despite the strange life they grew up with, lived with, Amber still believed in all those things. She still believed they could have a wonderful life. That is, Ivy thought, until today.

She couldn't take it back. She couldn't change what had happened. Ivy sucked in a breath. Now wasn't the time to deal with personal issues. Now was the time to pack up and get the hell out. Ivy threw her pack over her shoulder walked out.

Everyone was already outside. She could hear Gabe and Ryan arguing but couldn't make out the specifics. She turned on all the fail safes, hoping it would help buy them a little time if her father and his minions weren't able to get in and verify the place was empty.

She took one last glance and knew deep down inside that it would be a long time before she ever came back. She would be seventeen in just a short time. Once she was eighteen, Zachariah would have less of a hold over her. No more claiming she was kidnapped and getting the authorities to hand her over to him. They just needed to stay one step ahead for a little longer.

Ivy stepped out to be met with a breeze that had grown even colder than the last time she was out. The sun was setting, and soon she'd be able to see the stars. The boughs of the trees rocked their invisible babies with calm rhythm. The lake whispered its goodbye with each wave that hit the nearby shore. She glanced, first to Patricia's grave where Amber stood, likely saying her own personal goodbye, then her gaze was drawn by the increased volume coming from Gabe and Ryan.

"You're an ass!" Gabe shouted and pushed at Ryan.

Ryan stumbled back, but didn't appear to want to fight. Ivy thought he might have some sense after all. Gabe was tough to beat in a tournament, but she didn't want to see what he was like if he got really angry. Gabe was a pretty big guy for his age, but his real skill was his ability to move quickly. Big guys don't usually move as fast as he could, so it was his greatest weapon. That and his ability to size up his opponent and know what they were going to do next. Ivy couldn't help herself. She hoped Ryan got mad enough to fight. Was she a terrible person for wanting to see Ryan get his butt kicked? Probably, but she was strangely comfortable with that.

Amber stood at Patricia's grave as Ivy approached. "I'm sorry, but we really have to get out of here." Amber spoke softly, but Ivy couldn't make out what she was saying at first. Things were fragile between she and Amber, but that couldn't make them careless now. Patricia wouldn't want that.

Ivy frowned as the seconds stretched on and she finally began walking over to her sister. As she got closer she could hear Amber talking and could see her standing there with her eyes shut. Only then did she realize something was really wrong. Amber was saying the same thing over and over again like a mantra.

"They're coming. Run! They're coming. Run!" Over and over but with an eerie calm that caused goose bumps to rise on her arms.

"Amber?" Ivy spoke softly, and when she touched Amber her eyes snapped open and they were staring at each other. "Are you okay?"

"Ivy?" Amber seemed confused, then her eyes widened in fear. "Ivy," she whispered, "They're coming."

"Who?!" Ivy felt her heart begin to race as she watched Amber's eyes look beyond her and into the forest.

"Zachariah," she whispered. "He's here..."

CHAPTER 15

"How do you know Zachariah is here?" Ivy asked, shaking Amber's shoulders to bring her attention back around to her.

"I was told," Amber answered, but seemed distracted by something more than just the immediate threat.

Before Ivy could ask anything more, Gabe walked up beside her.

"I think we need to go now," he told her. "We just saw a huge flock of birds take flight about a quarter of a mile south. They rose up from the treetops like something had spooked them."

"Something is wrong with Amber." Ivy told him. "It's like she's in a trance. She says Zachariah is here."

"Grab her!" Gabe said as he turned to signal Ryan that they needed to get moving immediately.

Ivy took Amber's hand and pulled. Her sister came away without a struggle though she continued to look back at the grave with no outward evidence of panic.

Ivy would talk with Amber later, but for now there was enough going on that her sense of survival kicked in, and just like those birds, she was going to take flight. They all hurried toward the car.

As they approached Ryan, Ivy felt the cold hand of doubt reach down and grasp her heart.

"Are you going with Ryan?" she asked. She didn't want to sound desperate, but that's how she felt. Despite the training, she was frightened. She and Amber always thought they'd have someone with them. Patricia or John or Helena, so they'd not given a lot of real thought to having to be on the run without help. Of course they'd discussed this scenario, but it always ended at the safe house, they'd not progressed beyond that yet. There was supposed to be more training. There was supposed to be more time.

"I'm going with you," Gabe said and put his hand out. "But, I'm driving." He offered a half smile when Ivy paused in surprise. "I'm not leaving you, Ivy. It was my cousin who gave you up to those people. To your father. I'm not going to just leave you now."

Relief washed over her, through her and built up a few tears that held tight behind her eyes, refusing to gather and fall.

"Thank you," she said and she turned to Amber, who already had the keys out.

Amber handed the keys to Gabe and got into the back seat of Duster. Ryan approached them, and they both turned to have their last words.

"If you leave, my sister will die." Ryan's tone was desperate and sad.

"I told you, Ryan," Gabe said, "This isn't their fault. We're not having this conversation again."

"Listen to me Ivy," Ryan implored. "What would you do to save your sister? Wouldn't you do anything? I had to try. I knew he could save her. You understand?"

She did understand. She understood more than he could ever know. Ryan had no idea how Patricia really died. She'd purchased her sister's life with Patricia's. Someone she loved with all her heart. Ryan was trying to save his sister's life, and all he had to do was, in his eyes, return two kidnapped girls to their father. Two girls he didn't know, he had no attachment to. Even when he realized things weren't all they appeared to be, he had to make a choice and he chose his sister's life over them. Would she have done the same thing? Probably.

Ryan stood there, near tears in his desperate plea for her to sacrifice her freedom for another person's life. In Ryan's mind, he probably figured she'd be free to do what she wanted in just a couple of years. He probably thought she was the most cold hearted person on the planet for not sacrificing those two years for the life of a child. He had no idea that once she was brought into the community she would have to fight for her life to escape.

"Ivy, we need to go." Amber sounded so calm, but Ivy knew there was a sense of urgency enveloping them tighter and tighter as each minute went by.

"Come with us," Ivy invited Ryan.

"You'd trust him?" Gabe sounded shocked. "He has betrayed you, betrayed us, this whole time!"

"He was put into an impossible situation. And he needs our help." She looked from Ryan to Gabe. "Just like I need yours."

"Going with you isn't going to save my sister." Ryan's tone sounded defeated.

"That's where you're wrong," Ivy told him as she turned to look him in the eyes. "I couldn't save my mother from Zachariah, but Ryan, I can save your sister. I can fulfill Zachariah's promise."

"What?" Ryan looked as confused as he sounded.

"The ability he has to heal people?" Ivy paused. "I have that, too."

She didn't want to use her power ever again, but what else could she do? Besides, this was her opportunity to beat Zachariah at his own game. For once, he would have to consider her a threat.

"What do I have to do?" Ryan asked, frowning.

"For now? You'll need to give up your phone and come with us. And we take this car, not yours. After we're done in San Francisco we can go to your sister."

"I'll do everything you ask, but we see my sister first."

"Ivy, hurry," Amber called out the window.

It didn't really make a difference if they waited just a little longer to find out what was in that safety deposit box. It would still be there when they finished taking care of this. His sister was dying. There was no telling how much time she had left. Ivy nodded and Ryan immediately rushed to his car to pull out his things. He was in the Duster in less than a minute.

Gabe turned the engine over, and Ivy cast a final look at the cabin and the grave. The car moved forward and began to pick up speed. She turned back and looked out just in time to see the albino step out of the forest on Amber's side of the car, point his gun and shoot.

"Look out!" Ivy screamed as the car slid sideways, corrected and lurched forward.

The sound of breaking glass wasn't as loud as Ivy thought it would be and when she sat up to look at the damage she saw that it was little more than a small hole toward the bottom of the side window.

"Oh crap!" Ryan yelled. "She's been hit!"

Ivy turned around in her seat to find her sister's hand covering what looked to be a small dart lodged in the side of her neck. She pulled it out and threw it into the floorboard then covered the wound with her hand as blood trickled out the tiny hole. Ivy unbuckled giving little thought to the fact that Gabe had sped up, and they were about to make a sharp turn to get back onto the interstate. She knew those things in the back of her mind, but as she watched Amber's eyes begin to roll back into her head she couldn't think of anything except getting to her sister.

"Amber!" she cried out as she reached over the seat and grabbed Amber's hand as Amber closed her eyes and went limp.

Ivy was over the seat and next to her sister in seconds. Ivy's heart beat so fast it ached. She lost balance for just a moment, as Gabe took the turn onto the main highway, and slammed her head into the door, falling for a moment over Amber's limp body. She righted herself, but not before accidentally connecting her elbow with Ryan's nose, eliciting a line of expletives and causing Ryan to unbuckle and climb over the seat to what little safety there was in the car.

Ivy lay her hand over the bleeding hole and tapped into her power. The way Amber acted when she got hit by the small dart, Ivy figured it was full of some tranquilizer, but she couldn't be sure. These people didn't think like normal people, and they might very well be okay with killing one of them to prove a point.

Her power gathered in her center, and she pushed just a little bit to get things going when an electric shock hit her from where her hand touched Amber's neck. An intense electric current gave her a shock, a warning something wasn't right. Ivy cried out and pulled her hand back to find it blistered, as though she'd touched a hot pan. She shook her hand, blew on it, and stared in horror at the still limp Amber. What was going on?!

"Everything okay back there?" Gabe asked.

Ivy glanced at the rear view mirror to see his eyes dart back and forth between the road and the mirror.

"I don't know," Ivy answered honestly. "I tried to heal her, but something's not right!"

"Do we need to go to a hospital?" Gabe asked.

Ivy looked at Amber. Her skin was ashen, and she wasn't sure if a tranquilizer did that to someone or not.

"I think we're going to have to," Ivy answered.

Gabe gave a quick nod and turned his attention entirely to the road ahead. Ryan looked around, first looking beyond them and then into the backseat. Ivy spared a glance behind them as well. No one was following them. Now that they were on a busy highway she wondered if they would want to take a chance at getting pulled over and having to explain a tranquilizer dart. Or maybe they had someone up ahead, some look out.

"We need to get somewhere public where they won't want to cause a scene," Ivy said.

"They caused a scene in a police station and a busy diner in front of witnesses in broad daylight. You really think there's somewhere they won't be willing to go?" Ryan asked while looking into Ivy's eyes.

She saw the fear fighting with the frustration in his eyes. No wonder he wanted to just do what Zachariah told him. This seemed like an impossible situation.

"How is Amber doing?" Gabe asked.

"Her breathing is steady, but she looks pale to me," Ivy said as she pulled Amber into her lap and started stroking her hair. Tears burdened her eyes, but not her cheeks. She drew in a long, deep breath to steady herself.

"So, are you saying your ability to heal isn't working?" Ryan asked.

Just when Ivy thought things couldn't get worse, now she had to worry about Ryan doubting her and possibly betraying them again. She had no idea why her power wasn't working right. She looked at Amber's skin where she had touched her, but there wasn't a mark there. This wasn't the first time she'd felt something like this. She looked down at her leg. She wore Capri pants so fabric wouldn't rub on the spot there on her leg, right above her ankle. The spot that was shaped like a hand. She looked back at Amber and wondered if pushing all of Patricia's energy into her had somehow made it impossible to use her power on her. She had healed herself earlier without any trouble. She needed to know if her power would react to others like it was with Amber. If she couldn't heal Ryan's sister, they needed to know sooner rather than later. And the look on Ryan's face as his eyes fell to the burn on her palm told her that he'd be a ticking time bomb for them if she didn't figure out one way or the other.

Ryan pushed some napkins up into his nose, but it was still bleeding pretty badly. Ivy looked at it closely. It didn't appear to be broken, but she'd nailed him pretty hard. She reached her hand out toward his face and he flinched away.

"What the hell?!" he asked as he moved closer to the dashboard, or rather, as far from her as he could get.

"Do you want to know if my power works or not?" she asked.

He took a few seconds to contemplate his options. He looked at Amber. He frowned just slightly, bit his lower lip, and nodded with a jerk of his head as he leaned toward her.

Ivy moved slowly, leaning only slightly so as not to move Amber out of her lap. Her fingertips brushed his cheek and held there for a few seconds as she called her energy, first to herself, then pushed it out very slowly into Ryan. She watched as his eyes grew wide and he took in a sharp intake of breath. It was more shock than anything because Ivy had felt the energy hit its mark and there was no electric jolt coming back to her.

She dropped her hand and watched him remove the wads of paper from his nose. He gently touched there and brought his hand back. No blood. His eyes jerked up from his fingertips to Ivy, and a smile slowly spread across his face.

"Did it work?" Gabe asked, glancing again in the mirror just briefly.

"It worked," Ryan said before Ivy could answer. "It's going to work." He was nodding, his eyes still locked to Ivy, but his expression changed to something more thoughtful that she couldn't put her finger on exactly. The only other time she'd seen an expression like that was on Gabe, the night in the dojo when she knocked him down so hard he had skid burns on his cheek the next day. It was something akin to respect.

"What do you want to do about Amber?" Gabe asked. "I have an idea."

"What?" she finally asked.

"Dr. Scarborough might be able to help," he suggested. "He's not too far. He sometimes covers at the MMA fights when the regular guy can't make it."

The funeral home guy?" Ivy asked, surprised. She knew they all called him doctor, but she hadn't given much thought to it. She'd not had cause to attend many funerals for people, just a few older folks that had befriended John and Helena even before Patricia had brought them to town. The old guy was a bit eccentric, but very kind and very organized. "What kind of doctor is he?"

"He used to be a pathologist at the hospital in town until his stroke put him in that wheelchair," Gabe told her. "My mom says he's a great guy and really good at what he does. Or, did, anyway."

"But, don't pathologists work on dead people?" Ivy asked.

"They're still doctors. And they do testing and stuff on live people, too." Gabe sounded as though he felt he needed to defend the old doctor.

"I don't know." She sat back against the seat now, her gaze falling to her sleeping sister. "I'd feel more comfortable with a regular doctor at a hospital."

"Well," Ryan interjected, "these people are after us and they may realize they got a hit on someone, and where do you think they'll be searching to see if they made their mark?"

He was right. Zachariah and his community soldiers would likely check out the hospitals. That's what she would do. She'd check hospitals, old haunts, maybe the car garages, just in case they hit a tire or something else that might need fixed. They needed to stay away from any of those places. No one would look for them at a funeral home. The irony alone would probably rule it out. She nodded at Gabe. They needed to make sure Amber was okay first, then get back on the road to San Francisco and hope whatever it was in that safe deposit box could help them.

"Anyone following us?" Gabe asked Ryan.

"I don't know. I don't think so." He looked back again and Ivy turned around as well. If someone was following them, they weren't being obvious about it.

"I'm going to pull over at the gas station up there," Gabe told them. "I'll park around back. See if anyone pulls in and looks like they're searching for someone."

Gabe waited till the last second to pull off the ramp and turn right toward the gas station. They pulled in behind the station and parked between two semi-trucks.

Over fifteen minutes went by with no one seeming to follow them. It was just odd, and Ivy wondered what the next move was going to be if they weren't planning on following. They carefully made their way back around, pulled back onto the highway back toward town. Half an hour later, Gabe turned off another ramp, this time going left in the familiar direction of the funeral home and a sea of graves.

The weight of Amber's head in her lap was like the weight of the world on her shoulders. Nothing she did seemed to work out right with her sister right now. This huge chasm had wedged between them, and for the first time in her life Ivy felt alone. Her sister was always the voice of reason. She was the thoughtful one. She followed the rules, and none of that was helping her now.

The funeral home was nestled behind some tall pines, like a fence protecting the privacy of the dead. Gabe slowed as they turned down the long drive. The place resembled an old southern Victorian home, even though Ivy knew it was less than ten years old. There had been a big write up in the newspaper when the new building went up. Some people hated that the funeral home was farther away, yet some people liked the remoteness of it. Everyone in town used this place because everyone liked Dr. Scarborough. It was hard not to. Every time Ivy saw him at the diner in town he would tell her and Amber how pretty they were and tell John he'd better keep a shotgun and a shovel handy. Then he'd tease John that for ten dollars he'd let John bury the bodies in the cemetery behind the funeral home.

Ivy figured that was why he had the building built here as they pulled up and the landscape of protruding stones disappeared behind the large house. With Dr. Scarborough's difficulty getting around, this was a great solution for him.

He lived here, worked here, and didn't need to go far to do graveside services.

There was a round-about driveway, and Gabe pulled right up to the front steps and turned the engine off. Ivy heard the clicking sound of his buckle, then another as Ryan also unbuckled.

"You need to stay here," Gabe told him.

Ryan froze in mid-motion, frowned and then let his hands drop to his lap.

"You don't trust me?" he asked. "Even after Ivy proved she can help my sister?"

"It's just better this way," Gabe told him in a tone that said there was no way on earth Ryan was going in there with him. "I should probably talk to Dr. Scarborough before bringing Amber in."

"What are you going to tell him?" Ivy asked. She hadn't buckled back up, so she was able to easily move to toward the door, making room for Amber's head as she rested it on the seat.

"I'm going to tell him as close to the truth as possible," Gabe said as he opened his door and turned to stand up. "Someone was screwing around with dart guns and Amber got hit, but we don't know what they were using."

Ivy nodded and opened her door as well. The breeze blew warm with a kiss of brisk cold that made Ivy's arms breakout in goose flesh. She rubbed them as she stood and faced Gabe. She watched Ryan open his door and get out.

"Hurry," she whispered.

He reached out and put his warm hands on her arms, the contrast prolonging the goose flesh instead of getting rid of it. She knew he wanted to comfort her, but she wanted to get help for her sister, so she smiled and moved back enough that he dropped his hands. He nodded and walked up the stairs, not bothering to knock and going inside the beautiful home.

"I really need to pee," Ryan said as though it were the most natural thing to announce. "If I can't go inside I'm going to go around the corner. I'll be right back."

"You should stay here!" She did not want him out of her sight. Regardless of whether or not she could heal his sister, she couldn't trust him as far as she could throw him.

"You're welcome to come with me, but," he left it open ended for a moment then smiled, "someone should stay here with Amber, don't you think?"

With that he walked away from her. She was torn between leaving Amber there unguarded and following Ryan to make sure he wasn't giving away their position. They needed time here so Dr. Scarborough could check out Amber, help her. She watched him disappear around the house and bit her lower lip as she considered what to do. Glancing at Amber, she worried that maybe her situation would get worse, but her sister was breathing evenly and her color even looked better. Ivy wished she'd left the sleeping bag somewhere easier to get to. If Amber went into shock she'd need to keep her warm. Gabe had his jacket up front and she opened the driver door to get that and put it over Amber. It took a moment of looking at the front seat and feeling something wasn't quite right before she realized what it was. Gabe had nothing in his hands when he went inside. Where was his cell phone?

CHAPTER 16

IGHT NOW THEY WERE relatively safe, but if Ryan decided to betray them again there was no telling how long they would have before Zachariah and his people showed up. Ivy couldn't imagine they were that far behind them. She needed to stop him and buy more time for Dr. Scarborough to look at Amber. That was if Gabe could convince the old doctor to assume that kind of liability.

Ivy slammed the door and ran in the direction Ryan had gone. She stopped short as she turned the corner and scanned the immediate area. He wasn't there, but she caught the sound of whispers coming from behind the house and took off in that direction as fast as her legs could carry her.

Ryan leaned casually against the back of the house. He was facing away from her, but she could see how his arm angled and his hand covered his ear. He murmured something she couldn't hear through the pounding of her heart in her own ears. She moved slowly toward him trying to hear what he was saying. But, regardless of her practiced stealth, some sound she wasn't aware she was making or some sixth sense on Ryan's part brought him around to face her.

He didn't try to hide that he was talking on Gabe's phone. He looked at her with such a serious face, appearing much older than his eighteen years.

"Mom, stop crying," he spoke gently into the phone. "I'm sorry, too."

Ivy continued to walk toward him. He stood straight and motioned her to come closer. As she neared he put the phone on speaker so she could hear the woman – his mother- crying on the other end. He'd called to check on his sister. He wasn't betraying them.

"You need to get here soon, Ryan," his mother's voice sounded hoarse. She'd cried so hard she could barely speak.

"I'm coming, mom," he promised. "I'll be there in just a couple of days."

"Hurry." The one word, spoken through a sea of grief.

Ryan didn't say anything else, just hit the button that ended the conversation. Ivy doubted he could have said anything even if he wanted to. His body convulsed in jagged movements as tears streamed down his face. He closed his eyes so tightly she wondered if he was trying to force the tears back. He fell to one knee, unable to stand under the weight of all his grief. Ivy knew that feeling well. She kneeled down beside him, not caring that the grass and a few underlying pebbles dug into her knees. She put her arm around him, and he fell apart. She said nothing, just held him until the tears stopped.

He took the hand she offered to help him to his feet, then wiped his damp face with the back of his hand. He looked around, toward the graveyard, which seemed to frighten him, to the interstate that one could catch glimpses of through the tall trees, anywhere but at Ivy. She gently took the phone, and he gave it to her without comment. She turned and walked back to the car. He could follow her, or he could remain behind to gather himself if that's what he wanted. It wasn't that she didn't care, not exactly. But there was nothing she could do right at that moment for him except offer him space and time in his grief.

As Ivy rounded the corner of the house, she spotted Gabe walking out of the front door. Instead of taking the stairs, he walked to the ramp and that's when she noticed the funeral home door was open wide. An old man dressed in what Patricia would call his "Sunday best" rolled out in his wheelchair. He wore a thin bow tie and thick black-rimmed glasses that made Ivy think of Buddy

Holly. Dr. Scarborough saw her and gave a quick wave, but the quick smile she was accustomed to seeing when she ran into him outside of his work was missing. They were asking him to help them but not call the police or an ambulance. He couldn't be happy about that, yet he was, headed toward the car, nonetheless.

Ivy saw the car door was open, no one was inside.

"Where is she?" Ivy turned to Gabe. "Where's Amber?"

Ivy's heart beat fast and adrenaline pushed through her like fire. Where was her sister?

"Amber?!" Ivy screamed as though the fear could escape that way.

"Calm down!" Gabe went to hold her, but she pushed him away.

"My sister is gone!"

"She's not gone." Ryan's voice was uneasy, and turned Ivy around as though he had screamed it.

She followed his gaze. Amber stood in the graveyard among the dead, her hands out from her sides, her palms down as though she was feeling the air just above the dirt and grass and stone. Her eyes were closed, the look on her face serene. But, that wasn't what caused Ivy to stop in her tracks. It was graves themselves. An incandescent white cloud surrounded Amber. Within those clouds Ivy was horrified to catch glimpses of people. A face, a hand, a body. Anna was pulling souls from the graves.

First there were just the few closest to her, but there were at least a hundred hovering white clouds, all standing physically over their graves. They were all facing Amber.

"Amber?" Ivy called out, and when Amber opened her eyes it was like she was leading an orchestra of the dead. They all turned in unison to watch her as well. There was no malice, no emotion at all that she could tell, not even interest really. They just looked at her because Amber did.

The seconds stretched out, long and taut. This moment would be burned into her memory forever.

Ivy knew the moment her sister really saw her. Amber closed her hands into fists and relaxed her arms and just like that the clouds were gone. They just disappeared.

Ivy shook the petrifying fear off like a coat that had weighted down her body, and she ran to Amber stopping short of pulling her into her arms. Something was different about Amber, and for the first time in her life she was confused about what to do regarding her sister. For the first time in her life, she feared Amber.

As if sensing that fear, Amber's face softened, she offered a small smile. She appeared perfectly healthy and normal. Ivy had no idea what had just happened or how Amber had recovered from whatever drug the dart had injected, but when Amber held out her arms, Ivy rushed to embrace her.

Amber was cold and Ivy hugged her tighter hoping to warm her. Instead, Amber began to shiver so hard her teeth clicked together. She stepped out of the embrace and rubbed her arms for warmth.

"Are you okay?" Ivy asked.

"I feel wonderful," Amber answered, but offered nothing more.

"Let's get inside and have Dr. Scarborough tell us you're doing wonderful," Gabe said as he walked up next to Ivy.

Amber followed them away from the graveyard, without resistance.

Everyone moved at a leisurely pace to allow for Dr. Scarborough to move with them. He'd waved off Ryan's offer to push him and didn't seem to really need the help anyway. They went up the ramp and walked into the dark recesses of the funeral home.

Ivy's eyes slowly adjusted to the darker interior, and she was glad when Gabe's warm hand took her cold one. As she took in more and more of the place, she recalled how lovely it was, decorated in antiques from years gone by. There was something soothing about the way it was decorated, something that said, "Time is not a barrier to eternity." You felt like there were things that lived forever, that you could enjoy and love and admire forever as you passed each beautiful antique chair, table, area rug, and collectible. Ivy was always pulled toward the glass display case in the large room outside one of the viewing rooms. Dr. Scarborough had an impressive collection of miniature antique hearses from various periods in history. The tiny models drew her with a spell of morbid uniqueness. Before she got too close, Gabe tugged her hand. The others were following Dr. Scarborough through a set of lovely, ornate walnut doors that had a small sign held within a gold stand saying "Private."

They walked into Dr. Scarborough's inner sanctum. This was the home part of the large building. There were antiques everywhere. Ivy wondered who decorated the place and realized she had never seen a Mrs. Scarborough. Had the doctor hired someone to create the peaceful scenes from long lost, yet beloved years? Or maybe the old man was secretly a home decorating mastermind? Either way, the room appealed to her with feelings of home and peace and good old American apple pie values.

Dr. Scarborough led them into a parlor complete with settees and velvet chairs. Everyone took a seat with the good doctor in the center of the room.

"Normally, I would offer refreshments," Dr. Scarborough began. "But, first I think we need to get a few things sorted out.

"I understand from young Mr. Hennessey that there was some horseplay with dart guns and tranquilizers and that our young friend-of-the-grave here was wounded and needed help. But, that has obviously changed and I must admit to being on the fence about wanting to know any more than I do at this moment." He paused there and rubbed the end of his nose as though it itched. "I also admit, freely, that I am very curious about what this young lady was doing in the graveyard out back. And I'm not sure if you still require anything from me at all."

Amber was sitting on a lovely blue settee with white brocade around the edge of the seat and beautiful, dainty white flowers scattered across the blue material. She looked neither sick nor upset, but neither did she appear her normal self. She was staring out one of the two windows in the room, the one that looked out over the graveyard. She hadn't spoken and didn't seem to mentally be there with them, which made Ivy more concerned than when Amber had been completely unconscious.

"Dr. Scarborough?" Gabe began pacing nervously back and forth in front of the side window. "I don't even know what to say."

Ivy knew how easily these things could get out of hand. Something unexplainable often caused people to react in fear and do things they might not normally do. Dr. Scarborough pulled out a white handkerchief and blotted at his forehead. Ryan couldn't stop staring at Amber. When Ivy stood up, Gabe stopped pacing and all heads turned toward her except for Amber's.

"I think my sister was drugged with some kind of tranquilizer just like Gabe said. If you could just examine her and tell us if you think she's okay physically, we can get out of your hair."

Dr. Scarborough sat silently for a moment, then his gaze following Amber's out the window to the graveyard.

"Some people feel called to the dead," he said. This won him Amber's attention. "And sometimes the dead feel called to some people. I've seen things I can't explain. I have faith that the souls of the departed have a destiny we can't know until we are nothing but souls ourselves." He looked into Amber's eyes and there was a yearning there that Ivy couldn't understand. She thought he might ask Amber a question, but then he turned his attention directly to Ivy. "Your sister may well be reacting to whatever drug was in her system. But, we all know what we saw out there in that graveyard. We all saw it. And none of us were drugged. At least I wasn't."

Gabe moved forward until he stood next to Ivy.

"No one is denying what we all saw," Gabe said to Dr. Scarborough as he took Ivy's hand. "We just don't know any more than you do about what happened out there."

"Amber?" Dr. Scarborough asked. "Do you know what happened out in the graveyard?"

Though everyone turned to Amber, she only stared at the old doctor. A moment went by and Ivy could see Amber thinking. She knew her sister well enough to know the look on her face when she was considering how to answer a difficult question.

"They woke me up. They told me I would feel better if I came to them, and I did," Amber answered.

"They who?" Dr. Scarborough asked.

"The dead." Amber turned back to regard the graveyard though the window.

The hairs on the back of Ivy's neck stood on end.

"Are they speaking to you now?" he asked.

Amber nodded. "Some of them."

"What are they saying?"

"They say this place is safe," Amber answered, then cocked her head to one side as though she were trying to hear someone whisper a secret. "There is a lady out there. She's the keeper of the dead. She's trying to tell me things, but it's too much at once." Amber frowned and shook her head as though she were clearing cobwebs from her mind. "I think I need to sleep now."

With that, Amber stopped talking and leaned against the back of the settee, shutting her eyes and shutting everyone out.

"Listen," Ryan spoke for the first time since they'd come inside. "We're all tired, but my sister needs us now. She can't wait for us to get some shut-eye. I can drive now and then Gabe. We can take turns while Amber sleeps."

Ivy understood his position, but she wondered if it would be the best thing to move her before the doctor examined her.

"Dr. Scarborough, what do you think?" Ivy asked. "Would it be okay to move her?"

The doctor was staring out the window, but turned to face Ivy before answering. "I think you should stay the night and make sure she doesn't have any residual problems with whatever drug was put into her system. If she has seizures, or some other kind of reaction, you'll want her to have immediate attention."

"But..." Ryan started but Gabe stopped him with a quick shake of his head.

"We make sure Amber is okay first, then we do as you say and drive in shifts until we get to Mia," Gabe told him.

Ryan's fist flew out, and he hit the small side table next to him with a loud thump. Ivy looked to Amber to see if it had startled her, but she didn't move or even acknowledge the sound. Ryan stood abruptly and walked out of the room. Gabe sighed, let go of Ivy's hand and followed him out.

"His sister is ill?" Dr. Scarborough asked.

Ivy walked over to the settee and sat next to her sister as she nodded to the doctor. He wheeled himself toward them, stopping in front of Amber, reaching out to check her pulse. Ivy watched him as he leaned forward and took Amber's face in one hand, moving it from side to side as he examined her. She didn't budge. He leaned back in his wheelchair.

"She's breathing fine, her color is fine, but obviously whatever got into her system has affected her," he said. "It's as though she's been given a sedative, but when she's awake she's able to respond to questions and situations. I just don't know."

Ivy could hear talking outside the house in the direction of the front door. Gabe and Ryan were arguing, but she couldn't make out everything that was being said, only snippets.

Dr. Scarborough rolled his wheelchair to the window overlooking the graveyard. He stared out the window as the sun fell, casting colors and shadows over him as time changed partners from day to night.

Minutes passed. The sounds of arguing changed to a hushed conversation Ivy could no longer hear any of. She was startled to see Amber's eyes open, fixed on the doctor.

"She's the keeper of the dead, you know," Amber said softly.

Dr. Scarborough nodded, but continued to look out the window. "I figured as much."

"She's lovely. I really like her." Amber smiled as the doctor turned just enough in his chair to look at her.

"She always had a soft spot for troubled teens." He smiled back at her.

Ivy fought to keep her curiosity in check. She felt like she was eavesdropping into a personal conversation, but they both knew she was sitting right there. As the minutes ticked by, she became slightly annoyed, as no one offered to explain what was going on. It was like they were speaking a language they knew she didn't understand and it was frustrating.

"Who are we talking about?" Ivy finally asked.

"Years ago, I lost my wife to cancer." Dr. Scarborough wheeled himself slightly so he could face Ivy, but still glanced out the window when he wanted. The graveyard seemed to be like a touchstone for the doctor, and his constant glancing out the window appeared to give him peace. "She was buried out there." He nodded in the direction of the graveyard. "I couldn't stand to be so far from her, so I quit my practice at the hospital and built this funeral home here. And, I've been happier for it. Or, at least as happy as I can be until I'm with her again in the afterlife."

He smiled and finally wheeled himself away from the window and stopped in front of them. Amber reached out and took the old man's hand and smiled back at him.

"Does she say anything about me?" he asked her.

"Just that she's waiting," Amber answered. "She's very patient."

At that, Dr. Scarborough made a sound between a laugh and a sob, his eyes tearing but not giving way to gravity. The smile remained as he nodded.

"Amber?" Ivy spoke. Amber turned to her and for the first time since Patricia's death she smiled that loving, sweet smile Ivy loved. It was automatic to smile back at her when she looked like that and a heaviness in Ivy's heart lifted. "Do you know what's going on with you?"

Amber nodded. "I think so. I'm still not exactly sure, but I do know one thing; I can pull energy from the dead just like you can pull energy from the living."

"Are you saying you can heal using energy from ghosts?" Ivy's arms were instantly covered in goose bumps.

"Ghosts, souls, spirits," Amber started. "I can pull energy from them, but not for healing."

"Then for what?" Ivy asked. She recalled the day she found her own power almost by accident.

Amber regarded her for just a moment before she answered. "I don't know yet."

CHAPTER 17

D R. SCARBOROUGH WAS AN amazing cook. Ivy contemplated licking her fingers, but Gabe was sitting across from her at the large oak table so she thought better of it. The smell of fried chicken still lingered in the air, and regardless of the fact Ivy had eaten two pieces of chicken and a mound of mashed potatoes, the smell still made her mouth water.

Ryan was resting in a room nearby so he could drive in a few hours, so the doctor packed a meal for him to eat on the road. The plan was to eat and get a few hours of sleep then hit the road before the sun came up. Ryan wanted to get an early start at it. Gabe had returned from his conversation with Ryan looking worn out and unhappy.

"Is everything okay?" Ivy asked.

"Things aren't going well with Mia." He answered.

"I'm sorry, Gabe," she took his hand and squeezed it. "I should have asked you how you're holding up, too. I know you love your family. Mia's illness must be hard for you."

He nodded, squeezing her hand before letting it go and turning back to the group.

Amber and Dr. Scarborough talked about death as though it were was the most important topic in the world. Ivy half-listened for a few minutes, but none of what they said seemed relevant to her. Amber didn't know any more than she'd already shared, and Dr. Scarborough was really more interested in his wife and the inmates living behind his home. The doctor and Amber seemed to have grown close in no time, and though Ivy knew it wasn't right, she was a little jealous of their easy camaraderie.

"We should probably go to bed," he said as he leaned back in the chair and stretched his arms wide, then brought them back to rest on the table.

Ivy's heart skipped and she prayed that her expression did not give her away. Dr. Scarborough set up the downstairs guest room for the boys and the upstairs guest room for the girls, so Ivy was pretty sure Gabe just meant that it was time to get some rest.

"Right." Ivy gave a quick, and hopefully mature-looking, nod and scooted her chair back to stand up. She moved too fast and the chair fell back, crashing to the ground. Dr. Scarborough and Amber stopped talking and turned to look at her.

"Are you alright?" Amber asked.

Ivy could feel the blood rush to her cheeks. "Yeah, just a little jumpy I guess. I think we're going to head to bed." She stopped, halfway bent over the fallen chair, took in a deep breath and corrected herself as she righted the chair. "I mean, we really need to get some sleep."

Ivy glanced to Amber, then Dr. Scarborough, anywhere but back to Gabe. "You need to get some rest too." She nodded at her sister, but Amber wasn't moving.

"I'm going to stay up a little while longer," Amber said, glanced at Gabe, where she held her gaze a moment longer than what was comfortable for Ivy, and then she smiled as she turned back to Dr. Scarborough and began talking again.

Dismissed, there was little Ivy could do but begin to clear the table and hope Gabe left before her so he could, hopefully, forget about this by morning.

"Leave that," Dr. Scarborough told her. "I'll clear the table in just a bit. You need some rest. You can hardly stand."

"I really don't mind," Ivy protested.

"I know, but as the host I prefer to clear the table. Go on now."

"Come on, Ivy." Gabe encouraged.

He walked slowly toward the white door that swung open in either direction and led them out of the dining room and into the hallway that adjoined the sitting. Gabe took her hand and walked toward the stairs. She knew the guest room where Ryan slept was through an adjoining hallway beyond the stairway, and she thought he might say goodnight at the foot of the stairs, and her heart beat faster as she wondered if he'd kiss her goodnight.

He stopped at the foot of the stairs and pulled her into his embrace. A jolt of electricity flew through her veins, making her feel alive and on fire. He bent his head slowly and very softly pressed his lips to hers. Fleeting, electric, and addictive. Her entire body felt warm all at once, all from the touch of his lips to hers. He moved his lips to capture her lower lip. It was a mix of gentle pressure and her eyes shut without conscious thought.

Seconds, a breath, a few heartbeats and he pulled away. The distance between them acted like a string that opened her eyes as he pulled away from her. Her hand remained in his, and he gave it a gentle squeeze. His eyes read her face like he was reading the page of a book, then his gaze turned slowly to follow the stairs up and for just a brief second she thought he might take a step in that direction, and she wasn't sure she could say no if he did, but he looked back to her, shut his eyes for a few seconds and smiled before opening them again. He brought her hand in his between them, up to his soft, warm lips and pressed a kiss to her knuckles.

"Goodnight," he whispered, his voice a deep baritone that caused her to shiver even as it caused confusion and longing simultaneously. He released her hand, but didn't move.

Staring into his eyes, she felt the pull of something frightening and magical, natural and thrilling, but she wasn't sure what to do next. She wasn't a baby; she was nearly seventeen. That pull was something as old as time and, for her at least, a step toward casting aside the final remnants of girlhood, of innocence.

He took one step back and she felt the cool air of the room rush between them to cool her body.

"It's too much." The words escaped before she realized she was going to say them. So much emotion rushed through her there was no room for feeling embarrassed or even unsure. The Ivy of 24 hours ago would have been thrilled to take him upstairs, but now, romance was something selfish until she found John and Helena. Until she helped Ryan's little sister and figured a way for her and Amber to escape their father and the community. Her focus would shatter if she gave in now and that wasn't what she wanted to do. It wasn't who she wanted to be.

"It's okay, Ivy." Gabe took one step closer, and the air grew warm from his nearness for a brief moment as he leaned in and kissed her forehead before stepping away again. "I'm not going anywhere." He smiled, turned and walked down the hall beyond the foot of the stairs. She watched him open a door and disappear inside.

She pulled in a deep breath and let is out slowly before walking up the stairs and to the room assigned to her and Amber. That moment with Gabe played again and again in her mind as she looked through her backpack that one of the guys brought up for her. She pulled out a long t-shirt that would work as a nightshirt and got dressed for bed.

The room was done in white and lace, the obvious product of a woman's hand. There was only one bed, but it was big enough for both she and Amber easily. The room held the odor of antiques and some light lemon-based cleaner. Matching lamps on matching nightstands lit the room. Ivy turned hers off, but left Amber's on. Thoughts of relaxation, meditation and clearing her mind caused more stress than help as she tried to will herself to calm and find sleep. Thoughts of Gabe filled her mind, and she closed her eyes. When sleep overtook her she didn't even notice.

The next thing she knew something – some sound – pulled her out of sleep. She lifted up on one elbow to see Amber closing the bedroom door. A glance at the clock on Amber's side of the bed and marveled at how three hours had slipped by without her knowing it.

Amber got ready for bed and then slipped beneath the cool, white sheets next to her.

"You okay?" Ivy couldn't help asking.

"Oh yes," Amber answered as she reached over and turned her lamp off and then lay on her back. "I like it here. I wish we could stay longer."

Ivy wasn't sure how to respond to that. Her first inclination was to remind Amber that they had to figure out how to save John and Helena and Ryan's sister. But, she stopped herself, turned on her side to face her sister and waited for her eyes to adjust to the darkness. She wished she could make out Amber's features better, try to read her. Her sister had been through a lot and now there was some kind of connection to dead people that neither of them understood. If Amber was afraid, she didn't show it, but that didn't mean she didn't need her sister's support.

"I wish I could help you. I wish I could leave you here with Dr. Scarborough so you could feel safe." Ivy spoke softly.

"Thank you, Ivy." Was all she said before she turned over giving Ivy her back, dismissing her. "Goodnight."

Ivy turned and stared at a ceiling she could hardly see. "Goodnight."

Ivy's morning started without sunshine as Gabe tapped on their door before 5 a.m. She threw the covers back and her bare feet hit the cold hardwood floor as her arm shot out and she turned on the table lamp. Her breath caught in her throat, her hand coming up to her mouth to stifle a scream as she turned and saw a figure sitting in a wooden rocking chair across from the bed in the shadows. She recognized the figure before the scream escaped and released a loud rush of breath instead.

"Amber," she tried to whisper as her heart thumped loudly in her ears. She moved toward the door when the knock came again. "You scared the crap out of me!"

"Sorry," she said as she continued to rock, "I couldn't sleep."

Ivy opened the door to find Gabe standing there. He looked at her with a slight frown, then beyond her into the room.

"Everything okay?" he asked.

"Yeah," she sighed.

His gaze fell back to her and he offered up a half-smile. "Time to roll."

A quick nod sent Gabe on his way. Ivy turned back to face her sister and realized Amber was already dressed and ready to go.

"Why don't you get dressed, and I'll make the bed," Amber offered and got up from the rocking chair.

In no time, they were down stairs where Gabe, Ryan, and Dr. Scarborough were waiting for them in the dining room.

The smell of biscuits and bacon brought a smile to Ivy's lips. The table held a variety tasty options, and Gabe was already packing breakfast sandwiches, fruit, and bagels into a bag.

Ivy could feel Gabe's eyes follow her around the room as she picked at some fruit and then reached for the bacon.

"Bacon," Gabe said as he snatched a piece from her hand, "is the reward for being a carnivore." He smiled big enough that she could see a glimpse of his pearly white teeth.

"Well, not everyone is a meat eater you know." Ivy couldn't resist.

"Yeah, well not everyone deserves to be rewarded with bacon!" He winked and shoved the entire piece into his mouth.

"Some people deserve to be rewarded with a swift kick to the posterior, which is what will happen if you nab my bacon again."

Something about Gabe's smile and a warm breakfast seemed to lighten her heart and for that split second she felt something she was sure would evade her for quite some time—hope. She chanced a glimpse at Amber and was happy to see her sister smiling at her, chatting quietly off and on with Dr. Scarborough, who also seemed happier this morning. Even Ryan, who Ivy was sure had his own personal dark cloud following him, was at least sitting quietly, perhaps even contentedly, munching on a breakfast sandwich of bacon, sausage, egg and cheese on a toasted bagel.

"Eat up everyone," Dr. Scarborough offered. "Take what you can with you. Leave the clean up to me."

"We need to go soon," Amber added and her smile remained, but a seriousness around her eyes caused Ivy to take a closer look at her.

"I thought you wanted to stay here forever?" Ivy asked.

"Someone is coming, and we should leave before she gets here." Amber still held the smile, but now it didn't quite reach her eyes.

Ivy stopped in mid-motion, banana in one hand and a brown bag in another. She breathed out, continued the movement of putting the fruit into the bag and looked at the others in the room. They had stopped as well, the smiles all gone.

"Who's coming?" Ivy asked. The last time Amber predicted someone was coming, it had been Zachariah's crew.

"Don't be glum now," Dr. Scarborough interjected. "I'm expecting someone."

Ivy breathed out a sigh of relief, then thought about it. "This early?"

Dr. Scarborough handed the last of the biscuits to Gabe, who threw them in his ever-growing bag of food. "Soon enough," he answered. "I've been waiting for her for a long time and would like to have the house to myself when she gets here." He smiled again, and it seemed to infect the group as everyone went back to their light-hearted banter.

They packed everything up, and Dr. Scarborough followed them out as far as the front door. Gabe shook his hand and then turned to catch up with Ryan, who was already in the driver's seat. Farewells had been said and the final thank you repeated from each person. Ivy gave him a quick hug and waited as Amber did the same.

They walked together toward the car, and Ivy watched Amber turn one last time to wave goodbye.

"He's a really nice guy." Ivy smiled at her sister, who was so obviously fond of the old doctor.

"He's lonely," Amber said as she scanned the landscape ahead of them. "I'm glad she's coming for him."

"Who?" Ivy asked.

"His wife."

With that Amber began to walk a little faster, whether to beat the chill of the dark morning or the new reality she seemed cursed with, Ivy wasn't sure. Dr. Scarborough's wife was dead. Ivy was sure he'd said that. So, if she was coming for him...

Ivy glanced back as the reality hit her. This sweet old man that everyone loved, he was going to leave with his wife today, and he knew it. But he seemed okay with dying. He was even happy this morning at the table. He was glad, but for some reason Ivy felt a tug at her heart, knowing she would never speak to him again. There would be one less kind person in the world after today, and that thought made her melancholy as she reached the car and got in.

She leaned back in the seat, then reached for her seatbelt. As she buckled, she saw something move out of the corner of her eye just before a light blanket covered her lap. Amber straightened her part of the blanket, then glanced across and through the window for one final glimpse of the place. Ivy followed her gaze as the car moved slowly forward. Dr. Scarborough waved as they moved out of sight and in her mind she could see him waving and smiling long after they were on the interstate.

The sun peeked out over the horizon casting an array of color over the sky. Ivy leaned toward the light that filtered in through her window and closed her eyes. There was so much to consider, so much to get ready for, but all she wanted to do was soak up the pale sunlight and relax. She rested the side of her head lightly against the cool glass as the sun continued to shine through. She breathed in deeply and opened her eyes as she exhaled. She could see the side view mirror, and Gabe was leaning against his window, eyes closed, jacket tucked between his shoulder and neck for support. She envied his ability to sleep soundly in the car.

Gazing at him, she felt something stir in her chest. He was so tall and handsome—okay, dead sexy was probably the better descriptor here—but it was more than just his looks. Gabe was comfortable with himself. He knew what he wanted and took steps to get it. He was confident and smart and seemed totally unaware of those assets most guys would use to get everything. Get every girl they desired. He worked hard for everything he got. She had watched him do it. The martial arts tournaments, football, MMA training, she watched him sweat and bleed for everything he wanted. Now he wanted to help keep her safe. He wanted to help her find John and Helena. Knowing that Gabe was with her made her feel as though they could actually pull it off.

She had no idea how long she'd been staring at him before he opened his. This time she didn't feel her cheeks grow flush. This time she didn't want to look away and hope he didn't notice her staring. No, this time she held her gaze, and for a moment they simply saw each other, acknowledging the need to connect even if it were only through a glance. She smiled, he smiled back and then a loud sound of hard music pulled them both back into the reality that was sharing a long ride with Ryan.

"How long till we get to your house?" Ivy asked Ryan as she sat straight and glanced at him in the rearview mirror.

"Twenty-hours tops if we keep moving," Ryan answered then moved his gaze to Gabe to offer a frown as the music was turned down a few notches.

"How far from there to San Francisco?" she asked.

"About another twenty hours." Ryan said, but he was looking out at the road ahead as though he wanted to end the talking.

"Where does your family live?" Amber moved, pulling the blanket down so that it only covered her lap.

"Fort Collins, Colorado," Ryan answered, his eyes still on the road.

Ivy watched Gabe lean back against his door, resting once again with his jacket as a pillow. Amber pushed the blanket from her lap into the seat between them and yawned as she stretched out her arms, putting her hands in Ivy's face and wriggling her fingers under her nose with a giggle before moving back on her side of the car.

Ivy smiled and rolled her eyes at her sister. Her heart felt as bright as the morning sun, and the only thing more surprising than the realization that she and Amber were acting as though they were friends again was the realization that she felt happy without an immediate gust of guilt intruding on any hint of that happiness.

"You're awfully chipper today," Ivy ventured to find the source of this change in attitude.

"Yeah, I feel pretty good," Amber nodded. "Don't you?"

Ivy realized that she did feel pretty good. It made no sense. Was it some kind of post traumatic disorder maybe? Logic told her she had been slapped, metaphorically speaking, in the face by life with trauma and grief and should be immensely unhappy right now, but that's not how she felt. Looking at Amber, she wondered how her sister could know she felt good given all the reasons they should both be so miserable.

"Why are we happy?" she blurted out, disturbed to be disturbed by her own happiness. "What's going on?"

"Last night the Keeper of the Dead gave me a gift." Amber smiled, and it caused Ivy's heart to grow cold even though the smile seemed sweet and genuine. "Usually the dead stay where they're buried. That's what she told me."

Ivy nearly flinched at how cold Amber's hand was as her sister placed it on top of hers, entwining their fingers together, with Ambers on top. Ivy didn't know what to say. She kept silent, hoping Amber would continue, which she did.

"But, your gift Ivy," Amber paused and smiled again, "It's not meant to mix with mine, but it did. You pull energy from one person and put it into someone else. You pull from their life essence and for a moment those people are all connected."

Ivy felt the intensity of her sister's gaze as though Amber were waiting for her to have some epiphany from that little bit of information. When nearly a minute went by, Amber continued.

"You see, when she died, she died connected to me, so there was a way to bring her with us. The Keeper of the Dead opened that door and now she's here!" Amber became more animated as though she'd just given away an exciting secret she'd held for far too long.

"I'm sorry, Amber, I just don't understand. I don't know anything about the Keeper of the Dead opening doors, and I don't know how anyone with the title 'Keeper of the Dead' could have anything to do with us being happy."

Amber shook her head and rolled her eyes as though there was some sort of joke and now she was going to have to explain it.

"We're happy because she's here and because she's forgiven us. She said it wasn't our fault. We're released from the guilt. That's what you're feeling, Ivy."

Goose bumps crawled up Ivy's arms, and though the sun continued to beat down on her she felt a shiver of cold as though she stood naked in the snow.

"What are you saying?" Ivy's teeth even chattered a little and she reached for the blanket to pull it up to her shoulders. "Who forgave us?"

"Patricia, of course!" Amber announced with an almost childlike glee.

Tears burned at the back of Ivy's eyes, the only heat she could feel in her entire body. Her logical mind told her that something significant had happened to her sister. She'd found her own power and with that Amber's life would never be the same. But, Amber did appear to feel happy. She was happy this morning at the breakfast table. She hadn't played that horrible moment at the cabin over and over and over in her mind all morning like the mantra of guilt it had become.

Ivy looked intently at her sister, who seemed genuinely excited to be sharing this news. She recalled yesterday's events, the way her sister stood in the graveyard, the white clouds that hovered over the graves.

"When?" Ivy asked as her heart began to pound. "When did Patricia forgive us?"

"Last night she came to our room. She and I spoke while you slept. The Keeper of the Dead has forbidden her to say too much, but she is allowed to set our minds at ease and to help us when she can."

"Can she tell us where John and Helena are?" Ivy's body began to warm at the thought of rescuing them.

Amber's smile faltered, causing Ivy's heart to sink.

"Being dead doesn't make you all-knowing I'm afraid." Amber shook her head. "But, she remembers things. And she said we need to get to San Francisco fast. She said there's important things there for us."

"What's there? She put it there. Why can't she tell us?" Ivy was plenty warm now and threw the blanket off where it sat piled between them in the seat.

"She said John and Helena have information there as well and that we need to see it all together. She's not sure what is in their letter to us, but that everything we need is there."

"Is she here with us now?" Ivy looked slowly around the car, then back to Amber who was already shaking her head.

"She can only be with us when we're near the dead. It's like they are a transmitter or satellite tower or something." Amber frowned a little.

"Did she tell you anything about what's happening with you?" If Amber was right, Patricia had forgiven her and she was here to help them.

Amber nodded, her frown replaced by a seriousness that momentarily erased any hint of innocence or happiness that was there just moments before.

"She said faith healers get their power from a universal source that is not of this world, but that lives in this world." Amber spoke quietly, causing Ivy to lean in so she could hear. "The energy you pull from comes from that stream of power and manifests in healing and in life.

My power comes from a similar stream, but going in the opposite direction. I get energy from the dead. It can heal me, but only me."

Ivy thought about that for a moment and nodded. "But you can also see ghosts."

"It's more than that," she said in a whisper. "Where you can give energy for life, I can give energy for death."

Ivy's gaze jerked up to meet Amber's. "What does that mean?"

"Patricia says that I can touch someone and take some of their life away, like make them older, or drain their aura."

"What would you do with a power like that?" Ivy asked but knew she didn't really want to hear the answer.

"I can kill with it."

CHAPTER 18

GABE WAS SLEEPING AND Ryan tapped his hand on the steering wheel to the rhythm of the song on the radio. Neither had overheard their conversation and Ivy was grateful for it. It would take some time to process everything Amber had told her, and even then she just wasn't sure what to do with that kind of information even if she did understand it.

She'd given very little thought to where her power actually came from. That some cosmic stream of energy made up life and death wasn't something she'd even guessed at. She'd thought the energy was something her body made up, like static electricity. Knowing her ability tapped into something so powerful might have been useful to know before Patricia died.

Patricia. Ivy's heart sang with gladness to know Patricia forgave her. The rollercoaster of emotions was tiring, but her mind wouldn't let her rest. Patricia couldn't really tell them any more than what she already knew, so it was hard to say how much help there would really be. Still, Ivy couldn't deny that she felt lighter somehow, happier, because she'd been forgiven and because Patricia wasn't fully lost to them.

The morning sun beat down on her and she removed her hoodie, happy that she'd dressed in layers. It felt like they'd been driving for many hours, but really it had only been a couple, and Ivy sighed as she considered the long trip ahead. She couldn't even surf the web or play a game because she didn't have her smart phone. Patricia had forced them to leave those behind and bring burner phones instead. Yeah, it was going to be a really long trip.

Gabe woke, put his jacket on the seat between he and Ryan and turned to look at her. "Hey!" he said, a little groggily.

"Hey!" she answered as she noticed one side of his face had lines in it left from laying on his balled up jacket and that some of his hair on that same side was standing up like a cowlick. He must have noticed her because he smiled and rubbed at his face, then patted down his hair.

"Sleeping beauty awakes!" Ryan nodded at Gabe. "I figure we'll take a break and gas up in about an hour. Wanna drive?"

"Yeah, I'll drive," Gabe answered as he turned back around to look out the front.

"Don't you think it's odd that those people after the girls would go to so much trouble to find them and then, all of a sudden, they don't seem interested enough to follow us?" Ryan asked.

"I had that same thought," Gabe answered as he reached over to change the radio.

Ryan's hand snaked out and Ivy heard a loud thwack. Gabe instantly pulled his hand back.

"Dude!" Gabe complained as he shook his hand.

"When you drive," Ryan told him without a single ounce of guilt for slapping him so hard, "you can pick the tunes. Until then, driver picks, so keep your mitts off."

Ivy couldn't help it. She grinned. It was good to see them give each other a hard time. There was something normal in giving your cousin a hard time, or so Ivy thought, and she could use some normal in her life about now.

Ryan was right though. It was like Zachariah and his crew had just given up once Ivy and Amber hit the road. She wondered if maybe there was a tracking device they didn't know about or someone else who was watching them that they hadn't seen yet. Her gut told her they had not given up, but she wasn't sure what their game was either.

"Do you think they know we're heading to help your sister?" Ivy asked. It was the only logical answer she could come up with. Why chase when all you have to do is beat them there?

"Maybe," Ryan said. "Do they know you have the same ability as your father?"

"That's the million-dollar question," Gabe joined in the conversation. "If John and Helena know, then we have to assume her father and his cronies know."

"She healed someone in the diner the other day." Amber's voice cracked a little from still being groggy.

"Yeah, but I didn't make a big deal of that. They may have missed it."

"We have to assume they know and be ready when we get to Colorado," Ryan said, and immediately Amber nodded.

"They don't know about Amber." Gabe spoke to no one in particular and turned back to face the front. He removed his sweatshirt and Ivy could see he was wearing a plain white t-shirt that had their dojo logo embroidered on the left side.

He was right. No one knew about Amber's ability.

"Once we get close to Ft. Collins, we should call your mother, see if she's had any visitors there, any new people coming by. We need to stake the place out for a bit to make sure no one is watching it. There's really not a lot more we can do," Ivy said.

"We'll figure it out before we get there," Gabe answered.

Ivy nodded and relaxed back against the seat. No one spoke for a time. She shut her eyes against the sun and willed herself to clear her mind. She needed to stay level headed. She needed to concentrate on taking one step at a time. First, they needed to get to Colorado. Next they needed to get to Ryan's sister in the safest way possible. Then she prayed they got there in time and that she would have enough energy to heal Mia, because if she didn't someone was going to have to help her.

The music from the radio filled the empty air of the car, and Ivy begrudgingly admitted that Ryan had pretty good taste in music as some old southern rock began to play, then some blues. John would have loved this. For a fleeting second she wondered what music Gabe would listen to. Anytime she'd ever heard music on around him, heavy beats you could feel in your entire body.

The car jostled and Ivy jolted awake, surprised she had fallen asleep when she'd only meant to rest her eyes. They pulled up to a pump and Ivy unbuckled when they stopped. She got out, stretched, twisted, yawned and combed her fingers through her hair.

Amber and Gabe got out as well and they all began to walk toward the part of the gas station that was a mini-mart while Ryan gassed up the car. A quick trip to the bathroom, a cold bottle of water for everyone and they were on the road again. But this time Ivy joined Gabe up front as he took over the driver's seat.

"How long do we go for now?" Ivy asked as she started to reach out toward the radio, then remembered Ryan's rule and decided she'd just let Gabe choose the music.

Gabe smiled at her and pointed toward the radio. "I'm not a radio Nazi like Ryan. Go ahead.

We'll keep stopping every three hours or so until we get there."

Ivy nodded turned toward the old fashioned radio knob to see what music stations were available. She found something with a good beat and then leaned back and watched the car eat up the road for the next three hours.

They kept the conversation light, and the next time they stopped Ryan and Amber traded places with them. They'd bought fast-food for lunch and dinner. As the landscape changed, so did their mood. By the time they hit the Colorado state line, everyone was serious and somber. Night fell as they hit Ft. Collins. Ivy knew better than to think the darkness would hide them.

Ryan pulled over once they got into a suburban area. The houses were track houses and every sixth house started the same line up of houses.

Ivy and Gabe determined that they would get out and walk the perimeter while Ryan and Amber stood lookout within sight of the house. Ivy shoved her cell phone into her pocket and she and Gabe went around the block in opposite directions.

Staring out at the dark homes illuminated within, Ivy could almost imagine what it was like for Ryan to live here. It was an older neighborhood compared to the surrounding areas, but not run down. The area was clean and she could smell fresh cut grass from nearly every house she passed. Intermittently there would be the sweet smell of flowers, the sound of a barking dog, but no cars with people sitting in them and no one driving aimlessly around the neighborhood. Halfway around the neighborhood, she saw Gabe on the opposite side of the road. He glanced at her, but kept walking.

When she got back to Ryan and Amber, Gabe was in sight and soon arrived at the car.

"It looks clear to me," Ivy told them.

"Yeah, I went over to the house to peek inside and everything there looks fine too," Ryan said.

"Now what?" Amber asked.

"My mom said to come as soon as possible. I have a key. Now, we go inside," Ryan said and dug into his pocket to produce the house key.

Ivy followed Ryan. They left the car parked far away from Ryan's house just in case someone was watching the house from any of the neighbor's homes.

They went around the back of the house and quietly opened the back gate. Ryan swore when the motion lights went on and dogs in the neighborhood began to bark. So much for sneaking. Ryan's shoulders drooped noticeably, but Ivy could see him taking in a deep breath, squaring his shoulders and walking quickly to the back door where he inserted the key and opened it up for everyone to go in.

Ivy cast a glance about the back yard and as far as she could see beyond. If anyone was watching, they knew someone had just come into the house. The hairs on the back of her neck rose up as she imagined someone looking back at her from any number of the darkened windows within sight of the house. It seemed that some people were still up this late, and a few peered out their windows, but it was the windows she couldn't see into that bothered her most. There was nothing that could be done about it now, so she went inside and Ryan closed the door behind them.

A lamp clicked on and they turned to see a woman in her early forties standing there in pajama bottoms and a tank top. Her hair was disheveled and it appeared that she'd forgotten to remove her make up before going to bed, as her mascara was smeared around her eyes giving her that raccoon look.

"Ryan. Thank god you're here." Ryan's mom moved forward slowly arms extended toward her son.

Ivy knew the relationship between Ryan and his mom was strained, but she seemed genuinely happy to see him. Relieved even. She'd at least temporarily forgotten or forgiven Ryan for stealing from her bank account. Funny how such things were unimportant when someone you loved was dying.

Watching the two of them hold each other until they both began to cry, felt worse than accidentally eavesdropping on a private moment. She tried to turn away, to give them some privacy and noticed that Amber and Gabe doing the same. Ivy walked over to examine at a group of family photos hanging in a little alcove near the back door.

The photos showed a happy family, smiling, at the park, on the swing, in a sand box, posed and candid over a span of years. Ivy wondered briefly where Ryan's father was, since he was not in any the pictures. One picture in particular caught her attention. The photo showed Mia, Ryan and Gabe about three or four years ago. Mia looked happy and well, and the boys were playing in the sandbox with her. The photo was filled with so much happiness, Ivy could almost hear their laughter. She knew Ryan was close to his sister, but she had wondered how close Gabe was with the little girl. There was such an age difference, and they lived so far away from each other, but in this picture you could see he adored her.

She regarded another picture, this one posed like at some photographer's studio. It was Ryan, his mom, and Mia all dressed in blue tops with a gray background behind them. It couldn't have been taken more than a couple of years ago, and Ivy was shocked at how different Ryan's mom appeared compared to the thin, weary-looking woman.

"Mom, I'd like to introduce you to some friends," Ryan said.

Ivy turned to see that Ryan and his mother had ended their embrace.

"Amber, Ivy, this is my mom, Joyce. Mom, these are my friends who helped me get here."

Ivy stuck her hand out toward Joyce but, Joyce ignored it and took a step forward to embrace her in a hug. The hug was quick and hard, and Ivy could feel how truly thin and frail Joyce was under her clothes. Joyce then hugged

Amber and turned to Gabe, who got an extra long hug that Ivy was afraid might end in tears again, but Gabe patted her on the back and moved away before that could happen.

"I made up the guest room for you girls." Joyce offered a smile that only served to accentuate her weariness, and her voice cracked just a bit, so she whispered the last couple of words. "Boys, you'll stay in Ryan's room of course." She looked at them again and frowned. "Where are your suitcases? You must have more than just backpacks. Are you planning on leaving soon?"

Emotions ran across her face and changed just as fast from happy to sad to concerned to afraid.

"We're going to stay until Mia's better, Mom." Ryan stepped in and hugged his mother again, but this time kept it brief.

His mother stood there like a statue for a moment just staring at Ryan. Ivy thought she was going to speak, but instead a tear ran down her cheek and she bit her lip to keep it from quivering. Ryan leaned in again and held her, this time letting her stay in his arms as long as she wanted.

"It's going to be okay, Mom. I'm here now." Ryan continued to offer words of comfort as he held his mother, stroking her back and leaning his forehead down to rest on the top of her head.

Gabe moved toward them and joined in the hug. "We really need to get some rest. Let's do that, and then tomorrow we'll discuss what to do next."

Joyce nodded as she pulled away from Ryan, dabbing her eyes and wiping her cheeks. After offering food or drink, which they declined, she led them down the hall. Ryan and Gabe went directly into the first room on the right.

Joyce showed Ivy and Amber to a room on the left that contained a hide-a-bed couch already made into a bed. The room doubled as an office. There was a computer set up and a fax machine and several bookshelves built into the wall and filled with books.

"If you girls need anything at all, please help yourself or get me or one of the boys, okay?" She smiled that tired smile again as Ivy nodded and thanked her.

Then they were alone. Ivy turned to Amber, noticed that her sister was frowning as she stared in a darkened corner of the room.

"What is it?" Ivy asked.

"You should try to heal Mia tonight," Amber said.

"Why now? Why not after I get some rest and have more energy?" Ivy asked, but the look in her sister's eyes gave her pause.

"Mia's really tired and having a hard time holding on," Amber said.

"How do you know that?" Ivy asked.

"She just told me."

Ivy felt as though the wind had been knocked out of her. She turned, but it felt as though she were moving through water. Regardless of how fast she wanted to move, it wasn't fast enough. She opened the door into the darkened hallway and she thought she could hear a faint heartbeat, not of her own pounding hard and fast in her chest, but one that was slow, quiet and unsteady. Ivy followed that sound further down the hallway. Either she would walk into Mia's room or she'd be explaining herself to Joyce as to why she was roaming around the house opening doors. At this point it didn't matter. If Amber could already see Mia it might be too late. Ivy's eyes adjusted enough that she could see two doors. One was on the right and one was straight ahead at the end of the hallway. She grabbed the doorknob on the door to the right and pulled it open. The sound grew louder, the smell of sickness was almost overwhelming at first.

A nightlight shaped like dancing slippers sat on a table near the small bed and cast pink shadows against the wall, illuminating the little body tucked into bed. Tears filled Ivy's eyes. The girl seemed so very small in the bed made up of ballerina sheets and a pink bedspread. An oxygen tank stood on the other side of the bed and a tube was secured in the little girl's nose. She was so pale that her dark hair seemed almost black against her skin. Dark circles shadowed her eyes, and her lips were so pale they were nearly white. Ivy checked Mia's chest for signs of breathing. The soft intake of breath was ragged, stuttering. The soft sound of a heartbeat grew so faint that Ivy could no longer hear it over the roar of her own. She was afraid she was too late.

The sound of footsteps on carpet and the opening of the door made Ivy glance over her shoulder. Amber had had come in and brought Gabe and Ryan with her. Gabe stood beside her and Ryan walked around the bed to stand across from her as Amber found her way to the foot of the bed. She met Amber's gaze and silently nodded her thanks. Using Amber's energy might not a good idea given all the changes they'd both been through. But, it was good to have her sister in the room, supporting her, helping her where she could. And if she did need more energy she was certain Gabe and Ryan would help.

When Ivy her hands on Mia's cold arm Amber's quick intake of breath caused her to jump back.

"What is it?" Ivy asked.

Amber was looking beyond Ryan into the far corner of the room near the window. Whatever she saw there must have scared her, because her eyes went wide with worry and she said, "Hurry!"

Ivy immediately laid both hands on Mia. She pulled on her own energy and moved it through her and into Mia. She knew immediately that Mia was too far gone and she would need help if they were to save her. Her heart hammered hard as she considered the consequences. She glanced at Amber again, looking for some kind of acceptance or encouragement for what had to be done to save the little girl, but Amber was staring intently from the corner of the room, across the floor, beyond Ryan and to the bed as though she were watching something move in that direction.

"Ryan?" Ivy looked across from her and put one hand out to him. She thought he might hesitate, consider what he might lose, but he didn't. His warm hand grasped hers and a jolt of hot energy flowed through him almost as though he were pushing it as Ivy pulled it from him. Ivy felt it flow through her, go into Mia, move around there, lose some of its energy as it filled her up, healed her body. It wasn't enough. Ivy could almost feel the void that used to be Mia's lifeforce. She glanced at Ryan who was pale and starting to sway. His eyes started to roll back in his head and Ivy let go of his hand before he fell to the floor.

"He's fine," Amber said before Ivy could ask.

Amber moved around the bed, and Ivy thought at first she was going to check on Ryan, but instead she took Ryan's place.

"Amber, I don't think we should use your energy to try and heal her." Ivy glanced at Gabe who nodded and put his hand out to her.

"I'm looking to help heal her," Amber said as she raised her arms over Mia's body. Her hands were palm down, just like they had been in the graveyard that day.

"What are you doing?" Ivy asked as she grabbed Gabe's hand.

"I'm pushing her back," Amber said as she closed her eyes in concentration.

Ivy pulled on Gabe's energy and pushed it into Mia, leaving Amber to do whatever it was she could.

This time, when Ivy touched Mia, it didn't feel like she was pushing energy into a void. Instead it was like someone had capped the void, and Gabe's energy mixed with Ryan's began to fill Mia's lifeforce. Mia began to heal.

Ivy could feel the energy move through the small body, pause in spots and burn there, then move on. Ivy grew dizzy and looked over to Gabe, who was as pale as Ryan had been, but he was holding on and remained standing. He moved his mouth as though he would protest when she released his hand. Then he did sway but caught himself and slowly lowered to the corner of Mia's bed to sit down. He bent over and put his head between his knees.

Amber had taken a step back and no longer held her arms out. Ivy watched her eyes scan the room and then connect with her. She smiled as she looked down at Mia.

Mia reached over with her free hand to grasp Ivy's fingers. She rubbed them as though she weren't sure Ivy was real, then she smiled.

"Are you an angel?" Mia whispered.

"I am tonight."

CHAPTER 19

WHAT'S GOING ON?" Joyce's voice sounded panicked when she walked in to find Ryan lifting Mia from the bed, but at the first sight of her daughter, she stopped in her track. Her expression transformed into a mix of shocked disbelief and stunned joy. The physical change in her daughter was so marked, no one could have missed it. "Mia? Mia!" She ran forward. "My god! Oh, my god!"

Mia reached out for her mother, a big grin on her face, color in her cheeks and pink lips that her mother immediately put kisses to just before kissing her entire face.

"What's happened?" Joyce spoke through kisses and tears. "How is this possible?"

"Ryan brought an angel," Mia whispered as though she wasn't used to being able to speak up. She cleared her throat and spoke again trying out her voice by adding some volume to it. "Mommy, the angel healed me." Mia's gaze found Ivy and soon Joyce turned to look at her as well.

"What did you do?" Joyce asked.

"Mom." Ryan's voice was commanding and Joyce turned to him. "We should probably go sit in the living room and talk, but we should get Mia back to bed first."

"I'm not tired!" Mia protested.

"I know baby girl." Ryan walked over and took her back into his arms. "But it's important that you get as much rest as you can tonight. That way we can spend lots of time together tomorrow."

Mia pouted, and Ivy wondered if anyone had the strength to deny the little girl anything. But Ryan touched his forehead to hers and held it there for a moment before shaking it slowly.

"You need to let us talk in private with Ivy and her sister. I've come a long way to bring you help munchkin. Now I need you to help me and get some rest." Ryan kissed her nose and laid her in bed.

"I don't want to sleep in here alone," Mia whispered. "Mommy usually sleeps with me." She pointed to a large chair near the foot of the bed that Ivy had barely noticed when she came in. There were blankets in the chair, a small pillow, books on the floor beside it.

"I have been sleeping in here with her," Joyce said. "I was in my room getting ready for bed and checking my email before coming back here, then I heard the commotion and…"

Joyce stopped, and shook her head in dazed disbelief. Ivy put her arm around her, and Joyce turned to hug her hard. She sobbed a thank you against Ivy's shoulder.

"How about this, munchkin?" Ryan started and everyone turned to look at him. "we'll leave the door open and Mom can come back in just a little bit for you?"

After a few moments more, Mia grudgingly agreed. Ryan tucked the little girl back in her bed, while the rest of them headed out into the hall.

"Let's go into the kitchen and I'll make us some tea," Joyce offered as she led them toward the kitchen.

"Is she actually healed?" Joyce asked as she put the kettle on and moved around the kitchen preparing the cups. "Or is this temporary?"

"She's totally healed." Ivy said, but her gaze went to Gabe, then Amber. The next question would be harder to answer and she knew it.

The tea kettle screamed and Joyce removed it from the burner and began pouring into the cups. She had a small tray laid out and put the cups, honey, sugar, and spoons on it and walked it over to the table to pass them out to everyone. She sat down with her own cup, a delicate, feminine porcelain cup with little blue flowers decorating the outside. She stared into the cup for some minutes, and Ivy was glad to have a little more time to think over her answer for the question that would inevitably come next.

"Is it easier if I don't ask how you did it?" Joyce asked, her voice soft, her gaze still focused on the cup.

"It's easier for me," Ivy answered honestly.

"I don't want to sound ungrateful, but did you use any drugs I should know about?" Joyce asked.

"No, I didn't use any drugs at all," Ivy answered. "I'm not really an angel." She added it as an afterthought.

Joyce laughed and glanced up at Ivy for a moment before looking back at her cup. The smile didn't fade away entirely, and it gave Ivy courage.

"I'm at a loss as to what to say. Maybe it's shock? I hoped for a miracle, but I didn't think I'd get one. You really can't tell me how you did it?" She asked.

Ivy shook her head, hoping Joyce wouldn't press the issue. At least not now.

"I don't even care how you did it," Joyce admitted. "All I care about is that my daughter isn't dying anymore. I would never do anything to jeopardize the gift you just gave me."

Her voice cracked and Ivy watched her fidget with the cup as it dawned on her what Joyce was getting at. She didn't care how it happened, no matter what the cost and she didn't want to do anything that might reverse the outcome. In an instant, Ivy realized the power her father held. People would do anything to save the person they love. Anything. Zachariah wielded that power as though he had a right, as though he were some God. He took life and he gave it, and the ability made him think it was his right to do so.

Ivy felt the weight of that responsibility. She could heal and that was a great gift that people would pay for, kill for. That realization frightened her. She didn't want people to beg her to heal their loved ones. She didn't want anyone to feel beholden to her like that. And she didn't want the world knowing what she could do, making her beholden to the world because she had an ability people would want to exploit. For good or for bad people would want to exploit her and her life would no longer be her own. No, it was best not to tell too many people. She appreciated Joyce's discretion and her willingness to just be happy without an explanation.

"What you do need to know is this." Ivy looked directly at Joyce. "You can tell people she had some kind of new therapy treatment, new drug, a miracle, whatever you want to tell them, but I ask that you never tell people about me, about what happened here tonight."

Joyce was already nodding, steel determination in her eyes.

"One other thing," Ryan interjected. "You need to take a vacation for a little while. Go somewhere for a couple of weeks."

"Why?" Joyce asked.

Ivy's heart hammered hard as she looked to Ryan and then Gabe. "There's a very dangerous man looking for us. He would do anything to anyone for information about us. He would hurt you. And Mia."

"People may have seen us come in tonight. We need you to go away so you can pretend you took Mia for treatments before you come back here with her healed."

"Ryan?" Joyce asked. "Are you coming with us?"

Ryan hugged his mother. "I have to go. I have to help them. I owe it to them. *We* owe it to them. And Gabe is right. We need to have a story for Mia's recovery. You go. I promise I'll take care of myself and I'll contact you as soon as I can."

"I understand. It's not easy, but I do understand. I'm already on leave from work." Joyce was nodding emphatically. She stared right into Ivy's eyes as though she could prove her commitment to doing this with a look. "I can leave tomorrow if that helps?"

"It does," Ryan answered, even though the question was meant for Ivy.

Ivy nodded and offered a smile. She took a sip of the tea then picked up the honey and a spoon. "That would really help," Ivy said as she tested her tea again. It was sweet and smooth and chamomile. Even though there'd been a lot of excitement with the healing of Mia, Ivy was totally drained, and as she took another sip she watched Gabe get up and walk over to her.

"I know you're tired," he said as he put his hand out to help her up. "Why don't you try to get some sleep? We need to get back on the road soon."

"Where are you going?" Joyce asked.

As Ivy stood, she felt a little dizzy and must have swayed as Gabe pulled her closer to him, held her there for just a moment to steady herself, and then he took her elbow and turned her toward the kitchen archway that would lead back down the hallway to her room.

"We're headed west," Gabe answered for her then added, "Right, Ryan?"

"Right." Ryan answered.

Joyce grabbed Ryan again for a long, bone-crushing hug, then let him go. "Get some rest." She said. "All of you."

Gabe walked her to the door, squeezed her hand and let her go, making way for Amber to walk in after.

The loss of energy, the drain of it all hit her and she was so glad when her head hit the pillow and her eyes closed out the world.

IVY WOKE WITH A START. Her heart beat fast, her breathing was erratic, she was sweating even though the room was cool. Looking around the room, she realized she was alone. The sun shining through the crack in the curtains over the window told her it was time to get up. She doubted it could be very late in the morning. Someone would surely have tried to wake her.

Getting up, she swayed a little, but the dizziness passed quickly and she moved toward the door. It opened just as she reached for it, and Amber walked in with a tray of breakfast and a smile. The smile on her sister's lips caused her own to rise, and the dream residue melted into nothingness, forgotten.

"I figured you were tired and wanted you to sleep in as long as possible," Amber said as she sat the tray down for Ivy.

"Thanks!" Ivy smiled, then looked back into the bedroom with a frown. "You know me so well."

Amber sat next to her and sat her hand on Ivy's leg. "I do know you." Amber patted her sister's leg. "I know you love with all your heart. That you sacrifice a lot because of the life we have. I know that we're not perfect. Either of us. Mostly, I know that I love having you as a sister and I'm sorry for making you feel bad."

Ivy took Amber's hand and squeezed it. No matter what lay ahead, they would be okay. Courage born of love was the strongest Ivy knew of. Ivy was smart enough to know she needed to fear Zachariah and his people, but now she was less afraid.

Amber nodded and moved away so Ivy could close the door. In moments she was able to throw on some clothes, make her bed and get everything put in her backpack so she'd be ready to leave. She walked out and met up with everyone in the kitchen, where she heard laughter before she could even get inside.

Gabe and Ryan were passing Mia back and forth while the little girl squealed with delight at being the "toy" everyone wanted. Gabe pretended to try to run out the door with her, but Ryan blocked his path and pulled on his sister, who was thrown over Gabe's shoulder. Ivy couldn't keep herself from smiling as she sat at the table to eat and watch the antics.

Joyce sat across from her and Amber sat close by watching the happy family, but speaking very little herself. Joyce had some papers in front of her and stopped long enough to welcome Ivy to breakfast.

"If it had been up to me, I'd have let you sleep all day." Joyce smiled. "But, your sister seems to think you need to get back on the road, and she sounded pretty convincing."

Ivy glanced to Amber and nodded.

"So what's next for you?" Ivy wondered if Ryan would be able to leave his mother and sister before they left the house.

"Ryan insists on not knowing where we're going, but I have a flight booked already and a wonderful destination to take Mia for some fun and peace. We leave here in about an hour. Ryan and Gabe want to personally escort us to the airport."

"The airport's not far from here," Gabe said as he gently sat Mia back onto her feet. Mia skipped over to her mom and took a seat right next to her. "We'll take her and come back for you and Amber. You can shower and maybe pack up some sandwiches and stuff?"

Ivy nodded. It was best to let the guys take them. It meant not leaving Joyce's car somewhere that the community might realize she'd taken flight. The longer it took for them to find her, the better for everyone. And Gabe seemed to be a natural at ditching unwanted company on the road, so having him take her was probably her best chance at going undetected, at least once they got on the road.

The house was in a flurry of excitement and energy as everyone prepared to leave. Joyce and Mia hugged her and then Amber as they were gently pushed from the house by Ryan into the awaiting car.

Ivy used the hour they said it would take to get them dropped off to shower while Amber went through the kitchen taking anything they might need for the rest of the trip. Joyce insisted they take everything they want. When Ivy got out of the shower and walked into the kitchen, she realized that Amber had taken that to heart since there were two full brown paper bags full of food and drink stuffs.

Ivy sat down at the table as Amber packed a few other items like napkins and plastic utensils. Amber had been very quiet ever since she fell into the lake. Amber's anger had diminished to almost nothing. As a matter of fact, Ivy couldn't tell if Amber was mad at her at all, but she lacked the courage to outright ask.

"You seem to be adjusting pretty well." She thought that was a safe way to broach the topic of Amber's new-found ability. Since Amber didn't seem to lose her momentum as she answered the question, Ivy thought that perhaps things between them were healing in their own way.

"It's too new to really say," Amber answered while finishing the packing and taking a seat across from Ivy.

Ivy nodded. It had only been a matter of days since Patricia died and Amber's ability came to life. Had it been two or three? Ivy felt as though time had no discernible lines by which to measure it. The days had melded together, and even the hours seemed to take on less meaning. She had taken to measuring the number of miles or the number of stops.

Ivy wondered if Amber felt the same, but that was less important at the moment.

"What did you do with Mia?" Ivy asked, but watched Amber's body language carefully to ensure she didn't upset her. "I mean, I know you helped. I just don't know exactly what you did."

Amber sighed and then glanced in the direction of Mia's bedroom, then back to Ivy.

"I could see her soul," Amber said. "When she was nearly dead I saw her, but as she was actually dying, leaving the world forever, I saw her soul take on that white cloud form like in the graveyard. I don't know, I just knew I could hold her in place if I pushed my energy into her life force. It just seemed natural, so I did it and it worked. I held her until you could call her back."

Ivy marveled at how calm Amber was about it. She knew what her sister was saying though. Her own ability was like that. Somehow she just knew what to do. It was as natural as breathing even though she had never been trained to use her ability by anyone.

Amber got up, and Ivy watched her as she poured some coffee into a cup. She nodded toward her as though she were offering to get a cup for her, but Ivy wasn't really ready for coffee so she shook her head and waited quietly until Amber sat back down.

"I don't think we should have any physical contact when we use our abilities. Do you agree?" Amber asked as she took a sip of the steaming brew.

"Yeah, that doesn't seem to be working well for either of us I think." Ivy nodded. She was a little sad that there was now this one thing they had between them that they couldn't share. Amber was her best friend in the world. They had always shared everything. But now they had to be a little leery of each other's abilities. Ivy wasn't sure why, but it seemed unnatural to have that between them.

"I need to go ahead and pack. Do you mind cleaning the kitchen?" Amber asked.

They went about busying themselves. Ivy kept watch out the window, being careful not to be seen, but being diligent about making sure no one was coming near the house while they waited for the guys. Joyce had given them the keys to her car just in case, but Ivy hated the thought of leaving the guys behind. Even Ryan.

Ivy thought about how Gabe and Ryan were so happy this morning playing with little Mia. It reminded her of how they were back home, close, friends, not just family. And Ryan seemed to undergo some change from the inside out. He appeared happy as opposed to his nearly constant brooding. He was a nice looking guy and she recalled that Amber had had a little crush on him when they first met. She wondered if her sister still thought he was cute, or if the water under the bridge was too much. Now didn't seem like the time to ask. Amber had enough to think about. They both did. With Mia healed and on her way to somewhere safe, they could all concentrate on Zachariah and the community. Even Ryan seemed determined to stop the community now that his own family had to be wary of them. Zachariah could want revenge on Ryan for helping them, and that had to be scary for Ryan. Now that he'd crossed that line and chosen a side, he seemed determined to see it through. He'd gone from wanting to go with his family in order to keep them safe to wanting to get to San Francisco as quickly as possible. She thought he probably wanted all of this behind him and wondered if it ever really would be.

Those thoughts naturally segued to thoughts of Gabe. His mother had gone home the day before they arrived, supposedly to get Gabe and bring him back to Colorado for Mia's final days. She'd overheard him on the phone with her telling her Mia had recovered and telling her she should call Joyce and maybe meet up with her to celebrate.

She wasn't sure what he'd told her about why he wasn't going on the celebration tour, but he never said anything to her about changing his plans.

She heard a car pull up and quickly went to peak out the window. The guys got out of the car and as they approached the front door Amber walked into the room.

Before ten minutes had passed, they were packed and on the road again, this time to San Francisco. Answers awaited them there. Ivy was sure of it. Of course she could never have imagined how devastating some of that information would be.

CHAPTER 20

IVY COULD SMELL THE ocean. It was early in the morning but light out. It was cold, and Amber lay quietly up against her window in the backseat, and noticed she had her part of the blanket pulled up to her chin as well. She smiled to see that they matched, just like old times. It was too cold to roll the window down, but Ivy cracked it to get some fresh air, then left it open just a little so she could pull in the cool salt air. The contrast between the cool air and the warmth beneath the blanket caused goose bumps to rise up on her arms.

"You're killing me, Ivy." Amber was looking at her in the reflection of the window.

"I love the ocean air," Ivy protested, which only won her a frown, but the frown didn't last so Ivy left the window slightly down and continued to enjoy the scent of the sea air.

"The bank won't be open this early," Ryan said.

"Yeah, I was thinking we should go ahead and get the lay of the land there, make sure there's nothing suspicious around, then find a nearby restaurant and grab some breakfast where we can keep an eye on the bank until it opens," Gabe replied.

"I want to recap the plan before we get there." Ivy said. "The idea is that we need to get into the community. If Zachariah's people find us here, Amber and I will go with them. They'll likely separate us. That's a pretty standard tactic.

Gabe, you and Ryan will wait a few hours and then call the police to report us as kidnapped. Patricia has given Amber the address in Montana where they'll be holding us. You give that to the authorities, tell them we're there against our will, being abused. That will send the FBI, not local cops who might on Zachariah's payroll."

"I don't like it." Gabe said. "I don't like the idea of watching them take you and not knowing what's happening to you, either of you, once you're taken to that place."

"Duly noted. Again." Ryan interjected. "It's a solid plan. And the only one that lets them get in and look for their parents."

"Right." Ivy agreed. "Amber and I will use our time there to try and find out where they have John and Helena. We just need to know where they are. Once the feds arrive we can have them get John and Helena out. That minimizes danger directly to us. We all leave with Zachariah and his people answer to authorities."

"Two issues to consider though." Amber added. "What if they don't have them there? And what happens if Zachariah claims we'd been kidnapped and brainwashed against him. What if the feds decide we need to stay with our biological father?"

"You're underage, taken across state lines by force, under duress," Ryan joined the conversation, surprising both Ivy and Amber at the serious thought he'd put into the plan. "Even if Zachariah claims you were kidnapped and stolen from him, the feds will remove you from his first, investigate and then decide what to do. By then you'll have an attorney and a good case against him, especially if they find John and Helena there."

"And if John and Helena aren't there?" Gabe asked.

"They have to be there," Amber rubbed both her arms as though the temperature dropped and she couldn't get warm. "But, if they aren't maybe we'll get a clue as to where they are. Either way, we have an exit strategy."

"And if no one comes for us," Ivy rolled her window up. "Helena mentioned a reservation near the community. I think that's where John grew up. Apparently no one on the reservation likes Zachariah and his people. Maybe we could get them to let us stay there while we case the place trying to find John and Helena? Especially if I'm right and those are John's people."

Amber nodded.

They drove until they found the bank. Even that early in the day, before the bank opened, probably before most of the bankers that worked there were out of the shower to prepare for their day, they were making plans for when they got inside. Ivy's name was on file at the bank and she had her identification with her. Still, her heart beat faster to be this close to finding out what information had been left to them. She figured John and Helena would tell them not to do anything dangerous, and of course they would ignore that. They planned on going to a cemetery afterward so Amber could speak to Patricia about whatever they found there in the bank.

Ivy wondered at how morbid her life had become. Her mother, murdered. Her sister drowned and brought back to life. Her own ability tied so closely with pain, dying and misery. Even if it was a healing power, someone needed to be healed in order for her to be needed. John and Helena may or may not be alive, or in Montana at all. Patricia dead, the only way to contact her was to visit a cemetery, and not to visit her body, but to talk to her ghost. There was only so much a person could take, and Ivy hoped and prayed that whatever they found out at the bank would give her peace and put things to rest. Or, at the very least, enlighten her as to where she should go next, what she should do.

They must have driven around the bank ten times, taking different routes, moving in larger circles around the building, then moving back in. Gabe identified a little diner that was within sight of the bank. It was busy with people moving in and out, staying to eat or picking up something to go. They found a table there that allowed them to watch the front of the bank.

Ivy ordered an egg and cheese sandwich and some orange juice, watching the comings and goings, hoping she might recognize any one of those people as someone she'd seen from the community. Not knowing if they were out there was almost worse than knowing for sure. But, no albino, no one she remembered from the diner. Thinking of the albino, she thought of Patricia. He was her brother. Briefly she wondered if he would even care that she was dead. Perhaps he saw the grave and already knew. There didn't seem to be any love between them that day at the diner. As that scene replayed in her mind, she became aware of the waitress dropping off their order and absently she picked up the sandwich.

Amber stared intently at her, but as she was about to ask her how her breakfast was her eyes shifted out the window and she immediately tensed up. The curiosity was like an itch for Ivy, but one she knew not to scratch. She continued to watch Amber's reaction as she pursed her lips and bit at her lower lip. She picked up her glass of water and took a sip, gaze shifting back to her.

"The albino is standing at the bottom of the steps in front of the bank."

Both of the guys continued to eat, but they glanced without moving their heads. Ivy ventured a look, but leaned back in her chair so it would be harder to be seen. They needed to all act normal and not call attention to themselves just yet.

He was there, and though he stood alone, Ivy had no doubt there were others from the community nearby. Her mouth went dry, and she nearly knocked her orange juice glass over reaching for it as she continued to stare out the window. Gabe caught the falling glass before too much spilled over. It drew Ivy's eyes to him, and he nodded at her. He knew how important this was. If they were caught, they might not find out what was so important left there at the bank.

"The good news," Ryan spoke softly. "If they know you're here, someone told them. The only people who would know would be John and Helena. Right? They must be alive."

Ivy grasped onto that like a life preserver. That had to be true. John and Helena must still be alive. And though she was so happy to know that, she immediately wondered how horrible things must have gotten for them to give away their position.

"It's possible they followed us from Colorado." Ryan said.

"And let us get this far from their home base before stopping us?" Amber asked. "Not likely. Possible, but not likely."

"I'm going to get you a shot at getting in there," Gabe said. He was so confident she thought he'd follow up with just how he was going to do that, but instead he stood up, threw down some cash on the table and walked out of the restaurant.

It was like watching a horrible accident and knowing you can do nothing to save anyone. Ivy stood, but by the time they got to the door Gabe was standing in front of the albino and blood was everywhere.

It wouldn't take long before the police showed up. Gabe punched the man straight in the nose, and it took him a minute to recover before throwing back any punches at Gabe. People were gathering around them, some taking pictures with their cell phones, some making calls, probably 911.

Warmth filled Ivy's hand, and she felt Amber's hand in hers. Looking up at her sister, she knew what had to be done. They ran.

Her heart beat fast and her lungs burned from the energy they put into moving as fast as possible. Across the street and up the stairs, as they reached the door the security guard was opening it, looking beyond them to the fight just outside the bank. Ivy worried for just a moment that he might close and lock the doors because of all the commotion, or because two crazy girls were rushing the doors, but instead he pulled the door wide open for them. They were the first in the door. First to the teller.

The woman looked as though she had skipped her coffee and was regretting it. She moved slowly, spoke slowly, and needed to be told three times before she comprehended what they were asking for. Finally, she called for someone else to come help them and asked them to step aside.

Ivy watched every person that walked through the doors. She wondered where Ryan had gone. She worried about Gabe. It took several minutes before she realized the bank was cold, and it finally penetrated her clothes and she shivered as she waited. Amber had taken to pacing back and forth in the small waiting area they were sent to. Like her, Amber kept watching the people who came out.

Ivy saw the flashing blue lights just outside. It occurred to her that Gabe may have caused the fight to buy them time initially, but he'd likely end up in jail. He'd have to call him mom for help and Ivy hated the thought of that. But, Ryan could still call the authorities. The plan was still in place.

An older, tall man came up to them and asked for identification. Ivy produced her ID and the key to the box. The man nodded and the three of them walked inside another room where they stood while he unlocked a barred door.

They walked into a room with several steel boxes of varying sizes. He walked her to a small one opposite the door. Amber followed in silence. Ivy and the banker opened the small box with their keys and the man asked if she wanted to be left alone. She nodded, and he left, walked out where he stood just beyond the open door.

There was a table and a few stools in the middle of the room. Ivy took one stool and Amber took the other so they were on either side of the box. Ivy pulled in a deep breath and let it out slowly, opening the box on the exhale.

Inside was a manila envelope and she removed that. She found a bundle of money, thousands of dollars it looked like. There were passports, one for everyone in their family, but with different names. Ivy gave those a cursory glance and zeroed in on two letters addressed to her and Amber jointly.

The first was from John and Helena.

> *Girls,*
>
> *If you are reading this without us, we are likely dead. Do not seek revenge. Do not do anything dangerous. Do not take any chances. Take the money and your new identities and head to New Orleans. There you will find Patricia's father, who is no friend of Zachariah. There is a map in this envelope. This tells you how to find him and what to do next. He tried to contact Patricia in the past, to tell her he wanted to see her, but it was too much of a chance that Zachariah would find you, so she never responded to him. Now she can find her father and hopefully get the help he promised her.*
>
> *Know that we love you as our own. We would never change anything about our lives because we got to live it as a family with you. We are proud of you. Now live your life with caution, but with happiness.*
>
> *John & Helena*

Ivy wasn't surprised that they wanted them to go on and stay safe. Still, the tears burned, spilled and refused to stop. She closed her eyes for a minute, trying to will herself to be calm. They were not dead. She refused to believe that. And they would just have to be mad at her and at Amber for disobeying them. They would find them. They would get revenge.

When she opened her eyes, Amber was staring at her, dry-eyed, but patient. She glanced down at the remaining letter, the one from Patricia.

Ivy nodded and reached in for the envelope. It wasn't sealed, so she removed the letter, opening it, finding two pages of instructions telling them pretty much the same thing John and Helena told them, telling them where to find her father and to be careful because she didn't really know him that well. She had an email address for him and a cell number. No address other than New Orleans.

It was the second page that brought Amber closer, leaning over her shoulder, reading the words over and over just as Ivy read them. She felt numb at first, then angry that she'd never been told. Emotions ran faster and faster through her until she realized she was panting heavily, as though she'd ran a race.

> *Dear Ivy and Amber,*
>
> *You must forgive us for not telling you this, but we knew that if you found out you have another sister you would do anything to find her. We always planned to tell you about Elizabeth when you got older.*
>
> *She was so small and we thought she was dying so we left her at a hospital where we knew she had a chance to survive. Where we thought Zachariah couldn't find her. We hoped she would survive and be adopted by a nice family who would love her and keep her from harm.*
>
> *A year ago, a friend who lives on the Sioux reservation near the community emailed me a picture, which I have included in the lock box. He's kept tabs on Zachariah for years. The people on the reservation don't trust him. The man was a friend of John's and helped Helena escape many years ago.*
>
> *I know you will want to save Elizabeth from him, but you need to realize that she will only know what Zachariah has told her. You can't trust her. She will be dangerous. Keep to each other. Wait until you're older and have the training to find her outside the community to talk to her.*
>
> *Don't go to the community compound. If you do, you will likely never be allowed to leave it. Not alive.*
>
> *Love,*
> *Patricia*

Ivy stared at the letter a few more minutes before reaching into the box once again. There was one piece left behind and she pulled it out. It had been printed on regular paper, but it was a photo of a young girl about fifteen years old. Her hair was dark. And though it was hard to really tell, her eyes appeared dark as well. But, there was no denying that she was looking into a face she knew very well. Her own. Amber's. She had another sister. Triplets. Elizabeth.

Ivy took in a deep breath and let it out slowly. It was as though she were meditating, feeling herself grow calm, blanking her mind and slowing her heart. She felt empty for just a few seconds, and like the passing of the eye of the storm, the calm broke and the storm took on a life of its own. The heat of anger burned in her chest, giving life to warm tears that spilled down her cheeks unchecked. Betrayal, grief and anger swirled like a tornado, and she felt herself sway from the force of it all.

Warm arms grabbed her and held her tightly. Amber was breathing hard, but instead of heat she had grown so cold it was painful to remain so close in contact with her body. Looking up, Ivy moved away from her but caught her gaze, holding there as wordless pain was shared between them.

"How could they keep this from us?" Ivy's throat hurt from being so tight with grief. "This isn't some little factoid they could give us later about our life. This is our sister."

Amber nodded. "What do you want to do?"

The emotions swirling around began to calm as Ivy changed her focus from the betrayal of having such an important fact withheld by the people she trusted most, to searching her mind, her heart, for a plan.

"We stick to the plan." Ivy felt her heart rate slow, become normal. "We try to find Elizabeth, too. Find out if she wants to come with us." Looking at Amber nod in agreement, she went on. "First we get John and Helena out. Then Elizabeth, if we find her and she wants to leave. If we don't, we can always go back for her."

Amber walked the few steps it took to be near her again. The cold was still there, but not to a degree that Ivy refused her hand when she placed it in hers. Amber's power had flared, but Ivy's wasn't active, so touching was okay. Amber knew what had to be done. She knew what had to come next, but she waited patiently for Ivy to voice it.

"We need to get into the community. Now."

Ivy closed the security deposit box, stuffing the letters, picture and other items into the satchel she'd brought for that specific purpose. She stood up and glanced to where the banker stood outside the door and nodded to him. They were ready to go.

The breeze outside was cool, but the sun kept the day warm. Ivy stood at the foot of the steps of the bank, Amber by her side, and scanned the area. Since neither Gabe nor Ryan showed themselves, she had to assume one or both of them had gone to jail over the fight Gabe started with Patricia's brother, or they'd gotten away and were watching them from somewhere nearby. A twinge of guilt at having put Gabe in that situation rode the cold breeze, making it hard to enjoy the warm sunshine. An emptiness in her heart, knowing she would likely not see him for a while, took away any remnants of the ability to enjoy what was turning into a beautiful day.

Ivy had no doubt that once Zachariah had them it would be extremely difficult to get away. She hoped the plan worked. The only choice was to fight for the ones they love. No matter the cost.

She watched the faces of those people who passed them by. No albino. A slight smile tugged at the corner of her mouth as she thought about Gabe beating the crap out of the man who would betray Patricia, his own sister. The smile faltered as she thought about how Patricia had betrayed her and Amber by keeping a secret from them that should never have been a secret to begin with.

It was only she and Amber in the end. She reached out and took her sister's hand finding it still cold, but not so much that she couldn't hold it in her own.

From across the street, near the restaurant they had been waiting at, a young, pretty brunette in heels so high Ivy wondered how she could move in them headed their way. As she grew closer, a man in a dark suit and dark sunglasses joined her. By the time they reached them, another woman, more military looking with her pony tail, camouflage pants and olive green tank top, stood next to them as well.

"Will you come peacefully?" the woman in the high heels asked.

Ivy nodded, and the woman looked to Amber. She turned and the woman with the pony tail walked behind them while the man stood beside them. As though it had all been choreographed they stepped in time, surrounding them, forcing them to walk in time along with them. Their small group didn't go far before a dark van pulled up alongside the street, the side door opened and they were pulled and pushed inside.

There were benches inside the van and Ivy refused to let go of Amber's hand so they both sat on one side next to each other. The three who had walked them to the van sat opposite them and a large, muscle-bound man in casual clothing who had pulled them in sat next to them. Ivy took in the interior, looking at the railing that ran down the side of one side of the van. She could imagine that was there to tie or cuff someone to, but no one had made a move to secure them to it. If any of them had weapons she couldn't tell. The inside was dark and her eyes were still adjusting.

A sound from the front of the van caught her attention and she watched a man in the passenger's side next to the driver turn his body around so he could face them.

He was tall, older, dressed in a suit much like the man who walked them to the van. His cologne drifted up to her and she hated to acknowledge that it smelled good when everything inside her wanted to hate everything about everyone. His hair was mostly gray, but there was still some streaks of black in it. With the light behind him coming through the windshield it was hard to make out his facial features, but his voice boomed loud, confident and with a bass tone that have been called soothing if she didn't recognize its predatory cadence.

"Hello girls." The effort to sound charming only irritated Ivy. "Welcome home."

"This isn't our home. The community isn't our home." Ivy felt bile rise up in her throat.

"Home is where your family is." He continued.

"And you have our family, don't you?" Ivy wanted someone to tell them where John and Helena was. Now that they had given themselves over to the community, she wanted something in return. A little information. A little hope.

"I am your family." He said as she leaned forward and Ivy could see his face.

"Zachariah." Ivy's heart felt as though it had stopped. In her mind she had seen his face, so different from her own. She wanted to be nothing like him. But she was. They shared a similar ability. And, looking into his eyes, his face, she saw a likeness she never imagined. One she knew she would spend a lifetime trying to forget. All she had to do now is survive.

CHAPTER 21

IVY HELD ON TO Amber's hand as long as she could, but they took her. They held each other through a locked gaze until Amber was put into a dark sedan. No longer able to see her sister the cold fingers of fear crept into her heart. She was totally and utterly alone now. She knew this was likely to happen, but that didn't stop the apprehension growing in her heart. Her concentration, her attention, was split between the fear she held for what might be happening to Amber and the fear of what was about to happen to her as she sat in the van with her father, waiting for a private plane at a small airstrip near SFO.

She understood why they would want to split them up. If the goal was to brainwash them, this was the best way to start. Take away everything. Leave nothing but fear. Then offer to make things better, gain trust, give small tasks that would be rewarded. Ivy had no doubt she would play along until she knew where Amber was. She had been in her father's company for less than two hours and already she hated him.

The door of the van slid open and the young man in the dark suit helped her out. She heard the passenger side door open and close, but she didn't look. She followed the guy in the suit to where a small plane awaited them. She was helped inside and soon her father joined her.

"Where's Amber?" Ivy couldn't help herself. She needed to try to find out what happened to her sister since Amber didn't seem to be joining them on the plane.

"She'll be along in good time." He said and then offered her a bottle of water that she refused. He smiled, took one for himself and sat back in his chair, put the bottle down long enough to buckle up and took out his cell phone.

Ivy wasn't going to give them the chance to tell her to buckle up, she just did it. She listened to her father tell someone they were coming and that he had both she and Amber. It was a short call and it told her nothing of where her sister was.

Ivy leaned back and closed her eyes, hoping that would close out her father's attempts to draw her into conversation and that seemed to be working since he left her alone for the remaining two hours they were in the air. She had no idea where they landed, but there was another dark sedan similar to the one where they'd just left and Ivy's gaze held to it, hoping Amber might be inside.

They got out and she was lead to the car, but when the door was opened for her she saw it was empty inside. Her heart sank, but she got inside and moved over to make room for Zachariah.

The man in the dark suit got in on the driver's side and soon they were on the road. She did her best to track where they were going, every turn, every mile. There were no big cities, but she did see a couple of gas stations and one small town big enough for golden arches. The signs they passed told her they were in Montana.

The exit they took brought the car around a sharp turn and beneath an underpass that put them on a two lane road lined with trees so thick it caused shadows to mimic the night. Half an hour later they turned onto a dirt road that was difficult to see from the road. Only fifteen minutes on the dirt road and they crested a hill brining her within site of the infamous community compound.

Two large steel gate doors stood open with a couple of sentries standing guard. They nodded as the car drove through and into the compound. Ivy could see a tall fence nearly ten feet tall surrounding the buildings, making the compound secure. It was difficult to say how big the place was. There was a large white building toward the front where they drove in which appeared to be a community center. She saw a general store, a gas station, a shop with what looked like homemade clothing in the window. As they continued on their way she saw other buildings that she thought might be a medical clinic, vet, dentist and in another area was a cluster of stores with signs on them that she couldn't make out, but they appeared to be stores of some sort.

Several people walked throughout the compound with purpose, carrying various item, or empty bags. The women were dressed modestly. None of them were smiling.

Five minutes went by as they drove slowly away from what made up the main compound and soon they were in what she would consider the residential area of the compound. There were shacks, well made, but small, larger homes, and then at the end of a cul-de-sac there was an elaborate two story home, white with pillars in the front, very southern looking. The landscaping around this house was immaculate and beautiful with fountains, rose bushes and statues everywhere. The car pulled in front of this house and stopped. Of course this would be Zachariah's home.

A woman walked out of the front door and Ivy's full attention followed her as she came to meet them. She was too old to be Elizabeth and Ivy's heart sank. The door opened and the woman looked first at her, then beyond her to Zachariah. Something passed silently between them and the woman turned a big smile on Ivy as she extended her hand.

"Welcome!" She said, bright and cheery.

Ivy ignored the hand and got out on her own, which pushed the woman back a few steps in order to make room for Ivy to stand there. The sound of another door opening and then footfalls crunching on gravel told her that Zachariah was out of the car.

"Come inside Ivy." Her father's voice was still smooth and calm, but the hairs on the back of her neck stood up as she looked at the open door of the large house and realized it was like a gaping mouth, about to swallow her up.

Her convictions were still there. She needed to be here and she kept telling herself she was here because she wanted this to happen. She wasn't captured; she tricked them into taking her. Of course she worried that she'd still not seen Amber. She took in a deep breath, straightened her shoulders and walked up the steps and into the house.

Her eyes adjusted quickly to the darker interior. It was as elaborate on the inside as it was on the outside. Everything appeared pristine and white on the walls, but the furniture was all dark wood, antiques. The smell of honeysuckle filled her nose, a smell she normally liked, but knowing this was Zachariah's home's smell she thought she may never enjoy honeysuckle again. She wondered briefly if this was the house her mother lived in. Was this the smell she woke up to every day? The smell that road the air of the last breath she breathed?

The woman who greeted them stood near her at attention like a little soldier. As Zachariah removed his jacket she rushed to take it and draped it over her arm, looking up at him as though she waited for further instructions.

"Mabel, this is my daughter Ivy." Zachariah finally introduced them. Mabel smiled and nodded at her.

Ivy took inventory of doors, items that could be used as weapons and any idea of where Amber or John and Helena might be.

"I am happy to meet you." Mabel said as she smoothed the jacket in her arms like someone might a favorite pet. "I will have the sister wives prepare your room and set you up for a bath and a fitting."

Ivy stared blankly at the woman. Sister wives? It was one thing to hear Patricia talk about this place, these people, but to hear it spoken like it was a natural way to live, it felt surreal. For a moment she thought to protest, just because she felt the need to. But, she knew that would not help her fulfill her real goal. Cooperation would get her closer to what she needed. She nodded and when Mabel motioned for her to follow she spared a glance for Zachariah who watched her every step of the way. If he were waiting for her to fight, to make a scene, he would be waiting a bit longer. She turned and followed Mabel upstairs.

At the top of the stairs Ivy saw several plants in tall plant stands lining the path down the hallway. There were lovely paintings between the doors that lined each side and there were several doors. She wondered if the rooms were filled with sister wives and the thought of it made her shudder.

Toward the end of the hall Mabel opened a door on the left for her.

"This was your mother's room once." She smiled.

Perhaps she thought that would make her more comfortable, or less likely to destroy things or make a mess. Ivy wasn't sure what the woman thought the benefit of sharing that information would be, but Ivy couldn't deny the curiosity. She walked inside and Mabel followed her, closing the door behind her.

She may have just stepped through a time machine because the room appeared as though it was decorated in the 1950's and left that way as part of some museum display. She tried to imagine her mother here. Was this the same décor? Did she lay in that bed and look up at that ceiling?

"I was there the day you and your sisters were born." Mabel said behind her making her jump just a bit and sending her heartbeat pounding.

Ivy turned toward the woman. She was in her late forties if Ivy had to guess. Older than Patricia for sure. Her hair was dark and pulled back into a bun. Her clothes were modern, but modest. No make-up, but she did wear simple gold band on her ring finger of her left hand. The smile she used to greet her was gone entirely, replaced by a severe straight line of the lips and a slight furrowing of the brow. Ivy imagined that this was the real Mabel and she was glad to see it. Everything would be easier if she could just hate these people for letting her mother die. She didn't want to have to save anyone else. She had her hands full just trying to figure out what to do about finding John and Helena.

"Really?" Ivy asked, but would not give her the satisfaction of any emotion at all.

"Your mother was not well liked." She said as she walked to the bed, sat down Zachariah's coat and smoothed the covers. "She died right here in this bed." Her eyes cut to Ivy's face, but Ivy had already shut down. Nothing this woman said was going to get a reaction. At least not the one Mabel wanted.

"I'm sure my mother was just heartbroken that she wasn't popular with the sister wives." Ivy dripped as much sarcasm into those last two words as she could muster. Still, her gaze wandered over the bed despite her trying not to show that she cared.

Mabel harrumphed and frowned, shaking her head. She picked up the jacket again and headed toward the door.

"Someone will be here soon to get you situated. Stay in this room, understand?" She asked.

Ivy nodded and turned her back on the woman. The door closed quietly and Ivy was glad to be alone for a few minutes. She immediately went to check the window, but it was barred. There was a door in the room that lead into a small bathroom that also had a barred window.

Her gaze was pulled back to the bed and she walked there and ran her hand over the pillow. Kicking off her shoes, a habit ingrained in her from Helena, she laid down on the bed and stared at the ceiling. She closed her eyes and imagined she was her mother and wondered what she might have felt being pregnant so young and with triplets. Married to a man she didn't love, then murdered by him because she wanted to give her daughters a different life.

"Mom," Ivy whispered into the room, tears burning behind her eyes.

The click of the door opening brought Ivy up and she swung her legs over the side of the bed. A young woman about her age walked in with a towel and a robe. Like Mabel, she smiled when she saw her.

"Hi! I'm Sarah! I've been assigned to you. I have everything you need for your bath." She seemed genuinely happy as she walked into the room, closing the door behind her. Ivy thought it was strange that anyone could be happy here. For any reason. She'd not seen any of the other women look cheerful as this girl was.

Sarah eyed her for a moment and Ivy prepared herself for more hateful remarks like the ones she got from Mabel, but instead Sarah's eyes lit up.

"I think we're the same size!" she remarked as she walked around Ivy. "You can use some of my clothes until your own come in!"

Sarah reached out touched Ivy's hair, which made Ivy take a step away. Friendly or not, no one here under Zachariah's roof, under his influence, could be trusted, not even the seemingly happy-go-lucky Sarah.

Sarah didn't appear to notice Ivy's reaction.

"Let's go get started getting you familiar with how things are done here. The day is lovely out. I'll ask if we can tour the compound. I'm not sure if I'm to do that or if you'll need to wait for your sister." Sarah held the door open, motioning Ivy to follow.

"Where is Amber?" Ivy hoped the young girl might divulge that necessary information. "Amber?" Sarah asked quizzically. Then she paused and her expression changed to understanding. "Not Amber. Elizabeth!" Her smile was wide as though she had just delivered the best news ever.

"Elizabeth?" Ivy could only hope that her other sister would be willing to say where Amber was being held.

"Does Elizabeth live here, too?" Ivy asked as she patted down her damp hair, buying a little more time with the young, talkative girl. "How many people live in this house? It's very big and very beautiful."

"Elizabeth isn't married yet, so she lives here. There are ten sister wives, Elizabeth."

"So if Elizabeth lives here, is Amber here too?" Ivy hoped she'd get more information, but Sarah stopped, seeming to reflect.

"I'm not allowed to tell you anything. I've already said too much." Sarah looked genuinely worried.

"Well, I don't want to get you into any trouble. I was just curious as to when I'd see my family. Don't worry, I won't tell anyone you said anything." Ivy was more concerned that Sarah might tell someone that Ivy was asking a lot of questions. Ivy would need to find out information in small bites it seemed. That was fine. Often, being quiet and cooperative lead to others feeling comfortable enough to talk. And Ivy wanted people to talk to her.

The communal bathroom was further down the hall and quite large. There was a shower in one corner and a bathtub in the other. A vanity that had three sinks in it and a large mirror over it was located between the shower and tub. There was a small enclosed room that contained two toilets sitting side by side. Ivy cringed just a little at the thought of sharing a bathroom with so many other women at the same time and couldn't even imagine sitting next to someone while she went to the toilet. Could these women really feel like sisters just because they were married to the same man, or was there a closeness between them that went beyond that. Nothing she saw so far showed even friendly camaraderie. They were from the same community. Ivy wondered about the dynamics of the women's relationships, growing up led to believe they became real sisters perhaps through the joining with one of the men. The entire thought of it was disgusting to her and she tried to stamp that out, telling herself that just because they had a different belief system didn't make them bad or wrong. Right on the heels of that thought she remembered that these girls were forced to marry much older men when they themselves were young teens. She watched Sarah lay out toiletries for her. The lovely dark-haired Sarah couldn't be more than seventeen and she was already a sister wife. Ivy swallowed hard as she thought about her father and Sarah together. Yeah, that was disgusting, and if there were any way to do it, Ivy wanted to get all of these young girls away from this place.

"There's no lock on the communal bathroom," Sarah smiled as she walked toward the door." Sarah informed her. "So you may want to hurry if you're shy."

The door clicked behind Sarah and Ivy stood in the center of the room alone. Part of her wanted to remain there alone, away from the stress that was coming, the danger, the heartache. But, something stirred deep inside her and warmth flooded her veins, forcing her to move. More than needing peace was the need to find her sister, her family and get the hell out of this place. She wondered how long it would take for the authorities to respond and whether or not Gabe got away before the police arrived. It could be that there wouldn't be a lot of time to search for John and Helena before the FBI showed up. With that thought Ivy rushed to the shower and moved as fast as she could to complete her task. Within minutes she was finished and sat on a nearby bench wearing only a towel until Sarah walked in with clothes in hand.

The young girl smiled brightly at her as she handed over a pale pink, simple dress made of muslin. It was something Ivy associated with the Amish, simple but pretty. Sarah's dress was off-white and Ivy wondered at the variety of the clothes they wore. The style was the same though.

"You're quick like a bunny!" Sarah told her as she handed Ivy the clothing. "These are for you. They're mine from when I was..." she paused, blushed deep red and looked away before continuing, "before I was married."

It didn't even take a full second for Ivy to realize what the pink stood for; virgin. She didn't question why the dress wasn't white. She had no intention of learning the ways of the community. She smiled at Sarah and thanked her for the dress even though it made her blood run cold to put it on, to assimilate. But, fighting over clothing would do nothing but tag her as a troublemaker and she wanted to cooperate in everything that didn't really matter so she could be reunited with her sister. She just hoped that Amber had the same thought.

"Okay!" Sarah opened the bathroom door and motioned for her to follow. "Let's go! They've got dinner set up and we're going to celebrate finding you!"

Walking down the stairs Ivy took in everything she could just as she had when they walked in. The interior was much like Ivy's room reflecting bygone days. There were several pictures lining the wall as they descended the stairs, but most of those were pictures of what she guessed to be the community itself over the years. She slowed down as she reached a photo near the end of the stairs where the picture showed five men standing in front of yet another iteration of the. This photo was easily the oldest one of those she saw on the wall. Her eyes grew larger as she recognized the man in the center as her father. The other men looked very much like him and she guessed them to be brothers or cousins. Her father had been quite handsome once. There was no mistaken him though, with his cleft chin, hard eyes and tall stature.

As her eyes passed over the men they were drawn to some scrawl scratched at the corner that was partially hidden by the frame. She could make out the number 18. Another picture had a number in the corner, but it was a date from the 1960's. Ivy couldn't imagine that the photo of Zachariah was dated in the 1800's. That wasn't possible. Of course, a lot of things about Zachariah weren't supposed to be possible.

Ivy reached for the picture to examine it more closely but the sounds of a deep gasp drew her gaze instantly to the sound. Sarah stood there with a stricken look on her face. Ivy's hand hung in the air near the top right corner where she would have lifted it off the wall. Immediately she withdrew her hand. Sarah's expression was enough to change her mind.

"It's your family." The deep baritone sound of her father's voice rang out behind her on the stairs.

Ivy's head whipped around, a jolt of adrenaline shooting through her body. Zachariah stood at the top of the stairs looking down on her.

"The picture looks old." Ivy remarked.

"Yes, it is. That was taken when we first moved the community here back in 1827." He began to walk down the stairs toward her.

Ivy felt pinned by his gaze. She couldn't move. As he moved closer, her heart pounded in her ears and her stomach lurched with fear. His expression still showed no signs of anger, but something about his approach screamed predator and it screamed danger. It was as though he wore his own power like armor. Not the power that healed or killed people, but a power of knowing he was judge, jury and executioner. For the first time she knew she had underestimated him. She'd always known that he could kill without remorse, change lives at a whim and should be avoided at all costs. Now she knew there was so much more to him than that. His power was nearly palpable. The fear that washed through her and held her in place was unexpected. She hadn't felt this when she first saw him. But, now she was in his lair. She was caught not only by him, but by everyone else who served and feared him. Now, looking into the most cunning and dangerous face she'd ever seen in her life she worried, she and Amber would never be let out of this place. The plan they'd come up with to escape seemed less solid as she stood there in Zachariah's presence. She had to hope. She had to keep moving forward with the plan.

He stopped directly in front of her and turned his attention to the picture on the wall. Something passed over his face, like a shadow of some emotion he was unused to. She watched that shadow of emotion soften the hard edges of his mouth just a little. Then it passed and his eyes grew even harder, his lips clamped tight and the look that replaced his mask of indifference caused her to take a step back from him. For that brief moment she saw the face of the man who murdered her mother. A sense of self-preservation made Ivy turn and continue down the stairs to join Sarah who stood there, face bowed until Zachariah walked by them wordlessly toward the rooms to the left of the stairs.

Ivy glanced one last time to the photo and thought about the date. He had to be in his late twenties in that picture. Maybe early thirties. The picture was taken in 1827. That put her father at well over a hundred years old.

"Never touch his things!" Sarah whispered in fear at her. "Girls are sent to the punishment room for less."

Sarah was breathing hard as though she had just run a mile. Their eyes locked and the smiling, happy Sarah appeared much older now, less like a sweet young girl and more like an animal caught in a trap.

She moved around Ivy, walking as fast as she could, putting distance between them, probably for her own self-preservation.

Ivy could only guess at what the punishment room held for these girls and women. She hoped she would never find out personally, but the odds were she'd find out soon.

CHAPTER 22

THE DINING ROOM WAS huge with a table that was eight feet long. At the head and end of the table were chairs of honor. Ivy knew these were special because the plates there were golden while the rest were all white. There were also red roses next to the golden plates, and then a large, matching bouquet in the center of the table.

Mabel walked in followed by several women who Ivy figured ranged in age from seventeen to fifty. Mabel took the place of honor at one end of the table. She stood just behind the chair and watched each of the others take a spot as though she were a mother hen making sure each chick was present and accounted for.

Only four chairs were left, the head of the table, the chair just to the right of that one and the one right next to that. Sarah led Ivy to the chair just right of the head of the table and indicated that she should stand there. Sarah took the one next to her. They all stood at attention until the door opened and Zachariah walked in, taking his place at the head of the table.

Once Zachariah pulled out his chair and stood in front of it the others pulled out theirs and followed suit. Zachariah bowed his head in silence, the others followed suit. This gave Ivy a chance to look around without fear of being seen. The room had two doors: the main door from the hallway was just behind Mabel and the door where Zachariah had entered was on the opposite end, behind his chair. A row of tall, thin windows lined one wall and the white curtains were embroidered with small red roses. Each curtain was pulled to the side, secured with a white ribbon so it was easy to see out the windows into one of the rose gardens that surrounded the house.

As Ivy squinted at the windows trying to see if they opened or not, the sound of movement snapped her attention back to the people circling the table. They reached out joined. Sarah took Ivy's left hand, then Zachariah took the other. Ivy flinched, trying not to show her aversion to the personal connection. She stilled herself and kept her gaze fixed forward.

"Will Elizabeth be joining us?" Mabel asked.

"She's still at the wedding." He answered. Before Mabel could ask another question he said, "You'll save her dinner for later. This wedding doesn't require a reception, there will be no food."

A couple of the sister wives stifled gasps making Ivy wonder if the wedding Zachariah referred to was forced since it sounded as though there was no celebration going on. Her heart went out to the poor girl forced to marry some older man against her will. That seemed to be the way of it. From what she'd seen, younger men worked, older men married. She could be wrong, she realized, but none of the younger men she'd seen so far had wedding bands on. She'd specifically looked, wondering how the relationship dynamic worked in a place like this. Her thoughts were interrupted when Zachariah began speaking again.

"We are here today to celebrate life and acknowledge the power that gives us the community we have here." Zachariah's voice boomed. "I am happy to announce that my long search is over and my daughters have been returned to me. But, more than that, I want to thank the great life essence that gives me power, that my eldest daughter, Ivy..." with this he pulled her hand up to draw everyone's attention to her, "is the first female in our bloodline to be blessed with the power to heal."

A collective gasp from the group drew Ivy's gaze from one woman to the next around the table. Some smiled, some appeared shocked, Mabel pursed her lips and furrowed her brow. Confusion clouded Ivy's mind for a moment. Was she really the first girl in their family to have this kind of an ability? The amazed faces around the table said it was true. Ivy tucked that information away to examine later.

"Ivy will be married next week to one of our own so that her special gift may be joined with a gifted male and bring a new line of blessed and powerful people to the community." Zachariah squeezed Ivy's hand causing her to look at him, revealing the shock she couldn't hide. He smiled broadly as applause erupted around the room.

He released her hand and that seemed to signal to everyone that they could sit. Sarah pulled on Ivy's sleeve. Ivy was the only one still standing.

Numb, Ivy knew she needed to be very careful about how she responded to the news of her impending marriage. Taking a slow, deep breath, she took her seat and kept her gaze focused on the plate in front of her. She didn't dare look at anyone for fear of revealing her growing sense of panic. If the FBI didn't hurry with their investigation Ivy wondered how the hell she was going to get out of this.

Ivy flinched when someone standing beside her plopped a piece of baked chicken onto her plate and broke her concentration. Pushing down the panic she glanced up at a woman wearing black and white as she turned and walked on the other side of Sarah to put chicken on her plate as well. In a quick succession several other servers walked in with various bowls and plates, but these were set on the table and Mable began orchestrating the passing around of these containers so the women and girls could choose from these. The sounds of people serving themselves, whispered requests, pouring of water or tea created a buzz that only served to poke holes in Ivy's calm.

"You need to eat." Sarah whispered. "There will be nothing else served until breakfast."

She couldn't even look at the girl. Her stomach rolled and pitched and bile rose up regardless of how hard she employed her meditation training. She swallowed hard and shook her head just once.

"Snacking isn't allowed here." Sarah implored her to eat. After a beat she leaned in closer to whisper as softly as she could. "He's looking."

A jolt of surprise caused her to look over at the young Sarah, but by then she was already giving all of her attention to the meal, loading up a roll to her plate and asking for the tea to be passed.

Was Sarah really as happy as she made everyone think? Did she simply want peace or was she concerned for Ivy's welfare? Was it possible Sarah might actually help her? Ivy tamped that down. No, she couldn't entrust anything to Sarah, not her fears, not her plans. Not only because Sarah might tell someone, but because Sarah could be punished for helping her. Ivy was on her own until she found Amber.

For nearly an hour Ivy forced herself to nibble at chicken, place salad on her plate, pour herself tea and sip it, but mostly she went through the motions, pushing her food around on her plate to make it appear as though she participated in the so-called celebration dinner. When her plate was removed and replaced with a small piece of cake the sounds at the table increased, more whispers and some soft laughter told her that desert was a novelty in this house.

She managed a bit and then cut it into small pieces so no one would know how little she ate. The plates were removed and when Zachariah stood up everyone else followed, standing at attention once again until Zachariah moved away from the table. Ivy breathed out a sigh of relief that was short lived as she heard her father's booming voice call out to her.

"Come with me Ivy."

There was nothing to do but follow him. A glance back at Sarah told her she would be following him alone. He led her through a confusing maze of hallways. Ivy did all she could to try and take in every detail, storing the information for a possible escape route later. They entered a small library and Zachariah motioned to her to take a seat in front of the empty fireplace.

The room smelled slightly of cigar smoke, but there was a faint lemon scent that covered it and Ivy wondered if they used that to mask the smoke smell. Zachariah stood near the mantel.

It wouldn't serve her to disobey or be impolite. She still had questions, she still needed to see her sister. So, she sat quietly.

"I realize you've been through a lot, but this time next year you'll be fully integrated into our way of life. You'll have a husband, maybe even a child by them. All of this will be a memory and you'll look toward the future instead." His tone was flat, less encouraging and more authoritarian. He could care about her feelings, she realized as she watched him open a box that sat on the mantel and pull out a cigar. "Your husband will help you assimilate. You will have a good standing here since you are so unique." He fished for something in the box, brought it out and used it to snip the end of the cigar.

"Elizabeth also has a unique ability. It seems that only Amber was denied a blessing of power. But, she will serve a purpose here as well, as everyone here does." He took a seat in the other chair near the fireplace and reached for a lighter that sat on the small table next to him. The lighter was one of those old fashioned ones that required flint and fuel. He flipped the lid open and used his thumb to spin the wheel that lit the flame. He took a puff on the cigar, another puff and the shut the lighter lid down, extinguishing the flame. Another puff and he leaned back as though the smoke relaxed him somehow.

Ivy watched closely, waited quietly, but her mind was a storm of fear and confusion. At least he didn't know about Amber's ability. That could have condemned her to an unwanted marriage as well. But, what Amber's so-called "purpose" would be sent ice racing through Ivy's veins.

"Where's my sister?"

"Your sister is being prepared for her own type of service." His tone didn't change and he continued to puff on the cigar.

The smoke snaked through the air toward her as though she were prey. The smell was repulsive and Ivy leaned further back against the chair trying to escape it. She was trapped on so many levels.

"Will I see Amber today?" Her own voice remained level and she was proud of that accomplishment.

"Not today, but she will join us here tomorrow if all goes well."

"What does that mean? 'If all goes well'?" A slight elevation in the pitch of her voice brought a smile to his lips. She berated herself for slipping and giving him the satisfaction.

"If you cooperate. And if she cooperates, the two of you will be reunited soon."

"What is it we need to cooperate with?" Her voice was under her control again, but her heart was not. It beat hard and though the room was cool she felt herself flush as she tried to reign in her emotions.

"You'll marry in two days' time. You'll follow your training, wear what you're told, do what you're told and learn the ways of the community so you can be an asset to us."

"And Amber?" The steel in her voice held, but the ice ran again in her veins as she waited to be told her sister's fate.

"Oh, well, Amber just needs to learn our ways, follow them and obey her husband." He smiled again.

"You're going to force her to marry someone too?" Ivy knew they needed to get out right away, with or without John and Helena, they needed to regroup and find another way back here to find them. This was crazy.

"Oh, Amber was married earlier today. But, never fear, her husband is well respected in this community. She will be well cared for. She married her second cousin, Daniel. You may recall him, he's very unique looking. An albino."

The walls seemed to close in on her and she was grateful to be sitting already. Her mind blanked and adrenaline filled her body. The burn behind her eyes threatened tears.

Amber had followed her lead and agreed to come to the community in order to find John and Helena without having to ask Patricia for help. Thoughts of her sister's fear and disgust at being forced to marry Daniel filled Ivy's mind. Quickly on the heels of that came the thought of the wedding night, only hours away and that brought her back into herself. Determination rose inside her, fierce and furious.

Zachariah sat there puffing on the cigar, the smoke filling the room with its stench. Everything about him filled her with loathing. He was smug, so confident in his power to control everything and everyone. The violence within her rose up like a tidal wave, and the overwhelming need to launch herself at him and inflict any bodily harm she could manage was held in check by one simple fact: she still didn't know where her sister was. And now Amber needed her more than ever.

The door on the other end of the room opened, and a young woman dressed in white walked in. At first, Ivy thought it was Sarah, but, she had darker hair, long and flowing. She was more petite than Sarah, and walked with complete confidence. Ivy watched her as she would a predator. When the girl stopped in front of Zachariah, Ivy swallowed hard.

She knew she was looking at her sister, Elizabeth.

The room spun, then seemed to shrink in on her and grow cold. There wasn't enough air. Ivy began to breathe in shallow and fast as she wrapped her arms around herself for warmth and tried to take control of herself again.

Elizabeth looked very similar to Ivy and Amber, but her hair was dark and long. Her skin was lightly bronzed as though she'd been outside a lot, much like Ivy and Amber. Her eyes weren't like Zachariah's brown – or Ivy and Amber's blue. Instead they were a stunning shade of violet, so bright you couldn't help but look into them. She was slightly more petite, but appeared healthy. Looking at her Ivy couldn't help but wonder two things; did Elizabeth need saving, or would Ivy have to take her down along with Zachariah. From the haughty look Elizabeth was giving her, she doubted there would be any help from Elizabeth, or any love.

Moments passed by wordlessly. A tear spilled from Ivy's eyes, creating a warm, wet path to her chin. Ivy wiped at it and willed herself not to cry.

Her training had included meditation, concentration and of course Helena had taught them always take in what was around them, who was around them and consider what might be going on that she could *not* see. Falling back on those lessons she closed the door to the whirlwind of emotions that threatened to consume her. She willed herself to remain perfectly still as her sister moved further into the room, toward her.

"I'm Elizabeth." She said and her voice smooth, soft and warm. It was deep, like their father's, but feminine. She seemed older in a way that had nothing to do with looks. "I'm your sister."

"I know who you are." Ivy hadn't realized she'd been holding her breath and the words rushed out as she exhaled.

Elizabeth nodded, her face serene, her movements fluid. "Why don't we go see Amber?"

Ivy's gaze flicked up to where Zachariah still sat smoking his nasty cigar.

He said nothing, so Ivy nodded her assent and got up.

Elizabeth smiled and even that movement seemed elegant. Her hand reached out slowly as though she were afraid Ivy might bolt. After a brief hesitation, Ivy took Elizabeth's hand and followed her, leaving Zachariah sitting there with his cigar.

Elizabeth led Ivy through the house and out into a garden at the rear. Together, they followed a path made of red bricks. Each displayed the name of a woman and had a date below it, some with two dates. Elizabeth squeezed Ivy's.

"Those are father's wives." She said. "When he marries, they are given a brick in the garden. Each of them becoming a part of a path in the life of the greatest healer the world has ever known. It's an honor."

"Some honor." Ivy whispered. Elizabeth either didn't hear, or ignored the remark, so Ivy asked, "Some of them are dead?" Ivy had guessed at the bricks with two dates separated by a dash.

"Yes," she answered, "Then the bricks are a memorial to them. And they are buried in the community graveyard near the back of the town."

"So this is an official town?" Ivy tried to take in as much as she could of where they were going. She needed to know the lay of the land. "I saw some buildings when we came in that looked like stores and one that was a big building that I figure is a community hall or church or something."

They rounded a tool shed near some particularly fragrant yellow rose bushes. Ahead of them the brick path ended and concrete walkway began. The path ran alongside a gravel drive. Just ahead stood two white, simple single story homes. One had yellow rose bushes in the. Elizabeth steered her in that direction.

"Not a church." Elizabeth explained. "A town hall. And we're not officially a town, we have no post office, but we're self-reliant and have our own form of local government that everyone follows and respects." She slowed down as they grew near the house with the rose bushes and turned back to smile at Ivy. "We're here! This is Amber's house."

They walked up to the door and knocked. Almost immediately a young girl of perhaps twelve or thirteen answered. The girl's face glowed with excitement.

"Hello Elizabeth!" She smiled and opened the door wider allowing them to come in.

"Hello, Bea," Elizabeth answered. "This is my sister Ivy."

Bea turned her bright smile to Ivy. The girl was bronzed much darker than Elizabeth. She wore a lavender dress and not white or pink so Ivy wondered once again what it meant, but it was just a fleeting question pushed to the back of her mind as looked around the house for signs of her sister.

The house was immaculately clean just like Zachariah's. It was smaller and more simple and had more modern decor. She was surprised to see a television set inside a white cabinet, a box that she guessed was for DVDs and what looked like a box for a smart TV. There were speakers on opposite ends of the room against the same wall. They were also white as was most of the furniture. An archway led into a dining room, furnished with a chrome and glass table. A large bouquet of freshly cut yellow roses had been set on the table as a centerpiece.

"I'm not really supposed to cut the flowers," Bea said, leaning toward Ivy and lowering her voice to a conspiratorial whisper. "I'm not a gardener. I'm assigned to this house and Daniel likes yellow roses so I try to put fresh ones around the house."

"Where's my sister?" Ivy asked the young girl.

Bea's cheeks reddened and she cast her eyes to the ground as she answered. "She's getting ready for her wedding night. She's in the master bathroom right now and I'm not to disturb her until she calls for me."

"Where's the bathroom?" Ivy pulled free of Elizabeth's hand. She was more than willing to test Elizabeth's training when it came to hand-to-hand combat if that's what needed to happen in order to see Amber. But, Elizabeth didn't object when the young girl pointed to another open archway that led down a hallway. Ivy's feet took flight as she rushed by the young girl and down the hall. Hearing the sound of running water she knocked on the door. When no one came she began to pound on the door.

"Amber?" she yelled, her mouth close to the wood of the white door. "It's me, Ivy!"

Ivy heard the sound of a soft click of the lock being turned, and the door opened up just a crack. Amber peeked out, threw the door open to yank Ivy inside, then slammed and locked the door behind them.

Immediately Ivy put her arms around Amber and squeezed her tight. Amber winced, but held on tight.

"I knew you would come." Amber said, her voice so soft Ivy could hardly hear it over the running water in the shower.

Ivy had to pull away and that was when she saw the first of the bruises that covered Amber from neck to ankle. There were two distinct types of bruises: a series of small round bruises that looked like pinch marks, and an even more disturbing series of long, raised welts. The welts looked like they would bleed if you touched them roughly.

"What happened?" Ivy whispered.

Amber opened her mouth as if to answer, but only a sob escaped. She crumpled to the floor in a heap and started to cry. Ivy dropped to her knees beside her. She wanted to embrace Amber, but there was no place she could touch that didn't have some bruise on it. Finally, she leaned in and touched her forehead to Amber's, caressing her sister's head, whispering, "It's going to be alright," over and over again. They both knew was a lie, but she said it anyways.

Finally, after a few minutes, Amber's body stopped trembling. She used the top of the towel to wipe her face, breaking away from Ivy just enough that they could look at each other.

"They forced me to marry the albino." She said and fresh tears fell down her cheeks. "I said that I wouldn't do it, that it wouldn't be legal if they forced me without my consent. So they sent me to the punishment room."

With that she lifted her arms to expose more of the damage. The towel fell to her waist and Ivy gasped at the welts over her sister's chest and breasts, moving down over her stomach. Amber pulled the towel up.

"They beat you to make you marry him?" Ivy's stomach lurched.

"They beat me, but that's not what made me consent." Amber said, more tears gathering and falling down her cheeks. "Ivy, they brought Gabe and Ryan here, and they have John and Helena."

Ivy's heart felt as though it would shatter. She was glad to hear that John and Helena were alive, but if they had Gabe and Ryan then no call was made to the authorities. There would be no rescue. The plan had failed.

"We're on our own." Amber sat up straighter and pushed back hair that had fallen in her face. "There's no one to help us now."

Ivy felt a jolt run through her body and her mouth went dry. "Why would they take Gabe and Ryan?" Ivy had never considered Zachariah would take them.

"Collateral." Amber said as her eyes began to dry up and the first traces of anger replaced the sadness. "It's all about control. Ryan, John and Helena are all being held in the same place. It's a house, but it's more like the town jail. But Gabe..."

Amber swallowed hard and looked away before she continued.

"They were forced to watch the wedding. Ryan tried to stop it and when they started beating him Gabe jumped in." Amber drew in a deep breath. "He hurt a lot of them. But, when he bloodied Daniel's nose, they called in reinforcements. Gabe is still in the punishment room. I don't know if he's even alive. I heard someone say Zachariah told them to leave him that way as an example."

The sound of a key in a lock gave them only seconds before the door swung open and they reached for each other, embracing despite Amber's wounds. Elizabeth looked down at them, no emotion. She glanced up at the shower and frowned as she walked over and turned the water off. Ivy thought she heard her say, "Wasteful girls," but wasn't sure since it was said before the water stopped. Elizabeth turned.

"We are the Faith Healer's daughters." She said in a authoritarian tone. "We are expected to make our father proud. Do what we're told. Contribute to the community. I realize you two have been through a lot of trauma. I realize you've been lied to and are likely afraid of your new life right now. But, this is your home. We are your family. You will need to get it together and start learning the ways of your new life. So, get up," she looked at Amber directly. "Get dressed. And then join us in the living room so we can talk. Ivy? Come with me."

Ivy released Amber and stood, her blood growing hot as she thought of Amber being beaten. Gabe could be dead and there would be no cavalry to save them.

"Elizabeth, you need to listen," Ivy began, "We don't want to be here. Look at Amber. I don't give a damn about doing anyone in this community "proud". This is wrong. You must know on some level that this is wrong."

For a moment Ivy thought she saw the glimmer of compassion in Elizabeth's eyes as she looked at Amber still sitting on the floor.

"I wasn't there to stop them from beating her." Elizabeth said, her voice growing soft. "That shouldn't have happened, but Daniel has a temper. If Amber would have just cooperated she'd not have been beaten, and your friend…" she let the rest die on her lips.

"Help us," Ivy tried to reason with her. "You know what Zachariah is doing here is wrong. You can't just kidnap people, force them to marry. This kind of violence, is this what you think community is about? Is this what *you're* about?"

"I will ask father to come here and take care of Amber. You just don't understand our way of life here," Elizabeth took one step back just outside the door. "You'll learn though. But for now, Ivy, you need to come with me."

Ivy adjusted her stance, her feet slightly apart. "I'm not going with you. You're going to tell us where our people are and you're going to drive us off this compound."

Elizabeth's expression changed and she appeared a predator just as she had back in the library. "That's not going to happen."

"I think it is." Ivy challenged and took one step forward.

Elizabeth put one hand out in front as though to ward Ivy off. "Our father is no fool. People are reporting to him each time we pass certain areas. If I'm in this house more than twenty minutes, your friends will suffer for it. If I'm in this house more than half an hour, one of your friends will forfeit their life." Elizabeth looked at her watch. "It's been seventeen minutes. Even if you could fight me and win, I guarantee you it will take you more than three minutes to do it. And if I walk out of her bloody, which is the only way I'll walk out of here, someone will know what's going on and, well, I'm sure you can guess the rest."

Ivy wanted to slap her. She wanted to take her down and take Amber out of this place. But, Ivy had no doubt someone was monitoring their every move. Saving Amber could cost the lives of several other people. Thinking back at the look on Amber's face when Patricia died Ivy knew Amber wouldn't want other people harmed while trying to save her. This particular fight wasn't one she could win. Not really.

"Amber?" Ivy held her hand out to help her sister up, but kept her attention on Elizabeth.

"I don't want anyone hurt," Amber's voice trembled, "Not to save me. Go with her. Hurry."

"Come with me Ivy," Elizabeth's expression softened. "I'll check in and give you two ten more minutes together. Let's let her get dressed."

The front of Ivy's dress was damp from holding Amber close, but she didn't care. The coolness of the room where Elizabeth led her caused goose bumps to rise on her arms and she began rubbing them vigorously for warmth as she sat on one end of a white couch.

Elizabeth called in for twenty more minutes. She never mentioned the altercation between them. Ivy wondered if the half-hearted gift was an olive branch or a way for Elizabeth to deal with her guilt.

It wasn't long at all before Amber arrived dressed in pink, which gave Ivy a small amount of comfort. Not everything was lost yet.

Amber sat on the couch next to Ivy and they leaned against each other without thought, naturally needing the comfort only the other could provide.

Elizabeth sat in a large, over stuffed, white chair across from them. She watched them for some moments before speaking.

"Daniel's been healed of his injuries, but his temper isn't to be trusted right now, so Amber," she pinned Amber with a gaze that was part anger and part resolve, "You will continue to wear the pink dress until tomorrow night to give your husband a little time to cool down. After that you'll find green dresses in your closet. You'll be working in the gardens. Someone will be by to get you for training."

Amber said nothing, but Ivy felt her relax against her as she was told Daniel would be unavailable this evening to claim his marriage rights.

"Where is Gabe?" Ivy had to know what happened to him.

"Don't worry about your violent friend, sister. He is still alive and currently residing in the punishment room, where he will remain until after you wed George Thomas."

"And then?" Not that she was planning to stick around. Now that she knew where Amber was and Amber knew where everyone else was, they would be getting the hell out of here.

"After that Father will negotiate terms for the release of your friends." Elizabeth told her.

"Negotiate terms? With who?" Ivy asked.

"With you of course."

CHAPTER 23

ELIZABETH HAD NO INTENTION of letting them speak in private once she delivered her own message, which Ivy was sure was really Zachariah's. Elizabeth stood after announcing that it was time for she and Ivy to leave and promising Amber they would return once Amber's wedding night obligations were fulfilled.

"Elizabeth, what part of that is okay with you?" Ivy tried once more to reason with her.

Elizabeth's gaze fell to Amber and once again Ivy thought she saw some emotion flit across Elizabeth's face, empathy maybe, or concern or maybe she just imagined it. Either way Elizabeth stood tall and confident as she shook her head.

"We all have to deal with the consequences of our actions. That's why we have a punishment room. If you don't want to be *corrected* for your behavior then choose an acceptable behavior." The last was said more like memorization than a warning. "Amber is of age to marry and her husband is well respected here. She will be the first of Daniel's wives, which is a great honor and puts her in charge of the household even when he takes other wives. And as far as being here against her will...are you crazy?" Her tone finally changed and it took on a sharp edge. "You two were kidnapped, brainwashed and then left to fend for yourselves. You were compromised by those two boys. You could have died! I can't understand how you could be so selfish! Our Father, our flesh and blood father, your real family, has been searching for you for years! He never gave up! He was heartbroken! And you want to throw his gifts and his love in his face and spit on his good character instead of just being obedient daughters and showing some appreciation?"

By the time she finished her tirade her voice was booming and she was standing nose to nose with Ivy. Ivy was sure the flushed red cheeks on Elizabeth's face mirrored her own. As Ivy stepped back Elizabeth seemed to relax, confident she'd made her point. That was Elizabeth's first mistake.

Ivy brought her hands up and popped Elizabeth in the nose hard enough that blood ran out of both nostrils. Elizabeth staggered back, clearly stunned, tripped on a corner of the chair she'd been sitting in and fell hard onto the off-white colored carpet that was now speckled with blood.

Ivy turned and Amber was already standing there, eyes wide, jaw clenched. They both turned to Bea and the little girl blanched as she looked from Elizabeth to them again and again like she was watching a ping pong championship.

Amber walked to the girl and gently placed her hand on her shoulder. The girl appeared as though she might faint, but Amber ran her hand along the girl's arm, taking her hand and leading her to the dining room where she sat her on a chair.

"We aren't going to hurt you Bea, okay?" Amber said gently. Ivy saw her sister look around the room and walk to the drapes to remove the tiebacks.

"Twenty minutes of extra time may be the only time we get." Ivy told Amber. "We should have fifteen more minutes left to get everyone and get the hell out of here. Is there a phone here?" Ivy asked Bea.

Bea shook her head. "The men have cell phones."

Elizabeth began to stir.

"Stay down there Elizabeth and I won't hurt you." Ivy advised.

That only seemed to enrage Elizabeth and she moved with lightning speed up, leaping to her feet brining her hands up like a boxer. Elizabeth punched out toward Ivy's face, but Ivy was ready. She grabbed Elizabeth's fist and pulled her around so hard that Elizabeth lost her footing and fell to the ground. She scrambled to her feet, turned and faced Ivy once more.

Ivy was already waiting and lashed out for her sister's nose again. This time Elizabeth screamed out in pain, swayed and dropped like lead to the ground where she doubled over, holding her nose and rocking back and forth.

Amber ran forward and joined Ivy. Bea was tied securely to a chair in the dining room, her mouth filled with cloth and tied so she could not scream out for help.

They didn't need to discuss anything, they bent down and each took one of Elizabeth's arms to pull her up. They walked her into the dining room and sat her next to Bea. Amber ran into another room and came back with duct tape and a large knife. She began cutting strips of the tape and handing them to Ivy. Ivy took a napkin that was laying on the table and began wiping the blood off of Elizabeth's face.

"We can't tape her mouth shut if her nose is bleeding like this. And I don't want to heal her." Ivy said more to herself than to Amber. "Can you get me something more absorbent than this?" She needed to keep Elizabeth from calling for help, but she didn't want her to be unable to breathe.

She watched Amber disappear and come back with a washcloth, but when she went to get the knife to cut it into scraps of cloth Elizabeth elbowed Ivy and in one swift motion grabbed the knife and plunged it into Amber's side. Amber couldn't keep from crying out as she looked down at the protruding knife.

Ivy was on Elizabeth again, but this time she couldn't stop herself. She hit Elizabeth in the face over and over until Elizabeth lay unconscious on the floor. Amber was breathing heavily, still holding the knife as a red ring of blood flowed from it.

"No!" Ivy whispered. It was all she could think as she saw her sister's life's blood flow out of her. "No! No!" She grabbed the towel and tried to stifle the bleeding. Her hand went toward the handle of the knife, but Amber stopped her.

"I could bleed out if you remove it." Amber said, her face white, sweat already on her lower lip.

"I don't know that I can heal you. Our powers can't mix. I just don't know." Ivy felt the cold fingers of tragedy grasp her heart and it whispered the secrets of fate to her, her sister would die and with all the healing powers in the world, she couldn't save her.

"I know." Amber said. "You need to get out of here."

"I'm not leaving you." Ivy felt the heat of tears run down her cheeks.

"John, Helena, Ryan and Gabe all need you to focus right now." Amber's breathing became shallow and even her lips were white now. The blood was running out quickly and now it ran down the dress and dripped onto the carpet.

"No!" Ivy said with conviction. "This isn't the way things are ending for us." Something snapped inside her like a wall crashing down and behind it was her calm, her resolve. All of a sudden everything was crystal clear, every color was vibrant, she could hear everything around her and she just knew. She knew what she needed to do.

"There's a graveyard not far from here at the back of the town. We can make it there. That's your power. We get you there and maybe you can save yourself." Amber nodded. Bea was staring in horror at Elizabeth. Ivy followed Amber's gaze.

They must look like monsters to the little girl who had so obviously cared for Elizabeth. Ivy reached out her hand and placed it on Elizabeth. She pulled the energy that was inside her, let it flow down her arm, through her hand and into her sister. But when the power entered Elizabeth's body it was like the energy magnified and Elizabeth took in a deep breath, her eyes popping open wide and she sat forward, confused but no longer bleeding. Her broken nose had even healed and when she looked up Ivy thought she saw awe reflected in her eyes.

"You're no better than Zachariah and all his men beating and forcing them to do things against their will," Ivy leaned in close to Elizabeth's face, the venom of betrayal feeding each word. "No matter how you were raised, you know right from wrong. You would have your sister raped. You would have someone I love killed just to keep us here. You make me sick. If I was anything at all like you I would just kill you right now. But, I was raised by decent, loving people, not some whacked out psychopathic douchbag with delusions of godhood. I'm showing you mercy, because I know what it is. Ask yourself, Elizabeth, why you can't show mercy to your own sisters?"

Ivy stepped away feeling, not drained, but invigorated. The energy had flowed back to her from Elizabeth and she felt like a lit up Christmas tree full of bright energy. Ivy capped her power like you'd cap a bottle. She gagged Elizabeth now that her nose wasn't bleeding and took Amber's hand to lead her away from the house. Elizabeth had bought them enough time to try to escape. Now Ivy hoped there was enough time to get Amber to the graveyard so she could live.

Amber led them out the back of the house where a huge rose garden lined either side of a gravel walkway. She was limping, putting the least amount of weight and stress on the side that was bleeding.

"Amber? Do you know where the graveyard is?" Ivy whispered.

Amber nodded, "I can feel it."

Ivy put her arm around Amber taking as much of her weight as she could and they walked out the back door.

The rose garden opened up into a vegetable garden where several girls dressed in light green clothing were picking vegetables and putting them into sacks they had draped over their shoulder. They all looked up and stopped what they were doing, watching Ivy and Amber make their way across the field of greens and disappear behind several rows of corn.

Ivy waited to hear someone call out, or sound an alarm, but no one did. No one followed them, either. Amber began to stagger as they continued past the corn rows and into a clearing full of clover and grass, a stand of weeping willow trees on the far side. Amber lurched toward the trees. A small graveyard filled with crosses and headstones lay just beyond the trees.

The moment Amber stepped past the first headstone she pulled the knife out of her side. A sound that was something between a scream and a sob tore from her throat. The bloody knife fell to the ground and a few steps later Amber fell to her knees.

Ivy rushed to join her. "What next?" Ivy asked. If there was anything she could do she would, but her fear was that all she could do was sit there and watch helplessly.

"Keep an eye out for whoever comes after us. I'm going to need a little time." Amber's breath was shallow and each word sounded like she had to forcibly push it out.

Ivy grabbed the knife that Amber had dropped on the ground. She wiped as much of the blood off as she could so she could keep a solid grip on it. She glanced around the graveyard. They had some measure of cover with the trees, but she scanned the area looking for a better place to hide. She had no idea how long it would take Amber to heal. If it was going to be more than a few minutes they would need to hole up somewhere.

The sun was setting everything would be cast into darkness. The moon was only half full, so there would be little natural light. Ivy walked over to the crest of the hill and looked out at landscape beyond trying to find a safe place to bring Amber until they could figure out a plan. Ivy walked toward an ornately carved marble crypt with the name "Williams" over it. Glancing from headstone to headstone it was apparent the graveyard was as old as the town itself, with most of the graves being those of women, several children who seemed to have died within the first year of life, but those were mostly the older graves. There were men, some buried in the center of a group of women's graves. Ivy reached the crypt and pushed on the door. It opened easily and she looked inside. With the sun dropping, casing shadows within, Ivy wasn't sure she wanted to go inside, but the place was clean, well kept. Thinking to herself that it was better to hide with the dead than be found by the living she turned back and ran to Amber.

"Look," Ivy told her, out of breath and full of adrenaline, "right over the crest of that hill you'll see a crypt. The door is already pushed open. Go inside and close the door. Stay there until you heal. I just need to know where to find John and Helena. They'll help me get Gabe."

Amber nodded, getting to her feet and stumbling forward. Ivy caught her, but Amber righted herself quickly. There was already more color in her face, her lips no longer white.

"Follow the walking path from the east side of Daniel's home. It will lead you to the house they use as a jail." Amber struggled to speak, but it sounded less painful.

"There are a lot of dead people here." Ivy warned, wanting her to be prepared for when she crested that hill.

Ivy stood straight and on her own two feet as she nodded and began to walk. "Yes, I know. I'll be fine. Go get the others."

Leaving Amber to heal herself, Ivy turned and darted back through the willows towards Daniel's house. She knew better than to take the same path back and she circled around being careful not to be seen as she stepped through a curtain of flimsy limbs. The sun was gone, but it was still light enough to see her way in the light colored gravel. She passed the vegetable garden, but it was empty. As she neared Daniel's house she could hear voices and she fell back between some bushes, ignoring the scrape of thorns across her skin.

Elizabeth was standing with a group of men at the back of Daniel's home. She hadn't changed her clothes and was still covered in blood. Ivy shrank back more when Zachariah rounded the corner to join the group as though he might somehow feel her presence. She quickly collected her courage and leaned forward just enough to watch the group. Daniel was there and inside Ivy smiled as she saw the huge black eye and split lip that she figured came from Gabe kicking his ass.

A boy in his mid-teens came around the corner of the house with flashlights in his arms. Several of the people from the group helped themselves to a flashlight and then they all turned to Zachariah. Ivy strained to hear him, but his voice was so distinct and so loud it wasn't difficult to listen in.

"I want half of you to walk the parameter of the town, check all exit and entry points. No vehicles may leave until the girls are found. Understand?" His booming voice held a hint of anger and everyone was quick to nod in understanding. "George Thomas and his men will start going through stores and houses. Every building is to be checked. George?" He called out. And from around the corner came a very tall man that Ivy presumed was the man her father had promised her to.

He was tall like Zachariah, but that was the only similarity. Where Zachariah was thin, this man was very muscular, almost to the point of being deformed. She guessed his age as being in his mid to late forties. His hair was cropped extremely short giving her the idea that he was probably balding and trying to cover it up by keeping it buzzed. His clothes were tight had color and patterns; red with a tribal flair at the shoulders. His face was sharp and harsh. It appeared his nose had been broken at some point and the very end of it was bulbous and red. His brows were connected by a thick line of hair. The thought of being forced to marry this man made her skin crawl. He walked quickly for a large man and as he joined Zachariah and the group he began to speak, his voice as booming and angry as Zachariah's was.

"One of the women from the garden thinks she saw them heading toward the graveyard." George said.

"Very well," Zachariah answered. "Send half your men to check buildings and send half to the graveyard. I'll join Elizabeth at my home. Bring them there when you find them."

George nodded and everyone began to disperse. Zachariah cast a last glance across the area and Ivy's heart pounded as she pushed back as far as she could into the rose bushes, feeling thorns bite into her skin.

Several minutes passed and Ivy held on to the knife so tight her hand began to cramp. She ventured to peer out and saw that the back door of Daniel's house was standing open, but no one was outside. She stepped out into full darkness and kept her eyes wide open, searching the area with every step she took.

It was difficult to see inside of Daniel's house because the lights were off. She skirted the area staying close to the rose bushes until she found the path Amber had told her about. She looked up as far as she could see, most houses had lights on but she noticed one house with all the windows blacked out. That had to be it. The path seemed to stretch out for over a hundred feet, though in reality Ivy doubted it was really that far. The real problem was that there was no cover other than a rose bush here or there. She could see movement beyond another large garden and hear knocking on doors, voices, some yelling "Clear!" as they searched buildings.

She thought about just making a run for it, but a running woman would call attention faster than one walking, so Ivy steeled her nerves and palmed the knife, keeping her arm down at her side. She walked with purpose toward the house she hoped she'd find her family in. Halfway to her destination she saw a couple of men walk out from the rose garden and take notice of her. She could see they were discussing her, but she couldn't hear them. They began to walk slowly in her direction, but she was pretty far ahead of them. She picked up the pace a little, but not so much as to appear to be trying to get away from them.

She nearly tripped over her own feet as she strained to see everything around her, but focus on the house that grew closer and closer with every step. Just as she reached the house one of the men called out to her.

"Hey! You! Girl! Stop!"

She pretended not hear and rounded the corner out of their sight. Her heart beat hard as she scanned the area finding a young man of perhaps twenty years old standing guard on the porch. She smiled and waved at him, which brought him over to meet her as she walked toward him. She didn't see a weapon, but that didn't mean he didn't have one. She waited until he was close enough for her to pull up the bottom of her dress, freeing her legs and kicked him with everything she had.

She heard the air rush out of him when she connected. The look of surprise was all she needed to encourage her to follow up immediately with another kick, let go of the dress and start punching. He stumbled and fell, hitting his head on the porch railing. He lay there without moving, but she could see he was breathing. She reached out and touched him, this time she sent her energy in and closed her eyes. She willed herself to pull back on the energy, like pulling a punch, to make sure she didn't heal him back to consciousness. She'd never tried that before and hoped it would work, but with the nasty lump on his head from where he hit it growing immediately she wanted to make sure he didn't die. For all she knew he was the only good guy in this place. She wouldn't judge everyone here, not when she knew her mother, Patricia and Helena all once lived here and they were all wonderful human beings.

Time was not her friend, especially not when she knew those two men coming this way would be on her in just a few moments. She left the young man on the porch and ran to the door, heart pounding harder and harder. The door was unlocked and she opened it slowly. It opened into a spacious room with little furniture. It was a two-story house and she had to find everyone immediately so she took a chance.

"John? Helena? Ryan?" She called out. If anyone else was there watching over the prisoners she was about to meet them.

Immediately footfalls overhead sounded and she could mentally watch whoever it was running upstairs along the path that took him or her to the stairs. Her gaze concentrated on those stairs and soon a woman appeared. She was older than the man, maybe thirty, but larger than him. Ivy watched the woman descend the stairs and as she got halfway down Ivy prepared herself. A few more steps and Ivy started running. She aimed for the woman's knees and hit her so hard she nearly lifted her off the ground. The woman fell against the wall before falling down the last few steps. Ivy balanced herself, turned and jumped on the woman while she was still down and on her back. Again she heard the sound of air rushing out and a grunt when she landed on the woman, pinning her with legs on either side of her. Adrenaline spurred her into action and she just started hitting her, but the larger woman was not going down as easily as the young man outside. She threw Ivy off and got to her feet. The woman moved fast for being so large. She took a step back from Ivy and then put both hands in front of her, not exactly like she was surrendering, but it held Ivy back and caused her to look into the woman's face. Her eye was swelling already and her lip was bleeding, but she didn't appear enraged which is what Ivy thought she'd see there.

"Stop." She said, breathing hard as she continued. "I know who you are. I want to help."

Ivy considered that it was a trick, but time was running out as she heard the sound of feet coming up onto the porch, male voices mumbling and excited, then the door was kicked open.

The two men who had yelled at her as she was coming toward the house rushed them. One had what appeared to be a billy club in his hand, the larger man was armed with some of the biggest fists Ivy had ever seen close up and personal and that one swung out at her head the second he laid eyes on her.

Ivy moved back before he connected, then stepped back again as he swung out a second time. There was a fireplace nearby and her eye caught site of the poker standing against the brick of the fireplace. She moved again and again away from the slower man until she reached it and as he charged her she picked it up and swung out. The loud crack when it struck was sickening to her and he fell immediately, the hook on the poker was embedded into his head, his eyes already glazing over. She saw movement out of the corner of her eye and heard a loud crash which brought her attention to the other man with the club and the large woman fighting at the foot of the stairs. The man was wielding the club, striking out at the woman but missing the majority of the time, hitting objects or air. As he brought the club around and missed her again she took that opportunity to grab his wrist and pull him toward her then step out the way letting him fall into the steps, the club flying out of his hand. The woman jumped on his back, a loud crack filled the air again, but this time the man went still.

The woman was breathing so hard Ivy worried that she might be having a heart attack. But, when she turned her bruised face toward her she slowly smiled in triumph. She got up and walked quickly to Ivy, glancing at the man with the poker sticking out of his head, but seemingly unaffected by it.

"My name is Catherine, you can call me Cat." She extended her hand as she approached and years of conditioning brought Ivy's hand up to greet her. The hand was large and warm and strong.

"I have to hurry." Ivy spoke and realized she was nearly breathless herself. The woman had just taken out one of Zachariah's men. Ivy would give her the benefit of the doubt, especially given that she could really use the help about now.

Ivy reached out to see if there was any life left in the man she'd hit with the poker, but Cat's larger hand whipped out and grabbed her wrist.

"If you heal them, they will punish me." Cat looked directly into Ivy's eyes. The worry there was enough to make her stop and consider her choices. She was a healer; she didn't kill people. But, she also wouldn't put someone in danger who had helped her and her family.

"Come with us."

Cat shook her head. "I can't. My daughter, Sarah, is one of Zachariah's wives. I can't leave her here." She stood straight, wiped at some blood that ran from her lip as she pursed them. "There are girls here, even some of the boys and men, who want out of here, but no one dares cross Zachariah or his brothers. No, you get out while you can. Take your friends. But promise me you'll come back for us. You'll help us get out."

Ivy nodded, grateful to have an ally and happy to promise to put an end to the madness of the community. She reached out then and lightly touched Cat's cheek. The bruising started to clear when Cat stepped back leaving Ivy's hand in the air, touching nothing.

"I need the bruises." Cat looked at the other two on the floor and Ivy knew immediately why. Cat needed to appear as though she put up a fight.

"Where's my family?" Ivy asked.

Cat moved quickly as she motioned for Ivy to follow her, not upstairs, but to the back of the house. One large room was sealed off except for a single door that was metal with several locks to it. Cat brought out keys from her pocket and started unlocking the door. Ivy heard movement inside and the moment the door swung open she motioned for Cat to go in first and followed her.

John and Helena sat together on a cot meant for one and the moment they saw Ivy they rushed toward her. They nodded at Cat and Helena reached out to squeeze the large woman's hand. They smiled at each other for just one second, but it was enough to let Ivy know that Cat had been an ally to them as well.

Tears burned behind her lids the second John and Helena embraced her. Everything grew warm inside her, her heart felt as though it was swell and burst from her chest.

Helena was the first to pull back. She looked her over as though making an assessment. As she was checking her out Ivy saw movement beyond them on another cot and Ryan stood and walked toward them. His face was worse than Cat's, but he smiled just the same.

"Where is Amber?" Helena asked.

"She's hiding. We need to get her and get out of here." Ivy brought her attention back to Helena, but her eyes kept moving over to Ryan as he walked toward them, joining them.

She reached out to Ryan, pushed just a little, but immediately his face healed up. She wondered if her power was stronger here for some reason, or if it was just naturally growing. Something had supercharged her power because she was certain she'd never healed anyone this fast. Ryan smiled again.

"Thanks." He punched her lightly on the shoulder, something she considered brotherly and in that moment she forgave him. He was beaten like that because of Amber and Gabe. In the end he had chosen a side and it was theirs.

"Where is Amber?" John asked.

"She's in the graveyard." Ivy answered. "She's healing herself. I'm hoping she's ready to go by now."

"Healing herself?" John's expression changed instantly and the sweet, gentle man she knew disappeared, replaced by rage as she watched his face grow red, his jaw muscles tense. "Who hurt her? How bad is it?"

"Elizabeth stabbed her." Ivy answered and watched all that red drain out of his face until she thought he might actually faint. He didn't, but turned like he would walk out the door until Helena grabbed his hand to stop him.

"Just a second." she said. "We need to know the plan before we just walk out there." Then Helena paused for a minute and looked quizzically at Ivy. "She's healing herself?"

Ivy nodded. "It's a long story." She glanced at Ryan. "You didn't tell them anything?"

"Tell them what exactly?" Ryan shrugged. "I don't know what I saw that day. I mean, I overheard some of your conversation but even then I didn't understand it."

Ivy nodded again. She wondered how people would respond if they knew about her and Amber's abilities. Confusion was certainly on that list of possible responses.

"You can tell us when we get out of here." Helena said, bringing them all back to the issue at hand; escaping. "We'll have to follow you out of here. We came in with hoods over our heads. I have no idea if everything here is the same as it was when I was a young girl or not. And, John never lived here, he just delivered items to the general store."

"Gabe and I were blindfolded." Ryan added.

Mentioning Gabe's name brought her immediately to their next steps.

"We have to get Gabe! He's in a place they call the punishment room." Ivy felt overwhelmed with the need to get to Gabe. She had no idea how badly he was hurt and she wasn't leaving without him.

The room had grown suddenly silent. Her heart grew cold as she looked into Helena's tear-filled eyes.

"I'm so sorry Ivy," Helena said softly and gently took Ivy's hand. "Gabe is dead."

CHAPTER 24

"How do you know he's dead?" The panic found its way into her voice, which cracked just a bit as she said the last word. "How do you know for sure?"

Ryan stepped forward, his face a mask of pain. With all he'd been through Ivy considered him a pretty tough person. Tough as in able to withstand a lot of heartache. But, the look in his eyes, eyes that glistened with unshed tears, made her heart to fill with grief. She swayed and John reached out to steady her.

"I was there." Ryan spoke softly as though whispering it made the blow less harsh. "The albino beat him until Gabe lost consciousness, then Zachariah put his hands on him and I thought maybe he'd heal him so they could beat him again, but he touched him and Gabe grew perfectly still, his chest wasn't moving. His skin was grayish blue, like Mia when she couldn't get enough oxygen."

Ryan stopped then, growing silent and still, looking down at the floor obviously struggling with inner demons and hellish memories.

"They left you alive?" Ivy didn't mean it as an accusation, but Ryan flinched just the same.

"They seemed to think Amber and were together somehow. Maybe because I hit the albino when he said something about the wedding night."

"Daniel." Ivy said. "The albino is Daniel." Patricia's brother. Amber had to be so frightened. Ivy tried to imagine it, but it was just too much to deal with. Ryan began to speak again.

"They told her if she didn't cooperate with Daniel for the wedding night they would kill me just like they killed Gabe." Ryan's voice changed from grief to anger then and Ivy watched his close his eyes as she flexed the muscles in his jaw and balled his hands into fists. The moment passed, he got himself under control and opened his eyes to look at her again. "They left him hanging in that room."

Ivy did her best to reign in her emotions. Too many of the people she loved were now dependent upon her to get out of this mess. She needed to prioritize, organize and make her decisions. But, no matter how she worked things out in her mind she couldn't find a place for Gabe's death. It just couldn't be true. Until she saw it for herself she couldn't accept it. There was a remote chance Ryan was wrong. Zachariah may have put him in a coma to keep him out of the way. Anything was possible.

"I can't leave without Gabe." Ivy's gaze touched each of them one at a time. "I can't leave him here, dead or not."

Ryan's expression was something she would always remember. She'd never seen a look like that before. He lowered his head enough to see her directly in the eyes, his eyes made her think one word: death. He smiled, but it wasn't pleasant at all. That smile made the hair on the back of her neck rise up and she shivered though the room wasn't cold. But Ryan's expression was. He nodded and that cold smile widened. For a split second she was afraid of him. She wondered what all of this death, manipulation and destruction had done to Ryan's psyche. It had done something for sure. This was not the same guy she'd met in Coalville, and for that she was glad.

"Can you show me where this room is?" Ivy asked and Ryan nodded.

Cat joined their small circle and laid a large hand gently on Ivy's shoulder.

"I must stay here." Cat said as she slipped a key into Ivy's hand. "You'll need this when you get to the punishment room. Don't forget us."

"I won't. I promise." One way or another, she would come back for Cat and

Sarah and any of the others who wanted out of this place. She placed the key into the single pocket of her dress.

Ryan headed for the back of the house, Ivy, John and Helena close behind him.

They slipped quietly out the back door. All of them kept her eyes open, senses alert for potential threats, as they hurried after Ryan. They moved in the direction of Zachariah's home, but abruptly turned south instead of north to enter the house, ducking behind buildings or bushes to avoid the search parties combing the compound

Finally, they reached a sort of graveled cul-de-sac carved out among more of the tall bushes. In the center was a building not much bigger than a two car garage. The door was made of steel with a large padlock on the outside.

"This is it," Ryan whispered, and Ivy dug inside her pocket for the key Cat had given her.

The paddock opened easily. She removed it and opened the door. Inside it was dark and hot and smelled like sweat and old socks. The stench stung her nose and she wrinkled it until her eyes squinted.

A hand touched lightly on her shoulder and she turned to see John holding his forefinger to his lips. He squeezed her shoulder and moved in front of her. Not long ago she'd have been irritated to be pushed behind as though she needed to be protected, but things were different now. Now she knew needing help wasn't being weak. And that someone wanting to protect you was part of love. She wished she could tell John how much she appreciated him, but now was not the time. Besides, she'd do better to show him and was sure she'd get that chance.

Movement in the far corner caught Ivy's eye and she broke away from John and Helena to follow Ryan to the far right of the building.

Ryan found a lamp that cast a soft light in the room. There were exam tables, to the back of the building and chairs with metal cuffs bound to the arms. In the center of the room was a chair with Gabe's body still in it.

"Gabe!" She pushed Ryan out of the way to get to the slumped form. He was covered in blood and welts. He was cold to the touch and as she pushed her energy into him she felt the black void of death greet her. It was like dropping a single grain of sand onto the beach, it made such a small difference as to make no difference at all. Her heart sank as fast as she did as her knees hit the floor in front of him.

Ryan stood above her shaking Gabe's shoulder as though to wake him. Gabe only slumped deeper into the chair. No response. Not even a breath. She heard John and Helena walk up behind them. She felt warmth at her back as John leaned forward to check for a pulse. Ivy dropped her chin to her chest closing her eyes against what was to come as though doing so, delaying the words, would buy her just a little more time to ready herself.

"I'm sorry, Ivy." John whispered into the room as gently as he could.

She kept telling herself that it wasn't too late. It couldn't be. This isn't the way it was supposed to end. This was more tragedy than she could take and she pulled again at her power as she touched his leg. Darkness. Void. Tears. She was too late.

"We're not leaving him here." Ivy said.

"Of course not." Ryan's barely contained rage spewed out in clipped words.

"We can't carry him out of here. It's not safe." Helena pointed out.

Ivy looked up at Ryan and saw her own decision reflected in his eyes. They had to. She stood up and walked over to Gabe's body. A small silver key sat on a table nearby and she took a chance, using it to unlock his shackles. They came open and she unlocked them all. Ryan moved in and pulled Gabe's body forward and over his shoulder. Ryan was breathing hard, but he got the body up on his shoulder and turned to face them.

Ivy watched John and Helena exchange a look that clearly said this is a bad idea, but they back toward the door without a word. Ryan moved slowly now with the weight of Gabe pushing down on him. Ivy followed behind him, glancing one last time to the punishment room.

They walked out together into the night air, cooler, cleaner but still full of danger. Helena told John to follow her and they made their way out of the cul-de-sac to head toward the weeping willow trees a couple hundred yards away. John had found a large bowie knife. He held it in his grasp, clearly prepared to guy anyone who threatened them.

They could see flashlights moving in the distance and when the wind shifted from time to time they caught snippets of conversation about the progress of the hunt. They stayed out of the path of those lights, hugging the wall of rose bushes then ducking beneath the willow branches as they entered the graveyard.

Ryan tripped on a protruding stone and grunted hard as he landed on his knees, dropping Gabe as he fought for balance. Without a word, John lifted Gabe's slung him over his shoulder in a fireman's hold and turned to follow Helena. Ivy helped Ryan to his feet. Together, they turned and followed John and Helena.

Before long they were near the center of the graveyard. A figure stepped out from behind a tall stone cross and everyone stopped. Amber wore a dress when they came to hide here, but the silhouette of this girl showed her to be in pants, with long wavy hair.

Ivy moved up quickly to stand in front of Helena and greet her sister.

"Elizabeth." Ivy nodded at her and immediately scanned the area for more of Zachariah's people, but she didn't see anyone. "What are you doing here, *sister dea*r?" Ivy let sarcasm drip from the endearment.

"I sent Sarah to get help a few minutes ago when I saw the crypt door was open. It won't be much longer and this will be over." Elizabeth looked at Ivy and then beyond her. "For all of you," she added.

"Where's Amber?" Ivy asked. She was certain Amber would have secured the crypt, so either she'd had to leave quickly or she was healed and was already gone.

"I haven't seen her, but I'm sure she's around here waiting for you. Did you heal her?" she asked.

Of course Elizabeth would assume that, she had no idea about Amber's ability. Ivy worried about what might happen to Amber if they found out about her power.

Elizabeth glanced at Gabe's body and Ivy thought she saw a hint of regret pass over her sister's face, but before she could be sure it was gone and her gaze pinned Ivy in place with its fierceness.

"If you and Amber weren't so selfish that boy would still be alive." Elizabeth said.

The remark hit its mark and her heart stung with guilt. If she hadn't drawn Gabe into all of this, he would still be alive. He fought for her, for her sister and he paid the ultimate price for it.

"Your father killed that boy," Helena said and took a stop forward. "Just like he killed your mother right after you were born."

Elizabeth looked at Helena and her brows grew tight together. "That's the lie you're telling them?" She asked. "Our mother died in child birth, like lots of mothers do. Father is been wracked with guilt because he arrived too late to save her and he has done nothing but spend his life trying to get his daughters back from the people who stole them!"

"That's not true." From the shadows Amber stepped forward. Her dress was ruined but she looked remarkably well. "He killed her and he's brainwashed you."

Elizabeth tracked Amber's movements as she joined Ivy, putting her arm around Helena and glancing at John, then Ryan with a nod for each.

"Zachariah is our father. We are his children. There's no reason for him to want to kill our mother or harm us," Elizabeth argued.

Ivy stepped forward and took Amber's hand. It was cold and reminded her of Gabe's lifeless body. Anger burned inside her.

"Zachariah is mad with his own power," Ivy said, her voice raising just enough to make Amber squeeze her hand and keep her grounded. "Our mother wanted to leave this place, like a lot of people want to leave this place. She wanted her freedom. So he murdered her. These people saved us. They saved you, too, but you were sick and they had to leave you at the hospital. I'm sorry Zachariah found you. I truly am. But, I think in your heart you know there are a lot of things wrong here. I think you know Zachariah isn't everything he makes himself out to be. In your heart I think you know everything I'm telling you is true."

Elizabeth was already shaking her head and took one step closer to Ivy. "You're wrong! You couldn't be more wrong!" her tone was changing, the pitch higher, the volume louder. "These people wanted a child, children, and they took you. You trust them because they gave you some story about your father killing your mother? What are the odds of that compared to the odds of a childless couple wanting children at any cost?"

Ivy's hands balled into fists, her heart beating hard, her teeth mashing together so tight her jaw muscles ached from it.

"How do we prove to you we're telling the truth?" Helena addressed Elizabeth with a gentle tone.

Elizabeth was shaking her head.

"There's nothing you can say to convince me." Elizabeth said with finality.

"Perhaps there's nothing *we* can say," Amber's tone was soft like Helena's had been. "But, if our mother told you the truth herself, would you believe it?"

Ivy felt a jolt of excitement and fear. She looked at Amber and saw absolute calm in her face and her manner. Elizabeth seemed to waver, she was confused.

"What are talking about?" Elizabeth asked and took a step back from them. "She's dead."

"Yes. Dead and buried." Amber said and took another step forward. "Buried right here in this graveyard."

Amber walked closer to the Elizabeth and Ivy felt herself pulled in her wake. She followed Amber until the three of them stood in a small circle, looking at each other.

Amber's cold hand reached out and Ivy placed her warm one it. The hand was soft, familiar, but there was something just under the skin, some tightly leashed power that ran like a river through her veins.

"Ivy," she whispered. "This might hurt a little."

The energy sparked between them, cold and warm, life and death. And it hurt. Ivy willed herself to keep hold even though the energy from Amber began to bring her own to life, the stronger it became, the more it hurt.

That's when Ivy saw her, the woman standing near the crypt.

The woman walked toward them. She was small and young, her hair long and flowing. The moon cast light on her as though it guided her and Ivy knew the moment she caught sight of her face that this was Abigail. This was their mother.

Shock, excitement and fear clashed inside her, dulling the pain of her rising gift. When Abigail joined her daughters she smiled with both sadness and warmth.

Ivy felt tears run down her cheeks as she looked at the mother that risked everything to save them. Amber looked awe-struck, tears threatening to over-flow. But, Elizabeth was looking at them as though they were some science experiment gone wrong. Ivy realized then that Elizabeth couldn't see Abigail.

Amber reached across and took Abigail's hand. Ivy knew of only one way for Elizabeth to see what she and Amber saw. She reached out to her sister and took her hand, binding all of them with a touch.

"Elizabeth." Ivy said, but the moment their hands met Elizabeth's shocked gaze was on the ghost she was now linked to. "Meet Abigail. Our mother."

Touching Elizabeth caused an energy to spark painlessly between all of them. The pain of sharing energy with Amber disappeared entirely when Elizabeth joined their circle and Ivy glanced down to make sure she and Amber were still connected. Amber's head snapped over to Elizabeth, then to Ivy.

Ivy's eyes widened, as the energy between them moved like water between all of them. Her gaze moved to Elizabeth whose shocked expression seemed to have less to do with the warm energy that flowed through and between them and more to do with seeing Abigail since Elizabeth's gaze was cemented to Abigail's face.

"Mother?" Elizabeth whispered.

Their mother could have been another sibling she was so near their age. Her eyes were violet like Elizabeth's only they shined bright in a way no human's could. Her hair was long and wavy and blond.

"My girls." Abigail said and her voice was like a soft caress. "I've longed to see you. But, I wish you weren't in this place."

"We wish we weren't here, too." Ivy said and she blinked hard against the burn of gathering tears. "Gabe is dead. Father has lied to Elizabeth and we don't know how to stop any of it."

Abigail nodded and looked to Amber expectantly.

"We've been talking," Amber shared, "and I know how to escape this place. The question is, will Elizabeth go with us?"

Elizabeth still appeared stricken, but now it was her turn to lose the battle with tears. She didn't speak and Ivy wondered if she was in shock.

"She needs you to tell her." Ivy said to Abigail. "Tell her about Zachariah."

Abigail looked pained at the speaking of their father's name. "What they've told you is true, Elizabeth. I'm sorry."

Elizabeth's expression changed as the truth began to sink in. Moments passed, the wind grew cooler, no one spoke and the void was filled with a low hum Ivy hadn't noticed before. White clouds, much like those Ivy had seen at Dr. Scarborough's, hovered, growing closer. Occasionally Ivy could see hints of a person inside those clouds and it was unnerving. One of those clouds was a visitor, the only ghost who could move from cemetery to cemetery: Patricia. She gasped and it caused Amber to look at her, then follow her gaze to Patricia. Amber smiled at the apparition then turned back to their mother. The guilt of taking Patricia's life filled Ivy immediately and the energy that flowed grew cooler causing Amber to squeeze her hand to get her attention.

Looking at Amber she followed her gaze back to their mother who was staring at her.

"She doesn't blame you." Abigail told her in that soothing tone. "You did the right thing, baby."

The relief Ivy felt, the comfort of her mother's absolving her of guilt, was overwhelming and tears fell unchecked down her cheeks.

Thinking of guilt and death she glanced again at the white apparitions moving around the graveyard and tried to see inside them, hoping to find one more person. When she didn't see him she looked back to Amber.

"Where's Gabe?"

John was kneeling beside Gabe's body on the ground. Ryan stood nearby. Amber felt her power flex, the need to make things right overwhelmed her.

"He was already dead when I found him." Ivy's voice was barely a whisper when she spoke.

"There was nothing you could do." Amber assured her. "When you saved me I wasn't entirely dead, and my spirit wanted to hold on. Mia's spirit wanted to hold on. Gabe was being tortured. His only release from his pain was death. His spirit was ready to leave his body."

"Sometimes souls are caught, trapped, where they are killed because no Keeper will admit them and their body isn't buried yet." Abigail told them. "His spirit is still here somewhere."

"What happens to him now?" Ivy asked, worried now for Gabe's soul. She hated the idea of him being trapped here and knew she'd done the right thing by bringing his body with them.

Abigail looked back to where Ryan was standing and her expression was as curious as Amber's. She closed her eyes for a moment and her head fell back slightly. Their mother raised her head and opened her eyes with a nod.

"We need to form a circle, all of us, around the body," Abigail said and then quickly added, "but do not break this circle. Hold on to each other and don't let go of me."

They moved, holding on to each other until they reached Gabe's body.

The moment the body in the center of their circle Ivy cold see the white cloud that was Gabe's soul. It hovered over the body, not quite as solid as the other apparitions in the graveyard. For a split second Ivy saw Gabe. Then he was gone, nothing more than the thin, white cloud.

"You are a powerful healer, Ivy." Abigail said. "And Amber is the only Keeper of the Dead to ever walk the earth still living." She glanced at Amber and smiled, then turned to Elizabeth, "And you my sweet girl, you remarkable as well. You amplify power and you are a conduit for it, but you have not yet come into your own power. It is coming, though, I promise you." Abigail smiled at Elizabeth, but it was that sad smile that made Ivy wonder what fate was in store for her sibling. Abigail turned to Ivy. "Your friend's soul is unclaimed. Elizabeth will amplify our power, Amber and I will force the soul back into the body, but you, sweet Ivy, you will need to sacrifice a piece of your own soul in order to keep his bound to his body and bring him back from the dead."

Ivy's heart raced at the thought. Fear and excitement rushed through her and the energy between them sparked. She looked at Gabe laying between them. She wasn't being asked to heal Gabe, she was being asked to bring him back from the dead. And it was going to cost her a piece of her own soul.

The wind picked up and brought sounds of men. They all turned toward the crypt and saw a dozen lights walking toward it, accompanied by low murmurs and dark shadows. One shadow was taller than the rest and as they walked into the light cast by the moon Ivy saw Zachariah approach the crypt. Before he took the first step up to the where the door still stood slightly open he froze in place. And though he only stood there for a matter of seconds, Ivy's heart felt as though it beat a hundred times as she watched him turn around and stare across the graveyard at them. He didn't move until all of his men had joined him.

As Zachariah took his first step in their direction Ivy felt their energy spike and it brought her attention back to the circle. Abigail was staring at her and the look on her face turned Ivy's blood cold. Ivy wondered what could terrify a ghost?

CHAPTER 25

WE MUST HURRY!" ABIGAIL turned her back on her murderous husband. "Ivy!"

Ivy couldn't take her eyes off of the group headed up by Zachariah. From what she could tell the men couldn't see Abigail, they just knew they had found their prey, but looking at the tall man they all stood behind, the way he stared directly at Abigail, he knew exactly who was helping them. Her mother called her name.

"He can see you?" Ivy asked, her eyes wide.

"He is made of light and dark, of life and death. Yes, he can see me. He's not powerful enough to control me, or even to see me at will, not like Amber can. But, when there's strong energy from the stream of death, or the stream of life, he can see me clear enough." She rushed the words together, but Ivy caught it all.

"Can he stop us?" She asked.

"Yes, but once you tie your soul to this boy's soul not even Zachariah can harm him. Your light is so much stronger than his." Abigail smiled then, like any proud mother might. "Now pull your energy hard, take from us all and light up the night with your soul daughter."

A glance toward Zachariah and his half dozen minions and Ivy's heart sank. John, Helena and Ryan ran forward, putting themselves between Zachariah and his daughters.

Trusting them to deal with Zachariah and his minions, Ivy closed her eyes and focused her attention to the task at hand. Her energy sat there at the forefront of her mind, waiting for instructions, but instead of sending it out to Amber and Elizabeth or her mother, she pulled. She pulled hard, like taking in a deep breath when there was no oxygen to be had. She pulled hard, trusting that her mother would help keep them safe from the power and its ability to take all the energy in its path.

She felt the cold of Amber's power, not painful, not as long as Elizabeth was nearby acting as a conduit, a buffer. Amber's power, pulled from death, was every bit as powerful as her own, but then another pull of energy and Ivy tapped into Elizabeth's ability to magnify their power and all of a sudden it was like oxygen being pushed into her lungs. Ivy filled and filled and filled with such a powerful energy, cold and hot, warm, soothing and then suddenly it was too much, painful and she couldn't take any more, but more poured in. Ivy opened her eyes, looked down at Gabe's body where she could clearly see the white cloud aligned with the physical body, waiting for her. She focused all that energy and she screamed.

A bright light poured out of her, riding the scream and pouring itself through the white cloud and into Gabe's body. The cloud disappeared inside him, but the light kept pouring out. A cloud streamed out of Ivy to join the light.. Just as the tip of the cloud entered Gabe's body Abigail pulled away and Amber dropped her hand. The energy stopped so abruptly, the light shutting off, Ivy screamed one last time before falling to the ground in a heap next to Gabe.

There was only darkness and Ivy realized her eyes were shut tight. She forced them open and saw Gabe still lying there, eyes closed. She tried to move, but it was impossible. She didn't have enough energy to even lift her head, but then someone touched her, a cold hand turned her over onto her back. She looked up at the concerned face of her sister, Amber. Her mother was no where to be seen. She heard a commotion, loud voices, in the background, but she just couldn't concentrate enough to understand them.

"You're going to have to try to move." Amber told her, but the sound of her voice was odd, like she was calling out down a long tunnel. "We don't have much time."

It all came rushing back to Ivy, the graveyard, her mother, Gabe. She found the strength to look back at Gabe, but this time his eyes were open and her eyes widened, filled with tears and she willed her arm to reach out toward him. He seemed to be struggling as much as she was, but as her hand touched his he threaded his finger through hers. That one touch sparked her energy and she tried to let go of him, fearful that she might accidentally take his energy, but he squeezed her hand and frowned at her. Energy spiked from him, into her and then she returned it to him. The energy spiked between them, not draining, but feeding.

Her body filled and she turned to Amber who was watching Ryan and Zachariah square off. The adrenaline filled Ivy, met with the energy and she stood, full and ready to fight. Movement behind her brought her reeling around, ready to take someone down, but it was Gabe, standing there with eyes blazing with rage and something else.

His eyes were glowing.

"Your eyes!" Ivy exclaimed.

Gabe looked down at her, those softly glowing eyes moving over her.

"Yours, too." He smiled at her for just a moment and then looked back at the fighting going on in front of them.

Amber had already run to join John, Helena and Ryan. Something moved near the crypt and Ivy's mother appeared again like a white cloud, with only glimpses of her face flickering in the white mist. Abigail's arms extended and hundreds of white clouds rose up from the ground to surround the perimeter of the graveyard. Just beyond them were more of Zachariah's people, but they appeared unable to get through those white clouds.

From the corner of her eye, Ivy saw Zachariah grab Ryan by the throat. Ryan kicked out hard enough to break ribs. Zachariah flinched but held tight, and Ryan's struggles grew weaker. It was as though Ryan's energy was being drained. Together, Ivy and Gabe began running towards their friend.

One of Zachariah's men ran to intercept them and Ivy launched herself at him. As she fought the short, stocky man, Gabe plowed into Zachariah like a linebacker, throwing all his weight at Zachariah's legs, bringing her father down and Ryan down with him.

Pain filled Ivy as her opponent landed a hard blow to her ribs. She was certain one or two of those ribs broke, but she couldn't spare the energy to heal herself until after she brought her attacker down. He moved in closer and Ivy slammed heel of her hand into his nose with all her strength. Cartilage crunched and blood squirted. He went down, and she kicked him in the ribs. Hard. Tit for tat.

When it was clear he wasn't getting up, Ivy ran forward again. John had joined Helena to take down a particularly large and formidable fighter, but John was big, too, and the man was on the ground before Ivy reached them. She swerved right to help Amber fight a young woman who had clearly been trained in martial arts.

"I don't need any help." Amber called out when she caught sight of Ivy. "Help Ryan and Gabe!"

Sudden pain struck the center of Ivy's chest and she gasped. For several long seconds, she thought someone had driven a knife into her heart, but then her pain-glazed eyes fell on Ryan, Zachariah and Gabe, and she realized what was happening.

Ryan was on the ground, not moving, and Zachariah now had Gabe in his grip. One hand grasped Gabe's neck, but the other was laid flat against Gabe's chest. Zachariah was trying to kill Gabe with the power he called on from the stream of death. Ivy could feel it -- so cold it burned right in the center of her chest. The pain became so intense she dropped to her knees. She watched Gabe struggle harder, it was as though he were rallying against the pain he must surely feel as well. With one hand around Zachariah's at his neck he extended the other toward her. As though her power knew what to do, she felt it build inside her and her own arm reached out toward Gabe. Just as Amber had pulled energy from the graveyard with her palms down toward the graves, Ivy's hand came out, palm held out toward Gabe and the power rushed there. It was lightning fast, and though she felt it leaving her body, it was not painful. Light, white and glowing, not the misty white lights of the souls in the graveyard, but pure, clear light like the strongest bulb in the world shot from her palm toward Gabe's extended hand.

The light hit him and the moment it did Ivy saw Zachariah stumble back as though he'd been shot. He pulled his hand off of Gabe's chest and dropped him. Gabe landed on his feet and started hitting Zachariah with all he had. Zachariah fell hard to the ground and Gabe followed him. Ivy rushed over to Ryan who was unconscious but alive. As she started to heal him she heard her mother call out.

"You need to leave!" She said and her voice was more in Ivy's mind than her ears, but she saw Amber look in the direction of the crypt when it was said. Amber limped toward her, the young woman nowhere Ivy could see.

Ivy rushed to Gabe, pulling him off of an already unconscious Zachariah. The moment she touched him, he whirled, fists up, his face a mask of rage. The ferocious expression faded almost immediately.

"We have to go now," she told him.

Gabe stood up. He was moving slow, but he was moving on his own.

"Where's Elizabeth?" Ivy called out to her sister.

"I don't know. The fighting started and she just disappeared," Amber said. John and Helena rushed to join them.

"Follow me," Helena said and turned toward the crypt.

Ivy glanced back at her mother, but the white cloud that housed Abigail faded in and out. Gabe took her hand and pulled her forward. Helena ran behind the crypt and down a path into the woods. They hit a tall chain link fence and Helena turned to them.

The trail continued for nearly a mile, leading to a tall chain link fence. The posted signs up and down the fence announced it was electrified.

"What now?" Ivy asked.

"The electricity is off," the voice was masculine and came from the other side. An older Native American man walked out from a copse of trees.

"Tom?" John approached him, Helena at his side.

"We still keep an eye on this place." Tom said. "I was told something was going on near the graveyard. I came out to see for myself and, since this was where the last two escapes from this place happened, I thought I'd wait and see if anyone showed up. This section of the fence isn't getting any electricity, so why don't we get you all through and get to the reservation before we have company?"

Tom walked over to a section of the fence and moved it, opening it where someone had cut the fence previously. It peeled back and everyone walked through, following Tom to an old battered pick-up truck.

"Will they follow us to the reservation?" Ivy asked as she sat next to Gabe in the back of the truck near the tailgate.

Tom was pulling out a tarp to throw over them.

"Likely he will lick his wounds first. By the time he thinks to check the reservation, you'll be gone." Tom said as he covered them and then got in the truck to drive.

Ivy lay in the bed of the pickup. A warm hand took hers and Gabe gave a gentle squeeze. He pulled her hand to his lips and kissed her knuckles lightly. The half-smile was familiar and welcome and she smiled back.

The truck continued at its slow pace and Ivy closed her eyes as she thought about her mother and Patricia. Then she thought about Elizabeth and wondered if her sister had changed her mind about Zachariah now that she had seen their mother. And what about Cat and Sarah? It wasn't over, but for now they could rest. They could regroup. They could appreciate being alive and being together.

She squeezed Gabe's hand just for reassurance. The warmth felt so good as the cool air ran across her skin. They shared a soul now. Or, at least he had part of her soul in him. She wasn't sure what it meant, but she was glad he was alive.

There were more questions, but for now she would take the quiet void of uncertainty and wrap herself in it until she was ready to know the answers. That day was not today.

I DON'T LIKE IT," Ivy said for what felt like the millionth time. "There has to be a better plan."

Amber rolled her eyes at her sister, for the millionth time, and kept packing. Gabe sat on the corner of Ivy's bed watching the sisters argue. He'd already said all he was going to say on the topic.

"You saw what Zachariah is capable of," Amber tried to reason with Ivy and organize her toiletries. She had two bottles of shampoo and no conditioner. She really needed Ivy to let it go, but that would be too easy. Amber sighed. "Patricia says we have a shot at removing Zachariah's power to harm, to kill people. If we take away that weapon, we can help save the other people in the community being held there. They're all afraid of Zachariah and his power. Remove the weapon and those people may help us take Zachariah down."

"But, why Brooklyn? Why not somewhere here in Colorado?" Ivy asked and Amber was glad that at least it was a new question.

"The cemetery in Brooklyn is the second largest cemetery in the world. The only one bigger is in France and thought I'd love to go to Europe, I don't speak French and I doubt John and Helena would allow it, regardless of how important the mission is. Especially since Ryan is coming, too." Amber finished packing, hoped she remembered everything, and zipped up the suitcase.

"You know Ryan totally worked that out in his favor," Ivy smiled.

"It was the logical choice," Amber answered, "Unless, of course, you'd like me to pretend I'm married to your boyfriend and spend the next, however long it takes, pretending we're in love?"

Ivy scowled. "I just don't know why we can't all go to Brooklyn together until we get the information we need from the Keeper of the Dead at that cemetery."

"Because," Gabe made a grab for Ivy's hand, pulled her to him and kissed her cheek as he put her on his lap. "From here we can help keep an eye on Joyce and Mia, and my mom now that she's living with them. They're vulnerable. And, it's easier to hide a weapons training course and all the other stuff John and Helena have here now, than it would be in Brooklyn."

"I don't know about that." Ivy pouted.

"We have a plan and we're sticking to it." Amber said and made one last check of her things in the room before putting the suitcase on the floor to wheel downstairs. "You will help protect Gabe and Ryan's family. You'll work with John, Helena and Tom to keep tabs one what's going on at the community and get Gabe some real training."

"Hey! I'm the best fighter here and you know it." Gabe complained, pretending to be hurt by the remark.

"Maybe, but you need weapons training." Ivy reminded him. "Besides, I thought you said you're a lover, not a fighter?"

Gabe pushed her off his lap and onto the bed where he pinned her, not that she was putting up much of a fight.

"What I said was," he kissed her nose, "I'm a lover *and* a fighter."

"Oh just get a room." Amber sounded disgusted and began wheeling the suitcase out the door.

"Don't leave before I come say goodbye." Ivy yelled after her sister, but the door was already shut.

Gabe kissed her forehead, letting go of her wrists so she could put her arms around him. "I know you'll miss her. I know you're worried, but she's going to talk to some ghost. How much trouble could she find with that? Isn't she the ghost whisperer?"

Ivy laughed. "She's not a ghost whisperer. And it's not just a ghost. It's the Keeper of the Dead. A very powerful one if he's in charge of such a big cemetery. Or so Amber and Patricia think. And I doubt the trouble will come from any ghosts. It's more likely it will come from your cousin putting the moves on her."

"Amber can take care of herself when it comes to Ryan," Gabe said as he started planting little kisses across Ivy's cheeks and nose.

"I don't know. Ryan is pretty hot." Ivy couldn't help but laugh at Gabe's expression when he pulled back to look at her. "What? He is. That's not my fault."

"You just remember who you gave part of your soul to." He warned her with an extremely ineffective scowl that made her laugh.

Gabe stopped the laughter with a kiss that turned so hot Ivy thought she'd spontaneously combust. His lips moved to her chin, down her neck and back to her lips where Ivy was sure he was claiming more than just a small piece of her soul.

"I don't think it's my soul that you're after," Ivy smiled, then kissed him back.

"I'll take whatever I can get." He looked down at her, brushing a stray lock of hair from her brow.

"And what do I get?" She challenged.

"My whole heart, of course." The smile changed to something more meaningful and Ivy felt the rush of adrenaline send a thousand butterflies into her stomach.

"That's a good trade." Ivy smiled just before a car horn interrupted their moment and warned them John was on his way upstairs.

"If you don't want to have to heal me later, you'll need to let me up before John walks in," Gabe laughed and they jumped up from the bed just before John walked in.

Maybe their luck would last a while this time.

THE END

Made in the USA
Middletown, DE
30 May 2016